John Hannett

The Forest of Arden, its Towns, Villages, and Hamlets

A topographical and historical account of the district between and around Henley in Arden and Hampton in Arden, in the county of Warwick

SALZWASSER VERLAG

John Hannett

The Forest of Arden, its Towns, Villages, and Hamlets

A topographical and historical account of the district between and around Henley in Arden and Hampton in Arden, in the county of Warwick

Reprint of the original, first published in 1863.

1st Edition 2022 | ISBN: 978-3-37500-371-5

Verlag (Publisher): Salzwasser Verlag GmbH, Zeilweg 44, 60439 Frankfurt, Deutschland
Vertretungsberechtigt (Authorized to represent): E. Roepke, Zeilweg 44, 60439 Frankfurt, Deutschland
Druck (Print): Books on Demand GmbH, In de Tarpen 42, 22848 Norderstedt, Deutschland

THE
FOREST OF ARDEN.

THE
FOREST OF ARDEN,

ITS

TOWNS, VILLAGES, AND HAMLETS:

A

TOPOGRAPHICAL AND HISTORICAL ACCOUNT

OF THE DISTRICT BETWEEN AND AROUND

HENLEY-IN-ARDEN AND HAMPTON-IN-ARDEN,

IN THE COUNTY OF WARWICK.

ILLUSTRATED WITH NUMEROUS ENGRAVINGS.

BY JOHN HANNETT.

"Let fields and streams, purling through the valleys, be my delight; unambitious, may I court the rivers and the woods."--- *Virgil.*

LONDON

1863.

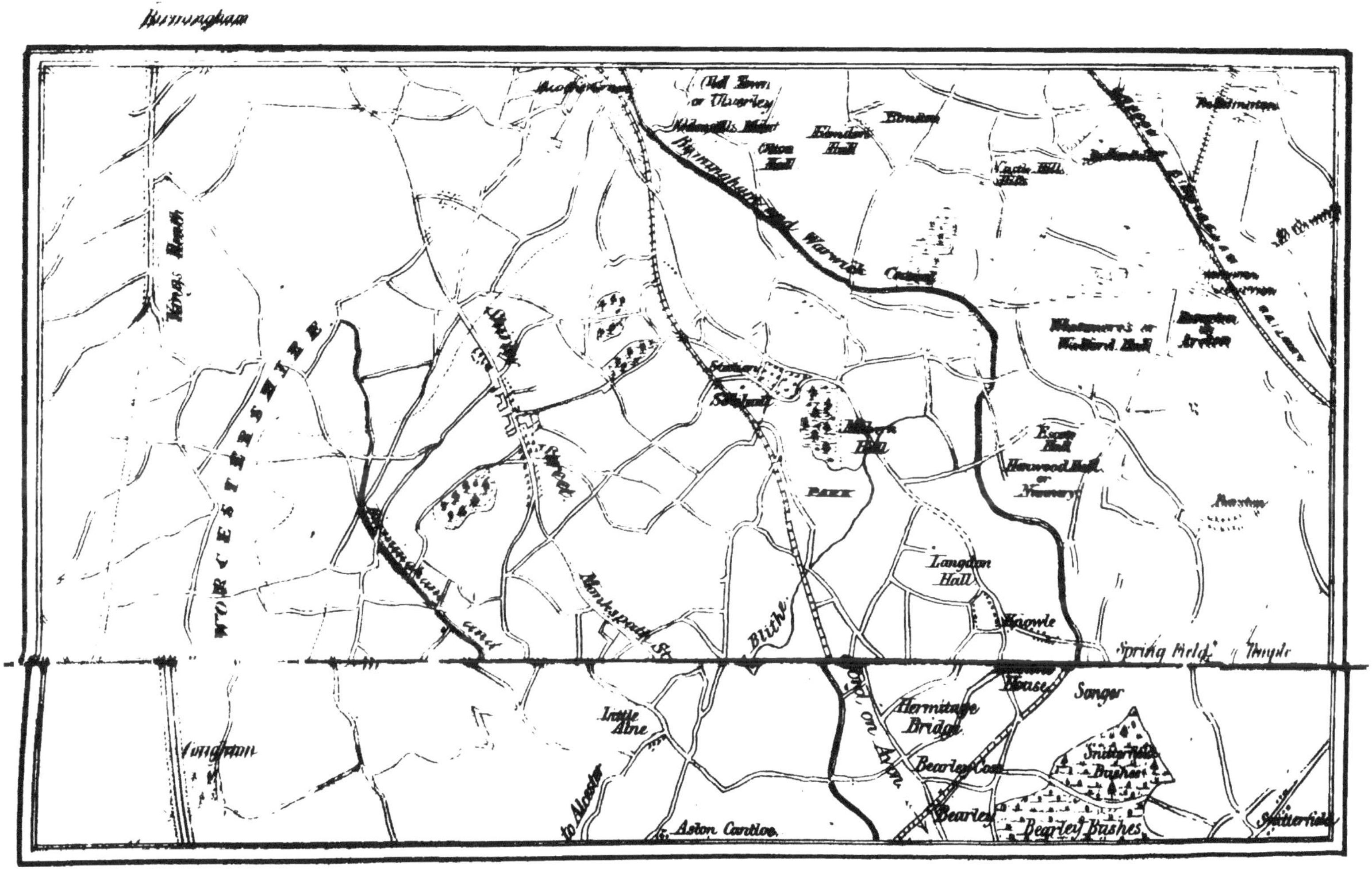
Birmingham
Birmingham and Warwick Canal
Worcestershire
Langdon Hall
Knowle
Spring Field
Songer
Hermitage Bridge
Bearley Cross
Bearley
Bearley Bushes
Snitterfield Bushes
Snitterfield
Blithe
Monkspath St.
Street
Little Alne
Aston Cantlow
to Alcester
Park
Kings Heath
Old Town or Ulverley
Elmdon
Elmdon Hall
Olton Hall
Hermitage Bridge
Wootton Wawen

Preface.

THE compiler of the following pages would deprecate a too rigid criticism of his performance, being sensible that the volume which he now commits to his subscribers and the public, is destitute of the merits which would have better corresponded with the liberal patronage and encouragement which, he is happy to acknowledge, have, from many quarters, been accorded to him during its progress.

The historical portion of the work has been mainly derived from the great Warwickshire historian, Dugdale, supplemented by the works of Leland, Camden, Tanner, and Stukeley, and by publications issued under the authority of Parliament. To these have been added numerous extracts from many interesting documents among the MSS. in the British Museum, the Record and Augmentation Offices, Parish Registers, &c., which have never before been made public.

The general plan of the work will be found to consist of a nine days' tour through the district laid down in the accompanying map. A description of the Churches, and an account of ancient and modern Mansions, Religious Houses, and other notable features of the country, are given at length, together with particulars of the characteristic scenery of this eminently rural district. These have been illustrated by upwards of fifty engravings, executed by Mr. E. Whimper, of London, principally from photographs taken expressly for the purpose.

Henley-in-Arden,

June, 1863.

List of Engravings.

Subscribers.

ABERGAVENNY, the Right Honourable the Earl of, *Birling Manor, Maidstone.*

AYLESFORD, the Right Honourable the Earl of, *Packington*, two copies.

Adams, Mr. Bookseller, *Stratford-on-Avon.*

Agar, Samuel, M.D., *Henley-in-Arden.*

Aston, Miss Harriet, *Rowington.*

BOSTON, the Right Honourable Lord, *Hedsor, Beaconsfield.*

Ball, Mr. John, *Nuthurst.*

Barber, Mrs., *Barston Hall.*

Barker, Rev. Joseph, *Barston.*

Barnes, Mr. Thomas, *Pillaton, Staffordshire.*

Bayley, the Rev. John Arden, Chaplain to the Forces, *Dover.*

Beard, J., Esq., *Hillfield Hall, Solihull.*

Beard, Mrs., *Hillfield Hall.*

Beck, Mr. J., Bookseller, *Leamington.*

Bedford, John, Esq., *Sleaford.*

Bedford, Rev. W. K. Riland, *Sutton Coldfield.*

Birmingham Old Library.

Birt, Miss, *Henley-in-Arden.*

Bolton, Mr. W., *Finwood.*

Bomford, Mr. B., *Little Alne.*

Boulton, John, Esq., *The Laurels, Solihull.*

Boulton, T., Esq., *Studley.*

Boutflower, Rev. H. C., *Elmdon.*

Brierley, Mr. T. H., *Knowle.*

Brooks, Mrs., *Bristol Road, Birmingham.*

Bullivent, Mr. G., *Wootton Wawen.*

Bullock, Mr. W., *Newnham, Aston Cantloe.*
Burd, Rev. C., *Lapworth.*
Burman, Charles, Esq., *Meifod, North Wales.*
Burman, Mr. John, *Henley-in-Arden.*
Burman, Thomas, Esq., *Waring's Green, Tanworth.*
Butler, Mr. James, *Ullenhall.*

Calwell, Rev. E., *Studley.*
Cartwright, Rev. T. J., *Preston Bagot.*
Cattell, Mr. Henry, *Knowle.*
Cattell, Joseph, Esq., *Hardwicke Farm, Studley.*
Chamberlain, Mr. T., *Henley-in-Arden.*
Chambers, Miss C., *Daventry.*
Chambers, Rev. J., *Garsden, Malmesbury.*
Chattock, Mrs., *Solihull.*
Cheston, Charles, Esq. *Henwood Hall.*
Clark, Mr. George, Sen., *Wootton Wawen.*
Clark, Mr. George, Jun., *Ditto.*
Clifton, Mr. F., *Henley-in-Arden.*
Codd, Rev. E. T., *Tachbrooke.*
Collett, Mr., *Oldberrow.*
Collins, Mr., *Leamington.*
Cooke and Sons, Booksellers, *Warwick.*
Cooke, Mr. H. T., *Warwick.*
Cook, Mr. John, *Oldberrow.*
Cooper, Edward, Esq., *Henley-in-Arden.*
Cooper, Mr. William, *Impsley.*
Coppage, Mr. W., *Henley-in-Arden.*
Corns, Mr. George, *Birmingham.*
Couchman, T. B., Esq., *Henley-in-Arden.*
Couchman, Rev. John, *Thornby, Northamptonshire.*

Dalby, Mrs., *Coleshill.*
Dartnell, G. Russell, Esq., I.G.H., *Arden House, Henley-in-Arden.*
Davidson, Mr. J., *Birmingham.*
Davies, Mr. John, *Wootton Wawen.*
Davis, Rev. F. R., *Coughton.*
Dawes, John, Esq., *Barston.*
Diamond, James, Esq., 5, *Belgrave Street, London.*

Digby, Rev. J. Wingfield, *Coleshill.*
Dolben, Rev. C., *Ipsley.*
Dowler, George, Esq., *Highfield House, Knowle.*
Draper, Mr. R., *Newnham, Aston Cantloe.*
Dugdale, J., Esq., *Wroxhall Abbey*, two copies.
Dunn, Mr. Bryan, *Henley-in-Arden.*

East, Mr. C., *Henley-in-Arden.*
Edkins, Mr. G., *Ditto*
Edwards, Miss R. A., *Solihull.*
Elliott, R. H., Esq., *Studley.*
Endall, Mr. W., *Henley-in-Arden.*

Fagge, Rev. J. F., *Aston Cantloe.*
Faulkner, Rev. William Andrew, *Beaudesert.*
Fawcett, Mr. William, *Sleaford.*
Fayrer, George, M.D., *Henley-in-Arden.*
Fetherston, John, Jun., Esq., F.S.A., *Packwood.*
Findon, Mr. J., *Henley-in-Arden.*
Flower, Edgar, Esq., *Stratford-on-Avon.*
Freer, Charles Thomas, Esq., *Billesdon Coplow, Leicester.*

Galton, Mrs. Darwin, *Claverdon Leys.*
Gem, Miss, *Moor Hills, Rowington.*
Gibbs, Edward, Esq., *Stratford-on-Avon.*
Gibbs, Mr. W., *Songar.*
Gillott, Joseph, Jun., Esq., *Olton Cottage, Solihull.*
Glover, Mr., Bookseller, *Leamington.*
Goldney, Rev. Horatio Nelson, *Tunbridge Wells.*
Goodricke, Sir F. L. H., Bart., *Studley Castle.*
Griffin, Mr. J., *Henley-in-Arden.*

Hackett, Mr. Richard, *Market Rasen.*
Hall, Egerton F., M.D., *Henley-in-Arden.*
Hall, Mr. Benjamin, *Birmingham.*
Harding, G. J., Esq., *Solihull.*
Harding, William Judd, Esq., *Baraset, Stratford-on-Avon.*
Hardy, Mr. John, *Stratford-on-Avon.*
Hardy, Mrs., *Bromsgrove.*

Harper, Mr. J. B., *Great Malvern.*
Harris, Mr. G., *Henley-in-Arden.*
Hawkes, Mr. A., *Thornhill Square, Islington.*
Hawkes, Mr. Thomas, Jun., *Henley-in-Arden.*
Heming, Mr. W. T., Bookseller, *Redditch.*
Hemming, Mr. F., *Henley-in-Arden.*
Heritage, Mr. C., *Aston Cantloe.*
Hewitt, Rev. Peter J., O.S.B., *Wootton Wawen.*
Heynes, Mr. J., *The Leasowes, Tanworth.*
Hildick, Mr. Benjamin, *Lapworth.*
Hill, Mr. A., *Studley.*
Hill, Mr. Richard, *Birmingham.*
Hill, Mrs., *Shottery.*
Hoddinott, William, Esq., *Barston.*
Hodges, Mr. George, *Lapworth.*
Hodgkins, Mr. D., *Henley-in-Arden.*
Hoitt, Mr. S., Representatives of the late, *Clifton, Bristol.*
Hoitt, Rev. H. T., *Bream, Gloucestershire.*
Holyoake, Mr. John, *Little Alne.*
Holmes, Mr. J., *Wootton Wawen.*
Homer, G., Esq., *Solihull.*
Hopkins, Mr. W. F., *Henley-in-Arden.*
Hopkins, Mr. W. F., Jun., *Ditto.*
Hopkins, Mr. Daniel, *Sandhurst, Australia.* two copies.
Howe, Rev. J., *Knowle.*
Hudson, Mr. Robert, *Lapworth.*
Hunt, Mr. William, *Sleaford.*
Hunter, Rev. Alexander, *Tanworth.*

Jabet, George, Esq., *Handsworth.*
Jervoise, Rev. F. Ellis, *Leamington.*
Jervoise, F. J. E., Esq., *Herriard Park, Basingstoke.*
Johnson, Mr. F., *Henley-in-Arden.*
Johnson, Rev. R. W., *Packwood.*
Johns, Mr. Henry, *Henley-in-Arden.*
Joiner, Mr. William, *Ditto.*
Jones, Rev. Thomas, *Ditto.*

Kemm, Mr. W., *London.*
Kemp, Mr. J., *Claverdon.*

Kempson, Rev. E. A., *Claverdon*, two copies.
Kimbell, Miss, *Solihull.*
Kimbell, William, Esq., *Tanworth.*
Kimbell, J. H., Esq., *Knowle.*
Kimbell, Mr. Henry, *Ditto.*
Kimbell, Mr. Edward, *Ditto.*
Kirshaw, John, Esq., *Warwick.*
Kirshaw, Miss, *Henley-in-Arden.*
Kirwan, Rev. E. D., *Wootton Wawen*, two copies.
Knowle Reading Society.

Lane, Rev. H. G., O.S.B., *Stratford-on-Avon.*
Lea, Rev. Thomas, *Tadmarten, Banbury.*
Lea, Miss Harriet, *Douglas, Isle of Man.*
Lea, Miss Mary, *Tanworth.*
Lee, Mrs. William, *Barston.*
Lewing, Mr. G., *Aston Cantloe.*
Lindsay, Mr. William, *Lapworth.*
Lord, Mr. William, *Henley-in-Arden.*
Lord, Mr. Z., *Ditto.*
Lowe, Mr. C., *Ditto.*
Lowe, Mrs. J., *Ditto.*
Lowe, Thomas, Esq., *Solihull.*

Marshall, Mr. J. S., *Knowle.*
Martin, Philip Wykeham, Esq., M.P., *Four Ashes, Knowle.*
Medens, Miss Ann, *Wootton Wawen.*
Middleton, Miss, *Preston Bagot.*
Mildmay, Rev. A. St. John, *Lapworth.*
Moilliet, Theodore, Esq., *Skilts House, Studley.*
Moore, Mr. Thomas, *Preston Bagot.*
Mordaunt, Sir Charles, Bart., M.P.. *Walton.*
Morgan, Mr. J., Bookseller, *Stratford-on-Avon.*
Morrall, A., Esq., *Studley.*
Morrall, F., Esq., *Ditto.*
Morris, John, Esq., *Henley-in-Arden.*
Moss, Mr. Thomas, *Ditto.*
Muntz, George Frederick, Esq., *Umberslade Hall.*
Muntz, Mrs., *Beaudesert Park.*

Muntz, Philip Henry, Esq., *Edstone Hall.*
Musgrave, Christopher, Esq., *Leamington.*
Mynors, Rev. Thomas, *Salter Street, Tanworth.*

Newberry, Mr. John, *Aston Cantloe.*
Newbery, Mrs., *Rowington Green.*
Newey, Mr. J., *Henley-in-Arden.*
Newling, Mr. A., *Liverpool.*
Newman, Mr. J., Bookseller, *London.*
Newton, Mrs., *Barrells Hall.*
Noble, Mr. F., *Lymington.*
Norman, W. P., Esq., *Langdon Hall, Knowle.*

Osborn, Mr. Joseph, *Lapworth.*
Osborn, Mr. William, *Ditto.*
Osborne, Mr. John, *Redditch.*
Over, Mr. W., *Henley-in-Arden.*

Palmer, W., Esq., *Ullenhall.*
Palmer, Mrs., *Claverdon.*
Palmer, Mr. C., *Derby.*
Palmer, Miss, *London.*
Parker, George, Esq., *Snitterfield.*
Payne, Mr. John, *Sleaford.*
Penn, Mr. G., *Birmingham.*
Perry, Thomas Aloysius, Esq., *Bitham House, Avon Dasset, Banbury.*
Peshall, Mrs., *Oldberrow.*
Phillips, Miss, *Leamington.*
Phillipps, Mrs., *Hurst House, Henley-in-Arden.*
Pippet, W., Esq., *Coughton.*

Radburn, Rev. William, *Henley-in-Arden.*
Rawlins, John, Esq., *Handsworth, Birmingham.*
Rich, John, Esq., *Bearley.*
Richards, Mr. Frederick, *Camp Hill, Henley-in-Arden.*
Roe, Rev. Ramsden, *Kendall's Hall, Elstree, Herts,* two copies.
Rogers, Charles, Esq., *Sleaford.*
Rudhall, Miss Emily, *Leamington.*
Rudhall, Miss Selina, *Ditto.*

Rutherford, Mr. John, *Claverdon.*
Rutley, Mr. I. F., *London.*

Sackett, Mr. W. J., Bookseller, *Birmingham.*
Salmon, Rev. H. W., *Oldberrow.*
Salt, Mr. J., *Ullenhall.*
Seymour, Rev. Richard, *Kinwarton.*
Shakespeare, S. G., Esq., *Hampton-in-Arden.*
Sharpe, Mr. C., *Sleaford.*
Sharpe, Mr., Bookseller, *Warwick.*
Shirley, Evelyn J., Esq., M.P., *Eatington.*
Simonds, Robert White, Esq., *Hampton-in-Arden.*
Simpkin, Marshall, and Co., Booksellers, *London,* twenty-five copies.
Skinner, Mr. C., *St. John's, Worcester.*
Smedley, Mr. Joseph, *Sleaford.*
Smith, J. R., Esq., *Birmingham.*
Smith, Mr. Charles, *Copt Heath, Knowle.*
Smith, Mr. Joseph, *Henley-in-Arden.*
Smith, G. T., Esq., *Goldicote.*
Smith, Mr. John Russell, Bookseller, *London,* six copies.
Smith, William, Esq., *Redditch.*
Smith, Rev. William, *Moreton Hampstead.*
Smith, Mr. Alfred, *Gainsborough.*
Smythe, Sir C. F., Bart., *Acton Burnell, Shrewsbury.*
Smythe, Rev. Patrick M., *Solihull.*
Stark, Mr. John Mozley, *Hull.*
Stephenson, Rev. Nash, *Shirley Street.*
Stilgoe, Mr. J., *Henley-in-Arden.*
Street, Mr. J., *Ditto.*
Sumner, Mrs. A., *Sleaford.*

Tarleton, Mr. John, *Wootton Wawen.*
Tempest, J. F., Esq., *Wootton Hall.*
Thomas, Miss, *Hall Green, Yardley.*
Thomas, Mr. A., *Ditto.*
Thompson, Mr. Thomas, *Solihull.*
Thompson, Mr. William, *Stratford-on-Avon.*
Thursfield, Rev. R., *Ullenhall.*
Timmins, Samuel, Esq., *Edgbaston.*

Tite, Mr. John, *Beaudesert.*
Todd, Rev. G. A., *Morton Bagot.*
Tonks, E., Esq., *Solihull.*
Treacher, Henry, Esq., *Park House, Wimbledon Park, Surrey.*
Treacher, Henry, Jun., Esq., *Wimbledon Park, Surrey.*
Turner, Mr. W., *Ullenhall.*

WORCESTER, the Right Reverend the Lord Bishop of, *Hartlebury Castle.*
Wakefield, Mr. John, *Knowle.*
Walton, Mr. James, *Stratford-on-Avon.*
Warde, Charles Thomas, Esq., *Clopton.*
Warden, C., Esq., *Stratford-on-Avon.*
Warriner, Rev. G., *Bloxham, Banbury.*
Watts, J., Esq., M.D., *The Mount, Shrewsbury.*
Webb, John, Esq., *Birmingham*, two copies.
Webster, Mrs. Thomas, *Sleaford.*
Whitehouse, Miss, *Studley.*
Whitehouse, Mr. Joseph, *Wootton.*
Whittington, Mr. T., Jun., *Wootton Wawen.*
Wilden, B., Esq., *Solihull.*
Wilkes, Thomas, Esq., *The Laurels, Knowle.*
Williams, Mrs., *Malvern Hall, Solihull.*
Williams, Mr. Edward, *Henley-in-Arden.*
Williams, Coopers, and Co., *London.*
Wilson, Miss, *Wootton Wawen.*
Wright, Mr., Bookseller, *Alcester.*
Wright, T. B., Esq., *Perry Barr, Birmingham.*
Wyatt, Mr. T., *Banbury.*

Yeadon, Rev. Edward, *Basingstoke.*
Yeales, Mr. William, *Claverdon.*

OAK AT PACKWOOD.

The Forest of Arden.

FOREST OF ARDEN.—BRITISH AND ROMAN PERIOD.—SAXON PERIOD.—NORMAN PERIOD.—PRESENT ASPECT.

A HUNDRED and two miles from London, on the Oxford and Birmingham turnpike road, and fourteen miles from the latter place, stands the quiet old town of Henley-in-Arden, so called from the district once known as "The Forest of Arden." It may, however, be questionable whether such a Forest ever existed in that special sense in which we speak of Sherwood, Epping, Windsor, and other well-known forest tracts. As the Ancient Britons and Gauls employed the term "Arden" of woodland in general, the district probably derived its designation from its peculiarly woody character.[1] And this inference is supported by what Cæsar says of Britain, at the time of his invasion, who describes the interior as "one great horrid forest." Strabo, as will be seen, also favours the same conclusion. Originally, "Arden," perhaps, served to designate the whole of Warwickshire, and parts of other counties, including the central region of England. Berkshire, in this way, obtained its name from "Berroc," the title of a well-wooded portion of the county. "Arden," on the other hand, in the course of time, became limited in its application, and was restricted to the locality including the towns of Henley and Hampton, together with the neighbourhood of those places.

In the time of the Romans, this part of Britain formed the province or country of the Cornavii.[2] Far inland, and covered with dense woods, it can hardly be matter of doubt, that, at the invasion by that warlike people, it was inhabited by the aborigines of the island, driven by the Belgic colonists[3] from the coasts. Cæsar states these colonists to have introduced agriculture and other useful arts, and that they were more polished in their manners than the inhabitants of the interior. He says, "Most of the inland inhabitants do not

---

1. The Abbé Expilly, in his *Dictionnaire Geographique*, &c., dated 1761, under the article "Ardenne," says, "Ce nom vient d'Arden, ancien terme Gaulois, qui signifioit forêt." This name comes from the ancient French term Arden, which signified a forest.

2. The Counties of Warwick, Worcester, Stafford, Salop, and Chester, by Ptolemy's account, formed the country of the Cornabii or Cornavii. There is no trace of the name now, though it appears to have continued in use up to the decline of the Roman Empire.—*Gibson's Camden*, ii, 327.

3 The Belgæ (so called from their warlike habits, Belgæ signifying "Men of Tumult") came from Gaul about three centuries before the arrival of Cæsar, who, when he had acquired the sovereignty of the continental and island Belgæ, brought over a considerable reinforcement of the former, and enabled the latter to extend their possessions into the interior regions of the country.—*Whittaker's History of the Britons*, 64, 65.

sow corn, but live on milk and flesh, and are clad with skins. All the Britons dye themselves with woad, which occasions a bluish colour, and, thereby, they have a more terrible appearance in fight. They wear their hair long, and have every part of their body shaved, except their head and upper lip. They are ignorant of the use of wool and garments, although, in severe weather, they cover themselves with the skins of sheep and deer."* Their dwellings, according to Strabo, were formed of branches of trees wrought together, a confused group of these huts, generally built in the centre of a wood, constituting a town, all the avenues to which were guarded by mounds of earth, or by trees felled and laid across. Diodorus Siculus states that their houses were made of reeds or wood, that they laid up corn in granaries, that they were simple and honest in their dealings, and that the island abounded with men, subject to various kings and princes. Dio Cassius, speaking of the more northern nations, says that they tilled no ground, that their food was game and fruit, that they lived in huts naked, had wives in common, were inured to hunger, cold, and other hardships, and, when in the woods, could live on the bark and roots of trees.[4]

Too much stress, however, must not be placed on this description, for it is notorious that the haughty and polished

---

4. Whittaker says there was no great difference between the real Belgæ and the real Britons on the arrival of the Romans. They constructed their edifices in the same manner, used the same pieces of brass or iron for money, painted their bodies, and threw off their clothes in the hour of battle. Both wore their hair alike, and prosecuted their wars on the same principles. In all great features of national character they agreed, and several of the latter concurred with the former in attention to agriculture, and in wearing garments of woollen, the only difference being that the commerce of the country rested in the hands of the Belgæ.—*History of the Britons*, 84, 85.

* *Commentaries*, bk. v, s. 14.

Romans generally designated the nations they conquered as barbarians; and it is more than probable they had little opportunity of gaining correct information of the domestic habits of the Britons. Although the dwellers in this district of Arden may have been as little advanced as any of the tribes[5] of the island, still they were acquainted with many arts, which, by the Roman writers' own showing, prove that they were not the ignorant barbarians their invaders wished the world to believe. That they had the mechanical genius to construct chariots and train horses in harness Cæsar himself testifies,* for he says, "they drive about in all directions, throw their weapons, break the ranks of the enemy, leap from their chariots and engage on foot. They retreat and advance, and are so expert as to check their horses at full speed, and to manage and turn them in an instant." These charioteers are stated to have numbered four thousand on one occasion.[6] Besides these they had a well-trained cavalry, but their principal strength lay in their infantry, who fought with darts, large swords, and short targets.† They had bits, made of ivory, and were found to be possessed of bracelets, vessels of amber and glass, agates, pearls, and abundance of tin.[7] They navigated in barks, the keels and ribs of which were formed of light materials, the other parts being made of wicker, and covered with the hides of oxen.

---

5. Britain, when first known to the Romans, was divided into seventeen independent states on the south of the Tyne, and thirteen to the north of that river.—*Pomp. Melius*, bk. iii.

6. "Their strength lies in their infantry; but some tribes fight in chariots. The more noble acts as driver, and his retainers are combatants."—*Tacitus' Life of Agricola*, 12.

7. Tacitus says, "Britain produces gold, silver, and other minerals, the profits of our victory."—*Ibid*, 12.

* *Commentaries*, iv, 33. They are said to have had six varieties of wheel carriages.

† *Richard of Cirencester*, i, 3.

The Romans, from their conquests, were well qualified to judge of population, and we have the testimony of Cæsar that "the number of people was countless, their buildings exceedingly numerous, and the number of their cattle great,"* a statement which shows that the Britons had made considerable progress in the arts favourable to life. Though some of these, such as ship building, and the employment of marl as a manure for land, may have been introduced by the Belgic settlers on the coasts, still the construction of chariots, and the training of horses for these and for their cavalry must be attributed to native ingenuity and skill. They possessed, likewise, the softening influences of poetry and music; for besides the Druids,[8] they had their bards, who sung in heroic measures the deeds of their gods and heroes, accompanied with the sweet notes of the lyre.†

To these testimonies to the comparative civilization of the Ancient Britons must be added their religion, which, organized and regulated as it was, if we are to believe the statements of Cæsar and others on the subject, is no mean evidence of their advancement in humanizing attainments. Their worship, superstitious as it may have been, can scarcely be regarded as the sign of a people in the depths of ignorance and degradation. Their Priests were persons of no slight and superficial cultivation: these, the Druids, had the management of things sacred, conducted the public and private sacrifices, and interpreted all religious matters. They had also great authority in civil affairs, decided all

---

8. DRUID. A name derived from the word *Daru* in the British and Celtic language, equivalent to *Drus* in Greek, and signifying an oak, beneath the shade of which they celebrated their worship.

* *Cæsar*, v, 12. † *Richard of Cirencester*, i, 4.

controversies, arbitrating in disputes relative to inheritance or boundaries of lands, decreeing rewards and punishments, and instructing the youth, particularly those belonging to the chief families. They used written characters in most of their public and private matters; but in the preparation of youth intended for the priesthood, they taught them to commit to memory the doctrines communicated to them. This they did for two reasons; first, that they might be kept secret from the mass of the people; and, secondly, that their disciples might, by practice of this kind, find it easy to remember transactions of which they were hereafter to be the historians. They inculcated, too, the principle that souls do not become extinct, and imparted to youth knowledge of the stars, their motion, the extent of the world and the earth, the nature of things, and the power and majesty of the gods.*

Like other nations, the Britons were idolaters; they are said to have offered human sacrifices, and to have attributed divine virtues to the mistletoe. The Druids, it is certain, esteemed nothing more sacred than the mistletoe, and the tree on which it grew, if an oak. They particularly delighted in groves of oak, many of which were consecrated to their worship, and they performed no sacred rite without the branches of that tree.9 But that they sacrificed their criminals, or the captives taken in battle, is not sufficiently certified to be implicitly believed. Taking all these cir-

9. The mistletoe is rarely to be found growing on the oak, but generally on apple and crab trees: In Packwood garden and other neighbouring localities, it grows in great profusion. "The Druids gathered the mistletoe with religious ceremonies, and at particular times. The sacrifice and the feast being prepared under the tree, they led thither two white bulls. The priest, clothed in white, ascended the tree, cut off the mistletoe with a golden bill, and received it in a white cloth. The victims were then slain, and the favour of the Deity invoked on the offering."—*Richard of Cirencester.*

* *Cæsar*, vi, 14.

cumstances into account, it is difficult to suppose that a people so ingenious, and with such knowledge and laws as they are thus reported to have possessed, would be living in dwellings of the primitive character of those depicted by the Roman writers, or that they would be without clothing in a climate like Britain, a country described by themselves as having days in winter of only six hours' duration. It is, therefore, reasonable to conclude that the constructions designated "towns," were more secure places of retreat than their ordinary dwellings, in cases of hostility between the native chiefs and their retainers, who, previous to the arrival, and after the final departure of the Romans, were frequently engaged in warfare against each other. To favour this interpretation, we have Cæsar himself stating that the Britons, on being repulsed by his cavalry, concealed themselves in woods, where they had secured an admirable refuge, prepared beforehand, in case of civil war. This, and others, he calls fortifications.* And again, he relates how when they have fortified the intricate woods, to avoid the incursion of an enemy, with an entrenchment and a rampart, they call it a town.† The Saxon Chronicle also records that, after a defeat, the Britons fled to the wood-wastes.

If any part of Britain formed the "great horrid forest," described as the prevailing feature of the interior, this portion of Warwickshire would be especially included in that phraseology, seeing how well wooded it continues to be. That the dwellers in this extensive forest tract may have been of a more primitive character than those nearer to the coast, is probable: Still the general characteristics of the whole race will apply to them, since they, no doubt, contributed their quota in the general levy of chariots,

* Book v, 9. † Book v, 21.

cavalry, and foot, in the many conflicts with the Roman invaders, as well as furnished money, and a portion of the hostages named as being sent for "from remote places." *

The Romans, after ruling Britain for four hundred and seventy years, finally left the country, A. D. 409. During this period the people who formed the province of the Cornavii, like the rest of the tribes south of the wall of Severus, had been reduced to the Roman sway, and brought, by their great roads, into communication with the other parts of the country. This part was not immediately crossed by any great Roman Road, being situate within a triangle formed by three of them, viz. the Ryknield Street, the Fosse, and the Watling Street, from which many of the more ancient British roads and trackways led to the interior.[10] The Ryknield Street intersected the Fosse and Watling Street, one northward of Birmingham, the other at Stow-on-the-Wold. It was the only Roman road running through part of this district, and it is to it, and some supposed British roads, that we shall alone direct attention.

THE RYKNIELD STREET

Ran partly through, and close on the west side of this district. Entering the county of Warwick a little north

10. The Britons maintained a considerable foreign commerce, had formed towns or large communities, and employed chariots for war, and undoubtedly for civil purposes. Hence their internal communications must have been free and numerous. It is no surprise, therefore, after the lapse of so many centuries, marks of such *British roads* appear even at present to a careful observer, traversing the island in every direction. They differ from those made by the Romans, in not being raised or paved, nor always straight; but often wind along the tops or sides of the hills which lye in their course.—*Commentary on the Itin. of Richard of Cirencester.*

* *Cæsar*, iv, c. 27.

of Birmingham, it proceeded in a straight line west of Tanworth, Skilts, and Mapleborough Green, by Studley, to the station or city of Alauna, (Alcester,) and left the county a little south of Bidford. Stukeley, describing this road north of Birmingham, says, "Either our maps are wrong, or the Roman road goes very much winding, perhaps to avoid the great *Arduen* forest. The name of this forest is left in divers places, as Henley-in-Arden, &c." * He states further, "I find the *Rignig* Street way comes from Alcester directly north and south by Moseley, over a heath where the road appears now very broad;" † and "They call the *Rigning Street*, the Hickling Street at this place, (Birmingham,) and likewise Portlane." ‡ Some portions of it still bear the name of the Portway road.

On the right hand side of this road, a few yards from the tenth milestone from Birmingham, and nearly opposite to an inn called the White Lion, are some earthworks of great antiquity, designated, by the tradition of the neighbourhood, as Roman Remains. How far this may accord with the fact, is a problem for the antiquarian to determine: This much, however, may, with certainty, be affirmed of them,—that they are of very ancient date. If Roman, situated, as they are, midway between Birmingham and Alcester, they might form a small post, the area within the embankment being too inconsiderable for a permanent fortification or camp. The work consists of an embanked parallelogram, surrounded by a double moat, or fosse, three sides of which are clearly defined.[11]

Alauna, (Alcester,) situate close upon the south-west

---

11. The area within the embankment is 264 feet by 155. It is most probable, from the double moat, that it formed the site of the dwelling place of some powerful chief, in a very early period of our history.

* *Stukeley's Itin. Bor.*, 20. † *Ibid*, 21. ‡ *Itin. Cur.*, 61.

corner of our district, was, according to Richard of Cirencester, a city of the Dobuni,[12] one of the tribes forming the province or greater country of the Cornavii. Many remains of the Romans have been found near this place, such as coins, urns, &c. Two urns were discovered in 1812, and, a short distance from them, the skeleton of a man nearly seven feet in length, by whose side was placed a long straight sword; but, on being removed, it fell to pieces.*

The principal indications, however, of the presence of the Romans in the district of Arden, are to be found at Harborough Banks, in the parish of Lapworth, and in a small Post at Beaudesert, where the remains of fortified places are still clearly defined. To these works some secure means of approach from their great arterial ways must have existed, and there are still many signs of ancient roads and trackways, such as the Britons are known to have adopted, in close proximity to them. One of these (portions of which are yet in use) is discernible from the south of Lonesomeford, through Lapworth Street, by Harborough Banks, Packwood, and Baddesley, which formerly went, as shown in old maps, through Shirley Street, in a direct line to Birmingham, joining, near that place, the Ryknield Street. Hutton calls it a Roman road, and describes it as leading to Stratford-on-Avon. Another came southward by Wootton Wawen, along the present Edge Lane, commencing near Whitley, and separating the parishes of Beaudesert and Preston Bagot. From this point, it proceeds in a direct line to Camp Hill, the Roman Post before named, where it is now broken by inclosure; but traces remain of its

12. The Dobuni, formed of Dobh-buini, and interpreted the residents on a river, means, I think, the men of the valley. All the other terms applied to them signify lowlanders.—*Whittaker's Britons*, 88.

* *Archæologia*, xvii, 332-3.

continuance through the fields, where it formerly led into the road over Liveridge Hill. The road passing through Lapworth Street, ran, at that place, a short distance westward of the great work now known as "HARBOROUGH BANKS;" and, a little to the east of the course of this road, in the parish of Knowle, was found, in the year 1779,

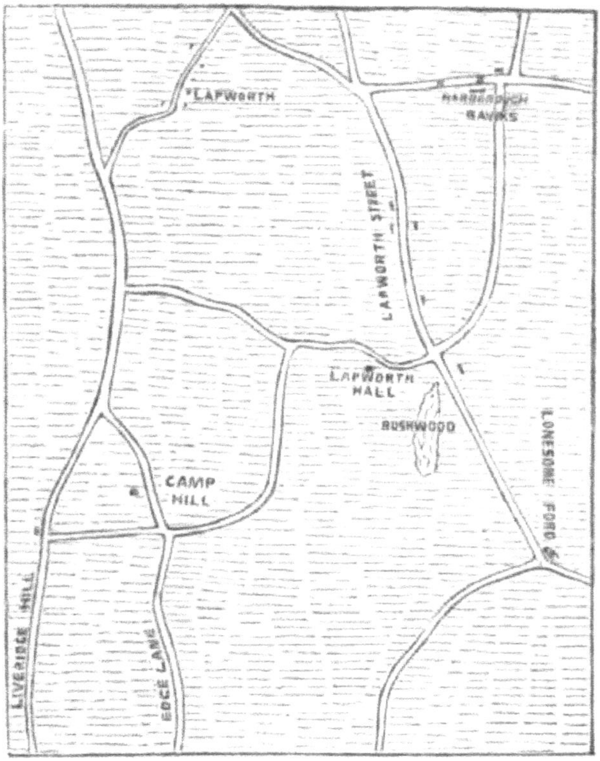

an earthen urn, containing a mass of Roman coins, weighing about fifteen pounds. They were mostly copper, or of that metal washed with tin or silver, and many of them of the Emperor Gallienus, his wife Salonina, the younger Tetricus, and other usurpers in Britain, during the reign of Gallienus.

They were found on an eminence, which, however, bore no marks of a tumulus.* The foregoing plan will show the situation of these works, and direction of the roads.

HARBOROUGH BANKS

Is within the manor of Brome Hall, in that portion of the hamlet of Kingswood, lying in the parish of Lapworth. It forms the remains of a Roman camp, or fortification, of some importance, as the earthworks, which still remain, from their extent show. The rampart, or circumvallum, which is laid down in the accompanying map,[13] incloses an area of about twenty-six acres, the eastern part sloping down to the brook, whilst the western portion is elevated, such being the usual situation chosen by the Romans for these defences.[14] Cæsar states that this kind of fortification formed a line of circumvallation around the camp, by the construction of an earthen barrier, defended generally by a ditch, in which stakes sharpened at the top, and hardened by fire, were driven, being held firm by trampled clay. The rest of the ditch was covered over with osiers and twigs, to conceal the stakes. Within the inclosure, forage and corn were provided, according to circumstances.†

Nothing of importance has been met with here beyond the spout of an ewer, discovered some years ago in digging for gravel. This, when melted, proved to be metal, resem-

---

13. An Inclosure Act having been obtained, these remains are in course of destruction, and by the time this meets the eye of the reader, little trace will be left of this interesting work of an ancient people.

14. The Romans preferred the plain for their places of defence, for the convenience of rivers, and possessing confidence in the art of war, they were the more indifferent in regard to the natural advantages.—*Archæologia*, v, 53.

* *Archæologia*, vii, 413. † *Cæsar*, vii, 73, 74.

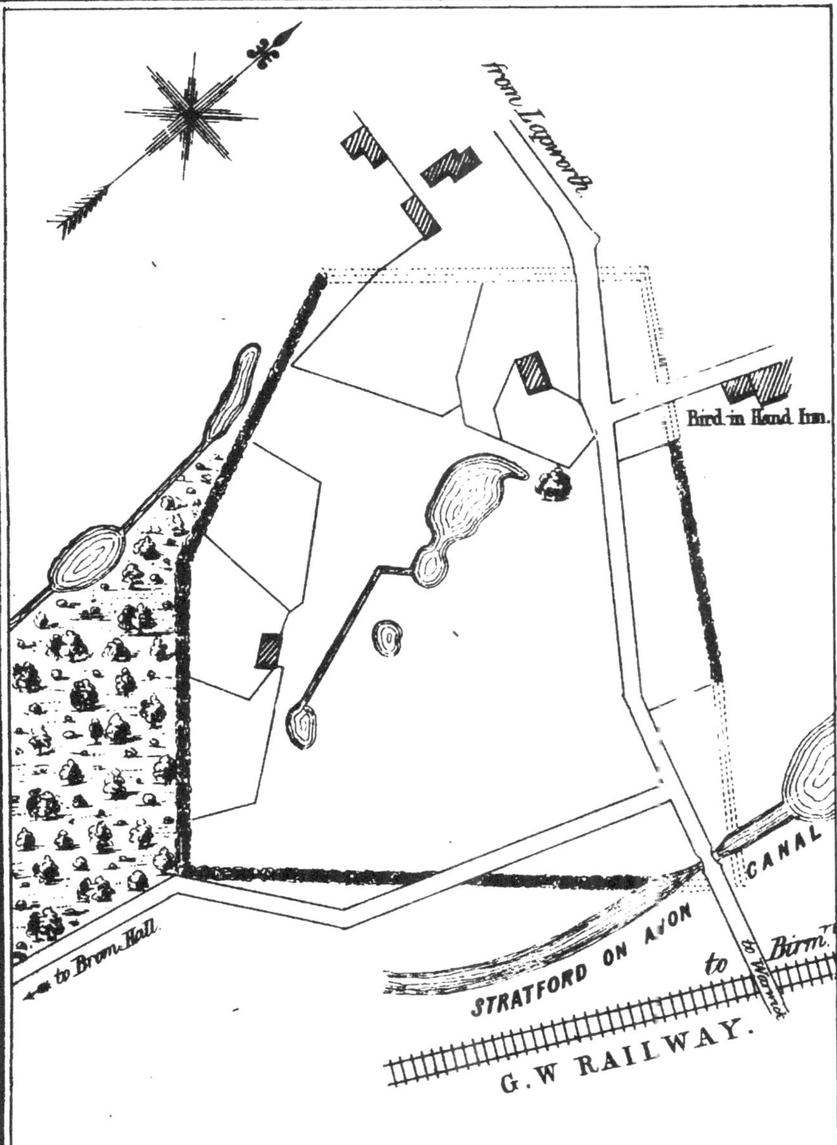

HARBOROUGH BANKS.

bling Prince's metal, a kind of Aurichaleum.* A few miles south eastward of this camp was Ausona, or Avona, (Warwick,) where the Prefect or Commander of the Dalmaian Horse was posted.†

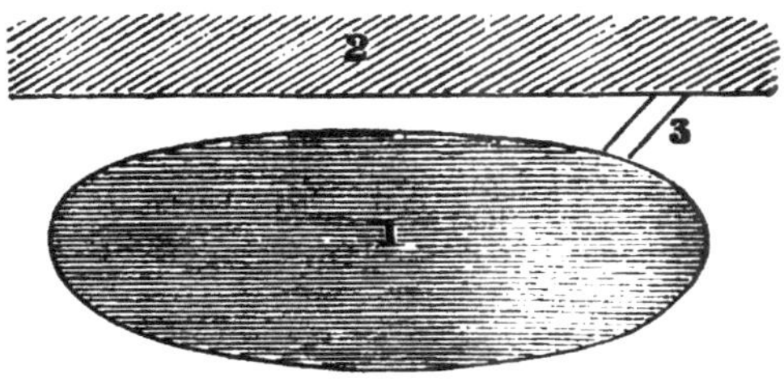

1. CAMP. 2. DITCH. 3. ROAD.

The Roman Post that has been referred to, lies about a mile and a half to the west of this last, on the right of the turnpike road leading to Birmingham from Henley-in-Arden,

* *Thomas's Dugdale.* † *Gibson's Camden.*

This elevated part retains the name of "Camp Hill," and the work from which it acquires this title, is considered, by some antiquaries, to have been an outpost connected by an ancient road with the former. Its outline will be best understood by the preceding view and plan. The road already described as passing along Edge Lane, ran close by it.

After the submission of the Britons to their conquerors, the Romans, fond of agriculture, induced the several tribes to form themselves into communities, and thus towns of a better character, and settlements sprang up in various directions. The cultivation of the earth was encouraged, and the inhabitants became more civilized; but, on the departure of that people, and during their civil dissensions and broils,[15] and the attacks of the Picts and the Saxons, the country relapsed into much of its former state. The Saxons, who spread themselves over the whole of Britain, destroyed great numbers of the towns, laid waste the land, and, according to Gildas, "In the streets lay the tops of lofty towers, stones of high walls, and human bodies covered with blood, with no chance of being buried, save in the ruins of the houses, or in the ravening bodies of wild beasts and birds. The living fled to the mountains, to the thickly wooded forests, and to the rocks of the seas." *

Under the Saxon Heptarchy, this part of Britain formed a portion of the kingdom of Mercia;[16] but these adven-

---

15. Tacitus, speaking of the disposition of the natives, observes, "that they were divided by factions and animosities among their chieftains," even in the time of the Roman occupation."—*Life of Agricola*, bk. xii.

16. The Anglo Saxon kingdom of Mercia included the counties of Chester, Derby, Nottingham, Lincoln, Salop, Stafford, Leicester, Rutland, Northampton, Huntingdon, Hereford, Worcester, Warwick, Gloucester, Oxford, Buckingham, and parts of Hertford and Bedford.

* *Gildas*, s. 24, 25.

turers, soon after subduing the natives, were in constant tumult and quarrel amongst themselves, and turned their weapons against each other: Hence new disorders arose. To these elements of strife, the inroads of the Northmen and Danes added further sources of disturbance; and this part of the kingdom seems to have suffered some of the calamities of war, though not in so great a degree as the more exposed parts on the eastern coasts; for we find it recorded, A. D. 1016, that Canute, with his army, went into Warwickshire, during the mid-winter's tide, and ravaged, and burned, and slew all that they could come at.*

Throughout these successive desolations, the thickly wooded district of Arden would, from its peculiar features, escape many of the more pressing calamities of those early days, when rapine and plunder prevailed along the sea-board of the island,—especially along its eastern shores: Forsaking, therefore, further reference to these ancient distractions, we may remark next, in relation to this district of Arden, that the Romans, who were not great lovers of the chase, during their occupation of the island, left the woodland parts of the country in pretty much the same state in which they found them. The Saxons, however, hunters from their childhood, instituted a new order of things with respect to the forest tracts of ancient Britain. Ardent followers of the chase, they speedily made inclosures of the more woody districts; and appropriated, by well-defined boundaries, to the gratification of their passion for hunting, the primitive forests of the country of which they had become possessed. Indeed, hunting, with them, was the preparatory school for warlike achievement. The patience, courage, power of endurance, and address, requisite to the

---

* *Anglo Saxon Chronicle.*

reputation of a skilful hunter, were attributes equally essential to the renown of the warrior. Accordingly, no part of the education of a Saxon noble was more carefully attended to, than proficiency as a hunter, in testimony of which we learn, on the authority of Asser,* that King Alfred, in his youth, was a zealous follower of the chase, hunting with great assiduity and success; for, says he, "skill and good fortune in this art, as in all others, are among the gifts of God."

A region, therefore, like that of "Arden," would, doubtless, become a favourite hunting ground of the new possessors. Such lands as were not disposed of, were held to belong exclusively to the crown; and in these, secure from the presence of man, wild animals found a safe retreat. These lands, abounding in game of various kinds, were called "Forests," and were reserved to their especial use and gratification by those in authority, who imposed severe penalties upon all who presumed to encroach upon their pleasures.[17] Any freeholder, however, during the Saxon rule, had full liberty of sporting,—to start, pursue, and kill any game upon his own lands, providing he abstained from trespassing on the King's Forests. Great part of the district we are describing, appears to have been early parcelled out among the Thanes, or leading men, since little of it belonged to the king at the taking of Domesday. A portion

17. A law of Edward, in a volume of the Exchequer, states, "I will that all men do abstain from hunting in my woods, that my will shall be obeyed under penalty of life." Edgar, a most popular Anglo Saxon king, was so rigorous in his forest laws, that the thanes murmured as well as the lower husbandmen, who had been accustomed to use the woods for pasturage and boscage. Canute's forest laws were scarcely less stringent: Though he allowed bishops, abbots, and thanes to hunt in his woods, still the penalty, if a freeman killed one of the king's deer, or struck his forester, was loss of freedom, by being reduced to a penal serf.

* *Life of Alfred.*

of this, it may be inferred, would, at an earlier period, have been appropriated by the owners, to the preservation of game, and the enjoyment of those field sports, to which they were passionately addicted. Although the Saxons were great destroyers of the strongholds which the Britons had received from the Romans, and built very few others, still we may reasonably conclude, that on their possessions here many of them would erect abodes of some extent, where, with their retainers, they could more readily indulge in the pleasures of the chase.

There is, consequently, but little token of Saxon rule in this district, as few castles were built in their time, and but few grants, by charter, occurred before the Norman invasion. Lapworth was, however, given to the Bishopric of Worcester, by Kenulph, King of Mercia, in the time of Danebert, the ninth Bishop of that See, and so continued till the time of King Canute the Dane, when the then Bishop granted the village to *Hearluvinus*, as a reward for attending him on a special embassy into Saxony. The absence here of tumuli, or barrows, their usual mode of sepulture, so common in some counties, tends to show that no great battle took place within its area, and that none of their magnates had residence therein. The probability is that the whole of this district was, for a long period, kept strictly in a forest state, for the preservation of game and the amusement of the great landed proprietors, the principal of whom, before the Conquest, were the Earl of Mercia, and the Thanes Baldwin, Leuvinus, or Leofric, Wagen, Swain, Godric, &c., all of whom were displaced, and their possessions bestowed upon the companions of the Conqueror, the greater portion falling to the Earls of Stafford, Mellent, and Warwick, Nigel de Albani, the progenitor of the de Mowbrays, and Hugh de Grentemaisnill. The Saxons, nevertheless, during the period of their occupancy, introduced, and practised, agriculture, and the kindred arts; and at the time of the Norman Conquest, portions of the district, which we may designate "The Forest of Arden," are described as being under cultivation, although woods sufficiently extensive still remained to give it a forest appearance. To the partial cultivation of this tract, we have testimony in Domesday Survey. There we learn that, in *Wootton*, were nine ploughlands and twenty-two bordars,[18] having six ploughs, and a wood, two leagues long, and one broad. In *Beaudesert*, two ploughlands, two ploughs, and an inclosure, half a mile square. In *Preston*, six ploughlands, arable, two ploughs, and a wood, one mile long, and half a mile broad. In *Lapworth*, one ploughland, arable, and a wood, two miles long, and one broad. In *Rowington*, eight ploughlands and nine ploughs, with a wood, a mile and a half long. In *Hampton-in-Arden*, with its several hamlets, ten ploughlands, and woods, in extent, three miles long, and three broad. In *Solihull*, then called *Ulverlie*, eight ploughlands, and a wood, four miles long, and half a mile broad. And, in almost every other parish in the district, there is record of a proportionate extent of arable and woodland. Besides game, these woods supported a great number of hogs. In one, four miles long, it is stated there was keeping for 2000 hogs. The lands of the Saxon Thanes thus distributed among the Norman Barons, it was long before the country reached anything approaching to a settled condition. The change of masters was attended with much discontent

---

18. Ploughland, hide, and carucate, are supposed to have been the same in extent, and to have contained each about 120 acres, more or less, without any decisive computation. Bordars.—Husbandmen, who occupied a bord, or cottage, with a small parcel of land, for which they supplied the lord with poultry and eggs, and other small dainties.

and turbulence on the part of the aboriginal population. Although so large a proportion of the native aristocracy had been exterminated at the battle of Hastings, their memory was cherished by their retainers with a fond regret, which was, in no wise, diminished by the institution of those forest laws, which became a constant source of dissatisfaction and strife through succeeding generations.

Under the Conqueror, the feudal system prevailed in a rigour which was no mitigation of its intolerable burdens. After the Norman invasion, the whole land of the kingdom was either in the hands of the crown, or held in fief[19] by the vassals of the crown: And the property of all the animals of chase was held to be vested in the crown, whilst no person, without the express license of the king, was permitted to hunt, as in Saxon times, even upon his own estate. The Conqueror, who, as the *Saxon Chronicle* affirms, loved the red deer as if he had been their father, is alleged to have visited the slaughter of one of these animals with a heavier penalty than the murder of a human being. It is easy, therefore, to conceive what an amount of irritation and suffering these forest laws must have caused in a district, like the one we are describing, abounding in game.

The new proprietors of the lands, and their tenants, soon began to rebuild, or to enlarge the old houses, so as to make them secure against aggression.[20] Various strongholds, in the locality of "Arden," had sprung into existence,

---

19. The Normans held their lands under what was called knights' fees, or service. The land in England was divided into upwards of sixty thousand of these fees. For every knight's fee the proprietor had to provide a knight, or soldier, to attend the king in his wars, for forty days in a year.

20. A great number of castles were built in Stephen's days, by the nobles of the realm, either to defend the confines of their counties from invasions of foreigners, and violence of homelings; or as fortifications to themselves when they meant, or intended, any inroad or breaking in upon their neighbours.—*Holinshed's Chronicle*, ii, 110.

during the reigns of the early Norman kings. Amongst others, the castle of Beaudesert was built by Thurstan de Montford; that of Bickenhill, a member of the lordship of Hampton-in-Arden, was erected either by Nigel de Albani, or Roger de Mowbray, and that at Studley, by William de Corbuson: of these, however, no vestige remains. Edifices of equally substantial character, here and there arose,

"Such as the moated hall,
With close circumference of wat'ry guard
And pensile bridge, portends! * * *
* * * * Such the retreats
Of Britain's ancient nobles! less intent
On rural beauty, and sweet patronage
Of gentle arts, than studious to restrain,
With servile awe, barbarian multitudes;
Or, with confederate force, the regal power
Proudly to control. Hence they, their vassal troops
Assembling, now the fate of empire planned;
Now o'er defenceless tribes, with wanton rage,
Tyrannic ruled; and, in their castled halls
Secure, with wild excess their revels kept." *

The sites of these castles are well known spots in their respective localities. Nor are abundant evidences of buildings of less note wanting in the same district. Though now supplanted by modern dwellings, the traces of the moated inclosure are very common: More especially is this the case at Lapworth, Codbarrow, Baddesley, Langdon, and Packwood, where the "watery guard" of the "Halls" is to be found in pretty much the same state as when first excavated for the purpose of protection. In the first-named of these parishes, there is also a moated inclosure on a farm belonging to Lapworth Charity, and another, the fosse of which is very deep, on the farm called Lapworth Park; but without any buildings. Others may be found at Hampton-

---

* *Edgehill*, by Richard Jago, son of Richard Jago, rector of Beaudesert, anno 1709 to 1741.

in-Arden, and at Packwood Glass House; and we have moat-house farms at Studley, Ullenhall, and other places, as well as park farms at Wootton, Beaudesert, Lapworth, &c.[21]

The remains of some of the castles of the Norman Barons still in existence in England, enable us to form an opinion of their extent and strength; but, of the dwellings of the lesser landowners, and the labouring classes, little is now known. Britton observes that "the almost unceasing prevalence of internal wars, combined with the ravages caused by foreign aggression, have swept away almost every vestige of any domestic edifice, properly so called, which had been erected during the first thousand years of the Christian era: and in the three following centuries, the same rude hand of violence both prevented the erection, to any extent, of dwelling houses of a permanent character, and also wrought the destruction of the greater part of such as then chanced to exist. From the eleventh century, however, till the close of the fourteenth, occasional examples still remain, though, in themselves, few in number, and perhaps situated in positions widely distant from one another, from which the general principles of the Domestic Architecture of those days may be ascertained with tolerable accuracy." *

In this district, as it has been stated, the *moated* dwelling appears to have been the general characteristic, one ancient specimen of which is still existent: This is Baddesley

---

21. The evidence of grants of parks or chases is shown in the numerous fences in this county, still called Park fences, whereby the landlord claims nine yards of land beyond the apparent boundary, as his freeboard. A *park* was an inclosed chase, extending over a man's own grounds, and allowed by a grant from the king. *Free warren* was a similar franchise for preservation of beasts and fowls of warren, which the Norman kings invented to protect them, by giving the grantee a sole and exclusive power of killing such game so far as his warren extended, on condition of his preventing other persons.

* *Britton's Early Domestic Architecture*, 6.

Clinton, the site of a still older dwelling, some parts of the massive walls of which, are built up in the present structure. The engraving of this old Hall, on a subsequent page, will give the reader an adequate idea of the exterior of mansions of the period, with gateway, drawbridge, and lofty mullioned windows. The interior is, at the present day, modified to meet the requirements of modern times; but there is, fortunately, a document in existence, by which we can form an opinion of the plan, size, and interior arrangement of the structures erected by the landed proprietors in Arden, in the fourteenth century. The plan appears to have been, usually, a parallelogram, with or without wings. Within the moat, of which mention has been made in connexion with Lapworth, stood a manor-house, which Sir John Bishopden, knight, built. In the year 1314, 7th Edward II, it seems that he entered into a contract with William Hoese, mason, and John de Pesham, of Rowington, to build him a house of freestone, on his manor of Lapworth, which was to be forty feet long by eighteen broad within the walls, the end walls and gables to be three and a half feet in thickness, and those at the back and front two and a half. The doorway was to be in the middle of the house, and, on each side, a base chamber, with wardrobes and proper windows and doors; the chambers and doorway eleven feet in height. On each side of the entry, a stone wall, as high as the doorway, to which walls two columns of stone to be affixed, on which the door might be suspended. The doorway to be so constructed that a drawbridge might be fitted to it. Above the doorway and the two base chambers, was to be an upper chamber, of the length and width of the house, with two fireplaces and two wardrobes, and fitting doors and windows. This "chambre sovereyne" was to be nine feet from the floor to the rafters, whilst a parapet of stone, two and a half feet high, was to be raised above the roof timbers. The cost of the masonry was to be twenty-five marks, (about 200*l.*,) and the work completed within one year.* As there is no mention of the building of kitchens and offices necessary to such a structure, it is more than probable that those portions of the old manor-house remained. This, then, may be said to have been the general style of dwelling, standing, in the fourteenth century, within the various moated inclosures at Codbarrow, Langdon, Packwood, &c., the interior area of land within each being nearly the same.

Whilst the forest laws were enforced here, as elsewhere, in all their barbarous rigour, a power had gradually grown up by the side of the great Barons, destined to soften considerably the rude exercise of their authority. During the Saxon and Norman rules, large grants of land were made to the church; and the clergy shared, with the feudal lords, in the rights and duties of proprietorship. Forest tracts were vested in them, equally with the laity. With a taste and judgment, derived from their superior culture, they selected vast possessions in the most agreeable and fertile situations; and, amid the leafy shade and purling streams of the localities they had chosen, they built churches, founded religious houses, and defined the boundaries of parishes. In the not distant city of Coventry, societies of the Benedictine, Carthusian, and Cistertian Orders respectively established themselves; and from these, in due course, branched off minor corporations of the same class. These severally settled themselves at Wootton Wawen,

* *Parker's Domestic Architecture*, 5. Sir John de Bishopden engaged to lead the stone from the quarry at his own cost, and to find timber, carpentering, sand, and lime. Further details of this hall will be found on a future page.

Wroxall, Pinley, Studley, Henwood, and Temple Balsall, within the limits of "Arden."

From these religious fraternities a certain civilizing influence was constantly radiating. Themselves sprung from the people, they would, naturally, be imbued with popular sympathies. This bias towards the "lower orders" would also be increased by the humanizing spirit of their sacred profession: And holding, as they were supposed to do, the keys of both kingdoms, they were enabled to interpose, with considerable effect, on behalf of the subordinate classes of society. In the Priesthood, the people, at large, found powerful protectors. Bordar, soccage-tenant, and villein,[22] received at their hands a consideration to which they were strangers from any other quarters. The Church alone dared to resist and to denounce the encroachments and exactions of the nobility; and from its growing authority we may date the amelioration of the tyranny and extortion which had been long practised by the great landed proprietors. The services due to the landowner became less severe and better defined: Of this we have a signal evidence, in connexion with the district bordering on that we are describing. For it is on record that Thomas de Arden had in *Rieton* three servants, each holding a yardland and a half,[23] and paying a certain yearly rent in money, ploughing one day in winter each, and one day in Lent; mowing, raking, making hay, carrying corn, and gathering nuts—at each kind of work—one day. The cottagers, thirteen in number, besides their rent, worked one day each, at some of the

---

22. *Soccage-tenants*, or *Sokemen*, were freemen who held land of the king, or Lord of the Soke. By the Saxons they were styled "Lesser Thanes," (yeomen,) being free-born, and eligible to honourable service. *Villein*—a person in absolute slavery, the property of the lord of the soil, like the cattle upon it.

23. A yardland, the living of a ploughman or yeoman, was of uncertain quantity; sometimes larger than one plough could till, and sometimes so small, that one plough could till two.

before-mentioned labours;* whilst in Stoneleigh, (which remained in the hands of the crown, from the Conquest till the time of Henry II,) the inferior tenants paid a common fine, and at the general reap in harvest, called *Bederipe*, the sokemen, with their tenants, were summoned to reap the lord's corn, the sokemen to ride up and down on horseback with wands to see that they worked well, and to amerce those in the king's court that made default, or laboured idly.† The freeholders and tenants of Peter de Montfort, 7 Edward I, had also similar privileges in Wellesbourne Mountfort, and common in Kingswood, with pannage for their hogs and certain proportions of wood for fuel.‡

Whether, or no, any Forest of Arden, properly so called, ever did exist, certain, it is, that in the list of Forests in England, in the time of Queen Elizabeth, given by the celebrated antiquary, Sir William Spelman, no mention of Arden or any other forest in Warwickshire, is found. Considerable portions of the locality were, no doubt emparked and enforested, as there are many notices, in ancient deeds, of appointment, by proprietors of lands, of Foresters.24 We find, also, that Peter de Wulwardinton, (now Wolverton,) 18 Henry III, gave one mark fine to the king, for coursing in the Forest.§ Evidence exists, in Camden and Leland, of the state of the country in the time of Henry VIII. The former says, "Let us take a view of the woodland which lies north of the Avon, occupying a larger extent, being the

---

24. William de Bishopden, *temp.* Richard I, was enfeoffed of certain lands by his wife's father, Henry de Mountfort, to be held on certain conditions by appointment of his *forester*, and the fourth part of a wood at Baddesley Clinton. In the register of Stoneleigh Abbey, it appears, that the monks were to have Estovers in the outwoods by the oversight of the Foresters.—See *Dugdale.*

* *Dugdale's Warwickshire*, p. 33.

† *Ibid*, p. 177.

‡ *Ibid*, p. 410.

§ *Ibid*, p. 467.

most part covered with woods, though not without pastures, corn fields, and iron mines. As it is at present called the *Woodland*, so it had anciently the much older name of *Arden*, but, as I take it to the same purport, for Arden seems to have signified a forest to the Ancient Britons and Gauls."* Leland remarks "that the moaste parte of Warwykshire that stondithe on the lefte banke of Avon, is called *Arden*, and this countrye is not so plentifull of corne, but of grasse and woode."† At this time, however, the forest laws, still severe and terrible in their penalties, were in full force, and so continued, for many years after the reign of Henry VIII. His daughter, Queen Elizabeth, is said to have been fond of Hunting the Stag, and brought down many by the bow, in which she was skilled. This was also one of the principal amusements of the great landed proprietors of those days.[25] Drayton, a native of this county, gives a quaint but vivid descriptive picture of the Forest,‡ which, though long, is nevertheless, from its apt illustration of our subject, deserving of quotation :

---

25. Field sports, fishing, shooting, hunting, were the delight of every one, and although the forest laws were terrible, they served only to enhance the excitement by danger. Then, as now, no English peasant could be convinced that there was any moral crime in appropriating the wild game. It was an offence against statute law, but no offence against natural law; and it was rather a trial of skill between the noble who sought to monopolize a right which seemed to be common to all, and those who would succeed, if they could, in securing their own share of it. The Robin Hood ballads reflect the popular feeling, and breathe the warm, genial spirit of the old greenwood adventurers. If deer stealing was a sin, it was more than compensated by the risk of the penalty to which those who failed submitted, when no other choice was left. They did not always submit, as the old northern poem shows of *Adam Bell, Clym of the Clough, and William of Cloudislee*, with its most immoral moral; yet, I suppose, there was never pedant who could resist the spell of those ringing lines, or refuse with all his heart to wish the rogues success, and confusion to the honest men.—*Froude's England, temp.* Henry VIII.

* *Camden's Britannia*, by Gough, ii, 329.

† *Leland's Itinerary.*

‡ *Poly-olbion*, written 1612-1622.

"Muse! first of Arden tell, whose footsteps* yet are found
In her rough woodlands more than any other ground!
That mighty ARDEN held even in her height of pride,
Her one hand touching Trent, the other, Severn's side.
The very sound of these the wood nymphs doth awake;
When thus of her own self the ancient forest spake:
'My many goodly sites when first I came to show,
Here open'd I the way to mine overthrow;
For when the world found out the fitness of my soil,
The gripple wretch began immediately to spoil
My tall and goodly woods, and did my grounds inclose,
By which, in little time, my bounds I came to lose.
When Britain first her fields with villages had fill'd,
Her people wexing still, and wanting where to build,
They oft dislodg'd the hart, and set their houses where
He in the broom and brakes had long time made his leyre.
Of all the forests here within this mighty isle,
If those old Britons then me sovereign did instile,
I needs must be the greatest; for greatness 'tis alone
That gives our kind the place; else were there many a one
For pleasantness of shade that far doth me excel.
But of our forest's kind the quality to tell,
We equally partake with woodland as with plain,
Alike with hill and dale; and every day maintain
The sundry kinds of beasts upon our copious wastes,
That men for profit breed, as well as those of chase.'"

After describing the various birds and beasts of chase abounding therein, and a description of a stag hunt in Arden, he proceeds to a disquisition on the medicinal herbs, and the course of rivers of the immediate country, for which we must refer the reader to the work itself.

The sixteenth century was a time of progression in England; more land was taken into cultivation, and the material prosperity of the people promoted. The greater security afforded by the laws rendered the defensive appliances of the moat and drawbridge no longer necessary, or such situations desirable. Many of the old halls were abandoned, and other buildings erected, in more beautiful

* Referring to several towns, such as Henley-in-Arden, Hampton-in-Arden, Weston-in-Arden, &c.

and healthy situations. Hence a new class of lords' or manor-houses arose on hill sides or gentle slopes,[26] destined, in their turn, to be again deserted by the Lord, and appropriated to the Steward, or to the principal farmer on the estate. The latter, like his Lord, was given to hospitality; and partook, freely, himself, of the produce of the land; nor was the labourer, though badly lodged, less well fed and cared for.[27]

We have already alluded to the large proportion of lands once devoted to woods in this district, but, at the present period, these extensive tracts of forest ground have either altogether disappeared, or dwindled, comparatively, to the dimensions of plantation patches. It is, therefore, highly probable that the features of this district were, in the time of Elizabeth, advancing to the state in which they are now, in respect to covert and champaign; that is to say, well wooded at its northern and southern extremities, with a sterile heath, moor, or chase, four or five miles broad, and extending in length eastward of Knowle to Forshaw Heath, on the west. The dwellers in the district were then thinly scattered, in comparison with more open and cultivated countries, and the towns, villages, and hamlets, spoken of in the following pages, were found, A.D. 1565, to contain only 1051 families,* which, taken at five in each household, would make a population of 5255, not equal to the numbers in Solihull and Wootton Wawen, at the present time.

---

26. Hillfield Hall, Solihull, a residence of the Hawes and Greswoldes, is a specimen of this class. See illustration and description in the notes on that parish. Other remains of early manor-houses will be found described in subsequent pages.

27. The English farmers were choice in their beer; they called their best October "Mad dog," "Angels' food," "Dragons' milk," "Merry-go-down," and other names. A Spanish ambassador remarked "These English have their houses made of sticks and dirt; but they fare commonly so well as the king."

* *Harleian MSS.*, No. 618.

In this district, we may, without any very large drafts upon imagination, suppose Shakespeare to have studied the originals of many of his most exquisite descriptions of rural scenery; for he was, at the time, passing through the impressional period of boyhood. The beautifully wooded neighbourhood of Henley-in-Arden, within easy reach of that Stratford on which his fame has conferred an enduring celebrity, would furnish him with an ample store of images, from which in after years to pen those word pictures which yet vividly represent the prevailing characteristics of this part of Warwickshire. His frequent allusions to forest-shades, to babbling brooks, and flowery meads, and leafy grove, and sheltered dell, accurately correspond to the present aspect of the locality in question. In how many spots may still be seen

> "An oak, whose antique root peeps out
> Upon the brook that brawls along the wood!"

Such as was its general appearance in the time of the "poet of all hearts, ages, and climes," so is it now, with the exception that human industry has since done much towards fertilizing the once "waste and solitary places." Where, formerly, were unfruitful tracts, there are now abundant crops of grain; and, in the naturally more productive parts at each extremity of the district, owners and occupiers have united to effect improvements which will bear comparison with any similar efforts in other counties. Commercial enterprise has, too, effected its changes in the district of Arden. Canals and railways have been constructed, facilitating transit and promoting intercourse. Where, heretofore, stood the moated inclosure and crenellated castle, we now find the peaceful security of the farm-house and premises; where, once, the mailed warrior only trod, we now behold none but images of tranquil confidence; where, formerly, were wild solitudes, sacred to the rude sports and unbridled license of the few, we have now the rich promise of cultivated tracts, dedicated to the support and enjoyment of the many.

SOUTH ENTRANCE TO HENLEY-IN-ARDEN.

First Day.

PRESUMING the Traveller to have reached the old hostelry of the Swan, at Henley-in-Arden, it will now be desirable to commence a description of that town, to enter upon an inspection of its chapel, to inquire of its other objects of interest, and then to visit the villages, &c., in the district lying south of it, viz., Wootton Wawen, Edstone, Bearley, Aston Cantloe, Little Alne, and Shelfield.

HENLEY-IN-ARDEN,

A township in the parish of Wootton Wawen, is a small market town on the London, Oxford, and Birmingham road, 102 miles from the first-named, and fourteen from the last-mentioned place. The approach, from the south, is by a gentle ascent, on which stand *Arden House*, built by the late T. J. P. Burman, Esq., and *Hurst House*, erected by Major Noble, two neat outlying residences. The town does not appear to have been built before the time that Thurstane de Montfort established a market at his castle of Beaudesert, *temp.* Stephen, on the other side of the brook dividing Henley from that parish; and it is supposed that the first habitations arose for the accommodation of persons resorting thither; though, by others, from its name, being composed of the British word HEN, and LEY a place, it is considered to have had a much earlier foundation. It is not named in Domesday Book, and was, no doubt, accounted for in the lands of the parish of Wootton, granted at the Conquest to one of the Barons of Stafford. The first mention of Henley in any document is *temp.* Henry II, in the grant of a mill, by Henry de Montfort, to the monks of Wootton, and, soon after in a grant by Henry III, A.D. 1220, to Peter de Montfort, of a weekly market on Monday, and a yearly fair for two days, on the even and day of St. Giles. This was a removal of the market from Beaudesert Castle, for greater convenience; or a revival of that which had declined.[1] That the town had then become of some importance, may be inferred from its producing, in the eleventh of the same reign, xv*l* rent, the toll and escheats being valued at five marks; but it declined again after the battle of Evesham, when it was burnt down. In thirteenth Edward I, Peter, son of the above, claimed divers liberties here, viz., market, gallows,

1. Markets and fairs were exposed to considerable danger in early times, from open rapine or covert but determinate injustice. By a law of William I, it was decreed that all fairs and markets should be kept "in fortified cities, towns, or *castles*."

assize of bread, beer, &c.;* and, in the 24th of the same reign, the town is called "Burgus de Henley," and had then sixty-nine burgesses, who paid 7*l.* 18*s.* 10*d.* rent, possessing, besides, a park with two water mills; also pleas and perquisites of court 1*l.* 18*s.* 0*d.*, all of which were held of Edmund, baron of Stafford, by the service of three shillings, or one pair of scarlet hose. In 19th Edward II, (1326,) Peter de Montfort, grandson of the last named, granted a charter confirming to John de Lobbenham, various manors, &c. Among others, "One messuage called Park's Shepene, three water mills, three acres of wood within the Great Park, ten pounds and five shillings of rent and of service, to be received from all and singular the burgesses tenants of the borough of Henleye, together with all the borough of Henleye, with the tolls and all other liberties relating to the said borough." † The inhabitants had, 10th Edward III, obtained from the king a license, which shows that the market had again become well frequented. This license allowed them to toll all corn and commodities brought to market for sale, for the space of three years, the amount to be employed in paving the streets, which, not being accomplished, they obtained another patent extending the original term another three years; but, as this enlargement did not suffice to complete the work, a further extension of five years was obtained in 6th Richard II.

The manor came, by default of heirs, as will be found in Beaudesert, from the de Montforts to the Beauchamps, earls of Warwick; and next to the Botelers. Sir Ralph Boteler, knight, lord Sudeley, obtained a charter, 27th Henry VI, which granted various privileges to him and the inhabitants, con-

* *Rot. Hundredorum*, vol. ii, p. 228.

† *Cart. Cott.*, xxvii, 137. The witnesses to this charter are Sir John de Bisshopesdone, Sir Roger de Aillesbury, knights, and others.

firming the market before granted, and licensing two fairs, viz. one to be held on Tuesday, in the week of Pentecost, and the two following days; and the other, on the day and feast of St. Luke the Evangelist, and two following days.[2] From Sir Ralph Boteler, it came to Sir John Norbury, knight, and William Belknap, esquire, his cousins and heirs, from whom the king (Edward IV) obtained it by purchase. In 2nd Richard III, that monarch granted to "Thomas Cookesey Squier, th' office of Steward of o'r lordship of Henley-in-Ardern w'tin oure Countie of Warr', during his lif' w't the fees and wages of C*s*. of th' issues &c. of the said lordship. Also th' office of master of the game of the p'kes of Henley during his life with the wages and fees accustomed."* Edmund Brereton was bailiff of Henley and Beaudesert, 33rd Henry VII, and his Accounts show sums received, in that year, for

	£.	s.	d.
Rents of assize of the free tenants - - - -	8	19	8
Rents and farms outside the town - - - -	17	6	6
Sale of wood - - - - - - - -	-	-	-
Perquisites of the Court - - - - - -	1	15	0
	28	1	2

Six pounds, usually paid for the farming of the herbage of the Little Park was not included in the account "because it is retained in the king's hand for the support of the king's colts and mares there, called the stud."† The manor continued vested in the crown till the time of Edward VI, who in the first year of his reign, passed it by the name of the manor of Henley-in-Arden, alias Henley-Beaudesert,

2. These fairs still continue to be held. The original charter is still preserved in the High Bailiff's box, and a translation of it will be found in the Appendix.

* *Harl. MSS.*, 433, fol. 74b.

† Papers, *Warwick*, in Record Office, Chancery Lane.

with two parks there belonging, to John Dudley, earl of Warwick, and his heirs. This John Dudley was in high favour with Henry VIII and Edward VI: In the fourth year of the reign of the latter king, he was made Lord Steward of the Household; and, the year following, Duke of Northumberland: Being, however, attainted of high treason for the part he took in raising Lady Jane Grey to the throne, he was executed and his estates estreated to the crown, 1st Philip and Mary. The manor, &c., of Henley-in-Arden, and the living of Beaudesert, were, in the thirteenth year of the same reign, rated to John Digbye, esq., who appears to have either bought, or to have been negotiating for, their purchase.* At this time the lands, manor, &c., of Henley, comprised

	£.	s.	d.
Rents of lands and tenements - - - - -	7	8	10
Customary rents of the Manor - - - -	1	19	9
Rent of a mill, and one-horse mill with a water mill, and a pasture, called the Milkhouse - -	1	7	0
Rent of the Great Park in Henley, with the Lodge	26	13	4
Rent of the herbage of the Little Park - -	19	0	0
Perquisites of Court, on an average - - - -	-	16	8
	57	5	7
Fees paid out - - - - -	9	8	0
Clear annual value - - -	47	17	7

Will'm Petre. Ffrauncis Inglefield. Jo. Baker.
Exd. *p.* Jo. Swifte, Audr. 3

During the above reigns the town appears to have retained its ancient market, &c. Leland, *temp.* Henry VIII, writes, "From Stratford to Heneley, five miles. About the Est

3. The mills and milkhouse pasture were then let to John Whateley and John Wagstaff, the Great Park to John Whorwood, gentleman, and the Little Park to John Somervile, esq. The clear yearly value, rated at twenty-five years' purchase, it is stated, "amountethe to m.ccccxxij*li.* xiij*d.*"

* *Harl. MSS.*, 606, fol. 48.

End of Aulcester is the confluence of Aulne and Arrowe. Aulne runneth by Henley, a markett town five miles above the confluence, and hath divers wooden bridges over it. I learned at Warwike that the most part of the shire of Warwike, that lyeth as Avon River descendeth on the right Hand or Ripe of it, is in *Arden*, (for soe is the ancient name of that part of the Shire;) and the Ground in *Arden* is much inclosed, plentifull of Grasse, but not of Corne." *

In 1592, Henley is described as being, like "many other villages of lesser note, in Arden, as much as In the Wood. Near to this is *Beudsort* Castell, belonging to the Baron Mountforth. In the chapell of S. Collome[4] in the towne are divers armes but no monuments." †

The manor, &c., however, appears to have returned to the crown, for it was, 4th Elizabeth, granted by the queen to Ambrose Dudley, earl of Warwick, and his heirs males,[5] and in default of such issue to the earl of Leicester, by the name of Robert lord Dudley, and the heirs males.‡ Reverting again to the crown for want of issue, in the 31st of the same reign, it so continued, till James I passed it, with other manors, and lands, A.D. 1619, to John, lord Digby. It came, afterwards, into the hands of the Archer family, of Umberslade, Andrew Archer, esq., being lord of the manor in 1693-4, and remained with them till the partition of the estates among the coheiresses, when, in the division, it fell to Mrs. Musgrave, whose son, Christopher

4. Evidently a mistake, as the chapel is dedicated to St. John the Baptist.

5. The memory of the Dudleys being proprietors is preserved in the old sign of the Bear and Ragged Staff, which still swings over the door of an ancient inn.

* *Leland's Itinerary*, vol. iv, fol. 166-8.

† Notes taken by Mr. Vincent, *Harl. MSS.*, 2129, fol. 161.

‡ *Lansdowne MSS.*, 109, fol. 184.

Musgrave, esq., is now the lord of the manor.[6] The lord still occasionally holds his court here, when an election of a new High Bailiff takes place, and High and Low Bailiffs, Affearors, Butter Weighers, Beer Tasters, Brook Lookers, &c., are sworn in, whose duties are only preserved in the names which, doubtless, once gave the owners considerable power and importance.

THE CHAPEL,

Which is dedicated to St. John the Baptist, is a neat structure, and stands on the site of an earlier building, erected about 41st Edward III, at the cost and sole charges

6. On the division of the property, the valuation of the manor, &c., was as follows: viz.—Tolls of Markets and Fairs 5*l.*, Quit Rents 6*l.* 9*s.* 10*d.*, Cottage Rents 17*s.* 8*d.* per annum; Royalty and Rights appurtenant thereto 100*l.*; and Henley Mill 34*l.* per annum.

of the inhabitants; and arose, as stated in the confirmation made by the Bishop of Worcester, in consequence of the great distance and foul ways in winter time, between this place and the parish church of Wootton, and with the consent of William de Senye, then Prior of Wootton, and William de Perton, then Vicar. The inhabitants were assisted by the Bishop of Worcester issuing a bull granting to every one that would be openhanded in contributing, an indulgence of forty days. No part of the original building is apparent in the present edifice, which is in the style of the fifteenth century. It consists of a tower, behind which is the north aisle, and a small building, now used as a vestry room; with a nave, chancel, and porch on the south. The tower is embattled, with pinnacles, of a recent date, and has a large gargoyle at the south-east angle. The west window is pointed, and of three lights: Over this is a small pointed window, and above an obtuse angle arched belfry window; and similar to this are the upper windows on the other faces of the tower. On the north-east buttress, near to the north door, are the remains of a water stoup. The nave has a high ridged roof, extending, without external division, and of the same height, through, to the end of the chancel. There are five pointed-arched windows, of three lights, on the south side, the eastern window, which reaches to the roof, being of corresponding architecture, but with five lights and good tracery. The western window is more depressed in the arch, and is of four lights. Each of the gables is surmounted with a cross. The north aisle has two obtuse angle arched windows, with one of like character at the east end. The porch, which is west of the nave and embattled, is entered by a pointed-arched doorway, the interior one being of the same style, but more highly ornamented, the hood moulding having crockets, and springing from corbels representing the heads of a king and queen. The vestry, which has been higher than it now is, and which was probably, at one time, a chantry chapel, has two square windows without mullions, and appears to have been provided with no entrance from the outside. The interior presents no particular features. The north aisle is separated from the nave and chancel by four pointed arches, on plain octagonal pillars, and the north aisle from the tower by an arch of similar character. The entrance to the vestry or chantry chapel is by a pointed-arched doorway. The windows, as depicted by Dugdale, formerly contained a variety of coats of arms, viz., Henry VI, Stafford, Beauchamp, Boteler, abbeys of Evesham and Winchcomb, Trevill, Montford, Clinton, Catesby, Harewell, Aston, Company of Grocers, &c., all of which are gone. There appears also to have been formerly the effigies of one Thomas Kockin, grocer, with the subscription of "*Orate pro anima Thome Kockin*" in several of the windows, and in the east window of the chancel the picture of one Stokes, who is said to have been master of the Guild adjoining.* In removing the pavement of the Chapel in 1856, a monumental slab was found, about one foot under it, the inscription, on which, appears to be to the memory of this Stokes or Stoke.[7] It is on a very thick slab, bearing a Maltese cross, five feet six inches in length, thus:

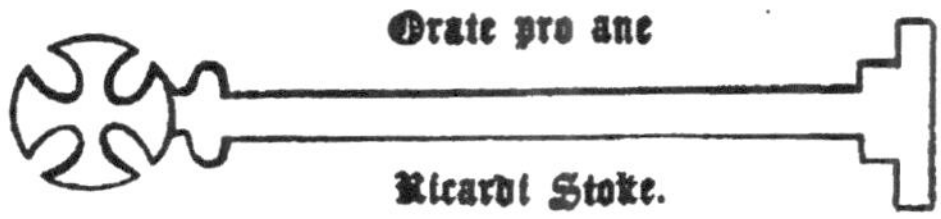

7. Of this family, probably, was Simon de Stok, who held lands in Preston Bagot, *temp.* Henry III and Edward I. *Testa de Nevill*, f. 98b. In 25th Henry VI, John Stokes held land in the Field of WHETLEY. See Papers in Record Office, Chancery Lane.

* *Churches of Warwickshire*, p. 136.

This slab is now placed outside near to the north door.

The chapel was repaired and restored in 1856, at a cost of 900*l.*, subscribed by the inhabitants and their friends. During the alterations, in removing a flat ceiling over the nave, the canopy of the rood loft, gilt and highly coloured, was found above, corresponding with the surbase below, from which the pillars of the screen supporting the rood had been cut. On one part of this surbase, was lettered, and in good preservation, in Old English characters,

"Nativitas D'ni nostri. Assu'ptio beatæ Mariæ. Resurrectio D'ni nostri."

The alterations consisted of the removal of two galleries (one over the communion table in the chancel), the throwing open the tower arch, the removal of the flat ceiling of the nave and chancel, the reparation of the fine timbered roof, the reseating the body of the chapel with open seats, the separation of the chancel therefrom by a neat screen, the erection of a new communion table and reredos, and the paving of the floors with Minton's tiles, the chancel part being of a rich character and of elegant design. The monumental records in the chapel are of modern date; and with the exception of the one before named, nothing of interest to the antiquary was found during the alterations. The font is a stone shaft, corresponding to the pillars of the nave. There are six bells in the tower.

The living is a perpetual curacy, in the gift of the parishioners, valued at 104*l.* The Rev. Thomas Jones is the present incumbent.

CHANTRY CHAPEL.

In the 43rd Edward III one William Fifhyde, of Henley-in-Arden, "gave one mark for license to give to a certain chaplain three messuages with the appurtenances, in Henley-in-Ardern, to be held in mortmain,"* for the founding of a Chantry in the Chapel, and the maintenance of one priest to celebrate divine service there daily, for the good estate of the said William. If this intention was carried into effect, the small building now used as a vestry, as seen on the north of the chancel in the engraving below, most probably, was the chantry chapel.

THE CHAPEL, N.E.

THE GUILD.

Sir Ralph Boteler, Lord Sudeley, owner of the town and manor, *temp.* Henry VI, founded a Guild in the Chapel, for four priests belonging thereto, to pray for the founder's soul. Little is known of the fraternity prior to the dissolu-

* *Rot. Originalium*, ii, 306.

tion of monasteries. In an account of the Rentals of Margaret Catesby in Henley and Beaudesert, 25th Henry VI, mention is made of a tenement between the lands of the Guild and of William Couper; and in a similar account, 3rd Edward IV, of the Croft of the Guild of Henley, and a tenement with a garden, which the Master of the Guild of Henley lately held.* In 1513, Sir Thomas Bownel, chaplain, and Sir Thomas Webbe, chaplain, paid each 6*s.* 8*d.*, in aid of the king.† On the Inventory taken 26th Henry VIII, the Commissioners report two priests only, as belonging to the Guild in the town of Henley-in-Arden, viz.:

	£.	s.	d.
"Sir Robert Colyns, chaplain in this Guild, in money paid by the hands of the Master there, for the time being, 106*s.* 8*d.* And Sir Thomas Bonell, another chaplain of the said guild, in money paid yearly 100*s.*, in all	10	6	8
The tenth part of this sum - - - - -		20	8"‡

In the following year the lands belonging to it were valued at 27*l.* 3*s.* 3*d.*, at which period three priests, one having 5*l.* 10*s.* 0*d.*, and the other two 5*l.* each, together with an organist, who had 2*l.* annually, constituted the establishment. By a deed, dated the last day of January, 2nd Edward VI, Richard Palady, gentleman, and Francis Foxhall, mercer, surrendered to the crown, "all those lands, meadows, grazings, pastures, and hereditaments whatsoever, with their appurtenances, now or lately in the tenure of Thomas Ffranke, or his assigns, lying and being in *Preston Bagott* and *Claredon*, in the said county of Warwick, heretofore appertaining and belonging to the late Guild of Henley in *Henley*, in the said county of Warwick, now dissolved, and part of the possessions then being, or

* Papers in the Record Office.

† *Taxatio ad Subsidium, Reg.* 26, f.97a.

‡ *Valor Ecclesiasticus.*

appointed for the support of four priests celebrating (divine service) in the chapel of St. John the Baptist, in the town of Henley, in the county of Warwick aforesaid, before the date of this grant. And all other lands, meadows, grazings, pastures, and hereditaments whatsoever, with their appurtenances, in Preston Bagott and Claredon aforesaid, to the said Guild of Henley heretofore belonging and pertaining, and parcel of the possessions there lately being."*

By inquiry made 1st Mary, it was found that Richard Budworth and Thomas Cosnel, late chaplains of Henley Guild, had each a pension paid him, the first of 4*l.* and the second of 2*l.* The brethren of these guilds generally possessed a house on the north side of the church.[8] Dugdale speaks of the one pertaining to this Guild, as being standing, north of the Chapel, in his time; and some portions of which are to be found in the building now covering the site. He also states that before the dissolution of this Guild, it was a custom, on all public occasions, (such as weddings and the like,) for the inhabitants to keep their feast in the Guild-house, in which they had most kinds of household stuff, as pewter, brass, spits, hand-irons, linen, tables, &c., and wood out of the little park at *Beldesert* for fuel, those who were at the charge of the feast paying only six shillings and eightpence for the use of them. All was then gone but the pewter,[9] which the chapel-wardens lent out for fourpence a dozen when any feast was made.

---

8. This situation was convenient for the Brethren, as their business was to pray, as well as eat. They bestowed alms on the poor, received travelling strangers, and did other acts of charity as far as their revenues allowed.—*Oliver's Sleaford Guild.* See further notes on Guilds, in Appendix.

9. Those remaining, viz. twelve dishes and seven plates, are now in the custody of the High Bailiff. It is a remarkable fact, that when the Reformation began to be agitated, the movable property of most religious establishments gradually decreased.

* Deed in Record Office, A.D. 1548.

THE HOSPITAL.

There was a Hospital built here, 26th Henry VI, for the relief of poor people and strangers; and, towards its support, the then Bishop of Worcester granted an indulgence of three years to all who made contribution. The site of this hospital is now unknown, though by some it is thought probable that the old timber-built house, now a butcher's shop, opposite to the County Police Station, formed part of it.

THE MARKET CROSS.

In the centre of the town, which is called the Market-place, stands one of the few Crosses remaining in this country, which is traditionally related to have been preserved from destruction in the seventeenth century by a shed which was built over it. This Cross is now much injured by time. The base, shaft, and capital are composed of three separate stones; the shaft being mortised into the base and capital. At the beginning of the present century there were niches on the four faces of the capital, containing the Rood, the Trinity, St. Peter with his key, and another subject defaced, all of which have now mouldered away, not a trace of the sculptured figures named being visible. Near the Cross was the Market Hall, a small, heavy, open building, supported on eight pillars, and being of no use has lately been removed. This building stood on the site of what was called "The Town House," taken down in 1793. On the old Town House was formerly a bell, removed from the chapel by license of the Bishop of Worcester, for the convenience of the school, in 1693-4, Andrew Archer, Esq., the lord of the manor, certifying that he would not claim any title or right to it. In 1727, the feoffees ordered the "Town House" to be repaired. In the middle of the seventeenth century, it would appear to have been the custom here to publish the banns of marriage in the market-place; for we find, in the Wootton register of that period, a memorandum that an intent of marriage between Roger Jennings of Wotton Wawen, and Margery Lambert of Shelfield, was published three several market days in the market-place of Henley-in-Arden, (January 8, 15, and 22, 1654;) no manner of persons excepting against it, or forbidding the same.

The other objects of interest are comprised in the numerous half-timbered houses scattered through the town. Some of these are peculiar, the beams of the upper portions hanging over the ground story, and others of them being of a more elaborately worked character. Occasionally, the removal of the plaster from houses that have been stuccoed, displays a fine specimen of this style, as happened during the repairs of the Swan Hotel in 1858, many portions of which, however, were in such a state of decay, that it was replastered, rather than incur the expense of a restoration.

The inhabitants of modern days, like their brethren to whom we have referred of the fourteenth century, appear to have had a taste for paving the streets, for according to a document in the Surveyor's Book, it was agreed at a meeting held April 18th, 1776, "That it would be to the great advantage of the Inhabitants, to have each side of the Street properly pitched," and that the right of commonage on certain fields should be discharged by the payment of certain sums per acre, to meet the expenses, which were estimated at 150*l.* What the improvement may have been at that time cannot be estimated, but the pavements then laid down are certainly now anything but pleasant to walk upon.

There is a neat Baptist Chapel in the place, and a small congregation of Primitive Methodists. Two large schools have lately been erected, and, under teachers of the National and British systems, the youth of the town are receiving an excellent education. The inhabitants in 1841 numbered 1223, and in 1861 had decreased to 1069. In 1563 the number of families was 113.* In 1730 the families numbered 115.†

Having now noticed what is worthy of remark in Henley, we may proceed southward from the town, on the turnpike road to Stratford-on-Avon, when we shall pass Mays Wood on the right, having a fine view on the left, over Wootton Pool, of Austey Wood, a well-known fox covert belonging to Sir C. F. Smythe, baronet. Proceeding onward through the toll-

---

* Extracted from the Return made by the Bishop of Worcester to the Privy Council, *Harl. MSS.*, No. 595.

† *Thomas's Dugdale.*

gate, and passing the National School, lately erected through the exertions of the Vicar, the Rev. E. D. Kirwan, the neat village of Wootton, with its church on the eminence in front, is approached.

WOOTTON WAWEN

Is the mother parish to Henley-in-Arden, as also to Ullenhall, Edstone, Aspley, and Fordhall, which we shall visit in the course of our rambles. It is a pleasant village situated two miles south of Henley, and is supposed to have taken its name from its situation among woods, as too from one *Wagen*, its lord before the Conquest, who resided here. According to Domesday, the manor then contained seven hides of land, with a church and two mills ; there were nine ploughlands arable, twenty-three villeins, and twenty-two bordars, having six ploughs, the woods being two miles in length and one in breadth, and the whole was valued at four pounds. These had been given to Robert de Tonei otherwise De Stafford, in which family the manor continued till the time of Henry VIII, when it fell to the crown by the attainder, for high treason, of Edward, duke of Buckingham. After this, it was obtained of the king by Thomas Grey, marquis of Dorset, whose son, Henry, being attainted in 1st Mary, the queen granted it to Sir John Grey, from whom it was purchased by Dame Agnes Smythe and her son, Sir Francis Smythe. His grandson obtained, 15th James I, a charter of free warren here, and left issue Sir Charles Smythe, knight, created 19th Charles I, lord Carrington, baron of Wootton, from whom (the title becoming extinct) the manor came to his kinsman, Francis Carrington, esq., whose daughter married Peter Holford, esq., whose daughter married Sir Edward Smythe, baronet, of Acton Burnell,

Shropshire, grandfather to the present owner and baronet, Sir Charles Frederick Smythe.

There was another manor, or estate in Wootton, for many generations in the Harewell family. Towards the end of the reign of Henry VIII, its then possessor, John Harewell, had two sons and five daughters. The eldest son, Thomas, died without issue, and William, the other, being a priest, the estates were divided among the daughters; and thus Wootton, with lands in Henley, Preston Bagot, Edstone, and Stratford, came to Agnes, the wife of John Smyth, one of the barons of the Exchequer. His widow, dame Agnes, as seen above, purchased the manor, and the estates have been united since that period.

THE CHURCH

Is the principal object of interest in the village, and stands at the top of a gentle ascent facing the Parsonage House, which is a modern building close to the road. The patron saint of the church is St. Peter, and the building, for a village church, is of large dimensions. It was given by

Robert de Stafford to the monks of Conchis in Normandy, shortly after the Conquest, and appropriated to them by Roger, Bishop of Worcester, A.D. 1178. In 1291, 19th Edward I, the value, with the chapels belonging thereto, was stated to be fifty-two marks, the vicar's portion being seven and a half marks. In 26th Henry VIII, the vicarage was valued at 12*l*, less 10*s*. 5*d*. for procurations and synodals. In the Survey made of Church Goods 6th Edward VI,[10] there were, according to the Inventory, then at Wootton,

> i chalice and iij belles.
> iiij vestments one chamlet tow worsted.
> ij copes one silke oon worsted.
> iiij Altarcloths.
> iiij towells diaper old.
> ij curtens silke.
> ij candlestickes bras.
> Md. that the p'ishe have sold sithe the last s'vey oon bell to the buyldinge of theire churche and a oyle (aisle).

The church consists of a central tower, supported by Anglo Saxon arches, the upper portion being of a later date, a lofty nave with clerestory, south aisle, and chancel with a large chantry chapel on the south side of it, extending, with the south aisle, the entire length of the nave and chancel. The tower is embattled, with small pinnacles at each angle. The upper portion, or belfry, has a double pointed-arch window on each face. The nave has a plain parapet with gargoyles between each of the four clerestory windows, which are obtuse angled arches of three lights. The west window is a pointed arch of five lights, and one four light pointed window is in the north wall, east of a

10. A Commission to Sir George Thogmorton, knight, John Digby and Thomas Marowe, esquires, to take inventory and certificate of all the Goods, Plate, Jewels, Bells, and other Ornaments in all Churches, Chapels, Guilds, Brotherhoods, and Fraternities, in the County of Warwick.—*Papers in the Record Office.*

half timbered porch, which covers the northern door. The south aisle has an embattled parapet, south and west, with pinnacles at the head of each buttress, large gargoyles projecting below the pinnacles. It has a two light pointed window west; and two flat headed windows of four pointed lights, south. The south doorway, covered with another half timbered porch, is a pointed arch, ornamented with the tooth ornament on the hood moulding. The chantry chapel and the chancel have high pitched roofs, the former containing two pointed windows, of three lights, on the south, and a large eastern one of similar character, with five lights. The eastern window of the chancel is large, and of seven lights, under an obtuse pointed arch. On the north are two pointed windows, set high on the wall, of three lights each.

The nave and south aisle are divided by three pointed arches, springing from plain circular pillars. The passage from the nave to the chancel, is under two Anglo Saxon arches, forming, with two semicircular doorways, north and south, the bottom part of the tower, and the oldest portion of the building. Two circular pillars, with three pointed arches, divide the chancel from the chantry chapel. A continuous pillar and arch runs on the south side of the tower, whilst a similar arch forms the division of the chapel and south aisle.

The windows, in Dugdale's time, contained the arms of Catesby, Harewell, Stafford, Hastings, Beauchamp, Wootton Priory, King's College, Henry VI, Abbey of Conchis, &c. Some remnants of stained glass still remain. There is also left a fine old oak church chest, strengthened in an extraordinary manner with iron-work, in the chancel; and the tourist will here find specimens of CHAINED BOOKS, a custom formerly adopted in all public libraries, to prevent abstraction.[11] They are in the chantry chapel, fixed to a reading desk, the ring at the end of the chain being attached to a bolt fastened to the shelf. The volumes consist of Works of Divinity of the seventeenth and eighteenth centuries, of no great value.

On the south wall of the chantry is a piscina of a fine ornamental character, and further eastward a low semicircular surbast arch, the hood moulding of which appears to have been partly cut and abandoned.

The monuments are numerous in the chancel and chapel. The engraving, at the beginning of this section of the work, represents the tomb of Sir John Harewell, (*obiit* 1428,) and is without inscription. Eastward of this, and within the altar rails, is a high tomb, with a dark marble slab, containing the brass figures of John Harewell, esq., and his wife, with smaller figures of five sons and five daughters. The following inscription runs at the head and down the south border of the slab:

---

11. So late as 1711, this precaution against pilfering continued; for it was then stated "Since to the great reproach of the nation, and a much greater one of our holy religion, the thievish disposition of some that enter into libraries to learn no good there, hath made it necessary to secure the innocent books, and even the sacred volumes themselves with chains—which are better deserved by those ill persons, who have too much learning to be hanged, and too little to be honest."—*British Magazine*, x, 391.

Hic jacet Johes Harewell armig' et dna Anna qondam uxor eius ac nuper uxor Edwardi Grey militis qui quidem Johes obit x die Aprilis anno dni MVV et que quedem Anna obit . . die . . a dni MV . . quorum aiab; ppitietur deus.

In the chancel are other inscriptions, commemorating several vicars of the church, with some of less note. On the north side of the chantry chapel is a high canopied tomb, with columns, surmounted by an escutcheon. On the tomb rests a mailed figure, representing Francis Smith, esq., with a Latin inscription to his memory: *obiit* September 3, 1626. This chantry chapel contains many monuments, some of them very large, to the memory of the different branches of the family of Knight, of Barrells Hall, in this parish, and those to whom they were allied. It has, too, one commemorating William Somervile, esq., author of *The Chase*, and a resident of Edstone Hall; as also a beautiful white marble mural monument, with a kneeling draped figure at the foot, to the memory of a recent owner of the last named edifice, John Phillips, esq. *Obiit* 1836.

In the cleaning of the interior in 1855, the scraping of the whitewash from the surface, brought to light a great number of subjects formerly painted in distemper on the walls, particularly over the arch in the nave leading under the tower, a space which was divided into numerous compartments, and filled with the principal events recorded in the New Testament. The royal arms, *temp.* Anne, were similarly emblazoned on the north wall, together with many other subjects on the south.

The pulpit is adorned with ancient carved woodwork; whilst, at the east end of the nave, there are specimens of open screen work, forming the inclosure of some large pews. The font is plain and octagonal. There are six bells in the tower, one as old as 1591.

The living is in the gift of King's College, Cambridge,

and the Rev. E. D. Kirwan, the present vicar. The living is returned, with Ullenhall, at 379*l.* They are now separated.

Coming out by the south porch, the village presents a pretty appearance from the church-yard, among the numerous memorials of which, near the north-east corner of the chancel, will be found the following lines, written by the Rev. J. Gaches, a former vicar, to commemorate one of Somervile's huntsmen, John Hoitt, of Henley-in-Arden, *obiit* 1802, aged 80.

"Here Hoitt, all his sports and labours past,
Joins his loved master Somervile at last;
Together went they echoing fields to try,
Together now, in silent dust, they lie.
Servant and Lord, when once we yield our breath,
Huntsman and poet, are alike to death.
Life's motley drama calls for powers, and men
Of different casts, to fill its changeful scene:
But all the merit that we justly prize,
Not in the part, but in the acting lies.
And, as the lyre, so may the Huntsman's horn
Fame's trumpet rival, and his name adorn."

At the northern extremity of the church-yard, are interred under plain flat slabs, the bodies of six vicars of the church. Near to this, is a small piece of land now used as a garden, by the vicar, which tradition assigns as the burial place of those who died of the plague in Coventry. There is no probability of any truth in this; but as the Carthusian monks, at Coventry, once held the Priory here by grant, this may be the only ground for connecting the little plot of land with that city.

THE PRIORY.

This was a small monastery of Benedictine monks, alien to the Abbey of Conchis, in Normandy, founded by Robert de Stafford, whose son gave to it the church here, with the tithes and oblations, one hide of land adjoining the church, and one hide called Doversdale. Subsequent confirmations and enlargements were made by his grandson, and his son in law Hervey Bagot, who came to the barony of Stafford in right of his wife. Many other benefactors contributed to enlarge the funds of the brethren here, by grants of land, mills, &c., in Henley-in-Arden, Offord, Mockley, and Beaudesert, in this county; East Wrotham, Linford, and North and South Pickenham, in Norfolk; the advowson of the churches of Wootton and East Wrotham; the mortuaries of Morton Bagot and Langley; and the tithes of Langley and Norton, which latter they exchanged for a pension.

In 16th Edward III, the Priory was seized by the king for rent to be paid during the wars; but restored to the Prior, with an allowance of three shillings a week for himself, and one shilling and sixpence for his fellow monk. It was again seized, 48th same reign, and so continued, till Prior John Maubert, 3rd Richard II, obtained a license to hold it during the wars with France, paying 40*l.* per annum into the exchequer. Three years afterwards it was granted to Robert Selby, priest, and another, for 46*l.* 13*s.* 4*d.* yearly. In 22nd Richard II, the Carthusians, at Coventry, obtained a grant of it; but it was restored by Henry IV. After many mutations in fortune, it was at length given by Henry VI, to the Provost and Fellows of King's College, Cambridge, recently founded by him; and to this foundation it still continues. The following is a list of the Priors from 1285 to the above period.

Roger de Pavilliaco, January 12, 1285.
John de Brocya, June 8, 1288.
William de Laverceye, November 8, 1309.
John de Tonnelier, July 26, 1328.
John de Silvaneto, January 2, 1340.
Guillerinus Pinchart, 1349.
John Maubert, March 7, 1370.
John Soverain, 1400.
John de Conchis, June 17, 1438.

There are no remains of the Priory, nor is the site certainly known, but the probability is that it was situated in the field west of the church, and immediately adjoining it.

Leaving the church-yard, we proceed again to the road, and come immediately to the lodge-gates of

WOOTTON HALL,

A substantial and well-built mansion, erected by the lord Carrington, before referred to, and the property of Sir Charles Frederick Smythe, baronet. The engraving presents the general external features of the building, which is, at the present time, the residence of Joseph Tempest, esq. The interior comprises numerous spacious and lofty rooms, having, at the back, extensive out offices, fish pools, and all the requirements of modern taste and civilization. The mansion is seen to the best advantage from the road, looking over the lawn in front, the sides of which are closely wooded with fine trees. On the north side of the Hall, stands a spacious ROMAN CATHOLIC CHAPEL, built in 1813, by the Dowager, Catharine, lady Smythe, at a cost of about 4000*l.*

The chapel, which is eighty feet long and thirty wide, was opened for divine service in 1814, and is dedicated to Saints Mary and Benedict. The exterior is of red brick; but the interior is of a more ornate character. The roof is divided into compartments for decoration, and the eastern window is of stained glass. The altar (sarcophagus shape) is of very beautiful marble, sculptured at and brought from Rome. The tabernacle (cupola shape) is made out of a solid piece of Carrara marble, and is surrounded by coloured marble pillars, having gilt capitals. The font is plain Gothic, and not in keeping with the rest of the interior. The pulpit is Grecian, put up in 1853, by the present pastor, the Rev. P. J. Hewitt, who also added other embellishments. There is a small organ of fine tone and compass, which was constructed, in the main, by the Rev. James Deday, a predecessor of the present priest.

Previous to the opening of this edifice, a smaller building, north of it, had been used, during several generations, by the congregation assembling here. In effecting some alterations on this spot in 1860, the remains of bodies, which had been interred many years ago, were discovered under the floor.

Leaving the grounds, and advancing through the village, we come to the bridge crossing the little river Alne, from which is a fine water view between an avenue of trees, including an ornamental foot-bridge in the distance, and two cascades, meeting at the foot of the bridge we are crossing, presenting, when the waters are high, a very pleasing picture. The next building is the ROMAN CATHOLIC SCHOOL. Education appears to have been well cared for in this village, for, besides the School, named as standing at the entrance to the village, we find here a flourishing School, instituted by the Rev. P. J. Hewitt, in 1851, and maintained by subscriptions from himself, from Sir Frederick Smythe, baronet, and others.

Passing the large Flour Mill, we arrive at the CEMETERY belonging to the same body, opened in 1852. It is laid out with taste; and, in the centre, is a chaste Mortuary Cross, designed by Welby Pugin, esq., the upper portion executed by Lane and Lewis. The ground was given by the late Sir Edward Smythe, baronet, and the cross and walls were erected chiefly at the expense of the Hon. Mrs. Carrington Smythe, and the pastor. The high road, which we are now following, passes under the short aqueduct of the Birmingham and Stratford Canal; and skirting the side of Austey Wood, brings us to the plantations and grounds of

EDSTONE HALL,

Which is approached by the lodge about a mile from the village. This mansion was built by H. Mills, esq., and finished by the late John Phillips, esq., who purchased it, and the manor, of him. The house is fitted up in superior style, and contains some good portraits of the family of the late possessor. The cellars are remarkable for their loftiness and as running throughout the whole extent of the building. The engraving presents a view of the house, as seen over the pool. Since the death of Mrs. Phillips, the hall has been let to P. H. Muntz, esq., who now resides here. On this spot, in a former building, dwelt the celebrated Somervile,[12] a great hunter, and author of *The Chase;* but of the house which he occupied, only a small stone, on which his arms are cut, remains, built up into the head of a doorway. The Somerviles were owners of Edstone from the time of Edward IV to the middle of the last century, deriving it by the marriage of Thomas Somervile with Joanna, the heiress of the Ailesbury family, alive in 1509. It descended to their son Robert Somervile of Edstone, and afterwards to John, of the same place. His son John Somervile "was condemned of high treason and sent to Newgate, with Arderne, his father in law, who was executed next morning, but Somervile hanged himself in Newgate."* The manor then descended to the family of William, the second son. It had successively come from the de Staffords and others, to the former of whom it was given by the Conqueror with Wootton. It is stated to have then contained five hides, valued at 3*l.*, with woods, half a mile long and half a furlong broad. Before this time it belonged to *Ailric* and *Uluvinus*, being then called *Edricestone.* The monks of Bordesley had common of pasture in this lordship for fifteen beasts, two draught horses, and two hundred sheep,

---

12. Himself and several branches of the family are buried in the chantry chapel in Wootton Church, and monuments erected to their memory.

* Note attached to Pedigree in *Harl. MSS.*

according to the large hundred, being the grant of Peter de Montford.

Here was formerly a chapel belonging to the church at Wootton, for Nic. Benet, Curat. de Edriston, was taxed to a subsidy in the year 1513, 4*s*. This chapel was built by William de Edricheston, *temp.* Henry III. Taurinus, then prior of Wootton, granted him license to do so, upon condition that it should be acknowledged as a grace and favour, and that he and his successors, priors, should have the power to annul the same whenever they pleased, as also that the chaplain, there officiating, should swear in all things to preserve the rights of the Church at Wootton. The witnesses were Joh. de Bec and Roger, then Vicar of Wootton.*

The population of Wootton, with Edstone, in 1851, was 704; in 1861, 675. In 1563, fifty-one families. The parish, with its numerous hamlets, &c., contained 2252 inhabitants in 1861.

Leaving Edstone, and travelling again on the turnpike road, we come to four roads where, as was usual at such crossings formerly, stood the Cross: [13] Hence Bearley Cross as now called; and the origin of the sign of the inn there. Turning to the left, about a quarter of a mile further, we arrive at the small village of

BEARLEY,

Called Burlei in the Domesday Survey, and said to have been then held by its former owner, one Alric, of Robert de

13. Many crosses were placed as marks of the boundaries of districts. Sometimes they were erected where the corpse of any great person had rested as it was carried for burial, and very often in church-yards to remind the people of the benefits vouchsafed to us by the cross of Christ; and in early times at most places of public concourse, or at the meeting of thee or four roads or highways.

* *Thomas's Dugdale*, 830.

Stafford, to whom the king had granted it, and to consist of one hide of land, value 10*s.* In Edward the Confessor's time, it had been rated at double that sum. The manor, or portions of the lands, were successively in the hands of the families of Cumin, de Cantelupe, and Burley, and were owned, *temp.* Edward II, by William de Warwick, who sold it to Robert Moryn, of Snitterfield, whose son, John, settled it on his mother and her second husband, John de Cumpton, for their lives, with remainder to himself and heirs. Since this time, 8th Edward III, it has been divided into several freeholds, and the principal owners now are Darwin Galton, esq., John Rich, esq., and others.

THE CHAPEL.

This is another chapelry to Wootton Wawen, and in the gift of the vicar of that parish. It appears to have possessed a chapel from the time of Richard I. By a Terrier made 1585 it appeared that Bearley paid no tithe or tenth to the Vicar of Wootton, but for the burial of any corpse fourpence. All tithes paid to the parson who is to fill the cure of Bearley. In 6th Edward VI, the church goods were

> j chalice & ij belles.
> oon vestment dornix.
> one cope dornix.
> one altarclothe.
> one towell.

The building now standing is a mean brick and tile edifice with no architectural pretensions. It consists of a small tower, under which is the entrance, and a nave and chancel. The nave contains a few modern monumental inscriptions, and a font which appears older than any part of the building, which in itself is very uninteresting to the visitor. The present incumbent is the Rev. Thomas Jones, and the living returned at 62*l.*

The population of Bearley was 231 in the year 1841, and 238 in 1861. There were nine families in 1563.

Before returning, if we direct our gaze beyond the village, a fine view is obtained of Snitterfield Bushes, a famous fox covert of great extent, and one of the most frequently visited covers in the county, rarely failing to furnish a fox, when all others in the neighbourhood have failed. As Somervile, who lived close by, sung, it may here still be said,

> "Hark! what loud shouts
> Re-echo through the groves! he breaks away—
> Shrill horns proclaim his flight! Each struggling hound
> Strains o'er the lawn to reach the distant pack.
> 'Tis triumph all and joy!"

Returning to Bearley Cross, we pass over the turnpike road, and in proceeding down the road to Aston, travel under the *Long Aqueduct*, erected in 1813.* It stands on thirteen lofty piers, and extends 500 feet, over a little stream and valley. It was, at the time of its erection, the wonder of the country round, whose inhabitants flocked to see this marvel of engineering skill, as they thought it, of carrying a

canal over a valley. About a field off, on the right, is SILLESBURNE, a farm house, situate near a little stream which is crossed on the turnpike road, by a bridge, still called the Hermitage Bridge. On the site of this house, once stood a Hermitage, mention of which is made in the will of John Harewell, who died 7th Henry VIII, (1428,) bequeathing his body to sepulture in the church of St. Peter at Wootton, and leaving *6l. 13s. 4d.* for repairs of the great roadway between the latter place and the Hermitage at Sillesburne. Passing along, the road leads by NEWNHAM on the left, a country of heavy land, and about a mile further on, we arrive at the village of

ASTON CANTLOE,

So called from its early proprietor, William de Cantelupe, to distinguish it from other Astons, in this county. In the Conqueror's time the manor was valued at six pounds, and consisted of five hides of land, a church, a mill, and woods a mile square. It was then called *Estone*, and had been recently given to one Richard, a noble Norman, and was then enjoyed by Osbertus, his son. So early as 6th John, it was obtained by the before named William de Cantelupe, and continued in that family till the time of Edward I, when, for want of heirs, it came to Henry de Hastings, who had married Johanna, daughter of another William de Cantelupe, *obiit* 39th Henry III. The Cantelupes were great patrons of the Priory of Studley, endowing it with lands here of the value of 41*l.* per annum, and other privileges, as also the advowson of the church in support of the hospital built at the gates of the said Priory.

From the above heiress the manor fell to John de Hastings, her son, who claimed, 13th Edward I, a Court leet, with assize of bread and beer, waifs, gallows,[14] and free warren within the manor, which were allowed.

By an Inquisition held at Stratford-on-Avon, 8th of this reign, the Jurors presented that the liberties of Aston and other places, impede common justice, because they do not permit the king's bailiffs, in any way, to perform their office, without their bailiffs. Also that John Clerk, bailiff of the bishop of Worcester, took of a certain inhabitant of Aston, imprisoned, 10*s.* for permitting him to escape.*

The family of Hastings possessed the manor for several descents, down to Lawrence de Hastings, created earl of Pembroke, 13th Edward III. Dying, 22nd of the same reign, it came to his son, John, then an infant, one year old. The king (26th) then committed to William de Clinton, earl of Huntington, the custody of the manor, to hold until the lawful age of the heir, rendering thence annually twenty pounds, and, afterwards, on his death, 29th Edward III,

---

14. A short distance south of the village is a place called "Gallows Green," where several human bones have been dug up. This may have been the place of execution of offenders whom the will or caprice of the lord might condemn to death.

* *Rot. Orig.*, vol. ii, pp. 226 and 228.

it was in like manner and terms, at the request of the executors of the will of the said William de Clinton, committed to the custody of Juliana, wife of the said earl.* John de Hastings dying without issue, the manor came, by entail, to Sir William Beauchamp, second son of Thomas, earl of Warwick, who was created lord Bergavenny, and it has, ever since, been in the same family, the present earl of Abergavenny being lord of the manor.

A castle and park are said to have existed here in the time of the Cantelupes. Of the former there is no authentic record; but of an extensive building evidence still remains north of the church, in an inclosure moated on three sides, the other being formed by the river Alne. Here are several mounds of earth, and the field now bears the name of "Stocking Banks." Materials and timber used in building have been found at various times, indicating the existence of a structure of some note once within its area.

THE CHURCH

Is dedicated to St. John the Baptist, and formerly belonged to the Canons of Studley Priory. It was valued at thirty-three marks in 1291, and was given to these Canons by William de Cantelupe, whose heirs repossessed themselves of it on two different occasions, on the latter of which they gave it to the Priory of Maxstoke. The Canons of Studley afterwards obtained possession, which led to great suits between them and those of Maxstoke, in which the latter at length prevailed. In 26th Henry VIII, the vicarage was valued at 10*l.*, less 10*s.* 5*d.* for synodals and procurations. The Church Goods, *temp.* Edward VI, are returned as

* *Rot. Orig.*, r. 3 and 11.

j chalice & iij belles, one litle bell.
ij vestments, one silke, one dosonton.
one cope, worsted.
one pix, bras.
ij artarclothes.*
ij towells.

Md. That the p'ishe have sold sithe the last s'vey to the maynten'nce of theire churche and the relief of the pore, oon bell.

The building comprises an embattled tower, with five bells, a nave, north aisle, chantry chapel, and chancel, the gray walls of which contrast admirably with the beautiful yard in which the edifice stands, and which is a model of what a church-yard should be, care being taken, by the

incumbent, to have it kept as a place really sacred to the memory of the departed, and not, as too commonly happens, in a state in which no one would suffer his homestead to be seen, rank with nettles, weeds, and rubbish.

The tower, like that at Wootton, is embattled, with

* *Sic* in MS.

pinnacles at each corner and a two-light pointed window on each face of the belfry. The nave and chancel have high ridged roofs. Some of the windows furnish fine specimens of tracery, and, with the doors, are generally pointed arches. The east window is lofty, with the tracery destroyed, the mullions extending to the top of the arch. At the east end of the chantry chapel is a massive mullioned window with heavy tracery, under a pointed arch. Over the north doorway is a curious specimen of sculpture inserted in a niche. This has evidently been brought from some other building, and placed here. The figures consist of a female in bed, with a child in swaddling clothes on the outside. The coverlet is brought over the body, up to the chin, whilst the head of a man is carved at the foot of the bed. The sculpture is rough in execution, and the subject of it has puzzled many to conjecture.[15]

The nave of the church was restored, the south wall rebuilt, a new open timber roof erected, and the interior newly seated with open benches in 1851, by subscriptions raised by the vicar. The nave is divided from the aisle by four pointed arches, springing from three octagonal pillars. The tower is entered from the nave by a similar pointed arch, springing from corbels in the wall. The chancel is very lofty, and of large dimensions, being nearly the size of the nave, from which it is divided by a lofty pointed arch, with a low stone wall and iron gates, restored in the year just stated. The chancel is fitted up with stalls[16] and altar, choral service being uniformly employed. A small window,

---

15. It is more than probable that this is a rude representation of Joseph, Mary, and the infant CHRIST; and, as it was formerly covered with plaster to show a smooth surface, may have been removed from the chantry chapel, and so hid from observation, to prevent its destruction.

16. One of these stalls is ancient, and the carved heads in good preservation; the others are modern additions, and of a temporary nature.

on the north side, has been filled with a modern stained glass representation of the Annunciation of the Virgin Mary, beneath which is the inscription, "Thank offering for many opportunities of Holy Communion." The roof, very old, is in circular form, with a carved cornice. It formerly bore the arms of Beauchamp, earl of Warwick, Clinton, earl of Huntingdon, &c. On the west wall were also the arms of lord Brooke. On the south side is a sedilia of three graduated seats, which have been lately restored, but the columns dividing them have, at some period, been cut off. The priest's door has been partly filled up, and a slab inserted halfway, to form a credence table. The vicar contemplates the restoration of this part of the church, which, when finished, will form a fine specimen of an ancient chapel.

The chantry chapel is separated from the chancel by two arches and one pillar, similar in character to those in the nave. The east window contains fragments of ancient stained glass. This chapel, as will be found by the account of the Guild very early established in this place, was devoted to the services of a priest of that fraternity, at the altar of the Blessed Virgin.

There are several monumental slabs and mural tablets in various parts of the church, but none of ancient date. A modern stained glass window, subject, "The Crucifixion," has been placed in the nave, behind the pulpit.[17] The font is octagonal, on a pillared shaft, the capital charged with quatrefoils, deeply cut. The Rev. J. F. Fagge is the present vicar.

The vicarage was valued in 36th Henry VIII, at 9*l.* 9*s.* 8*d.*,

---

17. This pulpit is considered to be the original one, and is of oak, standing on four buttresses, with finials, and divided into eight plain panels.

less synodals, &c., 18*s.* 11*d.* It is now returned at 93*l.* The vicarage house stands at the west end of the church-yard, but presents no feature worthy of particular note.

In the tasteful church-yard, with its neat walks, flowered graves, and well shorn lawn, many pretty memorials to the dead have been set up. One slab bears a cross, and an inscription to the memory of the Rev. H. Hill, *obiit* September 1, 1849, who resided here only a few years, but was a great benefactor to the parish. The old church-yard cross, opposite to the entrance to the church, has been restored, and the following inscription placed on the base: "This cross was restored in memory of Henry Hill, M.A., vicar of this parish, 1850." This gentleman erected the spacious and handsome school-room and house abutting on the church-yard, at a cost of about 1000*l.* to himself; and, by his munificence, a weekly average of sixty poor children now receive a good education in a village, where, not many years ago, instruction was little thought of, and still less cared for. The school buildings are in the early English style, erected by Mills and Son, from designs by W. Butterfield, Esq., of London, and harmonize with the architecture of the church.

THE GUILD.

The Guild here was of very early origin, being founded by the parishioners, who alone comprised the fraternity, to the honour of God and the Blessed Virgin. In 9th Edward IV a license was granted to Sir Edward Nevill, knight, the lord of the manor, for the maintenance of a Priest, daily to celebrate divine service at the altar of the Blessed Virgin, in the church, for the good estate of the said king, and Elizabeth his consort, as also for all the brothers and sisters of the fraternity, during their lives, and for their souls after death, and for the souls of all the faithful departed. In the return made 37th Henry VIII, this Guild was certified as follows:

	£.	s.	d.
"Sir Thomas Berdemore, chaplain in this guild, in money paid by the hands of the Master there for the time being, 106s. 8d. And Sir John Wryte, another chaplain there, in money paid yearly, 100s. in all	10	6	8
The tenth part of this sum - - - -		20	8"*

Tradition states that the residence of the Priests of the Guild, was a range of buildings, the foundations of which may be traced in a field, called "Parsons' Close," situate a short distance south of the church. It is, however, more probable that the half timbered house, with its projecting upper story, and porch, north of the church, was the Guild House.†

NEWNHAM

Contains nothing of interest to induce the rambler to visit it, consisting only of a few detached farm houses and cottages. Further on is another member of Aston, called

WILMECOTE,

Noted for its extensive stone quarries, and cement works, which furnish employment to a great number of workmen. It is mentioned separately in Domesday Survey, and then contained three hides of land, value 60s., held by one *Urso*. In 12th Henry III, it had become the property of William de Wilmecote, who took his name from the place, and in his family the manor continued till 8th Henry VII, when it passed from Henry de L'Isle and his wife, in trust, for Hugh Clopton, alderman, of London, and with the Cloptons

* *Valor Ecclesiasticus.*

† See Appendix.

it remained for a considerable period. The manor subsequently came to the earl of Abergavenny, whose descendants now hold it, with a great portion of the land of the chapelry.

THE CHAPEL.

Before the 12th Henry III, there was a Chapel here, for, in that year, William de Wilmecote had a suit with the archdeacon of Gloucester, relative to the advowson of the chapel belonging to the village. It was dedicated to St. Mary Magdalene, and was given to the Guild of the Holy Cross, at Stratford-on-Avon, in the time of Edward IV, by Henry de L'Isle and Elizabeth, his wife, who had become owners of the manor, she being heir to the Wilmecotes.

The chapel, now standing, was erected in the year 1840, at a cost of near 2000*l.* It is dedicated to St. Andrew, and is a neat stone building, consisting of a nave, two narrow aisles, and a small chancel, presenting no particular external features. Entering by the western door, under a pointed arch, the interior offers a more elegant appearance, being fitted up at considerable cost. The nave, as well as the aisles, have open timbered roofs, and are divided by four pointed arches, springing from circular pillars. The aisles are lighted with single lancet windows, some of them filled with stained glass. The western gable is pierced with two very lofty lancet windows, and the chancel, or east window, is of three lancets, the middle one higher than the others, divided externally by plain stonework, and internally by round columns with capitals. The centre one contains a representation of the Crucifixion, and other subjects, in coloured glass. On each side of the altar are two stone seats, under trefoil arches, with circular columns, and a piscina on the north side corresponding in design. The pulpit is of carved stone, presenting four faces to the front, and approached by steps under an arch leading from the priest's door. The font, which is circular, on a similar base, is also carved. The seats are all open, and divided from the choir and chancel by a low screen. As there is no tower, or bell turret, the bell hangs in a wooden campanile a few yards from the north door.

The living is a perpetual curacy, and the Rev. E. Male the present incumbent.

The school in the chapelry is a neat building, erected in 1846, and is conducted on the National system.

PATHLOW,

A third member of Aston Cantloe, is situate about a mile east of Wilmecote. It now consists of a few scattered farm houses and cottages, but anciently gave name to the Liberty of Pathlow. It had the title of a Hundred in the Conqueror's time, and is styled, in Domesday Book, *Patelau.* It was early granted to the Bishops of Worcester, and 4th Edward I, the then bishop had return of writs, assize of bread and beer, with other royal customs therein.[18] It remained with the see of Worcester till the time of Edward VI, when it was exchanged for divers lands in Worcestershire, with John Dudley, earl of Warwick, and his heirs, and it came to the crown, 1st Mary, on his attainder. Her successor, queen Elizabeth, granted it to Ambrose Dudley, earl of Warwick, but failing issue male, it again returned to the crown, and was by James I granted to Sir Francis Smythe, of Wootton Wawen, whose successors occasionally hold a court leet for the manor.

Another hamlet to Aston must be visited on our return;

18. It was in this part of Aston that the occurrence referred to at p. 63 doubtless took place.

so proceeding for a short distance on the road we entered Aston, and turning to the left, we come to the brook running from Wootton, a very dangerous place in winter, and frequently impassable for hours after a storm. Passing over a lofty bridge, of not very strong materials, used for foot passengers only, we enter the hamlet of

LITTLE ALNE,

Consisting of two farm houses and a few cottages. It was anciently possessed by the lords of the manor of Aston, and the lands, given by the Cantelupes to the Canons of Studley, were principally, if not wholly, in this place. The first William de Cantelupe erected a certain hospital near the gate of the Priory of Studley for the relief and entertainment of impotent people; and William, his son and heir, granted to them lands, for this purpose, in his manor of Aston, to the value of 10*l.* annually, which effects, 1st Mary, were granted to one Anthony Skinner, and comprised five tenements, a water mill, and a meadow. The estate remained in this family for several generations, and is now the property of Walter Hemming, esq., of Bewdley, whose father purchased it of Sir F. L. H. Goodricke, baronet.

SHELFIELD

Is another member of Aston, and lies about a mile to the left of Little Alne, and, like it, consists of a few farm houses and cottages. There are three remarkable conical hills on one of the farms, of considerable altitude. William de Cantelupe, as before cited, made considerable grants to the Canons of Studley, *temp.* Henry III; and, in defining these, the document describes them as bounded by the park of *Scelefhull.* Dugdale says that, without doubt, the woods, or great part of them, mentioned in Domesday Book as being then in Aston, were here situate, and that they "were imparked by the lords of the manor for their pleasure in hunting, it being a mountainous ground most proper for deer and conies." This park is described as being bounded by the highway leading from *Spernore* (Spernall) to Aston. The manor appears to have passed through the various families named in the account of Aston, and to have descended through them to the present owner, the earl of Abergavenny. The old manor house still remains here converted into a farm house, now called Shelfield Lodge. There is another large farm house, called Shelfield Square, the property of John Durnin, esq. In a manor house on the site of the former, doubtless lived the John Barret, 9th Richard II, who married Felicia, the daughter and heiress of Peter de Studley.

The population of Aston Cantloe, with its hamlets, was 1089 in the year 1841, and 1155 in 1861. There were fifty-three families in 1563.

Proceeding homeward on the Alcester turnpike road, and passing over *Round Hill*, from which extensive prospects of scenery may be obtained, we pass

OFFORDE,

On the right, formerly a small hamlet, with a manor house, but now having only a mill and a few cottages remaining. In the Domesday Survey it is described as containing five hides of land, with a mill, and woods a mile long and half a mile broad, the whole being of the value of 5*l.* It was granted to Robert de Stafford, having been the property of Waga, the former proprietor of Wootton Wawen. In the time of Henry II, one of the successors of the above

Robert, enfeoffed Robert the son of Matthew, and his heirs, of all his interest here, excepting the lands of three freeholders, and a wood lying on the left hand of the ancient way leading from Wootton to Morton Bagot. He residing here, assumed the surname of Offord, and married the granddaughter of Robert, son of Odonis, lord of Morton. In 25th Henry III, William de Blancfront was certified to hold Offorde, and in 36th of the same reign to have half a knight's fee there of the lord Stafford. His grandson styled himself lord of Offorde, 31st Edward III. It came again into the hands of the Stafford family, for, 46th of this reign, they are certified to hold the manor in fee.* The place afterwards became of little consequence as a village, and passed ultimately in the same manner as Wootton to the family of the Smythes, and has long been accounted as parcel of the lordship of that place. On the left is a farm house, retaining the name of the *Park Farm;* and beyond it, *Wavensmere,* an ancient member of Wootton Wawen. Here, having arrived again on our return, we plod our way to Henley-in-Arden, our original point of departure, which we speedily reach, glad to rest, yet not dissatisfied with the day's pilgrimage.

* *Inquisitions Post Mort.*

Second Day.

OUR next trip will comprise the places lying south-west of Henley, viz. Hungril, Nutlands, Oldberrow, Morton Bagot, Spernal, Studley, Mapleborough Green, Skilts, Outhill, Ullenhall, and Barrells.

Travelling by what is called the new road, turning west, at the south end of the town, we arrive at a few scattered houses, called *Hungril*, or *Hungerhill.* The road-way called Watery Lane, was, formerly, in the brook now running by its side. From its dangerous nature, however, the inhabitants of Henley, A.D. 1769, were induced to purchase the adjoining land, and to make a safe road, alienating, in order so to do, a portion of their rights in the common field.[1] Proceeding up the hill, which gives name to the place, and turning round by the guidepost towards Redditch, we have, on the left hand, a pleasantly-situated farm house, called *Nutlands*, so styled, most likely, from the

1. The parishioners were compelled to effect this great improvement to avoid further indictments, which it is stated in the Highway Book they had been subjected to "by reason of its *founderness* and *quicksands*."

character of underwood once growing there, and arrive, at the distance of two miles from Henley, at

OLDBERROW,

A small village, situated on a peninsula, or narrow strip of land, in the county of Worcester, stretching, like a wedge, of several miles in extent, into Warwickshire. This place is in the lower division of the hundred of Blakenhurst and Deanery of Warwick, and was, at the time of the Domesday Survey, called *Olberge*. It then belonged to the Abbey of Evesham, and comprised twelve hides of land, two swine-herds, and a wood, the value being 5*s*. Nash, in his *History of Worcestershire*, conjectures the name, Old-barrow, or borough, to have arisen from an ancient tumulus here. At the latter end of the reign of Edward III, there was a family of the Owlboroughs resident in the place; and their arms, three owls, were formerly in the church windows. In the 4th and 5th Mary, the manor was given to Valentine Knightley, in whose family it long remained. Afterwards it came to the Packwoods, who sold it to the trustees of the earl of Catherlough, from whom it descended, in direct succession, to the late Robert Knight, esq., of Barrells, at whose death the property was purchased by William Newton, esq., and others. There are several distinct properties in the parish, belonging to Philip Wykeham Martin, esq., Mr. John Cook, and other proprietors.

THE CHURCH,

Like the manor, belonged to the Abbey of Evesham, up to the dissolution of religious houses. It is a small structure, dedicated to St. Mary, presenting, as the engraving shows, a somewhat picturesque appearance. After the suppression of the Abbey of Evesham, it was transferred to the Knightleys; and remained in their patronage, until, by the marriage of Ann, heiress of the family, it passed to Robert Foley, esq., who sold it, A.D. 1705, to William Holyoke, junior, who afterwards disposed of it to the Rev. John Peshall, of Guildford, Surrey, in whose family it has since continued, the Rev. Samuel D'Oyley Peshall, lately deceased, having been the rector up to 1858. The Rev. H. W. Salmon is now the rector. Connected with the rectorial history of

this place, is a letter from Charles I (dated February 26, 1643) preserved in the archives of the bishopric of Worcester, commanding the authorities to expel Thomas Burrough from the living, because he was a rebel. Another rector, William Holyoke, 1725—1769, is frequently mentioned in lady Luxborough's letters to Shenstone, to which we shall more particularly refer when we come to Barrells House.

The church consists of a nave, chancel, tower, and timber-built south porch. The tower is also timber-framed, and rests on beams thrown across some solid masonry, part of the former stone tower, portions of which are supported by strong buttresses. The exterior is plain and unpretending, the walls being whitewashed up to the ridged roof, which is covered with tiles. The interior presents no special features, with the exception, perhaps, of the chancel, which is distinguished from the nave by a slight elevation of the ceiling. The windows are mostly small, all the mullions being obliterated, with the exception of one at the east end of the chancel, which is larger, perfect, and divided into three compartments by two mullions, with the corresponding tracery. In this window were, at one time, the arms of the Abbey of Evesham, and several figures, in the attitude of prayer, in the divisions between the mullions, together with an inscription, "*Orate pro animabus Joh's Owleboroughe (et uxoris) ejus.*" These have all disappeared, except the arms, now in the uppermost centre. On the south side of the communion table, is a piscina and locker, the ornamental portions of which have been destroyed. Opposite, on the north side, is another opening, which may have been used in the Easter celebrations.* The church, judging from the date, 1698, upon one of them, appears to have been pewed many years. Two only of the old open seats remain. A small gallery has been erected at the west end, over which an unsightly dormer window has been inserted. The font stands on a shaft of four connected pillars, is nearly circular at the base, ending in an octagon at top, with a face bearing some rude carving on three of the sections. There are no monuments, except two slabs on the chancel floor. Three bells occupy the tower.

The living is returned at 200*l.* per annum. In the reign

* See "Beaudesert."

of Elizabeth the parish contained ten families; in 1776 it had twenty-seven; and the population in 1841 numbered sixty-three, in 1861, fifty-six.

Leaving OLDBERROW, we re-enter Warwickshire, in which, about a mile and a half further, and over a road not very practicable for light wheeled carriages, and through a country not remarkable for beauty of scenery, we come to another small village, called

MORTON BAGOT,

Possessed, before the Conquest, like Wootton Wawen, by Waga, and bestowed by William I on Robert de Stafford, of whom, at the time of the survey, it was held by one Hervey. It was valued at 20*s.*, but was then worth 40*s.* In Henry II's time, Robert Odonis, or the son of Odo, was the owner, through the marriage of one of whose daughters with William Bagot, part of the property passed into his possession, and continued in his family for several generations. They resided here; hence the addition to distinguish the place from the other Mortons in the county. Two other daughters of Robert Odonis also possessed property in this village; for William Trussell, a descendant of one of them, held of the lord Stafford, 36th Henry III, half a knight's fee, along with Roger Bagot. The possessions of the other daughter were transferred, by Robert de Mora, her descendant, together with the advowson of the church, to the Canons of Kenilworth, about A.D. 1254. The celebrated Robert Bagot, son of the above William, and a great favourite of Henry III, likewise resided here. His son, William, was a knight, and sold the manor 24th Edward I, for 130 marks, to Roger de Coningesby, who, in the 31st of the same reign, obtained a charter of free-warren throughout all his demesne lands here. His son, John, was one of the knights of the shire for the county of Warwick, 18th Edward III; and, some years after, was one of the Commissioners for putting the statute for labourers into execution in this county. His son, dying without issue, the manor came to his daughter, married to John de Lee. For want of heirs in the next generation, it reverted to Thomas de Coningesby, a descendant of the second son of Roger de Coningesby, the purchaser already referred to, in whose family it continued some time. The Trussells of Bellesley, appear to have had the reputed manor and the presentation to the living in 1361, and at that period were designated "*Dominus de Morton Bagot,*" and continued lords thereof up to the year 1427. The manor has since passed through various hands; and now, with the greater part of the property in the parish, belongs to Sir F. L. H. Goodricke, baronet.

THE CHURCH

Is dedicated to the Holy Trinity, and was granted, as before stated, to the Canons of Kenilworth. These Canons presented to the living till 1361, when it appears that William Trussell presented Henry Copenhall, and his two successors, as vacancies arose. The Canons seem to have repossessed themselves of the living in 1432, for one year, after which the patronage appears to have reverted to the same family, and to have continued in their nomination till 1551. A lengthened dispute took place early in the reign of Edward II, between the Prior of Wootton and the Rector of this place, relative to the burial of persons who died in the parish, and the mortuaries arising therefrom. It was tried in the Court of Arches, and given in favour of the Prior, but the Rector disputed this in the Court of Chancery, and it was not settled till the 19th of the same reign, by a similar decision. The Church Goods, 6th Edward VI, are returned as

> one chalice one bell.
> one vestment, fustyan.
> ij altarclothes.
> ij towells.
> ij crosses, one bras, one leade.
> ij cruett.
> one sensor, coper.

In 1291, the living was valued at six marks and a half; in 26th Henry VIII at 6*l.*, and is now returned at 188*l.* per annum. It is in the gift of Sir F. L. H. Goodricke, who has lately presented to it the Rev. G. A. Todd.

The Church is situated on a rising ground, and is of a mean character, having no great interest for the lover of architectural details. It consists of a nave and chancel, with a timber-framed belfry resting on the roof of the former. The nave contains windows of two and three lights, under pointed and obtuse angled arches. The chancel side windows are similar in character, and the eastern window is of three lights under a semi-circular arch. The interior is nearly as uninteresting as the exterior. The nave, the roof of which is ceiled over, is seated with a few pews and some clumsy oak open benches, and on each side of the chancel are open stalls with carved heads and finials. The chancel arch is pointed, and the east window filled with figured quarries. There is a piscina on the south side, and on the north are some remains of the rood screen. The font is octagonal, resting on a plain basement. There are a few monumental inscriptions to the memory of the Holyokes and other families, all of modern date. Two bells occupy the belfry.

The population in 1841 was 170, and in 1861 numbered 150. Twenty-three families resided here in 1563.

Passing from Morton and travelling along the lanes, having a fine view of Studley Castle on the right, at a distance of two miles we arrive at another small village called

SPERNALL,

Anciently written *Spernore*, situate on the river Arrow, and in the time of the Domesday Survey the property of William Buenvasleth, held of him by one Hugh. It was rated at two hides, a mill at four shillings, and seven sticks of eels, with woods three furlongs long and one broad, all of which were valued at 40*s*. There were four villeins and seven bordars with three ploughs. The lands appear to have come by some agreement into the possession of William de Newburgh, the first earl of Warwick of the Norman line, as one of them, 2nd Edward II, was lord of the place, and granted it to the family of Duvassal, to hold the same in sergeantry, by the service of attendance on the earl, and his heirs, at certain times as chief butler. With the Duvassals it remained till the end of Edward III's reign, when issue male ceased. After this William Spernore, styled William Duvassal, *dominus de Spernore*, was seized of it as tenant for life, the reversion pertaining to Walter Holt, son and heir of one of the daughters of Nicholas Duvassal. This Walter Holt had livery of the manor, 5th Henry IV, and he enfeoffed the same to John Reve, vicar of Coughton. His heir, Thomas Reve, passed it, 7th Henry VI, to Thomas Wybbe, esq., but soon after John Throckmorton purchased the whole of the rights, &c., of the manor from the descendants of the coheiresses of the above Nicholas Duvassal, and in his family it has continued to the present time.

THE CHURCH,

Formerly a chapel to the neighbouring church of Coughton, is small, and represented in the initial letter of this chapter. In the reign of Richard I, the Bishop of Worcester decreed that the Canons of Studley, as in Coughton, should have the right of burial of such inhabitants as were not in a free condition. These tenants by bond service, dying of a pestilence, and the lords of the lands they occupied being obliged to dispose of them for others, a dispute arose, relative to these burials, between the Nuns of Cookhill and the Canons of Studley, the former having obtained the advowson of the chapel from the latter, 11th Henry III, hence their claim. In 30th Edward III this dispute was settled by the then bishop, who directed that the Canons should have the burial of those who died on lands formerly held in villeinage, and the Nuns the others, which rights were valued, A.D. 1291, as belonging to the Canons, at 25*s.*, and to the Nuns at 20*s.*

In 26th Henry VIII, the living was valued at 4*l.*, and is now returned at 154*l.* The Rev. C. Dolben is the present incumbent.

The Church, dedicated to St. Leonard,[2] consists of a nave,

2. St. Leonard, a French nobleman at the court of Clovis I, was converted by Remigius. He died about 559, and is implored by prisoners as their patron saint.

chancel, and porch, all of which were almost entirely rebuilt in 1844. The nave, which still preserves some portion of the old structure, is lighted on each side by two obtuse angle arched windows, of two lights, those most eastern being old, and the western ones rebuilt to correspond; the gable, supported by five ancient buttresses, is surmounted by a turret with one bell, under which is a two-light pointed window. The chancel, wholly rebuilt in the Norman style, has a small semi-circular arched window on each side, and a circular window, in six compartments, at the east end. Two round columns, with capitals, run up at the angles of the gable as high as the string course, and a cross forms the apex. The porch is modern, placed over the south doorway, which is flat headed.

The interior is fitted up with open seats, oak reading desk, stone pulpit, and font. The north eastern window of the nave contains a few fragments of ancient stained glass, and the opposite one some modern glass in the tracery. The two more western ones are filled with figured quarries and coloured glass borders. The chancel is divided from the nave by a semi-circular arch, and contains several marble tablets to the memory of the Chambers family, former patrons of the living.

The river Arrow is here broad and dangerous in flood time, as there is only a bridle and foot road across it. The prospects around possess little of an interesting character.

There were only twelve families resident here in 1563. In 1841 the population was 107, in 1861 only 106.

Passing from Spernall, another lane leads to the Birmingham and Alcester turnpike road, a portion here of the ancient Ryknield Street, referred to at p. 8. Turning to the right, and proceeding about a mile thereon, we come to the large village of

STUDLEY.

Part of this parish, at the time of the Norman Conquest, belonged to one *Swain*, and was after that event given by king William, in reward for services, to William de Corbuson or Corbezon. It then comprised four hides of land, on which stood the church and a mill. There were nineteen villeins and twelve bordars, as also a furnace, producing nineteen horse-loads of salt annually, and woods one mile in length and half a mile broad, the value of the whole being 5*l.* Another part, belonging to *Godric* in Saxon times, was, at the Norman Survey, the property of William Buenvasleth, and extended to one hide of land, with woods three furlongs in length and two in breadth, value 10*s.* From William de Corbuson descended Peter, called Peter de Stodley, a pious man, who gave lands to the monks of Bordesley, a mill and certain lands here to the Knights Templars, and founded the Priory of Studley; but his son and successor, another Peter, left little or nothing to his descendants, selling, to his tenants here, all his wood called *The Haye*,3 so that they might have common pasture therein for cattle, reserving to himself and heirs only the pannage and agistment for hogs. He gave also to Hugh de Montfort, of Beaudesert, who married his daughter Emma, large portions of this estate, and the park of Studley to Thurstan, son of Hugh de Montfort. The homage and services of certain tenants, with the advowson and patronage of the Priory, he granted to William de Cantelupe. With the Montforts it remained for some time. From them it passed to William Beauchamp, lord Bergavenny, to whom the other part of the estate passed from the Cantelupes in like

3. Is now a farm at Mapleborough Green, and still called "The Haye."

manner, as we have stated in Aston Cantloe. The same Peter de Stodley enfeoffed the then vicar of the parish in the manor, together with pasturage for a horse, called a hackney, in a meadow, called Castle Meadow, reserving a yearly rent of three broad arrowheads to the chief Lord of the Fee, for all services. This Peter had a daughter, Felicia, wife to John Barret, of Shelfield, to whom the said vicar assigned his rights in 9th Richard II. Their daughter and heiress, married to — Atwode, had also a daughter, wife of — Hunt, in Henry VIII's reign, from whom the Hunts, possessors of the old castle, derived their descent. This portion of the manor came afterwards into the hands of the Lytteltons; and, through them, descended to the present owner, Sir F. L. H. Goodricke, baronet, who has largely increased the estate.

Another large portion of this parish is that formerly possessed by the Canons of

THE PRIORY,

An establishment dedicated to St. Mary, and founded in the time of king Stephen, by Peter de Corbuson, or de Stodley, for Canons Regular of St. Augustine, first at a place called Wicton, in Worcestershire; but soon afterwards removed here. He amply endowed the house with lands, houses, salt furnaces, and the advowsons of several churches; but as the fortunes of his family waned, so did the means of the Priory decay, until there were only three Canons on the foundation, when granted to William de Cantelupe and his heirs. From this time till the dissolution of monastic establishments, the Priors and Canons of this house prospered. The Cantelupes largely increased their revenues and patronage. They built a hospital near the gate of the monastery, where impotent people might have relief and entertainment; and granted lands at Aston Canteloe, of ten pounds yearly value, for its support and maintenance. William, son of the above William de Cantelupe, besides many other grants of lands and immunities, obtained for them, 26th Henry III, a charter "that their woods, lying within the Forest of Feckenham, might be free to themselves, and no officer of the king's belonging to the forest to intermeddle therein, nor press upon them for hospitality, or entertainment, without their own good liking." At the Inquisition taken, 8th Edward I, at Stratford, referred to at p. 63, the jurors presented that the Prior of Studley and the Templars Hospitallers impede justice by preventing the king's bailiffs performing their office within their liberties. Also that the Prior of Studley had appropriated about half an acre of land in the village of Ipsley for five years past.*

The above and various other grants of lands and privileges, from different proprietors in the neighbourhood,4 yielded them such ample revenues, that, at the Dissolution, they were certified according to the Archer MSS., to be worth 125*l.* 4*s.* 8*d.* per annum over and above all reductions. Speed gives the gross valuation at 181*l.* 3*s.* 6*d.*, Dugdale at 117*l.* 1*s.* 1*d.* John Yardley, the then Prior, was granted an annuity of 15*l.* a year for his life. The site, with this portion of the manor of Studley, was shortly afterwards granted to Sir Edmund Knightley, sergeant at law, who dying, 34th Henry VIII, left his estates to the five daughters of his brother, this portion of them coming to Joane, the wife of John Knottesford, sergeant at arms, in whose family it

---

4. At the Dissolution they had large possessions in Studley, and various properties at Welvington, Great and Little Alne, Aston Cantloe, Coughton, Alcester, Sambourne, Donnington, Shottewell, Wheateley, &c., in Warwickshire, as also the like in other counties.

* *Rot. Hund.*, ii, 226.

continued till the death of John Knottesford, esq., in 1781. It was, after this, purchased by the Knights of Barrells, and is now the property of Mrs. Gooch, daughter of the late Robert Knight, esq., *obiit* 1855. The following were the Priors of the house:

Fromundus in the reign of Stephen.
Roger, time of Henry III.
John de Souche, July 10, 1338.
John de Gorcote.
John de Evesham, January 9, 1371.
Robert Wynby, September 27, 1431.
Thomas Bedull, time of Henry VI.
Richard Wode, March 8, 1454.
John Yardly, 26th Henry VIII.

The site of the Priory is approached from the village by an avenue of fine elms. The remains of the Priory have been built up, and now form the gable of a modern farm house, still called "The Priory:" They consist of a portion and the side and arch of what was once a window of the chapel. They stand, with a large garden and farm buildings, in a moated inclosure, the river Arrow forming part of it, and supplying the other portion with water, where not filled in. Part of it is bordered by some very lofty and graceful willows; and its extent, which is easily defined, shows that the religious community located here had no lack of worldly goods, a well-wooded, park-like ground still surrounding the place.

In proceeding to the Church we pass over the river Arrow, close to a large mill used in the manufacture of needles, on the site of which, most probably, stood the one belonging to the Knights Templars, given to them by Peter de Stodley.

THE CHURCH

Is situated on an eminence, nearly a mile from the village. It is dedicated to the Virgin Mary, and was given to the Prior and Canons of Studley by Peter de Corbuson, or de

Stodley, and remained with them till the dissolution of their house. In Dugdale's time the windows contained the arms of Montford, Attwood, Edgebaston, and Middlemore, formerly proprietors in the parish. One of the latter family, 7th Henry IV, viz. Thomas Middlemore, of Edgbaston, founded, in this church, a chantry chapel, for a priest to say mass daily at the altar of the Blessed Virgin, on the south part of the said church, for the health of his soul and his ancestors. This he endowed with eighty acres of land, ten of meadow, and 13*s.* 4*d.* yearly rent, all being in Studley, the revenues amounting, 26th Henry VIII, to 4*l.* 13*s.* 4*d.*; which sum was yearly received by the priest of Mr. Robert Middlemore, notwithstanding he did not duly attend here, but sung in other places at his pleasure. This chantry was then returned as under:

CHANTRY FOUNDED AT STUDELEY.

	£.	s.	d.
"Sir Martin Marten, Custodian of the Chantry founded in the parochial Church there.			
And it is worth in lands and tenements within the demesne of Studeley, annually	4	13	4
The tenth part of this sum - - - -		9	4"*

The Church Goods, 6th Edward VI, were much more limited in number than in many of the parishes we have quoted, viz.:

It'm there j chalice & iij belles, one cope velvett. One albe.†

In 19th Edward I, the living was valued at fifteen and a half marks; and, in 26th Henry VIII, it was rated at 8*l.*, being the stipend paid by the Canons of the Priory. It is now returned as of the value of 103*l.* The Rev. W. Godfrey is the present incumbent.

---

* *Valor Ecclesiasticus.* † *Papers in Record Office.*

The edifice consists of a low embattled tower, nave, south aisle, and chancel. Under the west window of the tower, a large obtuse-arched doorway has been cut, which forms the entrance to the church, the north and south doorways being filled up. The south doorway, with a pointed arch, had formerly a porch, which has been removed, but the north entrance still preserves a beautiful Norman arch, with zig-zag moulding, springing from plain round pillars with sculptured capitals.[5] Eastward of this are two pointed arched windows of three lights, and in the south aisle are windows corresponding in design. On each side of the chancel are two small pointed windows, the south one of which has been partly cut away, to form a doorway to a modern built vestry-room. There are two larger ones of two lights, under pointed arches north and south, at the east end. The east window is a depressed arch of three lights. The nave and aisle, as well as the chancel, have all high ridged tile roofs, in the former two of which, three ugly dormer windows have been inserted.

The interior, on first entering, gives the idea that the parishioners had determined to make it as *comfortable* as possible, as the roof, walls, seats, and galleries are plastered, coloured, and painted so well as to effectually hide the characteristics of the original building. The nave is divided from the aisle by two octagonal pillars supporting three pointed arches, and separated from the tower and chancel by arches of like character. With the exception of a piscina

---

5. "It is interesting to notice how very reluctant our forefathers were to destroy all traces of their predecessors' pious munificence, though anxious themselves to rebuild the church with additional splendour, and with the increased skill they had at their command. How very frequently a Norman doorway or font, carefully preserved, alone remains to attest the piety of a past generation."—*Brandon's Parish Churches*, vol. i, p. 61.

in the south wall of the chancel, there is nothing of architectural interest. The windows of the chancel are all filled with coloured glass and figured quarries, the gift, as an inscription on one commemorates, of the Lay-Rector, Robert Knight, esq., of Barrells, 1847. The chancel contains several tablets and monumental slabs to the memory of various members of the families of Knottesford, Petre, Phillips, Lyttelton, and Knight. In the nave and aisle are others to those of Chambers, Hardy, Dewes, and Holyoke. The font is a modern work and placed near to the pulpit. There are five bells in the tower, all bearing date 1688.

In the churchyard are several ancient tombs, the inscriptions obliterated. There is one at the end of the chancel to the memory of John Knottesford, esq., *obiit* May 10, 1781, "the last of a family, possessors of considerable property in the parish upwards of two hundred years." There is also a large vault on the north of the chancel, with stone canopy, the burial place of the Goodrickes. An ancient sundial lies prostrate in the church-yard, apparently the head of a former buttress to the church.

Passing out of the church-yard, and adjoining it on the north, is the site of the ancient Castle of Studley, built by William, son of William de Corbuson, or one of his descendants, most likely in the early part of the reign of king Stephen, who granted license to many of his subjects to build castles within their own grounds, A.D. 1135-40. As no record, however, containing mention of this edifice subsequent to that date exists, it is probable that it was demolished in the first of Henry II, 1154, when, according to Hollinshed, it was ordered "that all those castles, which, contrary to all reason and good order, had been made and builded by any manner of persons in the days of king

Stephen, should be overthrown and cast down, which were found to be eleven hundred and fifteen."[6]

Leland, writing in the time of Henry VIII, says, "The Lord Corporson, that was founder of Studley Abbey, had a fair maner place half a mile thens."*

Of this building no trace remains except the moat, now dried or filled up, though persons living remember part of it full of water. The house now standing within this inclosure is a half-timbered building with numerous gables, to which great modern additions have been made. It is large, but, though still called "The Old Castle," of no interest to the antiquary; and was formerly the residence of the Holyokes, ancestors of Sir F. L. H. Goodricke, baronet, whose property it remains.

Eastward of this building and the church, on a rising ground stands the modern-built

STUDLEY CASTLE,

Constructed with towers, keep, turrets, courts, and halls, with the varied accessories usual in buildings of this character in ancient times. It was erected by the present baronet, Sir Francis Lyttleton Holyoke Goodricke, under the contract of Grisel and Peto. The engraving will give a correct idea of the general design of the building, the park, gardens, and pleasure grounds around which are extensive. The views from the fronts of the castle, and from various

---

6. Many castles and holds were built by licenses from king Stephen, but, after his decease, Henry II caused them to be destroyed. Since that time also, not a few of those which remained have decayed, partly by commandment of Henry III and partly of themselves; or by conversion into dwelling houses of noblemen, their martial fronts being removed, so that at the present there are very few or no castles at all maintained within England, saving only on the coast, &c.—*Hollinshed*, vol. i, 327.

* *Itinerary*, vi, 74.

spots in the park, will be found of a fine and extensive character, reaching to the hills of the Lickey and Great Malvern.

The village of Studley is large, and keeps increasing in population and prosperity, for besides its agricultural wealth, it carries on a large trade in branches of the needle manufacture. It is situated on the turnpike road leading from Birmingham to Alcester, about four miles from the latter place, and six from the point of our departure on this day's tour. It contains a neat Catholic Chapel, and other places of worship belonging to various classes of Protestant Dissenters. A very neat and substantial schoolhouse and master's residence have of late years been built in the village, on land given by the late Robert Knight, esq., which are found of great benefit to the poorer inhabitants.

Leaving the village, and proceeding, over another bridge, on the turnpike road towards Birmingham, we soon come to one of its hamlets, an ancient manor, called

MAPLEBOROUGH GREEN,

Formerly an open waste, but now inclosed, having a few farm houses and cottage-dwellings thereon. It was part of William Corbuson's estate, held of him by *Goisfridus*, and contained one hide, and a wood one furlong wide and the like in length, altogether of the value of 15*s*., and, beforetime, the property of *Leviet*. This was the manor referred to as "The Haye" in Studley. In 19th Richard II, it had come into the possession of Thomas Middlemore, of Edgbaston, and was then certified to consist of two messuages, four hundred acres of land, sixty acres of meadow, and 1*l*. 8*s*. in rents. All these were in the possession of John Middlemore, of Edgbaston, in 10th Henry VI, and remained long the property of his posterity. They have since passed into various hands, Sir F. L. H. Goodricke being lord of the manor.

On turning from this place, to the right, where the roads to Redditch and Henley-in-Arden intersect the turnpike road, we have before us the grounds and woodlands of

SKILTS,

Another ancient manor of Studley, and formerly a grange or farm belonging to its Priory, called *Skyllus Grange*. The first notice of this place appears in a petition to the Bishop of Worcester, by Thomas Atwode, styling himself heir in blood to Peter de Stodley, the founder of the house. In this he complains that Thomas Bedull, the then Prior, *temp.* Henry VI, kept at Skilts a paramour, viz. Joan, wife to

John Green, with her husband's connivance, to which Joan he frequently resorted in secular apparel, allowing her wheat, malt, wool, and other articles, whereby the Monastery was much impoverished. The contiguity of the Priory to this grange, and the lonely and unfrequented nature of the neighbouring country, most probably led to the selection of this place by the Prior.

This part of the manor came, in the division of the estates of the Knightleys, 34th Henry VIII, (as before stated in the account of Studley,) to James Duffyld, in right of Frances, his wife, who sold it in 1549, to William East and others, together with a fifth part of the manor of Studley. In 1560, it was again sold to William Sheldon, esq., of Beoley, and at that time comprised two messuages, six hundred acres of land, sixty acres of meadow, six hundred of pasture, one hundred and twenty of wood, and one hundred of heath and furze; all of which he imparked for deer, and, on the south side thereof, built a very beautiful house of brick. From this family it came, by descent and sale, to other proprietors, and is now the property of Frederick Moilliet, esq., who resides at SKILTS HOUSE, which he has enlarged and much improved. Standing on an eminence, it is seen from a distance on the south, and commands itself most extensive views of a district of country extending over Studley, and far beyond Alcester.

Another member of Studley, called HOLT, consisted of the lands held by the Knights Templars, and afterwards by the Knights Hospitallers. This, at the Dissolution, also came into possession of Sir Edward Knightley. It was the property, 3rd Edward VI, of Henry Rishton, esq., and was then known as the manor and capital messuage of *Holt*, with the appurtenances in *Stodeleigh*, consisting of two messuages, three hundred acres of land, fifty of meadow, two hundred of pasture, and sixty of wood and underwood. All these Henry bequeathed to John, his son and heir; and, in the next generation, it was sold to Sir John Southworth, knight. It is still called "*the Holt Farm*," and is now the property of Sir F. L. H. Goodricke. Another member of Studley, the property of the Cantelupes, was called PADONGRE, but of this denomination of lands in the parish, all usage has expired.

The population of Studley, with its members, in 1861 was 2230, having increased 238 since 1841, when the numbers were 1992. In the reign of Elizabeth the number of families was fifty.

On rising the hill, from which a fine view of Worcestershire, the Ridgeway, the Lickey, and the Malvern Hills, is obtained, we come to a part of the Skilts estate, called *Outhill*, comprising two farm houses and a few cottages; and, descending the hill towards Oldberrow, we pass over the little strip of Worcestershire before spoken of, and proceeding on one side of Barrells Park, we arrive at

ULLENHALL,

A hamlet of the parish of Wootton Wawen. This place was also part of the possessions of Waga, before the Conquest, and it was given, after that event, with Wootton, to Robert de Stafford. It was then called *Holehale*, and contained one hide, the woods being half a mile long and a furlong broad, value 4*l*. From this Robert, Roger, earl of Warwick, obtained it, and he granted it in fee to one Roger, who took his name from the place. In this family it remained till the time of Edward I, when Robert, son of William de Olinhall, held the fourth part of a knight's fee of the earl of Warwick.* It afterwards became the

* *Rot. Hund.*, ii, 98.

property of the de Montforts, and fell to the crown by the attainder of Sir Simon de Montfort, knight, in the 10th Henry VII. He was descended from John, an illegitimate son of Sir Peter de Montfort, *temp.* Edward II. This Sir Peter had certain issue by one Lora de Ullenhale, daughter of Richard Astley, of this hamlet, and he took care for their advancement by bequeathing to them this and other estates. Sir John de Montfort, his eldest son by this connexion, having married Joan, daughter and heiress to Sir John de Clinton, knight, owner of the lordship of Coleshill, settled there, and his family remained in possession of Ullenhall till the attainder in Henry VII's time. By the crown, at this period, the manor was granted to Gerald, earl of Kildare, and Elizabeth St. John, his wife. From them it descended to their son, Sir James Fitzgerald, knight; but, in 1st Mary, came again to the crown by his attainder. It was then granted by the queen to Michael Throckmorton, esq., youngest son of Sir Robert Throckmorton, of Coughton, knight, in whose family it remained till purchased by Mr. Bolton, citizen of London. It came into the possession, afterwards, of the Knights, of Luxborough, in the county of Essex.7 From them, it descended through Robert, earl of Catherlough, to the late Robert Knight, esq., on whose death, in 1855, this portion of the estates was sold to various proprietors, the manor of Ullenhall, and mansion of Barrells, being purchased by William Newton, esq.

THE CHURCH,

Dedicated to St. Mary, stands on a considerable elevation,

---

7. The family descended from Nicholas Knight, of Beoley, in the county of Worcester (1st Richard III), William Knight, *obiit* 1580, being the first resident at Barrells. In 1682, William Knight, barrister at law, was living at Barrells, having a brother, Edmund, of London, mercer.—*Herald's Visitation, Col. Arms*, k, iii.

and may be seen for miles on the east and south. In the year 1256, Taurinus, prior of Wootton, granted the tithes of corn here to William de Romesty for eighteen marks. The Church Goods found here were, *temp.* Edward VI,

> j chalice & j bell.
> one vestment dornix.
> one cope dornix.
> ij towells.
> one altarclothe.

The building, which Dugdale calls "a fair Chapel," consists of a nave, chancel, south porch, and a timber-framed

belfry, containing two bells, with a turret or cupola over, resting on the roof of the nave. The nave and chancel are lighted by lancet and ogee windows, and have a ridged roof of equal height. The eastern window is a pointed arch of three lights. The gables of the nave and porch are each surmounted with a cross. The interior presents no very interesting features, the roofs of both nave and chancel having been covered with a coved ceiling in 1755, and the chapel seated with high pews, those in the chancel being nearly five feet in height. These with the unsightly gallery, and the two dormer windows in the roof of the nave, completely spoil the appearance of what might be made a very neat place of worship. The chancel is separated from the nave by a pointed arch, the half pillars, or piers, of which have been cut from the wall. A small portion of the rood screen remains. There is a piscina and locker in the south wall of the chancel, and the east and two side windows are filled with coloured quarries, the gift of Robert Knight, esq. Over the east window are the arms of Knight, painted on a shield. The communion rails are modern, bearing date 1820, the old ones, in the style found in many churches in the neighbourhood, being used as a balustrade to the stairs of the gallery at the west end. The porch arch is blocked up, and the porch serves for a small vestry or robing room. The font is an octagon in shape, and plain. In the chancel is a large mural monument to the Throckmortons, owners of the manor after the time of Edward VI, and another to the earl of Catherlough. A small tablet, south of the east window, records the births and deaths of various members of this family, whose remains were removed from the mausoleum in Barrells Park, on the 30th of October, 1830, and deposited in a vault here. The Chapelry formerly went with the vicarage of Wootton Wawen. It has recently been separated, and made a distinct living, W. Newton, esq., being now the patron. It is valued at 110*l.*, and the Rev. R. Thursfield is the incumbent.

The population in 1841 was returned with Wootton. In 1851 there were in Ullenhall and Aspley 459 persons, and in 1861 the number was 508. In 1563 there were forty-four families.

The hamlet of Ullenhall is extensive in acreage, and

numerous farm houses are scattered about its length and breadth, for a distance of three or four miles. Situate northward, are three other members of Wootton, viz. *Aspley*, *Forde Hall*, and *Mockley*, but of no sufficient interest to tempt the traveller out of his way to examine them. The early history of these places, as separate manors, is all that is now known.

ASPLEY.

The first mention of this manor appears to be in the 5th Henry III, when Robert de Chaucumbe was lord of it. Gilbert de Segrave, who had married Annabil, one of the coheiresses of this Robert, in the 26th of the same reign, became lord, and obtained a charter of free-warren, having an ancient manor house and park here. He departing this life, she granted it to John de Somery, a son by a second husband, on condition of his paying to her, and her son Nicholas de Segrave, and his heirs, a pair of gilt spurs, or sixpence annually. The manor afterwards returned to the Segraves, and was in possession of lord Berkeley, 26th Henry VIII. It was the property of John Sanders, of Honily, in 1698.

FORDE HALL.

The above John de Somery, in the early part of the reign of Edward I, granted this place to one Roger de la Forde, of Aspley, and Agatha his wife, and their heirs, at a rent of one shilling yearly. Hence it came to be called Forde Hall, and, 13th Richard II, was called a manor, one Robert Foulehurst being then lord. It came, about the time of Henry VIII, to John Fullwode, second son to Robert Fullwode, of Clay Hall, in the parish of Tanworth, and afterwards by one of the coheiresses of another John Fullwode, grandson of the above-named John, it fell, by partition, to Grace, one of six daughters, married to Angel Grey, esq. This and Aspley subsequently came into possession of numerous proprietors, and several neat residences have lately been erected by the present owners of the property.

MOCKLEY.

It is considered probable that the lands granted by Robert de Stafford to the Priory of Wootton, lay in this place, hence *Monklee*. The possessions of that Priory were given by Henry VI, to King's College, Cambridge, and these at Mockley have been enjoyed by the Provost and Scholars of that college to the present time.

Leaving Ullenhall, and travelling southwards, we shall now visit

BARRELLS,

Or *Barrels*, on the right of the road skirting the Park, on our return to Henley. What the old Hall may have been is not known; but that it was of no great pretensions, though, perhaps, equal to others of that day, is obvious from the letters of lady Luxborough,[8] who resided here from 1739 to 1756, and who, being a person of great taste and judgment, made many improvements. Shenstone the Poet, to whom these letters were written, describes her as a lady of "abundant ease, politeness, and vivacity, in which she was scarce equalled by any woman of her time." She

---

8. The honourable Henrietta St. John, wife of Robert, earl of Catherlough, viscount Barrells, and baron Luxborough, of Shannon, in the kingdom of Ireland. She was the sister of Henry, viscount Bolingbroke, principal Secretary of State to Queen Anne, A.D. 1710.

remarks, in one letter, April 28th, 1748, that "good carving is too fine for my humble roof. The room, consider, is only hung with sixpenny paper, and is so low that I have but five inches between Pope's head and the motto over it." But though she could not do much with the house, she appears to have been constantly adding to, or improving the grounds and garden round. We read of her Hermitage, Pheasant Yards, Flower Gardens, Bowling Green, Stable Court, (honoured with Mrs. Kendall's coach and six,) the stuccoing of her Summer House, by Mr. Wright of Worcester; also the making of the Ha! Ha! the Serpentine, and the Service Walks; the middle walk from whence you now see Claverdon; the planting of the lane which joins the coppice, and of twenty-seven good straight elms in the lower part of the long walk; also of the Piping Faun in the oak tree, and of the erection of statues and urns in the pleasure grounds, one of the latter to the memory of Somervile the Poet,9 once her neighbour at Edstone, the inscription on which she testifies great anxiety about. All these agreeable devices, which the countess had gathered round her previous to her death in 1756, have long ago disappeared. A poetical description of them, by the vicar of Coughton, making some little allowance for the exuberant fancy of the author, will not, however, be out of place here; and, although, perhaps, a somewhat flattering, may nevertheless, be accepted as a tolerably accurate account of Barrells, in a state which has long since departed. The lines occur in the "Dedication of a Pastoral Elegy to lady

---

9. She is not very complimentary to her Henley neighbours; for she tells Shenstone that she "thinks it [the urn] would be better done at Warwick, than it can be by the fools at Henley." She speaks also of the then Henley Incumbent as "Parson Hall, the little round, fat, oily man of God," as too of an "ill-natured rascal who is a weekly carrier from Henley to Warwick."

Luxborough, by Mr. Perks, of Coughton, corrected by Parson Allen,"[10] and are to the following effect:

"Here fragrant flow'rs refresh the musing fair,
Whilst zephyrs waft their odours thro' the air,
Luxuriant shoots, with one united blow,
Rival the colours of the various bow.
The warbling songsters, on the blossom'd thorn,
Stretch their melodious throats, and wake the morn.
The bee laborious, hums around the bower,
And sips the balmy sweets of ev'ry flower.
'T is thus the varied scene treats every sense;
Displays the charms of youth and innocence.
Within, new objects strike the wond'ring eye,
And strokes of sculpture with the pencil vie:
Here breathing shadows each apartment grace,
And meagre bustos show their marble face.
The robed Peer, full drawn, majestic stands,
And mimic miniature in motley bands.
There Nature's sports, from India's distant shore,
Or dress'd in lighter moss, or clad in ore!
See heaps of shells, old Ocean's glossy store,
Have left their briny cells, and weep no more;
Beneath the rolling wave no longer sleep,
Swept from the rocks and caverns of the deep:
Some skilful hand the pleasing task pursues,
And adds new lustre to their native hues.
The grotto's pride, when gaily interchang'd,
They shine, in regular confusion rang'd.
But O! the loveliest sight is yet conceal'd,
By human art never to be excell'd!
Here ev'ry flow'r that decks th' enamell'd meads,
Or thro' the grove its vernal beauty spreads,
In lively tints—so natural, so true,
A piece more perfect Titian never drew.
Thus Taste polite, and Judgment more refin'd,
Feast the admiring eye, and cultivate the mind."

The Hall was, in the latter part of the last century, greatly altered, and almost wholly rebuilt, by the late Robert Knight, esq. A new front, having a lofty portico, supported

---

10. The Rev. William Perks was vicar of Coughton from 1717 to 1767, and the Rev. Thomas Allen rector of Spernal from 1728 to 1753.

on fluted columns with Corinthian capitals, was erected, and the grounds kept in good order, till the breaking up of the establishment, when the extensive stabling and out-buildings were pulled down, since which period the hall, gardens, and grounds, were so neglected that it might, with truth, be said of the former glories of the place,

> "Sunk are thy towers in shapeless ruin all,
> And the long grass o'ertops the mouldering wall."

The property, as before stated, is now possessed by W. Newton, esq., who has taken down the portico, repaired the front, and built a lofty hall extending to a lighted cupola or lantern at top, with spacious kitchens and other suitable offices behind.

Returning eastward, through the once extensive park, along the long walk, the road rises up a short hill, surmounted by a large clump of trees. In this formerly stood a mausoleum,[11] wherein several members of the family of Knight had been interred: This was pulled down in 1830, and the bodies it contained removed to the vault before spoken of, in the chancel of Ullenhall Chapel, where a small tablet records their memories, thus:

Vicountess St. John, B. 25th February, 1723, D. 6th March, 1752.
Josiah Russell, B. 1674, D. 7th May, 1755.
Baroness Luxborough, B. 15th July, 1699, D. 26th March, 1756.
Honble. Henry Knight, B. 25th December, 1728, D. 15th August, 1762. S.P.
Countess Duroure, B. 21st November, 1729, D. 1st March, 1763.
Elizabeth Powell, B. 7th January, 1692, D. 11th March, 1765.
Caroline Knight, B. 30th July, 1772, D. 22nd August, 1772.
Henry Knight, B. 24th May, 1795, D. 14th November, 1800.
Count Duroure, B. 6th February, 1763, D. 24th September, 1822. S.P.

"The place thereof knoweth it no more!" So much for human greatness. Musing on the "vain, transitory splendours" of which this mansion was once the scene, we wend our way homewards; and, reaching the road adjoining Hungril, by which we set out, we return to Henley-in-Arden, and so finish our second day's ramble.

11. "Lord Catherlough, son of the famous Mr. Knight, cashier of the South Sea Company, has a seat at Barrels Green, about three miles off [Wootton], and built a tower in his grounds for his own burial, and that of his family, who were removed from their vault."—*Gibson's Camden*, ii, 342. They were brought from the chantry chapel of Wootton Wawen.

Third Day.

HAVING visited the places south of Henley-in-Arden, we may now proceed to those lying northward, viz., Botley, Tanworth, Salter Street, Umberslade, and Nuthurst, with their members. To do so we must journey for about a mile on the Birmingham road, after which taking the first turn on the left, we shall next reach

BOTLEY,

Now comprising an ancient farm house, opposite to which is a mill, and another farmstead, bearing the same name, but in a different parish. The manor of Botley, being a member of Wootton Wawen, was reckoned with that parish in Domesday Survey. Dugdale considers it to have been of much greater antiquity than this record, from its Saxon name *Botle*, which is equivalent to *Domus* in Latin. Robert de Stafford gave certain land in this place, *temp.* Henry II, to the Canons of Kenilworth, with the homages and services of several persons. He gave also, to Geoffry Malore and his heirs, all those lands, homages, and services, which he held of him here, reserving the payment of a sparrowhawk to himself and heirs. From this Geoffry, it descended to John Malore, who, 9th Edward III, obtained a grant of free-warren on all his lands here, as well as on other manors. From him descended another John, who with Ankitell, his son and heir, alienated it to Richard Archer, esq., and his heirs, by deed, 22nd Henry VI. In the family of Archer it continued till the death of lord Archer, of Umberslade, when it came, in the subdivision of the estates, to one of his daughters, wife of E. B. Clive, esq., who sold it to Bolton King, esq., in whose possession it remains.

There is nothing to detain the traveller at Botley, the mill being but a modern building, whilst the farm house opposite, though of considerable antiquity, presents no deviation from the style of half-timbered dwellings deserving of special notice.

The road leads on to *Dansey Green*, a cluster of houses very common in this part of the county: adjacent are several houses, now attached to farms, whose names, *Bickerscourt*, &c., once designated some particular manors, or members of the parish of Tanworth, of more note than at present. Leaving these, and at the distance of four miles from Henley, occupying an elevated site stands the village of

TANWORTH,

The church of which is a conspicuous object from the road which the traveller will pursue. The first mention of the place dates from the latter end of the reign of Henry I, when Simon, Bishop of Worcester, confirmed to the Canons of Kenilworth, the chapel of *Tanewrtha*, which had been given to them by Roger, earl of Warwick. This extensive parish had long been a member of Brailes, in the hundred of Kineton, and was, at the Domesday Survey, included in the enumeration of Brailes, in which it is stated, there were, at that time, forty-six hides of land, and woods three miles long by two broad, the latter of which Dugdale considers was chiefly in Tanworth. Before the Conquest, these lands were the property of the earl of Mercia; but after their seizure by the king they were transferred to Henry de Newburgh, when he had been raised to the earldom of Warwick. Tanworth continued in the possession of succeeding earls of this family till the 9th John, when it was assigned as dower to Alice, widow of earl Waleran, for her life, and afterwards, in like manner, to Ela, widow of earl Thomas, 26th Henry III. In 13th Edward I, it had returned again to the earls; for, in that year, William de Beauchamp, then earl of Warwick, claimed court leet, assize of bread and beer, free-warren, gallows, infangthef,[1] tumbrel, and waifs, within Tanworth, by prescription.

At an inquisition held at Stratford-on-Avon, the 8th of this reign, it was presented by the jurors that William de Morteyn took of William de Hayles, captive for the death of Thomas Dumbel, whom he killed, ten marks for delivering him, and admitted him, with certain of his neighbours, to bail; that afterwards Walter de Winterton came and gave them forty shillings for having him, to the damage of the king, and that the said William passed his land in *Toneworth* to the said Walter.* Also that William de Morteyn took of Richard, son of William de Merston, imprisoned for felony, five marks to let him go free, and that he said he was dead while yet alive.†

---

1. Infangthef was the liberty granted to lords of certain manors, to judge any thief taken within their fee.

* *Rot. Hund.*, ii, 227. † *Ibid*, ii, 228.

In 9th Edward II, Tanworth was in the king's hands, during the minority of Thomas, son of Guy de Beauchamp, and was then valued at 34*l.* 16*s.* 4*d.* per annum. As part of the property of the earldom of Warwick, it remained till the 3rd of Henry VII, when it reverted, with the other possessions of the family, to the crown.

In 34th of this reign John Wylaston, esq., was farmer of all the king's lands, tenements, and mills at this place, let by indentures for the term of .... years, by John Walshe, esq., lately the king's supervisor there, at a rental of 32*l.*, which he paid over to Thomas Godeman, the king's receiver.*

Tanworth was next granted, for 630*l.* 16*s.* 2*d.*, by Henry VIII, 36th of his reign, to Sir George Throckmorton, knight, to be held in capite, by the twentieth part of a knight's fee. With them it continued till it was sold by Thomas Throckmorton, esq., 2nd James I, to Andrew Archer, esq., of whose estate it formed a part up to the death of lord Archer, when, through default of male issue, it became the portion of one of his coheiresses, married to E. B. Clive, esq., who sold it, in 1826, to E. Bolton King, esq., who is the present lord of the manor of Tanworth. A considerable portion of the land in Tanworth belongs to earl Amherst, the descendant of another daughter of lord Archer.

THE CHURCH,

Dedicated to St. Mary Magdalene, was, originally, a Chapel belonging to Brailes. It was, *temp.* Henry I, granted to the Canons of Kenilworth; but in the 3rd of John, we find that it was designated a Church. At this time an arrangement was made, between these Canons and Waleran, earl

* *Papers, "Warwick," in Record Office.*

of Warwick, by virtue of which it was agreed that, on the living becoming void, the earl and his heirs should nominate a clerk to the canons, by them to be presented for induction to the bishop, and that the canons should receive from the incumbent, so presented, a yearly pension of two marks, in two payments, and a stone of wax on Candlemas day, for ever, which were afterwards regularly paid. All the glebe, however, was not given at the first foundation; for, *temp.* Henry III, Walter, the son of Peter de Wolvardington, granted a messuage, with the appurtenances, in Tanworth, to Richard Lungspe and his successors.

In 19th Edward I, the living was valued at fifty marks; but in 9th Edward II, at only thirty. At this latter period, it constituted part of the dowry of Alice, widow of Guy de Beauchamp. In 14th Edward III, the interest of the canons and earl passed to William de Clinton, earl of Huntingdon, the canons reserving to themselves and their successors the pension of two marks and a stone of wax per annum. It was at this time that a messuage, adjoining the church-yard, and forming part of the glebe, was granted to the canons by Thomas de Beauchamp, earl of Warwick. The transfer to the earl of Huntingdon, and the new grant to the canons, were both confirmed by the king. The earl of Huntingdon bestowed the advowson on his newly-founded Priory of Maxstoke, in this county. The canons of this establishment obtained the appropriation of the earl's gift, from Wolstan, Bishop of Worcester. By this instrument, the vicar was to receive a competent portion of the funds of the church, amounting to twenty marks per annum; whilst the two marks and stone of wax were to be paid, as heretofore, annually to the Canons of Kenilworth; together with a pension of two marks per annum to the Bishop of Worcester and his successors, and another of twenty shillings yearly to the Prior and Monks of Worcester.

In 26th Henry VIII, the Rectory of Tanworth was valued at 3*l.* 13*s.* 4*d.* per annum, the sum at which it was then let, and the Vicarage at 6*l.* 13*s.* 4*d.* They were given 30th of the same reign, by the king, to Charles Brandon, duke of Suffolk, who conveyed the former to his grandson, Robert Trapps. William Powlett, son of lord George Powlett, by Mary, daughter of a son of the said Robert Trapps, sold it, 44th Elizabeth, to Andrew Archer, esq. The advowson of the Vicarage had been purchased by him, in the 27th of the same reign. It is now in the gift of earl Amherst, the representative of one of the coheiresses of the Archer family, and is returned at the value of 500*l.* The rectorial tithes belong to Bolton King, esq., as Lay Rector.

In the return of Church Goods,* 6th Edward VI, it is stated that there were at *Tonworth*,

> j chalice & iiij belles, and sannce bell.
> viij vestments, iiij silke, iiij dornix.
> ij copes, silke.
> ij crosses, mastulen.
> ij crose, clothes.
> ij censors, mastulen.
> a payre orgayns.

The Church of Tanworth stands on a conspicuous eminence; this causes it to appear, as we approach it from Henley, of great altitude, which is not the case on a nearer inspection. The edifice consists of tower and spire, nave, aisles, and chancel. The tower contains a pointed belfry window on each face, but has no large western window or doorway. It is surmounted by a small and plain parapet, within which springs a simple octagonal

---

* *Papers in Record Office.* See p. 49.

spire. The spire was partly taken down in 1720, and restored a few feet higher than the old one. The south aisle contains three small windows of three lights, traces of one partly destroyed, and one at the east end. The porch entrance has been walled up, and a small window placed in the upper part of it, a barbarism which has been repeated in the northern aisle, doorways being inserted

further westward, so as to open under the interior gallery. The north aisle once contained several rich mullioned and tracery windows; but these were, A.D. 1790, replaced by lights, filled with plain lattice glass.[2] Of the nave there is now no distinctive feature, owing to the circumstance of one roof spanning the whole of the nave and aisles. The pitch of the roof of the chancel is the same as that of the nave,

2. These have, happily, now been restored, by the exertions of the Rev. A. Hunter, vicar, in promoting a subscription for the purpose.

with a cross on the summit of the eastern gable, the buttresses, at each angle of its rise, having short crocketed finials.

Entering the church, by one of the doors already named as opening under the gallery, the connoisseur of ecclesiastical style will have to deplore the havoc made by the Solons of the parish in the year 1790, who, in vestry assembled, November 17, 1789, resolved "that the church should be new pewed in a regular way, so as to be fit and decent for divine service." To provide for this, they took off the several roofs, destroyed the pillars and arches separating the nave and north aisle, and removed the porches. Proceeding to make the edifice *fit and decent*, they erected a roof of one span for the whole building, separated the tower arch from the body of the church by the erection of a large gallery, with closed screen under, pewed the body without leaving any central passage to the chancel; and thus, with a flat ceiling, having cornices round, and five circular central mouldings, gave to the interior much more of the aspect of a large concert room than a place of worship. As, therefore, there is nothing to praise, and much to deplore, let us leave these renovators, and hasten into the chancel, where, fortunately, they had no power, and describe the interior. It is divided from the nave by a high pointed arch, springing from piers or half pillars, but slightly defined, and has a coved ceiling. The south side has a pointed window of two lights, and two others of three lights, with a priest's door, and the north two of two lights, a third being filled up, and now partly forming the side of a modern vestry room. The east window is also pointed, and of five lights. It is exceedingly light and graceful, and would much improve the interior if filled with coloured glass. On each side of it, and nearly on a level with the sill, is a large carved bracket of exquisite workmanship, supported on shafts, considerable portions of which are hid by the raised floor. These brackets were once occupied by saintly images, and as there were formerly two chapels, or oratories, in this church, dedicated to Our Lady and to St. Catharine, most probably their effigies stood thereon, whilst the altars were placed beneath and in front. On the south side of the communion table are the remains of the sedilia, now reduced to one and a half complete stalls, the other portions having been cut away to introduce a monument to the memory of Andrew, lord Archer. Further eastward, is a piscina, under a trefoiled arch, with crocketed canopy and short finial. The chancel has, in some measure, been restored to its ancient state, by the erection of stalls for the choir, &c. The communion table is without ornament, and the font is a plain stone vase, placed in the nave, near to the entrance to the chancel.

The windows of the church in Dugdale's time contained the arms of Mowbray, Montfort, Tucket, Hastang, Crewenhale, Musard, Archer, and Waring; those of Beauchamp, earl of Warwick, and Clinton, earl of Huntingdon, gracing the parlour window of the vicarage house, having, no doubt, been removed from the church.

There were several monuments at Dugdale's visit: Those to the memory of Edward Archer, gentleman, 17th February, 1592, and two others mentioned by him, are totally gone; whilst those to the memory of the Fulwodes may be the dilapidated stones on the floor of the northern aisle. The other, named and engraven in his work, still remains entire. This is the brass plate, in a carved frame, on the north side of the chancel, representing a female at prayer before a faldstool, on which lies an open book. Below is an inscription to the memory of Margaret Archer, daughter of Simon Ralegh, of Farnborough, esquire, *obiit* 13th August, 1614. The chancel contains besides a large mural monument to the memory of Thomas Archer, esquire, and other members of the family. The monument referred to in the description of the sedilia is to the memory of Andrew, lord Archer, baron of Umberslade, the last male descendant of the family, *obiit* 25th April, 1778, aged 41. It bears the family arms, and has the draped figure of a female leaning on a pedestal, which bears the bust of the last lord. Another stone mural monument records the death of Thos. Spooner, *obiit* 1593, aged 93. In the nave and aisles are several tablets, and stones on the floor, to the memory of the families of Chambers, Hunt, and Willes. In the tower are six bells, all cast in the eighteenth century. A singular custom exists here of ringing one of the bells at the hours of nine, one, and eight o'clock, and which has been done time out of mind of the inhabitants.

In the church were formerly two chantries, one at the altar of the Blessed Virgin, the other at that of St. Catharine.

THE CHANTRY OF THE VIRGIN

Was founded by Robert Fulwode, the first vicar after the impropriation of the church to the Priory at Maxstoke: He granted, 19th Edward III, to Ranulph de Fulwode, and his heirs, his capital messuage at Tanworth, with the lands and tenements thereto belonging, situate in a place called Beaumont, and another messuage, also in Tanworth, to find a priest, chosen by twelve of the principal inhabitants of the town, to celebrate divine service daily in the church, at the altar of the Blessed Virgin, for all the living and dead of the parish, and for the benefactors to the said church and chantry. The priest was required to take oath, yearly, that he would faithfully perform such service, and likewise that he would daily say a *Placebo* and *Dirige*, with a special commendation of him, the said Robert, by name, and his heirs. This deed provided for a succession of trusts, in case of failure of heirs, and was witnessed by Sir Peter de Montfort, Sir Edmund de Trussell, Sir Roger de Aylesbury, Sir Thomas Blancfront, and others.

THE CHANTRY OF ST. CATHARINE,

It appears, was founded 14th Richard II, by one Thomas Collins, of Tanworth, who conveyed certain lands in trust, to find two priests to celebrate divine service here for ever. The disposal being made without license from the king, became forfeited, when he gave the property to John Swet, who obtained a patent from Henry IV, whereby they were assigned to Rose Montfort, (then a woman of consequence in the parish,) that she and her heirs should provide and maintain two chantry priests to celebrate divine service daily in the church of Tanworth, as well as for the good estate of king Henry during his life, and afterwards for his soul, as also for the souls of his mother and queen deceased; and for the soul of the said Rose Montfort, and the souls of her ancestors and heirs, and for other benefactors of the said chantry. This Rose gave, by deed, the lands unto John Blakenhale and Richard Boys, serving at the altar, to hold to them, and their successors, priests of this chantry, to celebrate divine service there for ever.

In 26th Henry VIII, when an account of these chantries was taken, it was certified that the parish was twenty miles in circumference, so that in plague and other sickness, the priests of these chantries assisted the vicar in the administration of the sacraments, &c.

The following is the return made of the chantries at the Dissolution :

CHANTRIES FOUNDED IN THE PAROCHIAL CHURCH OF TONWORTH.

"Sir Thomas Ilshawe and Fulco Flecher, custodians of the said Chantries.

	£.	s.	d.
And they are valued in lands and tenements there, beyond 32*s.* 8*d.*, allowed to the said custodians for rent repaid to the chief lords of the fief there, annually	12	0	8
The tenth part of this sum - - - - -	0	24	1"*

The lands of both Chantries were given, 7th Edward VI, to the Throckmortons and their heirs. In the year 1553 there was a pension of 6*l.* to Fulk Fletcher and the same to Thomas Yelsham, incumbents of these two Chantries. The precise locality of the Chantries, owing to the improvements of which mention has been made as the act of the vestry in 1790, can only be conjectured. Most likely, they were situated as has been suggested at p. 115.

The vicarage house is a modern building some distance from the church. The Rev. Alexander Hunter is the present vicar.

The churchyard, from its elevation, commands a most extensive view towards the south and east. Over the deep valley, "clustered in leafiness," running down to Henley and Wootton, are spread out the woods of Mays Hill, Austey, &c., whilst

"Far away the woodlands stretch"

to the extremity of Edgehills. From this point, and at no great distance, is seen the Leasowes farm, where a few years ago, under the church-yard hill, were dug up the remains of human bones and horses, a cannon ball, buttons, portions of a sword, &c., indicative of a conflict here, during some of the civil broils once common in "merrie England."

* *Valor Ecclesiasticus*, Henry VIII.

Close by is a farm still called "The Butts," no doubt designating the spot, common in every parish, when the bow was the principal weapon of warfare, where the youth of this village competed for prizes, on saints' and feast days.[3]

About twenty years ago a MAYPOLE, with vane and weathercock, stood in the open space west of the church, and many still recollect its gay garlands on Maydays long past.

The charities at this place are numerous, and the education of the poor well attended to in the large school connected with the church.

The village of Tanworth is larger than most others in this part of our tour, and is, from its situation, highly salubrious. The main street shows the singular nature of the division of parishes; for whilst the church and houses on the north side are in Tanworth, the whole line of street on the south, consisting of seventeen houses, is in Aspley, a hamlet of Wootton Wawen. The parish itself extends, from south to north, a distance of eight miles, some portion of it being land of superior quality, but a considerable tract on the line referred to at p. 28, is of a thin soil, on a gravelly substratum, and oftentimes taxes alike the pocket and patience of the farmer. The country, with this exception, is well wooded, and there are many spots of the shaded lanes in the parish that the traveller may well stay to contemplate.

---

3. In the time of Henry VIII, archery practice had fallen so much into disuse that an Act was passed, 1511, providing, among other matters, "that the statute of Winchester, for archers, be put in due execution; and over that, that every man, being the king's subject, not lame, decrepit, or maimed, being within the age of sixty years, except spiritual men, justices, and barons of the exchequer, &c., do use and exercise shooting in long bows, and also do have a bow and arrows ready continually in his house, to use himself in shooting." He was also to provide bows, &c., for every man child in his house, from seven years upwards.

Before leaving Tanworth village, it may be necessary to remark that in this extensive parish were formerly a great number of old manors, such as Umberslade, Sidenhall, Clayhall, Codbarrow, Beetlesworth, Lodbroke, and Crewenhale. All these possess some feature or other of historical interest; but as many of them now designate solitary farm houses, or small groups of cottages, we shall conduct the traveller to the most attractive sites, and notice the others in notes, in their respective localities.

Passing from Tanworth northward, at a short distance to the left is

LODBROKE PARK,

One of the ancient manors just spoken of. In the 8th year of the reign of Henry IV, Lodbroke Park[4] was found, by inquisition, to have been in the possession of Thomas Beauchamp, earl of Warwick, in the time of Richard II, and that he held it of the king as of the honour of Peverell. With this family it remained till the 3rd of Henry VII, when it came into the possession of the crown: In the 36th of Henry VIII, it was sold by the crown to Sir George Throckmorton, along with the manor of Tanworth, the whole of which was subsequently acquired by the Archers, through purchase, this portion of the Archer property ultimately passing, by marriage with a coheiress, to earl Amherst, the present owner, as has been already recorded.

The old house standing here was pulled down six years ago, and rebuilt. Round the garden was formerly a moat, now filled up.

---

4. John de Lodbroke, 19th Edward III, resided here, and had remainder of the endowment of the Chantry founded in Tanworth church by Robert Fulwode, assigned to him, in trust for its benefit. Richard III granted to William Catesby, of Lapworth, five hundred trees in Lodbroke Park, for rails to his new park there.

Northward of Lodbroke is a considerable district of the parish of Tanworth, forming the chapelry of

SALTER STREET.

It includes Earlswood, Warings Green, Illshaw Heath, and Monkspath Street, besides many scattered farm houses, and the old manor places of Cheswicke, Beetlesworth, and Sidenhall. Of these old manors, however, there is now nothing to attract the attention of the tourist.

CHESWICKE.

Dugdale considers this to have been a Roman work, *Wyke* meaning, in old English, a castle or fortification, but it is more probable the name was derived from a Saxon word, signifying to dwell. It was owned, in early times, by the ancestors of John de Broughton, who, 29th Edward I, had a grant of free-warren here from that monarch. In 42nd Edward III, Sir Thomas Broughton, knight, sold it to John Waring and Richard Gower, the heirs of the latter again disposing of it, in the seventeenth century, to one William Bache. In 1730 it had become the property of a Mr. Hall, and is now owned by Mr. John Cook.

BEETLESWORTH.

This was partly granted by William, earl of Warwick, *temp.* Henry II, to Roger de Ulehale, and passed to John le Archer. The manor, if such there were, was, in Henry III's time, granted by Ralph de Wilington (Wilmton) to Roger Durvassal, who obtained a license of pope Alexander IV to build a chapel here for the celebration of divine service, as by reason of its remoteness from the parish church, and the badness of the ways, his residence here was unprovided for:

Nicholas Longespe, then rector of Tanworth, assenting, reserved for himself and his successors a payment to the mother church of a wax candle of half a pound weight, on the feast of St. Mary Magdalene yearly. It afterwards passed to the Montforts and the Catesbys of Lapworth, and was sold, 36th Henry VI, by Robert Catesby, esq., to Thomas Green, and remained with his family for some generations. In 1730 it was in possession of the Rev. — Bonner, and is now the property of Mr. J. Heynes.

SIDENHALL.

This place gave name to the family of Sidenhall. It passed, 4th Edward III, by a daughter and coheiress of the house, to the Fulwodes, of Clay Hall, by one of which family it was sold to the Hugfords, of Henwood, with whom it continued till bought by Nathaniel Cookes, of Ingon. It was afterwards purchased by the marquis Cornwallis, and is at present the property of P. W. Martin, esq., his nephew. It is now a common farm house, near to which part of the old moat remains.

These, as before stated, are comprised in the district of the parish called *Salter Street*, the principal object of interest now being

THE CHAPEL,

Which is dedicated to St. Patrick, and was erected in 1839. It originally was a simple brick building consisting of a nave and chancel, and would accommodate about one hundred persons. In 1860 a composite tower of brick and stone was erected at the west end by Thomas Burman, esq., in memory of his father, the late Thomas Burman, esq., of Warings Green. The chapel is represented in the initial letter prefixed to this chapter.

The tower story consists of a vaulted and groined chamber about twelve feet square, forming a western porch to the church. It is entered by double doors, and has a doorway having a central column and highly enriched tracery head, in the principal division of which is a sculptured medallion of the ascension of our Blessed Lord; beyond this is an outer arch uniting the two westernmost buttresses, elaborately carved and having in the tympanun above a bust of St. Patrick holding the trefoil and in the act of benediction. This outer porch is panelled at the side to receive mortuary inscriptions of the Burman family, and is decorated with shafts of green Horton and red Mansfield stone.

The second stage forms the ringing loft, and is approached by a staircase external to the tower of peculiar character. The upper stage has a large three-light louvre window with a tracent head on each face. Over each of these is a gable the whole width of the tower, having at its eaves a figure of an angel holding the emblems of the passion, and at its apex a large wrought iron finial. The *four* ridges uniting these gables are coped with a wrought iron cresting, and a lofty and ornamented cross rises from their intersection. The cost was about 1200*l.*, exclusive of the ring of bells, which have been added by subscription of the landowners and inhabitants. The architect was Mr. G. T. Robinson, and the building executed by Mr. Ballard, the principal carving by Mr. Wood.

The living is a perpetual curacy, of the value of 150*l.* per annum, and is in the patronage of the Vicar of Tanworth. The Rev. T. H. Mynors is the present Incumbent.

Should the tourist have visited Salter Street, he will return southward, but if not, then leaving Lodbroke, he will proceed eastward, by Birchey Cross,[5] for some distance, turning to the right on a road which leads direct to

UMBERSLADE,

An ancient manor house, which, *temp.* Henry II, was partly given by Henry de Vilers, (sewer to William, earl of Warwick,) to Robert Archer and Seliit his wife, and their heirs. In this grant it is called *Terra de Ombreslade*, and recites that other part of the manor was given, by Roger de Ulehale, to the said Seliit only. William their son had, early in king John's reign, a grant of much land in Tanworth, by Waleran, earl of Warwick, which was set out by special boundaries. Pope Gregory IX also issued a special bull for a peculiar chapel[6] at this place, 19th Henry III. Of the members of this family, John, son of the before-named William, obtained a special charter from earl Waleran, for license to hawk and hunt in all parts of Tanworth, and to enjoy all other liberties belonging to the said earl within Monkspath[7] and Umberslade, on payment of twelve arrow heads and a couple of

---

5. BIRCHEY CROSS.—So called from a very large birch tree, once occupying the junction of the roads, upon which was a cross. Several other crosses anciently stood in the parish, viz., near to Umberslade, at Brown's Green, Jacob's Well, and Knowlesbury Cross, at Tanworth.

6. Dugdale says that in the windows of this chapel were the arms of Beauchamp, earl of Warwick, Clinton, earl of Huntingdon, and of the Archers, all of which were in good preservation, although of so early a date as the time of Edward III.

7. MONKSPATH STREET.—This was formerly a large tract of ground without any habitation, but a public house and a few farm residences now mark the locality. The manor was given, *temp.* Henry II, by William, earl of Warwick, to Roger de Ulehale; his great grandson, William de Ulehale, in the time of Henry III, sold it for forty marks to John le Archer, in whose family it continued till the division of the estates. Monkspath is supposed to have derived the name from the frequent journeying of the monks of Stoneleigh to Bordesley Abbey. There was another manor called Little Monkspath, held of the manor of Tanworth by the fourth part of a knight's fee, and belonging, in early times, to the Montforts of Coleshill.

capons, at Whitsuntide yearly. One of his sons was Lord Prior of the Hospital of St. John of Jerusalem, 14th Edward II. Thomas le Archer, grandson of William, 49th Edward III, granted license to Richard de Montfort and others, to amortize certain lands here, for founding a chantry in Lapworth Church, which will be more particularly referred to in a future page. This Thomas obtained from pope Boniface IX a special indulgence to appoint a special confessor, who might pronounce plenary remission to himself and wife of all their sins, which, with contrite hearts, they should make confession of at the time of their deaths. Richard, his son and heir, who died 11th Edward IV, by his will ordered his body to be buried in the church at Tanworth, giving to the fabric four marks, and directing that twelve pounds of wax be burnt round his hearse on the day of his funeral; and that there should be eight new torches made and lighted during the mass, to be held by eight poor men, each in a russet gown, who were to be supplied with meat and drink for that day. To this Richard succeeded three Johns, and then another Richard, Esquire of the Body to Henry VIII. His great grandchild, Sir Simon Archer, knight, born September 21st, 1581, was a gentleman well versed in the antiquities of his native county. With his descendants this and several neighbouring manors continued, in a direct line, up to the time of Thomas Archer, created, 21st George II, lord Archer, baron of Umberslade. His son, Andrew, succeeded to the family estates and honours, but died April 25th, 1778, aged 41, and lies buried, with his ancestors, in the chancel of the church at Tanworth, where his monument records that "He was the last male descendant of an ancient and honourable family, that came over with William the Conqueror, and settled in the county of Warwick, in the reign of Henry II, from whom his ancestors obtained grants of land in this county." He married Sarah, the daughter of James West, esq., of Alscot, by whom he left four daughters. In the division of his property, this part came, by marriage, to the earl of Plymouth, who sold it to Bolton King, esq., who has recently disposed of it to G. F. Muntz, esq., eldest son of the late member for Birmingham.

THE HALL

Is situated in a park of about three hundred acres, both of which have been much improved by the present proprietor. Near one hundred years ago, Jago sang of the scenery of this and neighbouring places,

> "Beneath the waving umbrage, Flora spreads
> Her spotted couch, primrose and hyacinth
> Profuse, with every simpler bud that blows
> On hill or dale.
> * * * * Such Umberslade,
> In the sweet contest joined, with livelier charms
> Intent t' illumine Arden's leafy gloom."

The old manor house was moated round, and had a gate-house. The moat was filled up in the reign of James I. The present mansion was erected by lord Archer. It is a large and handsome stone building, in the Palladian style of architecture, nearly square in form, having a western and eastern front. The eastern front had a portico, the pillars of which were of the Doric order, and was surmounted by a bust of the emperor, Titus Vespasian. The portico on the west had the arms of the Archers, with military trophies. The present proprietor has considerably improved the appearance of the west front, of which the engraving gives a good representation, by removing the portico, and erecting a colonnade extending from both wings.

On the borders of the park, southward is the site of the old manor of

CODBARROW,

Referred to at page 120. On this spot stood, in very early times, a mansion of some extent for that period. The moat, which is still very perfect, indicates the size of the dwelling it once inclosed. It is now approached, from the keeper's lodge, by a foot-bridge, but the space it incloses, 132 feet by 120, is used as a garden. Not a vestige of the edifice of which it has been the site remains.

This ancient seat belonged to the de Montforts, of Lapworth, and was in the possession of Richard de Montfort and Rose his wife, 37th Edward III. It descended to William de Montfort, their son and heir, and, by partition, came to Helen, one of his daughters, married to Richard Merebroke, who, in default of issue, by William, his son, and Alice, his daughter, entailed it upon John Catesby and Margaret his wife, and their heirs, this Margaret being the other daughter of William de Montfort. In the deed of disposition, it is styled the *Manor of Codbarrow*. In 1st Richard III, it appears to have been held in fee, as it is stated that "John Bigge hath the manour of Codbarowe in the countie of Warr., of the yearly value of xvi*l.* viij*s.*, with the issues of the same during his lif."* The manor came to the above-named Alice, who had married John Norris, knight, of Yatenden, Berkshire. He, 26th Henry VIII, conveyed it, in trust, for the benefit of William Willington, esq., of Barcheston. He, again, bestowed it upon Anne, his daughter, wife of Francis Montfort, esq., and her heirs. Their grandson, Sir Edward Montfort, (9th James I,) sold it to Simon Archer, esq., and it has been attached to Umberslade from that time to the present.

Near to this place is another old manor, viz.,

CLAY HALL,

Anciently called *Fulwode*, which gave the surname[8] to a family who resided here. The Fulwodes descended from a younger son of the Offords, of Offord, near Wootton Wawen. In 19th Richard II, John Fulwode obtained a license from Tideman, bishop of Worcester, for a private oratory at this place, which was renewed by the next bishop, 4th Henry IV. Clay Hall continued with his successors till 35th Elizabeth, when Robert Fulwode sold it to Thomas Greswold, whose executors, nine years after, disposed of it to Thomas Spooner. William Spooner, his grandson con-

---

8. Dugdale gives inscriptions on two monuments, to the memory of members of this family, extant in Tanworth Church when he visited it. One commemorated Richard Fulwode, *obiit* 23rd February, 1502; the other, Robert Fulwode, *obiit* 20th October, 1531. The founder of the chantry of St. Mary in the same church, was, doubtless, another member.

* *Harl. MSS.*, 433, fol. 67.

veyed it to Andrew Archer, esq., and it passed in like manner with Umberslade to the present owner, G. F. Muntz, esq.

Returning through the park, on the other side of the house, and on the eastern side of the grounds, stands an *Obelisk*, erected by lord Archer in the year 1749. Its form will be seen in the engraving of the chapel at Nuthurst, on a knoll near to which it is erected. It is mentioned by lady Luxborough, where she says, "I am to dine at lord Archer's next Tuesday, when I shall see the Obelisk, and be a better judge how it appears from the saloon it is seen from."*

In this neighbourhood was once a large oak, on which a cross was engraved. The parishioners, in walking the boundaries between Tanworth and Nuthurst, used to say a gospel[9] here. The tree was considered, by many, to be as old as the Conquest.

The parish of Tanworth, with its numerous members, contained a population of 2005 in the year 1841, of 1925 in 1861. In the return, *temp.* Elizabeth, there were 104 families.

Crossing the lane into the next field, we arrive at Nuthurst Chapel, erected for the convenience of the scattered houses of this ancient hamlet.

NUTHURST

Is a member of Hampton-in-Arden, from which, however,

9. The Gospel Oak was a boundary tree, and so called from the custom of reading passages from the Gospel at the spot, when the parishioners walked the bounds and limits of the parish. Different ceremonies were performed at the various boundary marks, in order that the localities might be impressed on the minds of the young, as they were attested by the recollections of the old.

* *Letters to Shenstone*, 107.

it is distant about nine miles. Like that place, and its other members, it belonged to the de Mowbrays, from whom it came to the de Montforts, and from them, 46th Henry III, to one of the Hastangs, of Leamington Hastang: It is, when possessed by this family, that we have the first mention of it, in a challenge by Peter de Montfort of certain services from Robert de Hastang. It had become the property of William Trussell in the early part of Edward I's reign: He obtained, 5th of the same reign, license of free-warren here, together with a special license to make a park of his woods in this place. From him it descended to the Trussells,[10] of Billesley, in this county, with whom it continued till sold, in the middle of the seventeenth century, to William Jesson, of Coventry. The property of the Trussells here, according to inquisition, 8th Henry VIII, consisted of one messuage, 200 acres of land, 300 of pasture, ten of meadow, thirty of wood, and 4*s.* rent charge. Nuthurst afterwards came to the Archer family, who sold it, with Umberslade, to Bolton King, esq., who has recently disposed of it to G. F. Muntz, esq.

THE CHAPEL.

Being a member of Hampton-in-Arden, there has been a chapel here from a very early date, which in consequence of its great distance from the mother church, had the privilege of burial accorded to it. Like Hampton, it was, 2nd Henry III, appropriated to the Canons of Kenilworth, by William de Cornhull, bishop of Worcester, who conferred

10. The Trussells were connected with the county from the time of Henry I, and held considerable possessions under the earls of Warwick. William, son of Sir Edmund Trussell, who first possessed Nuthurst, *temp.* Edward II, was chosen by the Commons to pronounce the sentence of deposition against that monarch. His lands were seized upon, as a rebel, by Edward III, but were afterwards restored.

upon these monks the tithes arising in the hamlet. In 18th Edward II, John de Olnefel, vicar of Hampton, granted a lease, for eight years, to Thomas Ketel, priest of the chapel at Nuthurst, of all the glebes, tithes, &c., reserving to himself all living mortuaries of the inhabitants deceased, and the burial of the bodies of all married persons and widows, with funeral oblations; and also pasture and forage yearly for four young beasts, steers, or heifers, and

the keeping of three or four hogs in harvest time, and for a month after Michaelmas. The grant stipulated that the said Thomas Ketel and his clerk should perform service daily, in the said chapel, honestly and decently, so that the vicar incur no blame; and keep the housing and chapel, with books, vestments, and other ornaments, in as good state as, or better than, he found them; but to cut down no trees, and to pay to the vicar, or his deputy, 20*s.* annually. Edward Fulwode, esq., of Clay Hall, further endowed the chapel here, by a grant, 9th Elizabeth. The old chapel in time went to decay, and was in ruins in 1730. A new building, the chapel now standing, was erected several years after. It is a small, unpretending edifice of brick, plastered over, consisting of a nave with four pointed arched windows on each side, a bell turret at the west end, under which is a small niche and a pointed arched doorway, which forms the only entrance. There is also a small chancel. The general appearance will be best understood by the sketch. The interior presents nothing remarkable beyond a stained glass window at the east end. It is seated partly with pews, and partly with open benches. The font is plain, standing between the pulpit and reading desk at the east end of the nave.

The living is a curacy, provided for by the vicar of Hampton-in-Arden. The Rev. J. Townshend is the present officiating minister.

The hamlet consists of three or four scattered farm houses, and some cottages, and contained a population of 132 in the year 1841, and 117 in 1861.

Leaving Nuthurst, we proceed down the lane leading to the turnpike road from Birmingham to Stratford-on-Avon, and by which road we again return to Henley-in-Arden.

Fourth Day.

IT will be necessary to-day to take the tourist over a portion of the Birmingham turnpike road already traversed, in order to visit Lapworth, Harborough Banks, Kingswood, Bushwood, Camp Hill, Buckley Green, and Beaudesert. From this road, at a distance of three miles from Henley, a lane to the right, overhung with leafy foliage and lofty trees, leads direct to the pleasantly situated village of

LAPWORTH,

The records of which are of an earlier date than those of any other parish in the district. Kenulph, king of Mercia, conveyed it, in the time of Denebert, the ninth bishop, to the see of Worcester, of which it formed a part till the time of Canute, when Brightegus, the then bishop, gave it to his servant Hearlewinus, in reward for his services in attending him into Saxony, whither he had been sent as escort to *Gunnilda,* the king's daughter, wedded to Cono, the emperor. The parish was then reckoned as half a hide, out of which twelvepence was reserved yearly, in acknowledgment of the right of the church. In the Conqueror's time, it was given to Hugh de Grentemaisnill, who returned it as containing half a hide, one ploughland arable and three villeins, the woods being two miles in length and one in breadth, the whole being valued at 20*s*. Before this, they had been the freehold of one Baldwin, who became tenant of the new proprietor. From the Grentemaisnills, it passed, by marriage, to the earls of Leicester, of whom it was held, in Henry III's time, by the ancestor of Henry Pipard, who fixed here his residence, and is styled in several deeds, *Capitalis Dominus Feodi de Lapworth.* He was a man of considerable rank in the county, holding several high offices during the reign of Henry III. On his death, the manor, &c., became the portion of one of his daughters, Dionysia, married to Sir Robert de Harecurt, whose son William, early in the reign of Edward I, granted to Henry de Braundeston, and his heirs, a certain part of his court and capital mansion here, viz., that lying to the west from the great gate of the wall, (which then extended to an oak standing before the door of the old grange,) together with the advowson of the church, and the homage and service of several freeholders. He also granted, or confirmed, to his nephew, Sir William de Bishopden, son and heir of the other coheiress, certain lands here, reserving for himself and heirs the payment of one barbed arrow yearly. The manor remained with the heirs of Henry de Braundeston till the reign of Edward III, prior to which, however, the family had acquired other possessions, here, by grants from Hugh de Lodbroke, one of which manors he granted or sold to Sir John Bishopden, knight, supposed to be that of Bushwood.[1] To the above Henry de Braundeston succeeded his son

1. These deeds with their subscribing witnesses are interesting, and correct translations of them will be found in the Appendix.

Hugh, who was frequently styled *Dominus de Lapworth*, having, 11th Edward III, obtained a lease thereof for forty years from Sir John de Bishopden. Dying without male heirs, in the 36th of the same reign, part of Lapworth came, by one of the coheiresses, to Richard de Montfort, and part to Philip de Ailesbury, who had married the other coheiress, a third daughter being a nun at Wroxhall. The whole of the estates afterwards came, by marriage, or grants, from the de Montforts and Bishopdens, to the Catesbys,* with whom they continued (with a slight interruption by the execution and attainder of William Catesby, esq., on the accession of Henry VII) till the time of James I, when Robert Catesby sold the manor to Sir Edward Greville, knight, from whom it was purchased by Sir Thomas Holte, of Aston, near Birmingham. From the Holtes, Lapworth descended to a daughter, married to Abraham Bracebridge, esq., of Atherstone, whose children, by Act of Parliament, sold the manors of Lapworth and Bushwood, with houses, farms, &c., in those places, containing 1014*a.* 1*r.* 28*p.*, and chief rents of Lapworth, 3*l.* 7*s.* 9*d.*, to Sir Charles Cockerell, baronet. These have since passed by purchase to W. W. Cooper, George Miller, and R. Dolphin, esquires.

THE CHURCH,

Dedicated to St. Matthew,[2] is situated, as the engraving shows, on a gentle eminence, and from the neighbouring hill, southward,

"At distance seen
Above its clustering group of trees,"

has the aspect of a building of superior character to any we

2. Dr. Thomas, in his edition of Dugdale, states it to be dedicated to "the blessed Virgin Mary," and cites his authority; but, as the wake or feast of dedication is still held on the eve of St. Matthew's day, we adhere to the earlier dicta of Dugdale.

* See Appendix.

have yet visited, an appearance which is fully borne out on closer inspection. It was given, *temp.* Henry III, by William de Harecurt, to John, son of Peter de Glen, who granted it to the Warden and Scholars of Merton College, Oxford, and, with a brief interval, it has remained in their patronage to the present day. It was valued, 19th Edward I, at seventeen marks and a half; in 26th Henry VIII, at

9*l.* 9*s.* 7*d.*; and is now returned at 428*l.* The inventory of Church Goods enumerates as here in 6th Edward VI,

j chalice & iiij belles, a saunce bell.
iij vestments, one vellet, ij dornix.
ij copes, one vellet, one silke.
iij albes.
ij altarclothes.
ij candlestickes, laten.
one pix, laten.
ij cruett.
a crosse, coper.
one sensor, laten.

Of the church originally given to Merton College, nothing remains but parts of the walls worked into the present edifice. In these remains of the ancient church are traces of windows that have been filled in. The more modern edifice consists of a tower with lofty spire, north and south aisles, nave, having what formerly constituted an open porch, with a chapel over it, at the west end, a chancel, and a chantry chapel on the north side of the latter. The tower was once independent of the body of the church, but it is now connected by a lobby or passage, leading through a pointed arch in the north aisle. It stands on the north side, exactly in a line with the eastern ends of the aisles and nave, and is lighted by pointed arched windows on each face of the ground story and the belfry. An embattled parapet surmounts the tower, which is approached by a projecting staircase at the north-west angle, covered with a pinnacle or coved roof. From the tower rises a graceful spire, which has, from its elevated situation, been, on two occasions, damaged by lightning. From the tower a very extensive landscape is visible on all sides, which will well repay the trouble of mounting to its summit. The two aisles are embattled, having crocketed pinnacles; the southern one contains three pointed windows of two lights, with crocketed mouldings and finials on the south, and a similar window at the east and west ends. The doorway is a pointed arch, and had formerly a half-timbered porch, removed during the incumbency of the Rev. H. A. Pye. The northern aisle has two similar windows and doorway, with a pointed three-light window at the west end. The nave has, on each side, four flat-headed clerestory windows of three lights, and a large western window, of five lights, rising over the western porch and chapel. It is embattled on the sides and on each gable, having five pinnacles rising from light buttresses at regular intervals on the former, and a cross on the apex of the latter. The gargoyles, which are large, are in the usual grotesque style. The western porch had two doorways leading from north to south, but one of these is now walled up. The chapel over is lighted by an obtuse arched window. It has a plain parapet, with pinnacles at the sides and cross in centre of the gable.

The chancel is the most ancient part of the building, and has been recently restored by the rector, from funds furnished by himself, Merton College, and other contributors. In the restoration nearly the whole of the south side has been rebuilt, the two obtuse arched windows and priest's doorway reinstated, the eastern pointed arched window, of five lights, reopened,[3] and a single-light window on the north side repaired. The other part of the north side of the chancel is occupied by the chantry chapel, which has two windows, one flat-headed, of three lights, eastward, and one pointed, of two lights, to the north.

The interior of the church is in true keeping with ecclesiastical architecture. The nave is separated from each of the aisles by four pointed arches, springing from pillars of different shapes and proportions, those on the north side being more massive than those on the south. The west window contains some ancient coloured glass, viz., four coats of arms taken from the west window of the south aisle,[4] and other portions from the chancel window, in 1807. At Dugdale's visit, the arms of de Montfort, Catesby,

---

3. The *renovations* of 1807 consisted of blocking up the east window, fitting the church with high pews, and breaking up the carved rood screen, bearing the arms of Catesby, Brome, and Arden, to form the altar rails and panelling of the walls of the chancel.

4. This was formerly called the Brome Hall window, and the arms removed were those of Catesby, Montfort of Beaudesert, Montfort of Lapworth, and Catesby impaling Montfort, quartered with Braundeston.

Braundeston, Arden, Arundel, Scrope, and others, were to be found in the windows. The roof of the nave is in ceiled panels, with cross beams and curved braces. The roofs of the aisles are plastered over, the southern one having a plain arched piscina, with a credence table at the east end. The western porch has no communication with the church. A staircase leads to the chapel above, founded A.D., 1374, by Richard de Montfort and others. On the south side of it is a piscina or water stoup. This building is now used as a vestry. The chancel, which is divided from the nave by a pointed arch, is now restored to something of its ancient form and style, under the superintendence of Mr. Street. The east window, blocked up in 1807, again throws its light over the interior, from which has been removed the wainscoting and wood-work, made from the rood screen at that time. The two south windows are filled with stained glass,5 shedding their rays on the ancient chapel opposite to them. Carved reading desks and stalls for the choir, a stone pulpit, and an oak lectern have been added, and the nave and chancel separated by pillars of Irish stone, resembling malachite, supporting a plain baluster of Bath stone. Over the communion table is placed an alabaster reredos, representing the Last Supper, executed by Mr. Earp, of Lambeth, the blank portion of the wall on each side being filled with encaustic tiles, as is the whole of the floor of the chancel.

The north chapel, separated from the chancel by a circular arch, is approached from the north aisle by a pointed arched

5. These windows were executed by Messrs. Clayton and Bell. One, a memorial to Alfred Lapworth, esq., presented by his family, represents the Nativity in the centre light, and the Adoration of the Magi and of the Shepherds in the two side lights. The other, the gift of John Fetherstone, junior, esq., the Baptism of Our Lord.

doorway. Dr. Thomas considers this to have been the chapel of Our Lady, but it is more probable that the altars of St. Catherine and St. James were here situated. On the eastern wall are two brackets, of different patterns, and near to each other. On these images once stood, and Dr. Thomas says, "in the loft, over the Lady's chapel, there is a hole in the wall just over the niche, where the image of Our Lady stood, wherein a man might unobserved, by strings, play tricks with the image; it seems to have been made for that purpose, for there is no other reason to be given for it."[6]

The church, which is pewed, has a gallery at the west end of the nave. It is in contemplation, however, to restore the interior so as to correspond with the chancel. The font is octagonal on a shaft of the like form, having a sculptured head at each angle. The tower contains five bells. The monuments are all of comparatively modern date, to the memory of a few of the rectors, and members of the Ingram, Camden, Bradbury, and other parishioners' families.

From the absence of any notice, it would appear that the church was devoid of monuments when Dugdale visited it; he cites only one inscription as being in the east window of the south aisle, viz.,

Orate pro bono statu Margarete Catesby
et Wil Catesby armigeri pro corpore regis.

THE CHANTRIES.

The Chantry dedicated to the Virgin Mary and to St. Thomas the martyr, was the western one described at page 138. It was founded, 47th Edward III, by Richard de Montfort, Roger de Ulbarwe, Roger Attye Greene, of Lapworth, and Richard Dolfyn, a priest, for the maintenance

6. These holes have lately been carefully searched for, but without any discovery of them being made.

of a priest to sing mass every day to the honour of the Blessed Virgin, St. Thomas the martyr, and All Saints, for the repose of the souls of the founders, and a long list of the neighbouring gentry, priests, &c., and for the souls of all the faithful deceased. The chantry was endowed with two messuages, two carucates of land, twelve acres of meadow, and sixteen shillings rent, all in the parish of Tanworth, which were, with the consent of the superior lords of that manor, settled, 49th of the same reign, upon John Jori, the first priest of this chantry, and his successors.7 The following is the return, *temp.* Henry VIII:

CHANTRY FOUNDED IN THE PAROCHIAL CHURCH OF LAPWORTH.

"Sir John Hynwood, custodian of the Chantry founded in the said Church.

	£.	s.	d.
And it is worth in lands and tenements beyond the demesne of Lapworth, annually	0	100	0
The tenth part of this sum - - - -	0	10	0"*

In the west window of the nave, as before stated, are the arms of the principal founder of this chantry, with this inscription:

Ri'us Montford fili' Petri Rose ux' et
Mo-ford d'ni de Bello deserto filia . . : . .

The Catesbys were great patrons of the church, and obtained an indulgence, A.D. 1467, of forty days, for all who attended mass at the altar of St. Catherine, to be celebrated daily for the souls of William Catesby and others.

---

7. 47th Edward III. Warwickshire. Richard de Monte Forti and others give ten pounds for license to be granted to the said Richard and others that they may be able to give and assign certain lands and tenements with their appurtenances in Toneworth, to a certain chaplain, who is to celebrate divine service every day in the chapel of Lapworth, founded in honour of Mary the Virgin and of St. Thomas the martyr, and All Saints: to be held at "mortmain."---*Rot. Orig.*, 34.

* *Valor Ecclesiasticus*, Henry VIII.

This altar, as well as that of St. James, once existent here, probably stood in the northern chapel, immediately under the brackets described at page 139, whereon would be placed their effigies. As the chapel is still said to belong to the lords of the manor, it may not be too much to assume the Catesbys to have been the founders of this chantry. In common with other churches, there were here also, previous to the Reformation, endowments for the maintenance of the rood and paschal lights, and for candles and lamps before the several altars. Ivo Pipard, on St. Leonard's day, 6th Edward I, settled a messuage, lands, and two shillings per annum, for the maintenance of two wax candles and two lamps in the church at Lapworth; viz., one candle to burn before the altar of St. James, on Sundays and holy days, at mass, and on all Saturdays when the mass of the blessed Virgin Mary is celebrated. One to burn before the said altar on other occasions; one before the reliques; and one before the altar of the blessed Mary in the chancel.*

The church at Lapworth had also, 18th Henry VI, certain lands given to it by George Ashby, the elder, comprising one hundred and six acres of arable, meadow, pasture, wood, and moor land, with two messuages, situate in Lapworth and Nuthurst, for the use of the then vicar, Ralph Perot, and his successors, to provide a certain lamp to burn there, and to perform other works of charity. These lands came to the crown, 1st Edward VI, and were conveyed, 18th Elizabeth, to — Grey, as concealed lands.

In the churchyard was formerly a fine old stone cross,[8]

8. Before the Reformation it was customary to erect stone crosses in churchyards near to the south porch of the church, to serve as a triumphant symbol of the faith and hope of the departed, and to designate that the ground was consecrated.

* *Thomas's Dugdale.*

built on arches, containing a pulpit, which had room for twelve persons: At the beginning of the seventeenth century, a renovating churchwarden, one Askew, removed it, the parishioners in their complaint respecting its removal, stating that it was pulled down by his privity, and employed to groundsill his house, and to build his chimneys.

The rectory house stands in a field west of the church, as shown in the illustration. The present incumbent of the living is the Rev. Arundell St. John Mildmay.

The village, occupying a gentle eminence, is of pleasingly rural aspect, and contains several good private residences. There are also extensive wharves here, on various parts of the Birmingham and Stratford Canal, by means of which a considerable trade in coal, lime, and corn is carried on.

The population of the parish numbered 729 in 1841; and 675 in 1861. There were forty-five families in 1563.

The charity estates here are large, and besides the relief to the poor, afford ample funds for education, which is conducted in the commodious school house near to the church.

On the eastern side of the parish of Lapworth is a spring, which divides into two streams, taking different courses, one going towards Balsall, and thence by various rivers, reaches the sea by the Humber; the other flows southward to the sea by the Severn.

Pursuing the road from Lapworth to Warwick, about a mile from the former, we come to

HARBOROUGH BANKS,

Of which some account is given in the introductory chapter, and which will be of interest to, and deserving of a visit from, the antiquarian. In addition to what has been stated as to its Roman origin, it is said to have been in military occupation in the time of the wars between Charles I and the Parliament. The report is, in some measure, sustained by the finding of a cannon ball and the remnants of a pistol some years since. That the Parliamentarians were in some force in this neighbourhood, and levied large contributions from the gentry, is shown by a document preserved in the deeds of the Ferrers family, (concerning whom more particulars will be found in another chapter,) the owners of Baddesley, Kingswood, and Brome Halls, in the vicinity. The items consist of horses, oxen, milk kine, corn, harness, arms, free quarters, and a contribution of 6*l.* per month, levied on the then proprietor, his son, and tenants, the whole amounting to the sum of 468*l.*, but whether or no the claim was paid is not stated.

A short distance from Harborough Banks, on the other side of the canal and railway, is

KINGSWOOD HALL,

Or manor house, the remains of which serve now for a small farm house. It consists of a front with two half-timbered gables, and porch in the centre. Near to this place, on the opposite side of the road, is a cottage having the arms of Beauchamp inserted over the door, doubtless a stone brought from some building in the neighbourhood, and placed here. At Kingswood Hall the family of Ferrers occasionally resided. Here died, October 10th, 1633, Henry Ferrers, esq., whose knowledge of antiquities, Dugdale states, gave a fair lustre to that ancient and noble family, whereof he was no small ornament. A curious document, still preserved, gives the account of expenses incurred at his funeral, which we quote as an illustration of the times.

The charges of the buriall: of Henry Ferrers, esq., who deceased att Kingswood in the p'ish of Rowington, the xth day of October, 1633.

		£.	s.	d.
Imp.	To Roberte Banister, of Henley, for meate - -	2	5	11
	To Thomas Vescy, of Rowington, butcher, for half a beef - - - - - - - -	1	12	0
	To Richard Lane, of ye same towne, butcher, for more meate - - - - - - - -	1	10	0
	To the same Vescy, for half a calf more - -	0	6	8
	To Thomas Rawbon, of Baddesly, butcher, for more meate - - - - - - - -	0	5	6
	To Richard Burtonwood, of Baddesly, for xi dozen of breade - - - - - - - -	0	11	0
	To Goodall, ye baker, of Balsall, for iiii dozen more of breade - - - - - - -	0	4	0
	Ffor breade and drinke for the neyboured at his house at Kingswood, before they broughte him to buriall to Baddesly Church - - -	0	4	6
	One hogshed of beere - - - - - -	0	10	0
	To Willa. Knighte, of Baddesly, for butter and cheese - - - - - - - -	0	5	0
	Ffor x cheeses more at viii*d*. the peice - - -	0	6	8
	Ffor the coffine - - - - - - -	0	7	0
	To the Vicar of Rowington for a mortuarie where he died - - - - - - - -	0	8	4
	Ffor makinge the grave - - - - - -	0	2	0
	Ffor ii sheepe more - - - - - - -	0	17	0
	To Widdowe Holder, for attendinge him in his sickness and for monyes laied out for him - -	1	10	0

Returning to Harborough Banks, on the south side of it stands

BROME HALL,

Or *Brome's Place*, now also a farm house. That a considerable mansion, surrounded by a moat, stood here in ancient times, is indicated by the remains of fish ponds of three falls, and pleasure grounds around. This, in all likelihood, was the seat of the Bromes, previous to the acquisition of Baddesley, by John Brome, the lawyer, of Warwick, his ancestors residing here for several generations. The first mention of them, in public documents, is of one Robert Brome, 20th Richard II, who was also a lawyer, and steward to Thomas de Beauchamp, earl of Warwick.[9] John Brome, his son, was returned by the burgesses of Warwick, to the parliament, 8th Henry IV. He married Joan, daughter and heir of Thomas Rodie, of Baddesley Clinton, by which alliance the estates at that place fell to the family of Brome, who fixed their residence there. William Catesby, grandson of Sir Richard Catesby, of Lapworth, by his second wife Elizabeth, daughter of William Astall, of Nuneaton, is described in the Catesby pedigree as of Brome Hall.* The east window of the south aisle of Lapworth church was formerly called the Brome Hall window, and the rood screen had several coats of arms of the lords of that manor painted thereon. The house now standing has been modernized by additions, the oldest part being the two chimneys and the half timbered gables. The interior of one part of the house still retains considerable portions of the ancient oak panelling.

Near to Brome Hall is THE HIGH CHIMNEYS, another farm house, so called from its ancient and lofty chimneys. Here there is a curious tradition relating to one of its former owners. On the inmates arising one morning, they found a basket, containing a child, at the door, which was taken care of by the parish; and, from being found on St. John the Baptist's day, it was named *John Basket*. By industry, in after life, he became the purchaser of this very farm, and it continued in his family for many generations,

---

9. The pedigree, Herald's Visitation, gives six generations preceding John Brome, the first being William Brome, of Brome.

* *Herald's Visitation, Harl. MSS.*

till it was sold to the late Benjamin Parnell, esq., of Solihull. Very near to this house, stands

LAPWORTH HALL,

Commonly called Bushwood Hall, from its being in that hamlet. This is an old moated manor house, the moat being full of water, and, with the exception of the eastern section, pretty much in its original condition. This manor belonged, as is mentioned in the account of Lapworth, to Henry de Braundeston, who passed it to Sir John de Bishopden, knight, by deed, bearing date 14th Edward II, with a special mandate to all his freeholders and customary tenants here. Afterwards, all the various manors in Lapworth became united (this among others) under Sir William Bishopden, knight, whereof Lapworth Hall, juxta Henley, is specially mentioned, 13th Henry IV.

The accounts of Simon Berebrown, collector of rents at Bushwood, 3rd Edward IV,* show some of the curious customary payments to the lord in the fifteenth century. Among others there were received as arrears, 2½*d.*, four barbed arrows, two roots of ginger, and one red rose. The rents of the free tenants amounted to 20*l.* 5*s.* 3*d.*, one pound of pepper, four roots of ginger, four wood hens, and four barbed arrows, as also of one red rose for a tenement called Fowlers.[10]

---

10. Some of the repayments illustrate the prices of labour and of certain articles in remote districts of the country, at this period, viz., for one two-horse load of hay, 3*s.* 4*d.*; for eleven quarters of oats, 15*s.* 4*d.*; for coals, 1*s.* 4*d.*; to the miller for four days' work, 8*d.*; to Wadwode for carriage of malt and wheat from Stratford, (about ten miles,) 2*d.*; for ringing swine, 2*d.*; for mowing, spreading, collecting, and carriage of hay growing in two fields, and ricking the same for the lord's use, 4*s.* 6*d.*; and to John Barnthurst, keeper of the park, 2*d.* per day.

* *Papers in Record Office.*

The general account of money received stands thus:

	£.	s.	d.
Arrears - - - - - - - -	0	0	2⅛
Rents of free tenants - - - - - -	20	5	3
Rents of assize - - - - - - -	4	9	9
Pasturage of the park - - - - - -	1	12	10
Pasturage of swine in ditto - - - -	1	5	0
Sale of wood - - - - - - - -	7	1	2⅛
Perquisites of courts - - - - - -	2	17	11
Sale of hay - - - - - - - -	1	13	0
	39	5	2

From the above Sir William Bishopden, by the marriage of Philippa, one of his daughters and coheirs, the whole came to Sir William Catesby, knight. The Catesbys henceforth had their residence generally here. Sir William, son of the above, was of great repute in the county, and held high offices under Richard III. Following the fortunes of this monarch, he was taken prisoner, stoutly fighting at Bosworth-field, and three days after beheaded. The estates were forfeited; but, in 10th Henry VII, were restored to his son, George, in whose family this manor remained till the time of James I, when it was sold by Robert Catesby to Sir Edward Greville, of Milcote, and it has passed through the various hands of the proprietors stated in Lapworth. This Robert Catesby was attainted, 3rd James, for participation in the Gunpowder Plot, and is said to have been slain, with Percy, at Holbeach House, Staffordshire. A tradition exists that he fled, after the discovery of the plot, to his house here at Bushwood; but, as he had before this time disposed of the estates to Sir Edward Greville, the truth of this is very doubtful. A tradition also exists that the plot was laid by Catesby and others, at a mill about a mile from the house. This mill has long since been removed, and the bed of the pool cut through, the only vestige remaining being an old barn, still called the *Mill Barn*.

The Hall stood nearly in the south east corner of the parish. A small farm house, built in 1708, out of the materials of the old hall of the Bishopdens, now represents it. Of the old mansion nothing remains. In the garden, within the moat,[11] foundations have been dug up, showing, by their extent, that the original edifice was of considerable pretensions. That there was a Hall, or Manor Place, in Lapworth, at an early date, is shown at p. 134; but whether on this site it is impossible to determine. If so, it is certain that it was removed to make room for a more convenient residence for the new proprietor in the time of Edward II: for Sir John de Bishopden entered into an agreement with William Heose, mason, and John de Pesham, of Rowington, to erect for him a stone mansion, at Lapworth, engaging to pay them twenty-five marks by instalments. The style of this house, together with its various rooms, &c., has been adequately noticed in the introductory chapter of this work.

Bushwood, though so long connected with the lords of Lapworth, is an outlying hamlet to Old Stratford, from which it is distant about ten miles. Dugdale considers that this place being, long before the Conquest, part of the possessions of the bishops of Worcester, was continued to that see, and held by successive bishops as part of the demesne of Stratford, and being a mere wood was called *Bissopswude*, afterwards corrupted to *Bushwood*. Here is still a large wood, taking the name of the hamlet, which consists of two or three farm houses and cottages, the population of which in 1861 was 35.

The adjoining farm to Bushwood is called *Lapworth Park*. On this, in a field called "Island Meadow," is a very deep moat; but no vestige of any building within its

---

11. The area within the moat, which is 21½ feet wide, is 176 by 148 feet.

compass, which is 123 feet by 119. William Catesby had a grant, 2nd Richard III, bearing date Kenilworth Castle, 28th May, of one hundred oaks, to be taken within the king's old park at Tanworth, and Earlswood in Tanworth, with five hundred trees, for rails, in Lodbroke Park, in the lordship of Tanworth, for making his new park here at Lapworth. This farm, from its name, denotes the situation of the park, and on it there are still large pools existing.

Keeping the road from Bushwood, and passing the two farm houses called "The Park" and "The Lodge," we come again into the Birmingham road, and, turning to the left, soon reach *Liveridge Hill*, where commences the parish of Beaudesert. From its summit a most extensive view over the southern part of the country is obtained. Near to this, in a field to the left, are traces of the Roman earthworks, called *Camp Hill*, described at p. 13. Southward is a small knot of houses, called

BUCKLEY GREEN,

A member of Beaudesert, the history of which is little known. Geoffry de Pauncefot and John Duvassal gave certain lands here to the Priory of Wootton Wawen, Gilbert and William de Monkelee, with Roger, then vicar of Wootton, being witnesses to the grant. In 1326, Peter de Montfort granted to John de Lobbenham sixteen acres of land in the field called Bockeleyffelde.* In the 3rd Edward IV, lands in Bockley were held of the Catesbys.†

The extensive parish of

---

* *Cart. Cott.*, xxvii, 137.

† *Rentals of Margaret Catesby, in Record Office, marked "Warwick."*

BEAUDESERT

Runs eastward of the road through Henley-in-Arden,[12] a short street leading to the church being in the centre of that town.

Beaudesert or *Beldesert* was so called from its pleasant situation in the once woodland parts of Warwickshire. At the Norman Conquest it was certified to have contained, under the name of *Donnelie*, (its after designation as Beldesert being given to it by one of its Norman owners,) one hide, with two ploughlands arable, six villeins and two bordars with two ploughs, having a park or inclosure half a mile in length and breadth, and of the value of 30*s.*, (formerly 20*s.*,) held by earl Mellent, heretofore the property of Alwold, who held it freely. From this earl Mellent, the greater part of his possessions here passed to Henry de Newburgh, his brother, the first Norman earl of Warwick, who enfeoffed Thurstan de Montfort, his kinsman, with this and other manors and lands. On the hilly part of Beaudesert, (where it is more than probable that a stronghold or military station, in the time of the Britons and Saxons, had existed,) he erected a large and strong castle, which continued to be the residence of his successors for many generations. In king Stephen's time he obtained, from the empress Maud, a charter for a weekly market on Sundays at his castle of *Beldesert*. This charter was renewed to Peter de Montfort, in the 11th Henry III, the market to be held on the Monday, at Henley-in-Arden. Henry, eldest son of Thurstan de Montfort, succeeded him, and was a liberal benefactor to Wootton Priory, giving to it

---

12. The initial letter to this chapter represents the fall of water, called "The Fletchers," a short distance north of Henley.

his mill at Henley, with a messuage and some land. After him was another Thurstan de Montfort, who was a munificent donor to Pinley Abbey, as will be seen in the account of that monastic establishment. Dying, 18th John, his son Peter, being then a minor, was placed under the guardianship of William de Cantelupe. In this Peter, Dugdale states, the family of the de Montforts was in the meridian of its glory. For his rebellious conduct towards the king, (Henry III,) his lands were seized, but, feigning great contrition, they were restored, and himself again in favour with that monarch, whom he shortly after attended into Gascony. In 34th of this reign, he obtained a charter of free warren in all his lands here and in other places, and the following year was made Governor of Horestan Castle, Derbyshire. In succeeding years he received many other special favours and honours, but again revolting, was taken prisoner, and confined in Windsor Castle. Liberated in a few weeks, he, two days after, took up arms once more against the king, who was made prisoner by the rebel barons. Escaping from their custody, Henry assembled a powerful army, and in the battle that ensued at Evesham, Peter de Montfort was slain. His lands here were, with his other possessions, seized by the crown, and a commission directed to the Abbot of Bordesley and Prior of Studley, to take an account of the number of acres of land, meadow, wood, and pasture, and the value of each; as also of those that held in villeinage, with the rents and services of the freeholders. This Peter gave to the canons of Studley all his demesne lands, called the Vineyard, situate at Studley, for the health of his soul, the soul of Alice his wife; as also of his father, mother, ancestors, and friends, whose bodies lay buried in the Priory of Studley. Peter, his son, was taken prisoner at the battle of Evesham, but afterwards found favour with the king, and his inheritance was restored to him, 51st Henry III. With the de Montforts Beaudesert continued till the 21st of Edward III, when, by the marriage of Guy, the last direct descendant of the house of de Montfort, with a daughter of the earl of Warwick, the castle and manor, with other lordships, passed to the Beauchamps. This conveyance of the de Montfort property here, was the result of an arrangement, by which an estate in tail was created in favour of the Warwick family, in failure of issue by the before-mentioned alliance. Thomas de Beauchamp, 50th of Edward III, granted, in the property thus acquired, a life estate to his son, William, afterwards lord Bergavenny, at a yearly rent of one red rose, payable at the feast of St. John the Baptist. It then passed to Sir Baldwin Freville and Sir Thomas Boteler, as recited in our first day's journey, p. 33: The Boteler portion continued under the same proprietorship till the 4th of queen Elizabeth, when it was granted to Ambrose Dudley, earl of Warwick, who, dying without issue, it reverted to the crown, with which it remained till alderman Cawdwell, of London, purchased the site of the castle, with the park wherein it stood. The other portion of the manor continued with the heirs of Sir Baldwin Freville, and was sold, 36th Elizabeth, by Sir Edward Aston, who married a sister of the last knight, to Francis Smythe, esq., of Wootton Wawen, by whose family this and the other portion are still possessed.

THE CHURCH,

Dedicated to St. Nicholas,[13] is of a more interesting

13. A native of Pataria, in Lycia. He was appointed to the see of Myra by Constantine the Great, in which office he died, A.D. 343. He is the tutelar saint of the Dominican Friars, and called the patron of sailors, virgins, and school children.

character than several of the churches in this neighbourhood, on account of the examples (in excellent preservation) of Early Norman architecture which it affords. It is not named in the taxation of 19th Edward I. In the valuation, 14th Edward III, it is stated that "The church of Beldesert is not enlarged because of poverty, but is of the yearly value of 40*s*." In the 33rd Henry VIII, when this place and Henley were in the hands of the king, 20*s*. were paid annually to the vicar for the tithes of the herbage and pannage of the parks.* The valuation of the living, 26th Henry VIII, was 7*l*. 16*s*., which was the sum valued for its sale to John Digbye, 13th Mary, on the forfeiture of the advowson by John, duke of Northumberland.† The Church Goods, 6th Edward VI, were

j chalice and iij bells.
vj vestments dornix.
ij copes saye.
iij altarclothes.
ij towell.
ij candlestickes.
ij shett.‡

The living is now returned at 292*l*., and the Rev. J. A. P. Linskill the present Rector.

The building consists of a western tower, a nave, with porch on the south side, and a chancel. The latter is the most ancient part, having, at the east end, a semi-circular arched window, as shown opposite, with highly ornamented mouldings, both internally and externally, supported by plain round pillars with capitals. The walls of the nave are of great thickness, showing their Norman origin. In the north wall, a door, having a semi-circular arch, has been blocked

---

* *Accounts of Edmund Brereton, in Record Office.*

† *Harl. MSS.* 606, f. 48.

‡ *Papers, "Warwick," in Record Office.*

up, the only entrance being by the porch, on each side of which are carved supporters of the seats, of Norman design. The tower is embattled, and has a large obtuse arched window of three lights in two courses on the west front. On the south side is a canopied arch, or niche, with ornamental bracket at the foot, from which the image has disappeared. In the tower are three bells. The walls of the interior are so defaced by colour-wash, as to hide the beauties of the old sculpture thereon. The nave

is separated from the tower (of a much later date) by a pointed arch, and from the chancel by a Norman arch, with zigzag moulding, which has sunk considerably, owing either to the failing of the foundation of the pillars, or to the superincumbent weight of the upper wall: it has, however, been strengthened by a pointed arch of wood underneath. The east window is similar in ornament to the outside, and is filled with stained glass, representing the Ascension, &c. It was presented to the church "In memory of W.

W. Lea, esq." The chancel was intended to have been finished with a stone roof; but the design was not carried out. Six pillars, or shafts, and brackets, from which the girders were to spring, appear to have been completed, and remain in tolerable preservation. In the north wall is a carved opening, or locker, which, most probably, at one time, was of a more ornamental character than it now is. In ancient times it served to represent the Holy Sepulchre at the Easter celebrations.[14] On the south side of the chancel is a piscina, and near to the south porch a Norman stoup, the outer portion broken off. The nave and chancel are ceiled, a practice which appears to have been very general in this locality. A few monumental slabs are found on the chancel floor, in token of former rectors, and one commemorative of Humphry Fairfax, of Ullenhall, 1688. The nave contains several marble tablets in honour of the families of Welch, Lea, and Charles, of Henley-in-Arden.

The Parsonage House, on the north of the church, is interesting as exemplifying the style of such residences in olden time. It is a large half-timbered gabled structure, with small low rooms, and has not been inhabited by any rector for more than a century. The church-yard contains several modern monuments and grave-stones of a character

---

14. These celebrations were typical of the interment and resurrection of Our Lord, and took place from Good Friday to Easter Sunday. Lights were kept burning before the sepulchre, and there are many entries of expenses connected therewith in old church accounts, such as payments for wax for the lights, and to the sexton for watching them. See SOLIHULL. A general belief prevailed in the early days of the Christian church, that Our Lord's coming would be on Easter Eve, hence the sepulchres were watched through the night until three o'clock in the morning, when two of the oldest monks would enter and take out a beautiful image of the Resurrection, which was elevated before the adoring worshippers during the singing of the anthem "Christus resurgens."

superior to what are generally seen in country church-yards, and it would be a very attractive place of sepulture, if the same care were bestowed upon it that we have had occasion to commend in the instance of Aston Cantloe.

The population of Beaudesert in 1841 was 205, scattered about an extensive parish, to which we have referred. In the year 1861 the numbers were 172. The number of families A.D. 1563 was only fourteen.

Leaving the church-yard and small cluster of houses near, the traveller will ascend the adjoining hill, called "The Mount," whereon formerly stood

THE CASTLE.

This edifice, as before stated, was built by Thurstan de Montfort. Dugdale writes that this "Thurstan, finding it so capable of fortification, erected thereupon that strong castle, whereunto, by reason of its pleasant situation, the French name, Beldesert, was given, which continued the chief seat of his descendants for divers ages; but, at length, through coheirs coming to such families whose principal mansions were in other places, to prevent the advantage, which in times of civil dissension betwixt the houses of York and Lancaster, might have been taken on either side, to the prejudice of its owners, (as I conceive,) was either demolished, or suffered to go to ruin; so that now there is not only any one stone visibly left upon another, but the very trenches themselves are so filled up, as that the plough hath sundry times made furrows in every part of them, to the great advantage of the industrious husbandman, whose pains, through the rankness of the soil, hath been richly rewarded with many a plentiful crop." What it was in Dugdale's time it is at the present day, the site, from which the very foundations have been rased, affording rich pasturage for cattle and sheep. The castle was in the possession of Peter de Montfort during the civil wars in the time of Henry III. Taking part with the rebel barons under Simon de Montfort, earl of Leicester, (of a distinct family,) he was slain, as before stated, at the battle of Evesham, in the 49th of that reign. From this period the fortunes of the family declined; and it is more than probable that the castle dates its decay, and utter dilapidation, from this rebellion. Certain it is that the materials used in its construction have all been removed; nor can there be much doubt that many of the timbers of houses in Henley once formed part of the castle, the mortices in the framework showing that the beams, &c., have been heretofore part of some larger building.[15]

In the 50th year of Edward III, Thomas de Beauchamp, earl of Warwick, granted by charter to William de Beauchamp, his son, for his life, "the castle and manor of Beaudesert, together with all the lands, tenements, rents, reversions, advowsons of churches, knights' fees," &c., in Henley, Whitley, Hazleholt, Forwood, and Studley, he rendering one red rose annually for all services, and doing for him and his heirs, to the chief lords of those fiefs the services due and customary by law.[16]

The latest mention of the castle occurs A.D. 1411, in the accounts of John Chamberleyn, constable of the castle, in

15. In building the bridge over the brook between Henley and Beaudesert, in the year 1854, a large timber beam was dug out from the foundation, which there could be little doubt had been so employed.

16. *Cart. Cott*, xi, 70. The charter bears date at Warwick, July 19th, 1377, and the seal of Thomas de Beauchamp, in red wax, remains. The witnesses are Henry d'Arderne, William Bretonn, Nicholas Lyllynge, Thomas de Byrmycham, knights, John Morhalle, John Wyard, William Durvassal, and others. Dugdale calls William de Beauchamp brother of Thomas de Beauchamp.

which is a memorandum that a trifling sum was paid "*pro emend' portic' castri.*"*

The chief outlines of the various works may yet be traced.17 The approach, or road up the hill, commences near to the church, at the end of Beaudesert Street, and winds gently round the eastern side of the first elevation, to the entrance of what was most probably the outer court. The whole of the top of the hill was inclosed by massive walls, having a deep fosse running all round them. This portion, the northern part, is remarkably steep at the top, and has evidently been made so by art, its height being several feet above the level of the southern portion. Parts of the ground have sunk considerably of late years. This elevated part was connected with the southern portion by a narrow way, most probably a covered one. At the extreme northern end, beyond the fosse, there appears to have been a barbican or outwork; and two others, one on each side of the covered way, seem to have been so placed as to command the defence of the ditch, or fosse, from one end of the hill to the other. It is also probable that there was a considerable outwork on the extreme south, commanding the approach by the road and its whole course up to the gate: so that we may

17. The disposition of these works appears to have been pretty similar to that of the many castles erected in feudal times. The first work was generally the barbican, a watch tower, flanked with walls, erected beyond the moat. A drawbridge united the barbican with the ballium, or space within the outer wall, the end of the drawbridge next the ballium wall being guarded by a portcullis, or strong gate sliding between two towers, having iron spiked cross bars like a harrow, and which could be raised and let fall at pleasure. Sometimes there was a second or inner wall and ballium. In the centre was the keep or donjon, the last resort of the besieged, and therefore the strongest of the works. The walls were of great thickness, and frequently the only light obtainable was through loop holes, windows being dispensed with, for the sake of adding to the strength of the building.

* *Churches of Warwickshire*, 147.

infer, from the extent, disposition, and nature of the works appertaining to the defences of this castle, that it was next to impregnable before the invention of gunpowder.

> "Reared aloft,
> And inaccessible the massy towers,
> And narrow circuit of embattled walls,
> Raised on the mountain-precipice! such thine
> O Beaudesert! Old Montfort's lofty seat!
> Haunt of my youthful steps! where I was wont
> To range, chaunting my rude notes to the wind."

So sung Richard Jago, A.M., son of a former rector of the parish, in the words of whose muse we will take our leave of a hill, from which, in this undulating country, one of the most extensive views, south and west, is obtained.

Fifth Day.

WE shall occupy this day's journey with the towns and hamlets lying east of Henley-in-Arden, viz., Whitley, Preston Bagot, Kington, Langley, Songar, Claverdon, Lye Green, Pinley, High Cross, Holywell, Rowington, Finwood, Lonesome-ford, and Bushwood. Taking our way southward down the street, and turning to the left at the end of it, we pass over Blackford Bridge, (near to Blackford Mill,) so called, doubtless, from the nature of the Ford over the stream here, whose floods frequently now render the road dangerous or impassable. Ascending Blackford Hill we arrive at

WHITLEY,

A member of the parish of Wootton Wawen, comprised in two small farm houses and a few scattered cottages. Whitley was formerly more populous, as, in 24th Edward I, it is certified to have had seven freeholders, who yearly paid 30*s*. rent, the pleas and perquisites being 2*s*. per annum. William the Conqueror gave Whitley, like Wootton, to Robert de Stafford, and it then contained one hide of land, a mill, and a wood, valued at 40*s*. It was held by one *Drago*, whose posterity, it is supposed, adopted the name of Whitley, according to the custom of that time. This family were long possessors under the de Staffords and the de Montforts, who held under the honour of Stafford. In the time of Henry V it had come to John, youngest son of John Harewell of Wootton, who styled himself *de Whitley;* and, in 17th Henry VII, his son passed the manor into the hands of feoffees. In 17th Henry VIII, Roger Harewell, son to the said John, sold it absolutely, for 60*l*., to John Smythe, the owner of Wootton, whose descendant, Sir C. F. Smythe, is the present proprietor. The Catesbys also held lands in Whitley, *temp.* Henry VI, and in the accounts of the rentals, 25th of that reign, particulars are given of land in the field of Whetley, extending into the *Marshes*, and near the land of John Stoke.*

Near to Whitley are two other small clusters of houses, called Kite and Preston Greens, belonging to the parish of Preston. Descending the hill we enter the village of

PRESTON BAGOT.

A public-house, with the sign of the Crab Mill, at its entrance, reminds us of usages long since vanished, a mill, of that description, having once occupied the site.

In Domesday Book this place was called *Prestetone*, and was then of large extent, comprising, Dugdale considers, greater part of Henley and Beaudesert, where there was then no habitation, and which were subsequently taken out of it. Its extent, at this time, was certified to be

---

* *Papers, "Warwick," in Record Office.*

ten hides of land; five, with a mill rated at 16*s*., and woods one mile long and half a mile broad. These five hides, &c., which had been the freehold of one *Turbern*, were held by earl Mellent, on whom the king had bestowed the whole, and were estimated at 50*s*. The other five, held by *Britnod* before the Conquest, were now held of the earl by one Hugh, and were valued at 40*s*. There were ten bordars, four bondsmen, one villein, and one stranger. From this earl Mellent, the manor passed, like Beaudesert, to the earls of Warwick, in whose proprietorship it continued till the time of Henry II, when it was sold to Ingeram Bagot, the earls of Warwick remaining chief lords of the fee. From the Bagots, who gave the distinctive name to the place, it was conveyed to the Knights Hospitallers, *temp*. Henry III, in which reign Simon de Stok and others held one knight's fee of the heir of Simon Bagot, and he of the Hospital of Jerusalem; and in 7th and 8th Edward I, the Hospitallers are stated to have held Preston for thirty years past.* In 21st Edward III, Nicholas le Messager, of Kenilworth, and Agatha his wife, showed to the king, that they had recovered in the king's court at Westminster, againt William le Muleward, chaplain, and Walter de Kington, chaplain, seisinam of three acres of land, with the appurtenances, in Preston Bagot.†

At the dissolution of religious houses, 30th Henry VIII, the manor was resumed by the crown, by whom it was granted to Edward Aglionby, of Balsall, esq., and Henry Hugford, of Solihull, gentleman. From these it came to the Throckmortons, of Haseley, and remained with them several generations. It has since passed through various hands: John Mills, esq., is now the owner of the manor.

* *Rot. Hund.*, ii, p. 226. † *Rot. Orig.*, 65.

The manor house is a large timber-framed building,[1] probably of the time of James I, and stands by the side of the Warwick road, close to the bridge passing over the canal. Lord Leigh, Sir C. F. Smythe, and others, also possess considerable property in the parish.

THE CHURCH

Is dedicated to All Saints, and crowns the summit of a very steep hill, immediately above the rectory, which was rebuilt, by the present rector, a few years since. The church is of a very poor character, with respect to architecture and general effect. It consists simply of one continuous nave and chancel, with a small brick turret for two bells, placed on the roof at the west end. The entrance is

---

1. In the reigns of Elizabeth and James I, timber frame-work became common in country manor houses. Wherever stone and brick were scarce they increased and multiplied. The carved pendants, the barge boards of the roofs and gables, were executed in oak and chestnut, with much beauty of design and a singularly pleasing effect.

by a timber-framed porch, through a Norman semi-circular arched doorway, a similar one, now walled up, having been opposite, in the north wall. Other traces of Norman architecture are found in several of the windows. At the east end are two trefoil-arched single-light windows, filled with modern stained glass, one representing Christ Blessing Little Children, and the other emblematical of Acts of Charity, each with suitable texts, "In Memory of Anna Cecilia, wife of the Rev. Theodore John Cartwright," *obiit* May 4th, 1856. A new window, similar in design to the last-mentioned, was inserted at the west end when the late alterations were effected. The windows formerly contained the arms of Montfort, England, Lancaster, and Beauchamp.

The interior was, in 1854, refitted with open seats, and other alterations effected, by the rector, aided by a subscription from the landowners and parishioners. The floor of the chancel was, at the same time, repaved partly with Minton tiles, the space within the communion rails being wholly so. The division of the chancel from the nave is effected by the reading desk and choir seats on the north, and by the pulpit on the south. The font is octagonal, with quatrefoils on each face.

There was formerly a monumental inscription in the church to the memory of John Randoll, 1626, and there are others still existing recording the deaths of several members of the same family. Other mural tablets to the memory of several rectors of the parish, and branches of their families, remain.

CHANTRY.

Peter de Montfort, the last male possessor of the castle of Beaudesert, founded, 20th Edward II, in this church, a chantry for celebrating divine service daily at the altar of Our Lady, for the health of his soul, and the souls of his ancestors and successors, endowing it with thirty acres of meadow, 5*s.* 6*d.* in silver, five strike of muncorn, and one strike of oats, to be yearly paid by certain feoffees and their heirs to a priest, for the performance of such service. As no further notice is found of this chantry, it is probable that the revenues were returned in the rentals of the Knights Hospitallers at the dissolution.

The patronage of the church has for many years been separated from the manor, and is now held by the Rev. Theodore John Cartwright, the present rector. In 1291, the rectory was valued at six marks and a half; in the 14th Edward III, at 4*l.* 6*s.* 8*d.*; and in 26th Henry VIII, at 4*l.* It is now returned at 385*l.* In 6th Edward VI the Church Goods here were

> j chalice & j bell, one hanbell.
> ij vestment, silke.
> ij copes, one silke, oon saye.
> ij albes.
> ij altar clothes.*

The rectory is a neat modern-built residence, pleasantly situated on the slope of the hill westward from the church.

The elevated situation of the church-yard affords to the visitor another of those extensive wooded landscapes, peculiar to this part of the country; and he will do well to rest awhile before descending the hill, and proceeding to Claverdon.

The population of Preston in 1841 was 238; in 1861, 220. There were only four families resident here in 1563.

---

* *Papers in Record Office.*

There is a small school kept in the village at the expense of the rector.

Returning through the village, and passing the old manor house already referred to, we proceed on the Warwick road; and, ascending another high hill, two miles further on we arrive at

CLAVERDON,

Which, before the Conquest, was the property of a Saxon, named *Bovi*, who held it freely. It is stated to have contained three hides of land, a wood one mile in extent, five ploughlands arable, and sixteen acres of meadow. There were within its limits a priest, fourteen borders, twelve villeins, and three bondsmen. This place was also a parcel of the lands given by the Conqueror to earl Mellent, which descended through various branches of the families of successive earls of Warwick.

In 7th and 8th Edward I, the jurors at the Inquisition held at Stratford, presented that the liberty of Claverdon impeded common justice by not permitting the king's bailiffs to perform their office there without their officers.* In 13th of the same reign, William de Beauchamp, one of the earls, claimed a gallows, with assize of bread and beer in the manor. It continued through several generations with the Warwick family, but was in the hands of the crown in the time of Edward IV, when a patent was granted to Edmund Verney, esq., as parker of the park of *Claredon*, on account of the minority of Edward, son of the late duke of Clarence, to hold during his minority;† and in the 2nd Richard III, a warrant was issued, dated Nottingham, September 27th, to "thauditours

---

* *Rot. Hund.*, ii, 226. † *Patent Rolls*, part i.

and receiu's of the lordeship of Clauerdon, to demaund nothing of Edmund Verney, squier, marshall of the hall, for the pannage[2] of the park of Clau'don, in counte of Warwik."*

The rentals of the manor, &c., 33rd and 34th Henry VII, are given in the accounts of William Hankorne, Prepositor there for the king,† viz.:

	£.	s.	d.
Arrears - - - - - - - -	0	0	0
Rent of assize - - - - - - -	16	5	2¼
Customary rents[3] - - - - - - -	1	14	2
Farm of the king's manor - - - -	2	0	0
Farm of the demesne lands - - - -	0	10	9
Farm of a horse mill - - - - - -	0	11	8
Herbage of the park[4] - - - - - -	0	0	0
Herbage of the king's meadow - - -	1	6	8
Farm of the fishery - - - - - -	0	3	4
Sale of wood - - - - - - - -	0	0	0
Perquisites of the court - - - - -	1	18	3
	£24	10	0¼

The crown, 26th Henry VIII, leased the manor to Roger Walford for twenty-one years; but Edward VI, in the first of his reign, granted the inheritance of it to John Dudley, earl of Warwick. On his attainder, 1st Mary, the queen leased it for forty years, at a rent of *27l. 4s. 1d.*, to Clement Throckmorton, esq., of the neighbouring village of Haseley;‡ but, in 4th Elizabeth, it was given to Ambrose Dudley, earl

2. Pannage or paunage.—This was a grant to graze and depasture horses and cattle, which the law calls *agistment*, upon an implied contract not to seize the same to the lord's use.—See *Blackstone*.

3. One of the customs was called *Fodryngsilver*.

4. Four pounds was the usual rent, but at this time, like the park at Henley, the herbage was reserved for the support of the king's colts and mares, called the stud. Also no rent was received for a certain meadow in *Closham*, because six cart loads of hay were annually cut from the said meadow and preserved for the support of the beasts in the park during the winter.

* *Harl. MSS.*, 433, folio 1906. † *Papers*, "*Warwick*," *in Record Office*.

‡ *Lansdown MS.*, No. 109, f. 184.

of Warwick, through whose death without issue, it came again into the possession of the crown. It was afterwards purchased by Thomas Spencer, esq., a younger son of Sir John Spencer, baronet, of Yarnton, Oxfordshire, whose granddaughter sold it to Andrew Archer, esq., of Umberslade, in whose family it continued till the death of lord Archer, when in the division of his property among his daughters, the manor came to the honourable Mrs. Musgrave, and it is now the property of Christopher Musgrave, esq., her son.

The objects of interest in the village are the church, and what is now called "The Stone Building." Proceeding to

THE CHURCH,

We find an edifice, almost new, in no very good architectural taste. It appears that there was a church here in Saxon times; and the building that preceded the present one consisted of a tower, (still standing,) nave, chancel, south aisle, and porch. The nave was wholly pulled down in the year 1830, when the present nave, south aisle, and chancel were built, at a cost of 1200*l.*, the funds being provided from a charity left by one John Matthews,[5] to whose memory a tomb stands in the church-yard, containing some verses relative to the gift, but of no sufficient merit to quote. The church is dedicated to St. Michael. The tower is embattled, having the bases of pinnacles at the corners, and has a projecting staircase up to the string course. The entrance is now through the pointed arched doorway of the tower; over which is a pointed arched window of three

5. The value of the estate is shown by the inscription on the tomb—viz., in 1617, Rent, 12 Nobles; in 1707, Rent, 12 Pounds; in 1825, Rent, 78 Pounds.

lights. The nave and south aisle are covered with a root of one span. The chancel has, like the nave, a high ridge roof, and contains on each side two flat headed windows, divided by mullions and transoms into six lights. The east window is larger and square headed, divided in a similar manner into eight lights. A doorway, having a plain pointed arch, is pierced between the windows on the south side. No

division by pillars separates the nave and aisle, and the roof is plastered between slight timber girders, with bosses at the intersections. A gallery, containing a small organ, runs on the south and west sides. The chancel is divided from the nave by a high pointed arch.

In the chancel is a lofty tomb, with pillars and canopy. Over this is a coat of arms, helmet, crest, and other insignia.

It is built partly in the north wall, against one of the windows, and bears the following inscription :

> Here lyeth the body of Thomas Spencer, of Claveydon in ye county of Warwicke, esquier, second son of Sir John Spencer of Althroppe, in the county of Northampton, knight, who deceased the 8th daie of November in the yeare of our Lord God, 1586. This Thomas Spencer married Mary Cheeke the eldest daughter of Henry Cheeke esquier and had issue by her one only daughter Alice Spencer married unto Sir Thomas Lucy knight of Charlcott in the said county of Warwick, knight.
>
> All the daies of my appointed time will I wait.—*Job* xiv, 14.

There are also mural tablets commemorating members of two families named respectively Wilcox and Deakins, and the Rev. Robert Wylde, a former rector. A late erection is one to the memory of Samuel Tertius Galton, esq., *obiit* 1844.

The font is a recent addition to the church, baptisms having been performed previously by the use of a basin placed on a wooden pedestal. It is octagonal, with sunk quatrefoils on each face, standing upon a like figured base and shaft. In the tower are six bells of good tone, which, from the elevated situation of the church, may be heard for many miles. On one of them is this inscription:

> "In wedlock's bands all ye who join, with hands, your hearts unite,
> So shall our tuneful tongues combine, to laud the nuptial rite."

In the exterior south wall of the chancel, under a projecting obtuse arch, is a tomb, with an inscription at the back, to the memory of Christopher Flecknoe, steward to Thomas Spencer, esq.

The south view from the church-yard is very pleasing, extending over a highly cultivated tract, rising to the upland in the distance.

Connected with the history of this church, it appears that, 23rd Henry I, Roger, earl of Warwick, gave to the newly founded Collegiate Church of Warwick, two parts of the tithes issuing out of the inclosures in the parish, and also of the pannage of all the woods.

In 1291 the living was valued at fifteen and a half marks, the vicar's portion being then six and a half marks. The vicarage, 26th Henry VIII, was valued at 6*l.*, the payments out being 8*s.* It is now returned at 265*l.* The archdeacons of Worcester have the patronage, which has been the case since A.D. 1269, or earlier. The Rev. E. A. Kempson is the present incumbent. The Church Goods* enumerated in the Inventory taken 6th Edward VI were

j chalice and iij belles.
iiij vestment dornix.
oon cope dornix.
ij altar clothes.
ij altar towell.
iiij cruett.
one crosse coper.
ij candlestick bras.
oon senser bras.

The vicarage is a modern built edifice, standing on the east side of the church-yard.

THE STONE BUILDING

Is situated northward of the church, adjoining a farm house. The portion that remains consists of a square building of three stories, as represented in the initial letter to this chapter. The front faces the east, and the entrance is by a pointed arched doorway on the south. This doorway is in a projecting portion of the masonry, extending half way up the side, before entering which another arched doorway in a wall, reaching from the building to the farm house, is passed under. Left of the doorway to the building

* *Papers in Record Office.*

is a window at foot of the staircase. The front, or east side, contains six windows, two in each story, of different sizes, but all with stone mullions and jambs. Two similar windows, walled up, are on the north side; and on the west are several single windows, which give light to the staircase. On this side also the chimney projects from the first story to the top of the building. The south side appears to have been connected with the other portion of the mansion, of which this square remnant once formed a part, by an open court. That its extent was considerable, there can be no doubt; for Dugdale says that the Thomas Spenser, esq., who purchased the manor of the crown, as referred to at p. 169, "obtained a lease from the dean and chapter of Worcester of certain lands in this place, built a very fair house thereupon, and for the great hospitality which he kept thereat, was the Mirrour of this County." This Thomas Spencer died in 1586, leaving one only daughter, married to Sir Thomas Lucy, knight, of Charlecote; but having no male issue, he settled this manor on Sir William Spencer, of Yarnton, Oxfordshire. The manor passed as before stated; but the land on which the remains of his mansion stands reverted to the dean and chapter of Worcester. It has lately been vested in the Ecclesiastical Commissioners for an annual rent charge, and since sold by them to Darwin Galton, esq.

On entering the arched doorway we find ourselves in a hall, or lobby, at the end of which is a room, approached by a similar arched doorway, having a low arched fireplace. On the left a passage, with another arched doorway, leads to a stone staircase, which rises to the top of the building. From this staircase, the rooms on the second and third stories are entered. These consist of two apartments on each story, one leading into the other. Each of the larger rooms has an open fireplace of carved stone, flat at the head, the smaller apartments having none, and appear to have been dressing rooms connected with the former, with which the arched doorways communicate. The windows of the larger rooms are divided by jambs and transoms into eight lights, and those of the smaller into four lights. There appears to have been a tower at the head of the staircase, the parapet surmounting it bearing evidence of pinnacles or globes having been affixed at each corner. The parapet on the other part also bears indications of a like ornament at the corners. What the extent of this fair house may have been, there are but few foundations left to indicate; but a careful inspection of the farm house adjoining will show that the building extended considerably on this side. The external portion of the chimney is large and massy, and the plinth and string course running along a considerable portion of the south wall. Inside is another massive wall now forming the side of a passage to the chambers, and the cellar presents nearly all round the walls some portion of the original building.

We may, however, readily assign to this mansion the importance Dugdale attaches to it by the evidences around of the extensive gardens and pleasure grounds once connected with the place. The length and breadth of these towards the east, though overgrown with rich herbage, is sufficiently defined to show that they covered several acres of ground. The raised terraces appear to be the same as when first thrown up, the central one extending in a straight line, about 220 yards from the building, and crossed at intervals twice by others running from one side terrace to the other. These were, no doubt, often traversed by the gentry of the county, when the "great hospitality" of the builder of the house and projector of the pleasure grounds, was dispensed to his neighbours.[6] All this glory has, however, departed, and nothing is known of the man save what his monument in the village church imparts. Whether this building stood on the site of a still older manor house must be left to conjecture. The earls of Warwick had, 2nd Edward III, a residence at Claverdon, as is evident by the grant of Spernall to one of the Duvassals to hold in sergeantry, viz., by the service of giving attendance upon the earl and his heirs at the castle of Warwick, or at their manor houses of *Claverdon*, Tanworth, and Sutton, at which of them he or they should happen to reside upon Christmas day, Easter day, and Whitsunday, then and there to perform the service of chief butler at those times, and receive a certain fee for the same.*

A short distance from the building is *Claverdon Leys*, the seat of Darwin Galton, esq., the owner of considerable property in this parish. It is a neat modern structure, to which great additions were made in 1858-9.

The parish is extensive, containing several distinct hamlets and manors. These the tourist may readily reach, if so disposed; but he will find nothing in them of interest

---

6. Towards the end of Elizabeth's reign and during that of her successor, the angular and circular windows gave place to those of a square and tall form, divided by transoms and placed in lengthened rows. Battlements were omitted, the pile was more massive, broken by a square central turret higher than those at the angles. The gardens of the period probably did not partake of a similar change. These were generally laid out in terraces and walks. The side walks were kept shady so as to afford shelter in the hottest sun. Some were like galleries for protection from the wind, hedged in at both ends and finely gravelled, whilst others had mounds breast high, and often level with the wall, so as to overlook the fields. Many had walks of turf dividing the garden into four equal portions. All around was redolent of sweet trees and flowers, whilst fountains, statues, obelisks, and other works of art contributed to the beauty of the scene. Bowling greens formed a portion of some, where "the old knights and chaplains daily quarrelled and made friends."

* *Escheat Rolls*, 2nd Edward II, 45.

sufficient to recompense him for such a deviation. They comprise Norton, which lies out of our district, two miles south east, Langley, Kington, Songar, and Yarnigale, and consist of a few farm houses and cottages.

The population of the whole parish, exclusive of Norton, in 1841 numbered 711, and 735 in the year 1861. In 1563 there were fifty-two families.

Here is a large National School, with residence, erected a few years ago, in which the youth of this and neighbouring parishes and hamlets are receiving a good education.

LANGLEY,

One of these hamlets, west of the church, was formerly of more importance than at the present day. At the Norman Conquest it was given to Robert de Stafford, with Wootton and other lordships. Langley was held of him by one *Judichel*, and contained one hide and a half of land, with woods one mile long and half a mile broad, valued at 40*s*. This in Saxon times had been the freehold of *Ernvi*. With the de Staffords the manor continued for several years. In 17th Edward II, Sir Henry de Lodbroke, knight, styled himself "*Dominus de Langele;*" and two years after, William Vaughan took the same title. The hamlet subsequently belonged to Sir Baldwin Freville and Richard Beauchamp, earl of Warwick; but, in Henry VI's reign, John Arden, of Park Hall, esq., who was then lord of the manor, settled it on his son and heir, on his marriage. Since then it has passed through several hands, and S. R. Solly, esq., is now the lord of the manor.

In this place was once a CHAPEL, which anciently belonged to the Church at Wootton. In Thomas's edition of Dugdale it is stated that about 1208, the abbot and convent of Conches (to which the priory and church at Wootton belonged) complained to the pope that the rector of Claverdon had unjustly detained the tithes and obventions of this chapel. On the cause being heard before the papal delegates the parson of Claverdon alleged that his church had had possession of them for more than forty years. It was proved, however, by the abbot and convent, that they had always received these tithes till the time of prior Ernulf, who granted them to W. Comin, the parson of Claverdon, for the time of his life, on his payment of a pound of incense yearly. It was also proved that before the late wars the inhabitants were baptised and buried at Wootton, and that during the reign of Stephen, the lord of Langley and his lady constantly attended the church at Wootton on feast-days, and that they were buried there, and it was further shown that Comin regularly paid the pound of incense, and that his successor for some time did the same, till the wars came on, when he refused to do so any longer.

The dispute appears to have extended over fifty years, for in 1257 an agreement was come to between the prior of Wootton and the rector of Claverdon, in which it was provided that, from that time, the chapel, with the tithes, great and small, should belong to the church at Claverdon, and that the inhabitants of Langley should bury their dead and receive the sacraments there, the rectors of Claverdon engaging to pay to the said prior, and his successors, five marks and eight shillings yearly. The priors of Wootton having lost the revenues of that priory (see p. 54) in the reign of Henry VI, the king gave the patronage of the church, &c., to King's College, Cambridge; and in 22nd of the same reign, a new arrangement was made, by which the archdeacon of Worcester, then rector of Claverdon, agreed to pay to the said college 40*s.* yearly, in right of their rectory of Wootton Wawen, and in default to forfeit double that sum, and pay all costs.

Of the chapel, whatever it might have been, no trace remains.

KINGTON,

Another manor, is near to Langley, and was, like part of Claverdon, held freely by *Britnod* in Saxon times; but, on the conquest, it passed to earl Mellent. It was then called *Cinton*, and comprised one hide and a half of waste, valued at 5*s*., the woods being estimated at 10*s*. The monks of Bordesley had, anciently, two carucates of land here, besides other possessions in Langley. At the dissolution of religious houses, this manor, designated "The Grange, Manor, or Farm at Kington," was granted to Clement Throckmorton, esq., of Haseley, and Alexander Avenor, and their heirs. The former died seized of it, by the title of "Kington Farm or Grange," 16th Elizabeth. With the Throckmortons it continued some time; John Parker, gentleman, was the owner in 1734; and it is now the property of lord Calthorpe.

The Grange, or Manor House, which is a rather large, half-timbered building, is still standing.

SONGAR,

A farm lying south of Kington, was a manor also possessed by the monks of Bordesley, to which it had been given, in the reign of Stephen, by William Giffard, and confirmed by Roger, earl of Warwick. At the dissolution of this monastic establishment, it came into the same hands as Kington, by the name of "The Manor, Farm, and Grange, called Songar Grange," and so continued for many years. It has followed the fortunes of its sister manor, and by sale has become the property of S. R. Solly, esq.

There are several other small clusters of houses in various parts of the parish of Claverdon, which need no special notice. One of these, *Lye Green,* we travel through on leaving Claverdon, and to the west of this is Yarnigale, having still a large common, which being hilly, is a prominent object in the landscape. Proceeding to the right, on leaving Lye Green, we soon come to

PINLEY,

An extra-parochial place, consisting of two farm houses and a few cottages, and anciently a member of Rowington. It then, like the latter, belonged to Robert, first earl of Leicester of the Norman line, who granted it to Robert Boteler, of Oversley, in this county. This Robert enfeoffed Robert de Pilardington, who founded, *temp.* Henry I, the

PRIORY OF PINLEY,

And gave to God and the nuns "all the land of *Pineleia,* with the consent of Robert Pincerne, of Oversleigh." Once established, the nuns (of the Cistertian order) were in no lack of benefactors. They dedicated their institution to the Blessed Virgin; and received grants of land, tenements, and tithes, in almost every parish and hamlet adjoining. The de Montforts, of Beaudesert, were amongst their most liberal benefactors. Thurstan de Montfort gave to the Priory the third part of all his victuals spent in his house; viz., bread, beer, flesh, fish, and whatsoever was dressed in his kitchen. Peter, son of the above, obtained the patronage of the priory from Roger de Pilardington, *temp.* Henry III. He allowed the same tenth of provisions as his father; as did also another Peter, his son. This Peter, 5th Edward I, is supposed to have redeemed this charge, by granting to the nuns a yearly rent of thirteen quarters of wheat and fourteen quarters of barley, on lands in Whitchurch, which they are stated to have acquired by purchase of Peter de Montfort, lord of that manor. This they were returned as possessing, 29th of the same reign.* Waleran,7 earl of Warwick, placed his daughter and niece under the care of the prioress and nuns of this establishment, and provided for their maintenance by a charter of which the following is a translation:

> "To all to whom the present writing shall come, Waleran, earl of Warwick, greeting. Be it known to you all that I have granted, and by this my present charter confirmed, to the nuns of Pinnelei, two marks of silver from my rents of Claverdone, to be annually received from my seneschal [or steward]: one mark at the feast of St. Michael, and the other at the feast of St. Mary in March [Lady Day]: so long, namely, as these nuns shall have the maintenance and guardianship of Gundred my daughter and Isabella my niece, whom I have committed to their care. But if one of these girls shall be removed from the charge and custody of the nuns, these nuns shall receive only one mark annually; and if each shall be removed by my desire, I will be quit [or free] from those two marks. Wherefore, if by any chance the said two marks shall not be paid to the before-mentioned nuns under the form prescribed, the nuns shall deliver the before-named girls to me or to my heirs. Moreover, I have granted, and by this my present charter confirmed, to the aforesaid nuns of Pinnelea, the redecimation of my demesne of Walton, as a pure and perpetual charitable gift, for the salvation of my soul, and of the souls of the countess Margaret my wife, of the earl R[oger] my father, of the countess G[undred] my mother, of the earl W[illiam] my brother, and of others my predecessors and successors. Witnesses—Thomas Prior; John de Kibbeclive; Richard, my chaplain; William, seneschal; Roger Murdac; Ralph Selvem; Wido de Oila; Roger, clerk; Symon, chamberlain, and others."
>
> [With the seal of earl Waleran.]†

In Pope Nicholas's Taxation, A.D. 1291, it is stated that the prioress of Pinley held at Pinley two carucates of land,

---

7. Waleran succeeded his brother William in the earldom of Warwick, A.D. 1184, and died A.D. 1204 or 1205. See *Dugdale's Baronage*, in which the above charter is mentioned.

* *Inquisitions Post Mort.*

† *Cottonian MSS.*, xi, 16.

each worth 10*s.* per annum, and a mill worth half a mark. The total income was 2*l.* 6*s.* 4*d.*[8]

The accounts of William Hankorne, 34th Henry VII, (see p. 168,) show an annual payment on account of lands formerly belonging to the earls of Warwick, "in a certain pension annually going out of this demesne to the prioress and nuns of Penley at 18*s.* per annum, from an ancient custom."* Divers immunities were also granted to these nuns in charters, by kings Henry II and III.

The establishment is stated by Tanner to have consisted of a prioress and three or four nuns. In the survey taken 27th Henry VIII, this house and its possessions were valued at 23*l.* 5*s.* 11*d.* over and above the reprises, amounting to 4*l.* 7*s.* 8*d.*, of which 16*s.* 4*d.* per annum was yearly distributed in alms to poor people, on behalf of the soul of Sir Peter de Montfort, and 12*s.* for the soul of Sir Ralph de Sudeley, knight. The high steward, Roger Wigston, esq., had a pension of 20*s.* yearly.

At the dissolution of the house, Margaret Wigston, prioress, was allowed an annuity of 4*l.* per year, during her life, but the nuns obtained no compensation. In the 30th of Henry VIII, the king sold to William Wigston, esq., son of the above-named Roger, the site of this monastery, with the manor of *Pinle*, and all the demesnes thereto belonging; as also the lands in Shrewley, *Clardon*, and Langley, with the croft at Hatton, and the said rent corn issuing out of the manor of Whitchurch. The purchase money was 342*l.* 11*s.*, for which consideration these possessions were conveyed to him and his heirs, to hold in capite, by the twentieth part of

---

8. *Pope Nicholas's Taxation*, folio, pub. 1802, p. 230. The return was erased, but it stands in the *Cottonian MSS.* below the taxable value.

* *Papers, "Warwick," in Record Office.*

a knight's fee, 1*l.* 16*s.* 9*d.* yearly, in the name of a tenth, being reserved to the king, his heirs and successors. The site and lands in Pinley were afterwards sold to — Cooksey, who held them in 1640, afterwards they were sold to Aaron Rogers, gent., whose son, John Rogers, rector of Fenny Compton, possessed them in 1734. They are at this time the property of Henry Wise, esq.

Besides the above these nuns had possessions, as found by the survey, in Haseley, Tanworth, Edstone, Watcote, Butler's Marston, Astley, Preston Bagot, Warwick, and Stratford-on-Avon, in this county; Byley and Chorlton, Worcestershire; Goodrickton, Gloucestershire; Sybford-Gower, Bedfordshire; and Shernford, in the county of Leicester.

The following were the prioresses:

Lucia de Sapy, November 5, 1269.
Helewysia de Langelegh, October, 1321.
Elizabeth de Lotrynton, March 4, 1324.
Matilda de Bret.
Amicia de Hinton, July 4, 1358.
Alicia Myntyng, March 12, 1426.
Margaret Wigston.

What remains of the priory is comprised in portions of farm buildings, which are situated in a sheltered valley, apart from any public road. The exterior aspect will be readily understood from the engraving, presenting only the arched doorway[9] to what was formerly the church or chapel. Over this doorway has been a large window, the lower parts of which are traceable inside. Of this portion, the front or south wall has been taken down, and brick pillars inserted, so as to adapt it for a waggon hovel and implement shed. The north wall, in places, preserves a

9. This doorway is more fully depicted in the initial letter commencing the next chapter.

Norman string course, together with the sills of two mullioned windows of three lights each, a third having, most likely, been destroyed by the insertion of large folding doors. The walls (two and a half feet in thickness) have, nearly to the level of these sills, been taken down, the present roof resting a few inches above them. The projecting portion at the east end, now a small stable, is

conjectured to have been a revestry. It was entered from the southern side of another apartment, now also a stable, through a pointed arch doorway, which, though much dilapidated, is highly ornamented with sculptured roses between the spandrels formed by the arch and square head. This latter building has a plinth and string course running on two sides of it, and west of the north door are the remains of what appears to have been a water stoup. There is also a rather lofty doorway leading into the remains of another room on the east, the sides still perfect, but the arch gone.

Another doorway appears to have been walled up in the

western side of the revestry. A stone coffin, with circular head, lies broken in the yard; and a fragment of a carved stone corbel is placed in the garden wall. A portion of the present farm house exhibits remains of further buildings, viz., in the stone chimney, and the plinth and string course on it and the walls running from it.

The grounds occupied three or four acres, surrounded by a moat, a considerable part of which, filled with water, still remains. No definite idea can be formed of their character, since nearly every clue to their original condition has been utterly destroyed: where once the prioress and her nuns enjoyed the pleasures of contemplation, the husbandman and his labours reign supreme.

> "The moaning blast will not declare,
> How great thy pomp,—thy cloistered dwellers, where?
> Thy vesper chimes are mute,—thy matin bell
> No more wakes echo from the flowery dell."

Leaving the abbey, and proceeding northward we pass Pinley House, a modern farm dwelling, with three other farm houses, called Cryer's (a corruption probably of Friars) Oak, Holywell, and High Cross, names of significance in times preceding the Reformation. This part of the country is not so thickly wooded as some we have previously traversed. Continuing our course, and passing for the first time over the Great Western Railway, we arrive at

ROWINGTON,

A considerable village, pleasantly situated on a hill, and commanding an extensive view to the south and west. This place was, in the Domesday Survey, called *Roclintone*, and was certified to contain three hides of land, a church, woods one mile and a half long, and eight furlongs broad. There were twenty-seven villeins, and twenty-four bordars, with nine ploughs. It was held freely by *Baldwin*, in the time of king Edward; but was, in the Conqueror's time, the property of Hugh de Grentemaisnill, and held of him by Roger, his undertenant. It soon, however, fell to the crown; for Henry I gave it and the church to the abbey of Reading, in Berkshire, which he had founded, which grant Henry II confirmed. In 1291 the monks of this abbey had here three carucates of land, of the value of 10*s.* a carucate, two water-mills, and one windmill, rated at 6*s.* 8*d.*; also in rent of assize 11*l.*, and the profits of their own store in this place, one mark; with pleas and perquisites, one mark and a half. At the inquisition held at Stratford-on-Avon, 7th and 8th Edward I, before referred to, it was found that the abbot of Reading had here assize of bread, beer, and other things, but by what warrant the jurors knew not; and that the liberties of the manor impede common justice, because they do not permit the king's bailiffs to perform their office without their bailiffs.* To these, in Edward III's time, Thomas de Rivere and Richard Goodman added, by gift, sixty-nine acres of land, and eight and a half acres of meadow, for the maintenance of one monk, being a priest, to celebrate divine service daily in the abbey church of Reading, for their good estate in this life, and for their souls after death. These lands were held of the barony of Stafford.[10]

After the dissolution of the great monasteries, the manor was leased to John Oldnall for twenty-one years, a lease which was soon surrendered, for five years later the king settled it on Katherine Parr, his sixth wife, on their marriage,

10. The revenues at the dissolution of religious houses are not available in this instance, the volume containing an account of the possessions of Reading Abbey being lost.

* *Rot. Hund.*, ii, 226.

as part of her jointure. On her death, 2nd Edward VI, it was resumed by the crown, and was, the 7th of the same reign, exchanged to John Dudley, duke of Northumberland, on whose attainder soon after it once more reverted to the crown. In 5th Mary it was granted to the above John Oldnall for another lease of twenty-one years, which seems also to have failed of fulfilment, since in 5th Elizabeth, the queen granted it to William Spinner, gentleman, Alice his wife, and their son. This grant, however, again failing from some cause or other the following year, the queen gave it to Ambrose Dudley, earl of Warwick, and his heirs; but, he dying without issue, it came once more into the possession of the crown, and so continued till the time of Charles I, who made it part of the dowry of his queen, Henrietta Maria, a settlement which, with the exception of the interval of the Commonwealth, continued in force till her death. The manor remained with the crown till the year 1806, being leased to various parties; but, in that year, it was purchased by William Smith, esq., of Rowington. Since this time it has passed through various hands, and is now the property of Edward Westwood, esq., who is enfranchising the lands of the few leasehold tenants remaining.

THE CHURCH,

Dedicated to St. Lawrence, is large, and of a better class of architecture than many we have had occasion to describe. It comprises a central tower, something similar to that at Wootton Wawen; but, in this case, rising near to the east end of the nave, instead of forming a division between it and the chancel. In addition to the nave there are narrow aisles, north and south, a small south transept, a chancel, and a large chantry chapel, extending from the north aisle, by the side of the tower, the eastern portion of the nave, and the whole of the chancel. The tower, which is supported on four pointed arches, springing from half pillars and piers, and rather low in elevation, is crenelated or embattled, bearing on two of the battlements shields. The belfry windows are of two lights, under a pointed arch, and within

are five bells and a clock. One of these bells, the fifth, bears a Latin inscription, which may be thus rendered:

"When I sound, if thou art not of willing mind,
Never to prayers wilt thou desire thy way to find."

The aisles are entered by pointed arched doorways, the south one having a modern brick porch, and, east of the northern one, is the remnant of a water stoup[10] in the wall. The aisles are each separated from the nave by two pointed

10. A basin, generally of stone, fixed usually on the east side of the great door, going into the church, which being filled with holy water, some sprinkled and others crossed themselves with it as they went into church.

arches, supported by octagonal pillars, and have, along with the latter, ceiled roofs formed of circular timber ribs attached to the rafters, horizontal ones dividing them into panels, which are plastered. The chancel is divided from the nave by a pointed arch, and is ceiled similarly. The east end contains a pointed arched window of four lights, with tracery above, the upper portion being filled with modern stained glass, representing, in the four compartments, the Birth, Baptism, Crucifixion, and Ascension of Our Lord: It has been thus ornamented as a memorial of the late William Aston, esq. The lower portion is covered with a white marble reredos, containing the Commandments, the Creed, and the Lord's Prayer, and is inscribed "the gift of Mr. Richard Reeve, citizen of London, A.D. 1750." Under the south-east window is a stone seat; but with no division into three stalls. This may have formed the sedilia: An apparent unsoundness in the wall, east of this, indicates the existence of a piscina, or the place where one has formerly been. The rood screen was removed some years ago, part of it now forming the outer gates of the porch.

The chantry, the roof of which is quite flat, is divided from the chancel by a carved screen. This was no doubt "The Chapel of the Blessed Mary," mentioned by John Hill, bailiff of Rowington, who directs, by his will, 15th Henry VII, that certain wax lights should be kept burning therein, "before the statue of St. Lawrence,"[11] to whom the church is dedicated.

The windows throughout the church are mostly square

---

11. This pious bailiff also left funds for the maintenance of the Rood Light, the Paschal Taper, and the Sepulchre Light, and for prayers at certain seasons for the souls of himself, his wives, and parents, for the abbots of Reading, and for all those whose bodies rest, or shall rest, in the church-yard of Rowington, *for ever*. *Churches of Warwickshire*, ii, 66.

headed, divided by mullions, and some of them foliated. The west window of the nave, which is placed over an obtuse arched doorway, is similar to the eastern one, but with more elaborate tracery. Above it, externally, is a blank shield, and, surmounting this, an obtuse arched niche beneath the apex of the gable.

The monuments in this church are numerous, and those of most ancient date record the memories of John Woollaston, Elizabeth Wolascott, John Hancockes, John Hill, Richard Reeves, with other benefactors to the church and parish. Two incised slabs with figures still remain, one on the chancel floor, and one in the north chapel; on the latter of which is the following inscription round the fillet or border:

> "Here lyeth Jhon Oldnall and Isbell his wife late bayliff of Rownton, a worthy man to be hadd in memory: who dyed the xi day of Augouste in the yeare of oure Lord God Mo. Do. Lviii, being of the age of threescore and xvi yere, upon whose soule Jesu have mercy."

The font is circular, without ornament, having a plain square pediment and round shaft. The pulpit is of stone, carved in panels, and stands on a half pillar at the south east angle of the tower, the adjoining reading desk and clerk's pew filling up the small south transept. There is a gallery containing an organ at the west end of the nave. In the nave and other places are a few open seats; but the principal part of the church is fitted with high pews, on many of which the initials of the owners have been cut or painted.[12]

---

12. On one of these pews figures in full, on a brass plate, the names of those who should occupy it: We say "should;" for we cannot but think that this vulgar practice arises from the infrequent attendance of the parishioners: It is, most probably, done to avoid inconvenient mistakes, the intervals at which they present themselves at church being so great, that without this contrivance they would forget their own pews.

The church-yard is small for the extent of the parish, and is crowded with graves, in connexion with which no memorials of any interest exist.

> "'They lived,—they died;' such is the sum,
> The abstract of the headstone's page."

On the north side is the vicarage, a newly-erected brick edifice with stone facings. Public schools on the National system are on the western side.

The abbot and canons of Reading, to whom the church was given by Henry I, formerly presented to the living. At the dissolution of religious houses the patronage reverted to the crown, with whom it still continues. The living was valued, 19th Edward I, at twenty marks, eight marks being the vicar's portion; and 26th Henry VIII, it was rated at 7*l.* 11*s.* 7*d.*, and 15*s.* 2*d.* payments. It is returned at 116*l.*, but the present value is 360*l.* per annum. The Rev. P. Brodie is the present vicar. The return made of the Church Goods, 6th Edward VI, was

> j chalice & iij bells, oon litle sance bell.
> vj vestments, oon vellet, iiij silke.
> oon cope, silke.
> v altarclothes.
> iiij albes.
> iiij stream's.
> iij ban' clothes.
> ij candlestyckes.
> ij cruets.
> ij crosses, oon coper, oon plate.
> vj towells.
> oon altar fronte, say.

There were eighty-seven families in the parish in 1563. The population in 1841 was 1046, in 1861 the number was 992.

The situation of the village on a hill or rock, whence its name, makes it one of the driest and most agreeable places in the neighbourhood; and, in consequence, several neat residences have been erected. Land here, which is divided among a great number of proprietors, accordingly realizes a better price than in less favoured localities. Standing near Rowington Green, the view, south and east, though not so picturesque as some in the district, is nevertheless sufficiently agreeable, and the eye may roam

> "O'er cultured plains, where hamlets tell
> Of homes where peace and plenty dwell,
> And, from its swelling hill, you spy
> Each mossgrown turret greet the sky."

Quitting the village proper, and descending southward by the road to the right, we come to one of several outlying hamlets, or clusters of farm houses, called *Finwood Green*, and, shortly afterwards, to another named *Lonesomeford*, a name, without doubt, derived from the former solitary character of the country where the ford crossed the little brook that still flows onward to the river Arrow, at Alcester. By Lonesomeford, the Birmingham and Stratford canal passes, and a considerable trade is done in coal, lime, and sand. Here there is a small chapel belonging to the Independent denomination of dissenters.

The road from Lonesomeford leads through the lands comprising the hamlet of *Bushwood*. On the right is a large wood known by this name; and the few houses belonging to the hamlet are scattered at wide intervals for the convenience of the farms. One of these, called Lapworth Hall, though in the hamlet of Bushwood, has, from its connexion in early times with the parish of Lapworth, been described in our last day's tour. Here was formerly Bushwood Common, inclosed in 1824, the improvement of which, since that event, has progressed so rapidly that it is now become a very fertile tract of land.

Having finished this day's ramble, the traveller may either

return to Henley for the night; or, if he desire to save the time required to reach this point on the morrow, retrace his way to Rowington, where he will find, at no great distance from the church, an inn capable of administering supplies to his weakness and rest to his weariness. Leaving him there, busily engaged in cultivating an intimacy with the viands and beverages that will soothe and satisfy his necessities, we wish him

> "Good digestion to wait on appetite,
> And health on both;"

That, so fortified, he may be ready on the morrow to resume his exploration of the beauties of the picturesque district into which he has penetrated.

Sixth Day.

LEAVING Henley-in-Arden, a longer walk or drive (as the case may be) will be involved at the commencement of this day's pilgrimage, which will bring us to Wroxhall, a parish in which we must pause awhile, for the sake of its ancient Priory. Thence we shall pursue our course to Baddesley Clinton, Packwood, and other places of minor importance, but affording much matter for passing observation and notice.

Proceeding, then, through Rowington, a road will lead us to the first-named in the list of places to be visited, that is to say, to

WROXHALL,

Not mentioned in Domesday Book. Dugdale conjectures that, owing to the barrenness of the soil, the lands here, like those at Hatton, though wooded, were not mentioned in that document. The first information we obtain of Wroxhall occurs in connection with the establishment of a monastery here. Of the origin of this establishment we have the following fabulous story, quoted by Dugdale, from a MS. in illustration of the superstition of the period. One Hugh, a person of great stature, son of Richard de Hatton, holding this manor and Hatton of the earl of Warwick, going to the wars in the Holy Land, was taken prisoner and kept captive for seven years. Reflecting, at length, that St. Leonard* was the patron saint of his parish church, he prayed earnestly to him for deliverance. The saint twice appeared to him in the habit of a black monk, and commanded him to go home and found a house of nuns of St. Benedict at his church. He made a vow to God that he would do so, after which he was miraculously transported in his fetters, and set down in Wroxhall woods, not far from his own residence. A shepherd, who was accidentally passing, found him, and though at first much frightened at seeing a person so overgrown with hair, he was persuaded to take a message to his lady, who, when she arrived at the spot, could not believe him to be her husband, till he produced part of a ring which had been broken between them, and which, when applied to the part in her own possession, fitted it. After solemn thanks to God, Our Lady, and St. Leonard, and prayer for direction, he was instructed where to build the monastery, by the token of several stones pitched in the ground, in the very place where the altar was afterwards erected. Two of his daughters became inmates; and a lady, named Edith, from the nuns of Wilton, was installed to instruct them in the rule of St. Benedict. Jago has sung this legend in his poem of "Edgehill."

The history of Wroxhall is dependent upon that of the priory, up to the time of its dissolution, as its nuns were owners of the whole of the lordship, besides other extensive manors and properties. The foundation of the legend we have referred to, is, most likely, that Hugh de Hatton had made a vow, during his sojourn in the Holy Land, in

---

* See note, p. 83.

acknowledgment of some great preservation. This, on his return, he performed by building the religious house here, in fulfilment of his pledge, sometime in the reign of Henry I or Stephen, and giving for its support the whole of the lands in "Wrocheshale," with lands and woods in the same place, the church of Hatton, and whatsoever belonged to it, as well as the land at Hatton which *Aytropus* had, and so much of the founder's royalty there as lay between the two brooks, with other property and privileges in that lordship. To this liberal endowment, many other persons added grants of land, advowsons, and payments from their estates, which king Henry II further enlarged by the gift of ten marks yearly rent, for the health of his soul, and the souls of his father and ancestors, to be paid out of his exchequer, until otherwise ordered. The fresh disposition of this grant occurred A.D. 1259, in the reign of Henry III, who assigned six marks of the original donation to be paid by the bishop of Worcester and his successors, and four by the sheriff of Warwickshire. In 13th Edward I the nuns made a claim of court-leet, gallows, and waifs in Hatton and Wroxhall, which was allowed. In 1290 Gifford, bishop of Worcester, made a visitation to this priory, and in 1309 another was made by bishop Landavon, at which time there were twelve nuns on the establishment. The church at least, if not the whole conventual fabric, Dugdale considers was rebuilt, or considerably enlarged, previous to 1315, as in that year Walter de Maydenston, or Maidston, then bishop of Worcester, consecrated the church and high altar. In 16th Henry VII, at the court of Isabel, then prioress, John Benet was admitted to a messuage and three crofts, to hold according to the custom of the manor of Wroxhall.*

---

* *Dugdale's Monasticon.*

The priory, like the whole of the smaller religious houses, was suppressed 27th Henry VIII. In the previous survey, 26th of same reign, the nuns were found to have possessions in Wroxhall, Hatton, Haseley, Beaudesert, Hampton on the Hill, Preston Bagot, Radford, Burton, Walston, Marston, and Brailes, in this county, besides other rents, &c., the whole valued at 78*l.* 10*s.* 1*d.*, less 5*l.* 15*s.* 3*d.* for various deductions. At this time, according to Tanner's "Notitia Monastica," there were five or six nuns; and on the dissolution, dame Agnes Lytle, then prioress, had a pension of 7*l.* 10*s.* per annum allowed. Sir Edward Ferrers was then high steward of the priory, receiving 3*l.* 6*s.* 8*d.* per year, and it was found that on every Maundy Thursday there were 20*s.* distributed to the poor people in bread and herrings, with 1*s.* in money, for the good of the founder's soul.[1]

In 36th Henry VIII the site of the priory, church, belfry, church-yard, and the lands in Wroxhall, with the rectory and tithes, were granted to Robert Burgoyne and John Scudamore, and their heirs. From this Robert the manor, church, &c., descended to Sir John Scudamore, baronet, of Sutton, in the county of Bedford, with which family they continued till the year 1713, when the estate was sold to Sir Christopher Wren. With his representatives, through Chandos Wren Hoskyns, esq., who married the heiress, it remained till the year 1861, when it was purchased by William Dugdale, esq.

---

1. In the MS. mentioned as recording the miraculous foundation of the priory, it is further stated, "The founder dyed the xix of Marche, [year not given,] and he lyeth buryed in our quier, under a marble stone, under the east dore of our close quier. His mother is buryed in our church-yarde." This would refer to a building standing here prior to the present church.

The prioresses were

Erneburga.	Emma.
Helena.	Matilda.
Sabina.	Cecilia.
Helena.	Ida.
Matilda.	Amicia.

Sibilla d'Abetot, April 5, 1284.
Isabella de Clinton, of Maxtoke, *obiit* 1300.
Agnes de Alesbury, December 6, 1311.
Agnes de Broy.
Isabella de Fokerham, October 25, 1339.
Alicia de Clinton.
Johanna Russell, July 2, 1356.
Horabila de Aylesbury, August 19, 1361.
Alicia de Aylesbury.
Isolda Walshe, September 3, 1425.
Isabella Asteley, July 20, 1431.
Jocosa Brome, *obiit* June 21, 1528.
Agnes Lytle, 28th Henry VIII.

The approach from the road to

WROXHALL ABBEY,

As it is now called, is by a fine avenue of oak and other trees, at the end of which stands the church, the conventual buildings, and the modern mansion, the latter forming the west side of the quadrangle that was once the court of the priory. Beginning with

THE CHURCH,

Occupying the northern part, the tourist will find it of one continuous breadth and height, without division of nave and chancel, with a brick tower at the end of the former, rising from the roof. The main building is embattled, as is also the tower, the turret of the staircase rising higher than the other part. On the north side are five pointed arched windows of three lights, the centre one being about half the length of the others, and having a corresponding arched doorway, blocked up, underneath it. On the south are two smaller pointed windows of three lights, and a third still smaller, the eastern portion of the wall having two pointed arches, walled up, originally intended to open on a southern aisle. The eastern, or chancel window, is pointed and of five lights. There are two entrances, one south from the quadrangle, and one north under the tower, leading from the church-yard, which is the one used by the parishioners. This had, formerly, a timber-framed porch attached, which is now removed a short distance over the pathway to the door. Entering by the doorway, which is a pointed arch, and exhibits a curious carved heading inside, we find the interior furnished with plain open seats, having carved finials to the heads; the pulpit and reading desk being towards the east, on the north side, and the font, a plain octagonal basin and shaft, westward, on the south side. The principal interest of the interior will be found in the stained glass windows and the monuments. The windows, on Dugdale's visit, contained the arms of Zouch, Say of Ricard's Castle, Beauchamp earl of Warwick, England, Latimer, Lodbroke, Montfort of Beaudesert, and others. Many remains of these still exist in the four northern windows nearest to the east. There are also, in good preservation, a figure of St. Benedict, under a canopy; the effigies of a saint or nun in the attitude of prayer; and many fragments of other figures, inscriptions, oak leaves, and similar kinds of ornament. The eastern window has a coat of arms in the four outward lights, the centre containing the rose and crown. The western, or belfry window, of three lights, possesses the arms of Nevile, earl of Warwick. The remains of a piscina exist under the south-eastern window, and a plain slab marks the sedilia. On the opposite wall, immediately under the sill of a window, are three curiously sculptured bosses.

Dugdale further states that, on a marble slab, was this inscription :

"Domina Jocosa Brome filia Johanis Brome et
Priorissa de Wroxhall obiit xxi Junij, anno Md. xxviii."

This is now gone; but there are remains of incised slabs on the floor, at the end now forming the chancel; whilst loose in the easternmost window of the north is the brass figure of a lady in the costume of the fifteenth century, of the original position of which in the church there is no evidence to show.[2] On the wall, north of the communion table, is a mural monument to the memory of Anna, wife of Sir Robert Burgoyne, baronet, *obiit* February 5, 1693, aged 51. On the south side, another mural tablet to the memory of Christopher Wren, esq., and Mary his wife, who died, respectively, in 1771 and 1773. Besides these, there are several tablets recording the deaths of members of the Wren family and others. Seven hatchments of the Wrens remain in the church. The roof is open timber-work, divided by cross-beams, &c. In the tower are three bells.

The Rev. H. J. Torr is the present incumbent of the living, a donative curacy in the patronage of the lord of the manor, but of which the value has not been returned to Parliament. As the church, which, up to the dissolution of the priory, formed part of the monastic establishment, was the place of worship for the parish, it was preserved and dedicated to the use of the parishioners, the parties to whom it was granted having the power to appoint the minister and pay his stipend.

The Church Goods found here, 6th Edward VI, were

j chalice & iij belles.
ij vestment, dornix.
oon cope, dornix.
one altarclothe.
one towell.

2. This figure is said to have been brought from the church of Brailes.

Leaving the church by the south doorway, we pass into a room adjoining, and thence into the quadrangle, or court of the priory, on the east and south sides of which the old conventual offices continue almost in the same state they were in when the religious community, located here, was dispersed. Passing a pointed arched doorway, leading to the garden, about midway on the east side is another, being the entrance to the chapter house, in the interior of which are six pillars with capitals, from which at one time a groined roof appears to have sprung. On the south side, near to the eastern angle, is an obtuse arched doorway, the wall, supported by massive buttresses, having pointed windows. This portion of the building was the refectory of the convent, and is now used, together with the entire range of offices, for the domestic purposes of the modern mansion. Ascending a staircase to the rooms over the chapter-house, opening on a long corridor, or passage, are a number of small rooms, the ancient oaken doors and frames, iron hinges, &c., being very perfect. If these were the dormitories of the nuns, as the cicerone of the place asserts, they are a striking contrast to what is now considered necessary for health. In one of them are still preserved several old full-length portraits of nuns, &c.

This priory, like so many others, had its special relics, the principal being the ring and chain named in the legend given of the founder.[3] These, however, like the potent

---

3. In ancient times every monastery, every parish church, had its special relics, its special images, to attract the interest of the people. The reverence for the remains of noble and pious men, the dresses which they had worn, or the bodies in which their spirits had lived, was in itself a natural and pious emotion. The people brought offerings to the shrines, where it was supposed that the relics were of the greatest potency. The clergy, to secure the offerings, invented the relics, and invented the stories of the wonders that had been worked by them. The great exposure of these miracles took place at the visitation of the monasteries.—FROUDE'S *England*. A more mercenary spirit,

virtues of roods and crucifixes, had no doubt, as Froude observes, "begun to grow uncertain to sceptical Protestants; and from doubt to denial, and from denial to passionate hatred, there were but few brief steps," so that when the "nuns were exposed to the wide world to seek their fortunes," there were few here to mourn their departure.

THE ABBEY,

As the modern mansion is called, stands on the west side of the quadrangle, the western front, shown in the following engraving, being built by one of the Burgoyne family, the

other portions of the nunnery being at the same time appropriated for offices. The interior of this mansion contains a wainscoted hall, dining and drawing rooms, with

---

according to other writers, actuated the king and nobility, in their suppression. See *Henwood Nunnery* in next chapter.

chimney pieces and various carvings. The front has a portico entrance and large bay windows. The entrance hall, which is forty feet long, is lofty, and the walls are covered with oak panelling. The dining and drawing rooms are also similarly embellished, the former having a fine carved oak chimney piece.4 The gardens, with a small lake, in front give a pleasing aspect, and the view extends over a quiet wooded country, but not so varied as some sites we have visited. Considerable additions and improvements are now in progress under the new proprietor.

Wroxhall in 1841 contained a population of 176, which had decreased to 145 in the year 1861. Twenty-four families resided here in 1563.*

Leaving the Abbey, and proceeding through the grounds in a different direction to that we approached it, we quickly arrive at the Birmingham and Warwick turnpike road, the northern course of which brings us speedily to Bedlams End, a cluster of houses called Chadwicke, and now forming a member of Baddesley. Taking the road to the left of the latter, and skirting Hay Wood, we soon reach

BADDESLEY CLINTON,

A small village in Hemlingford Hundred.5 This manor, formerly a member of Hampton-in-Arden, in which it was included in the Domesday survey, had at that time been

---

4. Previous to the late transfer of the property the hall contained a full-length portrait of Sir Christopher Wren, with a large coat of arms, and brackets with figures in armour, besides prints of the churches erected by him. The drawing room contained some portraits, carvings, and miniature effigies of the various orders of nuns.

5. The whole of the places before described are in Barlichway Hundred, as is the case with the next parish, Packwood. The remainder are all situate in Hemlingford.

* *Harl. MSS.*, 595.

given to Nigel de Albani, and was by him, or Roger de Mowbray, his son, granted to Walter de Bisege, *temp.* Henry I. In this family Baddesley continued three or four descents, till Sir Thomas de Clinton, of Coleshill, who had married Mazera, daughter of James de Bisege, granted it to James, the fourth son of the marriage, for his patrimony, he paying one penny per annum to his father's heirs, hence Baddesley *Clinton.* James was succeeded by Thomas, his son, whose two daughters afterwards came to the estate. With their descendants it continued almost uninterruptedly, till it was sold by one Nicholas Metley, a lawyer, *temp.* Henry IV. This Metley, by his will, ordered his body to be buried in the Temple church, London, and this manor to be sold by his executors, the proceeds thereof to be applied to the providing four priests to celebrate divine service for his soul and the souls of his ancestors, for one year after his death, or two priests for two years, and to provide another priest to do the same at Baddesley, for a like term, leaving his mother, his wife, and Robert Catesby, his executors. The first two sold the estate to the latter; but twenty years after, John Hugford, of Emscote, who had married Margaret, daughter of the above Nicholas Metley, gaining possession, Nicholas, son of Robert Catesby, seized and held it for several years, till he, in his turn, was ejected by the heirs of Hugford. Finding his title to be thus questionable, he sold it to one John Brome, of Warwick and Brome Hall,* who held lands in Baddesley prior to this time. This John Brome was high in office under the crown, in the reign of Henry VI, but ceased to have any public employment after the death of that monarch. In the 8th Edward IV he was mortally wounded by one John

* See p. 146.

Hurthill, steward to the earl of Warwick, in the porch of the Whitefriars' church, London, and was succeeded by his son Nicholas, who, three years after, slew John Hurthill in Longbridge field. The widow of Hurthill appealed against Nicholas Brome, on account of the murder of her husband; but through the mediation of friends, the matter was settled (12th Edward IV) by the latter agreeing to pay 100*l.* for the maintenance of a priest in St. Mary's church, Warwick, to say mass for one year, and to pray for the souls of John Brome and John Hurthill; and also to provide a priest, for two years, to sing mass in the church of Baddesley Clinton for the same souls. The manor and possessions at Baddesley after this came to Sir Edward Ferrers, who had married Constance, the daughter of Nicholas Brome; and in this family they have since remained. One of the family, Henry Ferrers, esq., (referred to at p. 145, as dying at Kingswood manor house, A.D. 1633,) left a curious poetical descent of Baddesley, in a document which was in possession of the family for some generations, but is now lost. The following is a copy:

"This Seat and Soyle from Saxon Bade, a man of honest fame,
Who held it in the Saxon's time, of Baddesley took the name
When Edward the Confessor did wear the English crown,
The same was then possessed by ——, a man of some renown;
And England being conquer'd, in lot it did alyghte
To Giffry Wirce, of noble birth, an Andegavian knighte;
A member Hamlet all this while, of Hampton here at hand,
With Hampton so to Moulbray went as all the Wirce's land.
Now Moulbray Lord of all doth part these two, and grants this one
To Bisege, in that name it runs awhile, and then is gone
To Clinton, as his heyre, who leeves it to a younger son;
And in that time the name of Baddesley Clinton was begun.
From them again by wedding of theirr Heyre, at first came
To Conisby, and after him to Foukes, who weds the same.
From Foukes to Dudley by a sale, and so to Burdet past;
To Mitley next, by Mitley's will it came to Brome at last.
Brome honours much the place, and after some descents of Bromes
To Ferrers, for a Daughter's parte of theyr's in match it comes:
In this last name it lasteth still, and so long—longer shall,
As God shall please, who is the Lord and King and God of all."

THE CHURCH,

Dedicated to St. James, stands on an eminence, some distance from any dwelling. It is small, and was at one time a chapel to Hampton-in-Arden, appropriated to the monastery at Kenilworth, with the church at that place and its other chapelries. The gift came from Roger de Mowbray, A.D. 1217, though it continued as a rectory, and was valued at two marks, 19th Edward I; at 3*l.* 6*s.* 8*d.* in 14th Edward III; and at 4*l.* 6*s.* 8*d.* in 26th Henry VIII. In 6th Edward VI the Church Goods were

> oon chalice, iij belles, a handbell, and a sacring bell.
> a pix, latyn.
> a cope, silke.
> iij vestm'ts, oon velvet, oon silke, oon dornix, w' iij albes to them.
> two altarclothes.
> a front of lether, gilt.
> two candlesticks, pewter.
> two cruetts, pewter.
> a pax, latyn.
> a corporys, w' a case.
> M'd. That the p'ishe have sold sithence the last s'vey to the repa'cion of theire churche, theis p'cells following:
> a cope, silke.
> a senser, latyn.
> a holywater tynke, latyn.
> a crosse, latyn.

The living is now united with Polesworth, and returned at 270*l.* The Rev. P. J. Brodie is the present incumbent.

The church consists of tower, nave, and chancel. The tower is embattled, having an external staircase at the corner adjoining the south side of the nave. The west doorway is a pointed arch under a square headed canopy or hood mould. Over this is a large pointed arched window of three lights, with good tracery heading. The belfry windows are of two lights, and the frieze or moulding under the battlements is ornamented with projecting carved heads, at the corners and centres of each face of the tower. This portion of the building is said to have been built, as a modern inscription on the south interior wall records, by "Nicholas Brome in the rayne of king Henry the Seaventh." Dugdale states that he had seen a document showing that Nicholas Brome, whom we

have referred to as killing John Hurthill, in revenge for the murder of his father, rebuilt the tower of this church from the ground, as also that at Packwood; and that he bought three bells for this, and raised the body of the church ten feet higher, all of which was noted in an inscription on his monument, then destroyed.

The nave and chancel have high ridge tiled roofs, and the windows of both are principally square headed, with the exception of the eastern window of the latter, which is an obtuse arch of five lights, in two ranges. The entrances to the church are by the southern pointed doorway in the nave, and by the priest's in the chancel, which is also pointed, having a flat moulding over the date, 1634, cut at the point of the arch.

The interior has been much neglected for years, and presents an unenviable contrast to the church last visited. The pews, with their once carved panelling, are fast falling to pieces, for want of timely repair; whilst a rickety gallery, with rough old stools for seats, appears destined to fall down from the same cause. A few ancient oak open benches remain. The open roof of the nave is of oak, nearly on a level with the point of a lofty arch separating it from the tower. The chancel division is by a low pointed arch, springing from piers in the wall, and a rude oak screen of no merit.

The upper portion of the east window is of stained glass. When Dugdale was here the figures and arms were perfect; and he relates that there were "portraitures of Sir Edward Ferrers, knight, and the lady Constance, his wife, with three sons and six daughters, all kneeling before St. George," with the scroll "*Sancte Georgi ora pro nobis,*" proceeding out of the knight's mouth, and accompanied with his and his wife's arms. This was in the upper part of the window. In the lower division was the picture of the same Sir Edward, and the lady Constance, with Nicholas Brome, her father, kneeling before a crucifix, another scroll from the lips of Sir Edward having "*Amor meus crucifixus est.*" Under these figures were four coats of arms of the Ferrers' and the families to whom they were allied. These, with the monument to the same Sir Edward, Dugdale intended to engrave, "that the beauty of them, which is so subject to perish by time and unhappy accidents, might have been represented to the world, for their lasting memory;" but the then heir of the family refusing to contribute to the expense, the intention of the learned antiquary was abandoned. What he feared might happen, has come to pass; the poor remains of what has escaped being now placed in the upper part of the window, in a miscellaneous manner. The centre light contains the Crucifixion, with a temple at the head. The northern light is filled in with Sir Edward and his wife kneeling before a faldstool, with books thereon, together with the scroll first named. The southern light has portions of figures, (heads and busts,) and the other scroll. The other two lights are filled with pieces of glass of no defined shape, such as heads, parts of animals, coats of arms, &c., evidently collected together and placed here for preservation.

The monument of Sir Edward, being of more enduring character, remains as Dugdale found it. It is an altar tomb with an arched canopy, and numerous armorial bearings, situate on the south side of the chancel. The following is the inscription:

> "Here lyeth Sir Edward Ferrers, Knight, son and heir of Sir Henry Ferrers and Margaret Hekstall his wife, of East Peckham, in the County of Kent, Knight. He died the xxixth day of August, 1535, leaving issue Henry, Edward, George, and Nicholas. Here also lieth Dame Constance his wife, daughter and heir to Nicholas Brome, Esquire, of this Mannour of Badsley Clinton, who died the xxxth day of September, 1551.
>
> "Here also lieth Henry Ferrers, their eldest son and heir, who married Catherine, one of the daughters and coheirs of Sir John Hampden, of Hampden in the Countie of Buck., Knight. He died Anno D. 1526, leaving issue Edward Ferrers, married to Briget, daughter to William Lord Windsor, of Bradenham, 1548, and died Anno Dom. 1564.
>
> *Ecce bic in pulvere dormimus. Hic nostræ resident gloria carnis. Disce mori mundo, Vivere disce Deo. Hodiæ nobis.*"

There were also several other monuments in honour of members of this family, and an inscription relating to the chancel, the latter of which only remains. It is on a stone over the priest's door, and to this effect, that

"Edward Ferrers, Esqvire, sonne &
heire of Henry Ferrers, Esqvire,
& Jane White his wife, did new
builde and reedifie this chauncel
at his owne proper costes &
charges Ano Domi 1634.
This Chvrch is dedicated to
Sainte James."

On the north wall are two hatchments, and a white mural tablet to the memory of Mrs. Helena Ferrers, late of Aylesbury House, *obiit* 29th January, 1840. Two old incised slabs are near to the priest's door, one having had a large brass plate and two coats of arms thereon. These, most probably, are the remains of the monuments named by Dugdale as "taken notice of" by Mr. Henry Ferrers in the time of queen Elizabeth, and then bearing the following inscriptions.

In the chancel upon a raised monument.

Hic jacet Beatrix Brome vidua, filia
Radulfi Shirley militis, quondam uxor
Johannis Brome de Badsley Clinton
armigeri; que obiit x die mensis Julii
anno Domini MCCCClxxxiii, cujus
anime propitietur Deus Amen.

Upon a marble slab, with a large brass of a man in armour.

Hic jacet Phillippus Purefey armiger
filius & heres Willielmi Purefey de
Shirford in Com. War. armigeri;
qui obiit xvi die mensis Septembris
anno Domini MCCCClxvi, cujus
anime propitietur Deus.

The communion table and rails are of plain old oak, the floor within the rails being paved with encaustic tiles. The font is an octagon without ornament, standing on a corresponding shaft. In the tower are three bells.

In the church-yard are several old grave stones, the inscriptions on all being illegible. It is a very secluded place, surrounded by woods and closely-timbered hedgerows; and it is only on the Sabbath that signs of life are seen here, and then but for a brief space. Then, indeed,

"Round its lone walls assembled neighbours meet,
And tread departed friends beneath their feet;
And new-briared graves, that prompt the secret sigh,
Show each the spot where he himself must lie."

Turning westward of the church-yard, we pass down an avenue of trees, and at the foot of the slope come to

BADDESLEY HALL,

The seat of the family of Ferrers, of whom frequent mention has been made. It is a fine specimen of the ancient fortified mansion; and since it is unique in the district we are describing, we may afford it a more particular and extended notice than other mansions have received. A dwelling house, belonging to John Brome, stood at Baddesley in the year 1450, as appears by a roll in possession of the family; but whether it is to be identified with the existing edifice is purely conjectural. The house, which is of low elevation, is of stone, encircled by a moat of considerable depth. It forms three sides of a square, the other side looking on to the moat from the inner quadrangle or court, which is now converted into a flower garden. A bridge of two arches, covered with ivy, conducts to the entrance. Here stood the drawbridge leading to

> "The strong postern gateway,
> Portcullised once,"

Which remains in its original state, under an embattled tower, the massive door strengthened with strong bolts and bars of iron. Passing through this gateway we come to the inner court, to the left of which we enter a spacious hall, in which there is an elaborately carved stone Elizabethan chimney-piece, with the arms of Ferrers in a circle in the centre, quartering Brome, Hampden, and White, surmounted with a helmet and the crest, a unicorn passant, ermine. In different portions are emblazoned other arms, scrolls, flowers, &c. This, as well as the oak panelling with which the hall is covered, was formerly painted, but has been recently restored by the present occupant, J. Muntz, esq. In the windows, too, are various arms and inscriptions connected with the alliances of the Ferrers family.

On the left of the hall is an oak panelled drawing room, having a large carved chimney-piece of the same material, containing the arms of Ferrers of Groby: The windows, likewise, abound in arms and memorials associated with family alliances. On the right is the dining room, which has a beautifully carved chimney-piece, date 1628, supported upon pillars of the Ionic and Corinthian orders, with arms,

Ferrers quartering White, in the centre. In this room are some good family portraits, and an additional series of arms and records of marriages embellishes the windows.

Ascending the stairs to the sleeping apartments, it will be found that nearly all are either wholly, or in part, lined with oak panelling, ornamented with carving or heraldic insignia. One chimney-piece, in a room called "The Ghost's Room," bears date 1634. The room extending over the gateway, named "The Banqueting Hall," contains portions of oak panelling round the windows at each end. These windows are square headed and of six lights, with stone mullions and transoms. In this room is an oak table extending the whole length; and on the walls are some family portraits. Beyond the Banqueting Hall is a small room formerly used as a chapel. In connection with the use to which this room was once appropriated, a curious bell is preserved, bearing a Flemish inscription, "*Jesus is* [*its*] *name*," and with the date 1548.[6] Several of the windows of the chambers, staircase, and passages, contain arms and other mementos of family history.

Descending by a back staircase, which leads to the kitchens and domestic offices, we find the walls of great thickness, differing much from other parts of the building, and indicating that they belonged to an earlier mansion once occupying this site.

Henry Ferrers, esq., and his son and successor, Edward, appear to have been the promoters of the embellishment of Baddesley House, if we may judge by the carvings and other ornaments, which are of this period: and it is not improbable that the former, who was well versed in anti-

6. This is probably the sacring bell enumerated at p. 205, and brought here from the church.

quities, was the designer of the alterations made in the hall; and also at the church, the chancel of which bears date the year after his decease, A.D. 1633.

The gardens, pleasure grounds, fish ponds, rookery, &c., outside the moat, are of some considerable extent, and well planned: From many points of these the view of the venerable remains is exceedingly striking and interesting.

The parish of Baddesley is extensive. Within its borders is a convent of nuns of the order of Poor Clares, which order was founded by St. Francis of Assissium, in the year 1212. It was established in 1850 by nuns from Bruges in Belgium, and there are now twenty-two nuns in the convent, Mary Victoria de Seille being the superioress. For many years previous to their settlement here, there had been a Roman Catholic Mission at Baddesley. The convent adjoins the chapel of the mission, and has no particular chaplain, the nuns attending all the services there. The present pastor is the Rev. B. Crosbie. The convent is a large brick building, but of no architectural importance.

In 1841 the population of Baddesley was 115, and 143 in 1861. There were only ten families in the year 1563.

Passing, by permission of the resident of the hall, through the private grounds, the road merges into another, leading the traveller to

PACKWOOD HOUSE,

A small mansion of the Stuart period, long the abode of the Fetherston family, a branch of the ancient stock of Fetherstonhaugh, of Fetherstonhaugh castle, in the county of Northumberland. They were here at an early period, and in the reign of Henry IV John Fetherston, and Emotta his wife, were members of the Guild at Knowle. In the time of the war between Charles I and the Parliament, another John Fetherston, residing here, appears to have been, in common with his neighbours, put to considerable expenses by one or both parties. In the following letter, still preserved among the family papers, he shows to what straits country gentlemen were reduced during this period.

"Good Brothr—I am in a great distraction concerninge my armor (being altogeither unable to satisffy my self in judgment and conscience what to doe) by reason of the genrall commands of the Kinge and Parliament: my protestacon putts me in mind that I am bound in conscience to serve both, and yet there seemes now a very great difference betweene them, wh I humbly desyer Almighty God, if it be his will, may be peaceably and timely composed and settled for the good of this throne and kingdome. I have not yet sent in my Armes, eyther to my lord of Northhampton, or Lord Brooke, because you know I am joyned wth Mr. Bettom, who is a known profest Papist, hee is to find the horse and man, and I ye armor and pettronells and sadle. If I should deliuer my Armes to Mr. Bettom's man, I should then haue done an act contrary both to the Kinge and Parliamt, who haue both declard that Papists are to be disarmd. I haue, therefore.......... my armor at yor house, and my pettronells I haue sent by my man now, and as for my sadle I cannot haue it from Mr. Bettom's: I understand that Mr. Dugdale lyeth at yor howse. I pray you prsent my Respects to him, and tell him my armes are there Ready, and I desyer they may be Imployed for the safety of the King and kingdome. And thus prayinge for a happy accomodacon of warr, with Remembranc of my love and best wyshes to you, I rest

"Yor dr louing Brother to his power,

"Jo. Ffetherston.

"My sistr & all my famyly are yet I thank God well, but now we are lately very much affrighted by Reason of a troup of horsemen, that cam to some of my neighbours howses and did disarme them and took away what they pleased undr coulor of taking of theire armes."

From the time of Henry IV until the year 1714, the estate descended from father to son, when Thomas Fetherston, esq., dying childless, bequeathed it to his great-nephew and namesake, son of William Fetherston, of Harbury. He dying also without issue in 1720, left it to his youngest sister, Dorothy, who married Thomas Leigh, esq.,[7] of Aldridge, in the county of Stafford. He assumed the surname of Fetherston before that of Leigh, and died at Packwood in 1755, leaving by his said wife, Dorothy Fetherston, one daughter, Catharine, who succeeded to the Packwood estate, and dying unmarried in 1769, willed it to Thomas, second son of William Dilke, esq.,[8] of Maxstoke castle, on condition that he and his successors, should bear the surname and arms of Fetherston only. This Thomas Fetherston, being killed by a fall from his horse, unmarried, in 1814, was succeeded by his brother, Charles Dilke, who also assumed the surname of Fetherston, and left two daughters, the elder of whom married, in 1833, her first cousin, John Dilke, eldest son of the Rev. John Dilke, rector of Packington, to whom the royal license was granted the same year, to bear the name and arms of Fetherston only, and who is father of the present possessor of the estate.

Packwood house was built on the site of one erected at a much earlier period; and it has since its erection been considerably altered. The park front, shown in our engraving, was built in 1634; but has been altered by the insertion of new windows, and the addition of a porch. A pillar sundial in front bears date 1660, and near to it is a dilapidated fountain, the water formerly spouting from a bear's head. The only part existing in its primitive style is one of the stables, which affords a rare specimen of the

7. He was great great-grandson of Sir Edward Leigh, knight, of Rushall, sheriff of Staffordshire, 26th and 44th Elizabeth and 1st James I, by Anne, second daughter of Sir John Fennon, knight, of Eston Neston, co. Northants, and Maud, daughter of Nicholas, lord Vaux, of Harrowden.

8. His mother was Mary, her half sister, only child of the above Thomas Fetherston Leigh, esq., by his second wife, Mary, eldest daughter of John Lane, esq., of Bentley Hall, and great-granddaughter of colonel Lane, who sheltered Charles II after the battle of Worcester.

massive oaken work of the period. The interior of the house affords nothing for special commendation, beyond a carved oak chimney-piece, two or three wainscoted rooms, and a few paintings by Vandervelde, Vandermeer, and Teniers, along with some family portraits.

The garden, adjoining the southern front of the house, is almost unique, remaining in pretty much the same state in which it was first laid out. It seems originally to have had, at each corner, a summer-house on a raised floor; and

three of these are yet to be found. By an iron gate we enter into another garden, or series of walks, the centre one bordered with Portuguese laurels, and columns of yews clipped into the shape of pyramids, &c. On each side of this gate are apertures, or niches, at the bottom of the walls, intended for an apiary, which was not found to prosper, by reason of mice and other vermin destroying the labours of the bees. Proceeding up the walk, or avenue, by a gradual ascent, we arrive at a terrace of similar character, having twelve yews rising, at equal distances, out of the thick clipped box hedge inclosing it; and in the centre of the southern hedge a spiral walk to an artificial mound, edged by a clipped box border of great thickness. The summit, which is crowned with a spreading yew, is equal in height to the house; and from it several beautiful views are obtained of portions of the park. Descending, it will increase the pleasure already experienced by the tourist, if he spend a little time in further exploration of the grounds of this

> "Rural seat,
> Whose lofty elms, and venerable oaks,
> Invite the rook."

The records of the family prove many of the trees to have been planted in the interval from 1669 to 1711. Amongst them are fine specimens of purple beech, flowering elm, variegated sycamore, &c. One large oak in the park, opposite to the stables, measures from the extremities of its branches one hundred and thirty feet.9 A pit, called "Spratt's Pit," of great depth, lies a little further southward: it was so designated in a deed of the time of Edward II.

About a mile north-west of the mansion are the church, the hall, and the parsonage, together with a few houses constituting the village of

PACKWOOD,

The greater number of residences belonging to which are scattered about, or near the different farms to which they appertain. The parish is of considerable acreage, and was once a member of Wasperton, near Warwick, and belonging

---

9. This oak forms the subject of the headpiece of the introductory chapter.

for some time to the monks of Coventry. The first mention of the place is in 7th Richard I, when it is stated that Philip de Kington levied a fine thereof to Roger de Charlecote. It was, however, again in possession of the monks of Coventry in 41st Henry III, when a grant of free warren in Packwood, as in all their other manors, was obtained; and three years after, on the appropriation of all the churches and tithes within their lands, this Packwood is specially noticed. On the foundation of the monastery at Coventry by earl Leofric, 7th Edward I, and the appropriation of lands here, he is described as lord of Packwood, amongst other places. At this time, the monks had two carucates of land in demesne, and two tenants, holding one yard of land by performing certain labours, being subject to such tax as the prior might impose: also six freeholders, who held two yards and a half of land at several rents, and suit of court twice a year. At the same time they had an inclosed park and an outwood, not within the precincts of any forest. In 19th Edward I, in the taxation of the temporalities of the religious houses, it is stated that the prior of Coventry had in *Pacwode* two carucates of land, with a water mill, and other privileges. These continued in their possession till the dissolution of monasteries. In the survey previous thereto, 26th Henry VIII, they had then here, rent of assize, 9*s*. 5*d*.; lands, tenements, pastures, and a mill, value 14*l*. 8*s*. 4*d*.; and the farm of the manor, 7*l*. 14*s*. 4*d*.; out of which was allowed to the bailiff, Thomas Hugyn, an annuity of 1*l*. 6*s*. 8*d*. On the dissolution, four years after, the king granted the manor and advowson to William Willington, and to William Sheldon who had married the latter's daughter, and to their heirs. This William Sheldon sold it to Robert Burdet, esq., of Bramscote; and by his grandson it was sold to Thomas Spenser, esq., of Claverdon, for 10,000*l.*, from whom it descended to Sir William Spenser, of Yarnton, Oxfordshire. It was afterwards in possession of Mr. Russell, of Warwick, who left it to his daughters, and who sold it to Sir Horace Mann. From him it came to the earl of Cornwallis, bishop of Lichfield, and is now the property of his great-grandson, Philip Wykeham Martin, esq., M.P. for Rochester.

PACKWOOD HALL,

With its moated inclosure, full of water, stands on the west side of the church-yard. Here, we may conclude, the priors and monks of Coventry maintained an establishment; and, from their well-stocked park of deer, and woods abounding in game, kept the refectory of their convent amply supplied. The hall is now occupied as a farm house, the moat extending round it, whilst an outer one, to the west, surrounds the agricultural buildings, rick yards, &c. The house has been lately rebuilt; but, to the curious in such matters, the moat, like others we have visited, exhibits a good example of those means of defence by which our ancestors provided for their safety in rude and troublous times.

Another farm house, southward of this, is still partly moated round. It was called "The Glass House," in the time of Charles I, from the number of its windows. In its original condition it occupied nearly the whole of the space inclosed by the moat. This house is on the Fetherston estate.

THE CHURCH,

Dedicated to St. Giles,[10] belonged, as before stated, to the

---

10. St. Giles was born at Athens, and after disposing of his property to charitable uses, travelled to France, where he became a hermit, and afterwards first abbot of Nismes, Charles Martel, king of France, having built that abbey for him. St. Giles died A.D. 795, and has, for some reason, ever since been regarded as the patron of lame persons and beggars generally.

monks of Coventry. It was reputed a chapel to Wasperton, in the reign of Henry VI, and therefore not presentative. The curate had then the small tithes and the altarage for his stipend, the monks retaining the tithe corn and all living mortuaries. His stipend, with the glebe, was valued,

26th Henry VIII, at 5*l.* per annum. In 36th Elizabeth, the chapel here was granted to Edward Wymerke, and is designated *Capella de Pacwode cum pertinentiis.*

The commissioners return as at *Pacwoode*, in 1551,

j chalice & iij belles, a handebell.
iiij vestment, two vellet, two saye.
ij copes, one silke, one saye.
one pixe, coper.
a crosse, laten.
ij cruett.
ij candlestickes.
ij sensor.
iij towell.
ij altarclothes.

The living is now a perpetual curacy, returned as of the

value of 100*l.*, but is really little more than 60*l.* The Rev. R. W. Johnson is the present incumbent.

The church,[11] or chapel, stands apart from the village, with no house near except the hall, and a cottage formerly the parsonage. It consists of a nave and a chancel, with tiled ridged roofs, and a tower with five bells, the first and fifth the gift of Thomas Fetherston, esq., in 1686, in which year the other three were recast. On the south side is a timber-framed porch, and on the north a brick-built transept, not at all in keeping with the rest of the building. The tower, which is embattled, is ascended by a spiral staircase, projecting from the south-east angle of the wall. It is in all its main features similar to that of Baddesley, being built, according to tradition, *temp.* Henry VII, by the same person and for the same reason. The proof of the latter is wanting; but evidence of the person who erected it may be gleaned from an inscription that formerly existed in one of the windows to the following effect:

"Orate pro anima Nicholai Brome qui Campanile de Pacwood fieri fecit."

The windows of the nave and chancel are of the usual pointed arch character, the one at the east end being of three lights. The interior is partly pewed, and partly seated with rough open benches, having a small gallery at the tower end, which has cut in two the oldest monument in the church, date 1610. The roof of the nave, by being ceiled, is hid in a very unsightly manner; and the insertion, at the time this was done, of six dormer windows, was no improvement. At the eastern end of the nave is a piscina, the arch and finial of which have been recently restored.

---

11. Here, as in the instance of Henley, we have designated this a church, because, as the sole edifice for parochial worship, it is generally so called.

The tower arch is pointed and lofty, and the chancel is divided from the nave by one of similar character, under which are remains of the screen and rood, surmounted by a large wooden cross, recently added. There is a piscina in the south wall of the chancel, under a pointed arch; and in the east window a representation of the Crucifixion in very ancient stained glass. Under this, a few years since, was inserted another subject, "The Descent from the Cross," after Rubens, the work of a young Birmingham artist, presented by the late Mr. Samuel Fullard.

The transept, as an inscription records, was erected in 1704, by Thomas Fetherston, esq., and a vault made under the same, "for himself and his posterity." The transept is lighted by a modern semicircular headed window; but, with the exception of the monumental tablets on the walls to the memory of members of the Fetherston family, some of which are of good sculpture, there is nothing of particular interest.

In the chancel there are several mural monuments to the memory of the Aylesbury family, former owners and residents of Aylesbury House. There is also a large mural monument in the nave, to the memory of John Fetherston, esq., of Packwood House, *obiit* 1679. The arms of Woodward are impaled with those of Fetherston, over the inscription. This gentleman had two wives, each named Isabella Woodward, daughters of two John Woodwards, one of Butlers Marston, and the other of Avon Dassett.

The communion table and rails are of the usual character we have described. The font is circular, on an octagonal shaft, and near to it is the parish chest; a venerable relic of the strength of materials applied to such articles in olden times.

The register of this church furnishes an interesting entry

of the marriage of the parents of the great lexicographer, Dr. Johnson, the time and place of which does not appear to have been known to his numerous biographers.[12]

1706. "Michell Johnsones of Lichfeld and Sara Ford maried June ye 19th."

The parsonage house, a modern building, is in a pleasant situation north of the church, and in the direction of

AYLESBURY HOUSE,

Formerly a mansion of some note in this part of Warwickshire. The family settled at it was a branch of the Aylesburys of Edstone, (see p. 58,) who possessed property here, in Solihull, and other places in the county. The branch located at this place occupied it for many generations, and several members of the family are buried in the parish church, as before related. The house, standing a field from the road leading from Packwood, is a plain brick building, of the time of the Stuarts, with a large open garden to the south. Traces of fish ponds, and of more extended pleasure grounds than now exist, may be easily recognized around the house.

A short distance west of Aylesbury House is

HOCKLEY HEATH,

A member of Packwood, consisting of a scattered group of

---

12. In the biographies of the Doctor, though particulars of his parents and birth are given, no mention is made of the time and place of their marriage. This entry can refer to no other parties. Boswell, *Life of Johnson*, says "His father was a native of Derbyshire, Michael by name, and his mother was Sarah Ford, descended of an ancient race of substantial yeomanry in Warwickshire." Quoting *Malone*, Croker says his father was born in 1656, and "died at Lichfield in 1731, at the age of 76. Sarah Ford, his wife, was born at King's Norton, in the county of Worcester, in 1669, and died at Lichfield in January, 1759, in her 90th year." Samuel Johnson was the eldest of two children, both boys, and was born September 18th, 1709. King's Norton is only a few miles from Packwood.

houses, that principally sprang up in consequence of the two inns, which in the old posting times, before railways were known, and when

"The twanging horn o'er yonder bridge"

announced the fast-going coaches then on the road between London and Birmingham, existed here for the convenience of travellers. These, in our days of express trains, are dim reminiscences. The glory of inns has departed; the larger of the two here has been converted into a private residence, and the other figures as a plain roadside public house.

The population of Packwood was 350 in 1841, and 292 in 1861.

Leaving this parish we may make our way to Knowle. In doing so, the traveller will pass the station on the Great Western Railway, and near to Darley Mill, probably the site of the prior of Coventry's mill in 19th Edward I: Afterwards his course will be in a direct line to that place, where he may rest for the night.

Seventh Day.

FOR this day's recreation of the traveller we shall confine our descriptions and journey to the considerable town of Knowle, the interesting hamlet of Temple Balsall, the nunnery of Henwood, and the ancient manor of Langdon. These are all of great historical interest, the churches of fine architecture, and will repay a lengthened inspection.

KNOWLE

Was anciently another member of Hampton-in-Arden, and is consequently not noticed in Domesday Book. It is first mentioned in king John's time, when William de Arden, of Hampton,[1] granted it to Amicia de Tracey, his wife, as part of her dower. In 35th Henry III, Hugh de Arden, his son, had grant of free warren in all his demesne lands in Knowle. William, son of the latter, had a lawsuit with

---

1. This William de Arden had also a residence here, for by an agreement, A.D. 1217, between himself and the canons of Kenilworth, relative to the advowson of the church at Hampton-in-Arden, it was provided that the said William, his heirs, and their families, should have liberty to hear divine service in his chapel at Knowle.

Peter de Montfort and others, relative to certain lands here; and, on his death, his widow had Knowle assigned to her as part of her dowry. This William and his brother Richard dying without issue, Knowle came to one of the coheiresses, Amicia, wife of John de Lou, who sold it to Eleanor, wife of Edward I. After her death, 20th Edward I, it, with other manors, was given to the monks of Westminster, on condition that, on the eve of St. Andrew, the abbot and monks should sing a *Placebo* and a *Dirige*, with nine lessons; one hundred wax candles, weighing twelve pounds each, being kept burning about her tomb, and every year new ones being supplied for that purpose; that those candles should be lighted on every eve of the same anniversary, and burn till high mass was ended; that, all the bells then ringing, they should sing solemnly for her soul's health, each monk saying a private mass, the inferior monks their whole psalter, and the friars' converts the Lord's Prayer, &c., for her soul and the souls of all the faithful departed. These and numerous other ceremonies and expenses, gifts to the poor, &c., were enjoined on the convent by a charter dated Berwick-upon-Tweed, 20th October, 20th Edward I, all of which being performed, the surplus of the revenue derived from Knowle was to be expended as "they themselves should best like."

The monks of Westminster leased these lands, 34th Edward I, for life to Ralph de Perham, and in 8th Edward II he paid a fine of twenty marks to the king for a confirmation of the grant of the manor of Knowle and Grafton, and other hamlets thereto belonging;* but afterwards they retained them in their own hands. They thus continued till

* *Rot. Orig.*, i, 230.

the dissolution of the abbey by Henry VIII, when Westminster becoming a bishopric, they were annexed to it.

The return made by the commissioners from the monastery of St. Peter at Westminster* was as follows:

Office of the Guardian of the Manor of Queen Eleanor.

Warwick.

	£.	s.	d.
Is worth in rents of assise, with rents & farms in Knolle - - - - - - - -	52	7	6
Site of the manor there - - - - - -	12	0	0
Perquisites of the court there, every year - -	0	58	4
Sale of trees there, every year - - - - -	0	50	0
In the whole as appears by the declaration, thence made - - - - - - - -	69	15	10

Dugdale† states the possessions of the abbey here to have been:

	£.	s.	d.
Rents of free assize & customary holdings - -	17	13	9
New rents - - - - - - - -	18	3	1½
Moveable rents - - - - - - -	0	5	2½
Rents & fee farms - - - - - - -	19	7	5
Tallages of customary holdings - - -	2	15	2½
Farm of the park - - - - - - -	0	13	4
Perquisites of the court - - - - - -	2	18	10
Farm of the manor - - - - - -	12	0	0

In 4th Edward VI, Westminster was made a deanery with secular canons, and the jurisdiction of the bishop united to London. In 1556, Edmund Bonner, then bishop of that see, leased the manor, for ninety-nine years, to Sir John Cope, who assigned it the following year to his son George Cope. On its resumption by the crown, 2nd Elizabeth, this queen, 13th of her reign, granted it to Robert, earl of Leicester, and his heirs, who exchanged it again, 23rd of Elizabeth, for other lands under the queen, so that it again reverted to the crown. King

* *Valor Ecclesiasticus*, i, 416. † *Monasticon*, i, 330; ed. 1830.

James, 20th of his reign, granted it to Sir Fulke Greville, knight, lord Brooke, to be held of the manor of East Greenwich, for the rent of 67*l.* 16*s.* 8*d.* per annum. With the Grevilles, who left several excellent charities for education, &c., it continued till A.D. 1743. It afterwards came into the hands of a branch of the Greswolde family, and in the division of the property in 1848-9, the manor and advowson of the church were sold to J. W. Unett, esq.

THE CHURCH.

This fine old collegiate church strikes the eye on entering the village, as far beyond the requirements of the parish. It was built in the latter part of the reign of Richard II, by Walter Cooke, canon of Lincoln, who, it is stated, "bearing a special affection to this place, from its distance from the parish church, did, for the health of his own and his parents' souls, erect a fair chapel here, with a tower-steeple and bells, on his father's own land." The place was then said to have contained about fifty houses, several inns, and a town-hall, and situate a mile from Hampton-in-Arden, though it is three of our present miles. The chapel he dedicated to the honour of St. John the Baptist, St. Lawrence the Martyr, and St. Anne,[2] and he added to it a church-yard, and endowed a priest to celebrate divine service, to baptize all infants born in the hamlet, and to bury all persons there deceased. To further this he obtained of pope Boniface IX a special bull, containing an indulgence for seven years for all who did penance, and made confession there, on certain saints and holy days, and who bestowed something at such times for the repairs. He also obtained, 1st Henry IV, a license to celebrate divine service from John Burghill, bishop of Lichfield and Coventry, and another the same year from the king, to Walter Cooke and Adam, his father, to found a chantry of one or two priests, to celebrate the same perpetually in the same chantry, the patronage of which the said Walter granted to the monks of Westminster.

The church consists of a tower, nave, north and south aisles, north transept or chapel, and a large chancel. The tower is embattled, and has a projecting staircase at the south-east angle. The nave has five clerestory windows on each side, and is embattled on the south, with pinnacles at intervals, the embattlement being a few inches lower over the fifth window, and taking line with the chancel. The

---

2. *St. Lawrence*, one of the most celebrated martyrs of the church, was by birth a Spaniard, and suffered a most cruel death in the year 258. He is said to have been, by the order of Valerian, prefect of Rome, laid on a gridiron, and live coals, nearly extinguished, thrown under it, where he remained calm, till death put an end to his sufferings.

St. Anne was mother of the Virgin Mary. The Latin church celebrated her day with great pomp, and attribute many miracles to her relics, which were brought from Palestine to Constantinople, and afterwards dispersed in the west.

pinnacles have huge grotesque heads, feet, and wings, as gargoyles, at their base. The north side, which has a plain parapet, has some of its pinnacles broken, the gargoyles remaining in tolerable preservation. The south aisle is embattled, and in other particulars corresponds with the nave, as does also the chancel parapet. The windows throughout the whole church are nearly all of pointed architecture, those of the chancel being larger, and exceedingly fine. Under each chancel window, nearest the east, are surbast arches, and on a buttress above a carved headless fowl. The church, which has no north or south door, is entered by a pointed arched doorway in the western face of the tower, over which is a pointed window of three lights. Passing through the tower, under a large acutely pointed arch, the interior of the church presents a pleasing appearance to the spectator. The nave is separated from the south aisle by four octagonal pillars supporting pointed arches, whilst on the north are three of like character, with pointed arches, and one half pillar and pier, with an obtuse arch, forming the division of the north transept or chantry. The centre light of one of the windows of the south aisle is of stained glass, illustrative of the woman touching the garment of Christ, with the verse "Thy faith hath saved thee; go in peace." It was placed here "To the memory of Thomas Satchwell," and others. The tracery in the north window of the chapel is filled with various fragments of ancient stained glass. The whole of the church has open timber roofs, the one in the chantry having carved beams and bosses. The chancel is separated from the nave by the rood screen,[3] there being no arch or depression of roof.

3. The rood loft had its name from the rood or crucifix, anciently set up in the middle of it. Here some of the lessons, and other parts of the liturgy,

This screen is one of the very few perfect specimens of such ornaments now to be met with. It is exquisitely carved, and had formerly, on the beam over it, painted whole length figures of the Virgin, of saints, and angels. It has been removed during the recent alterations, from the west to the east side of the chantry, but its removal leaves the chancel still spacious and imposing. The windows of the chancel, as before stated, are particularly fine, and the peculiarity of clerestory windows over two of them, is worthy of note as an unusual arrangement. In the upper part of the east window, portions of coloured glass still remain. In the chancel were formerly seven carved oak stalls on the north side, and six on the south.[4] In the south wall was a sedilia of four stalls, high in the wall and of unequal lengths, with carved arches and finials, and a cornice of oak leaves. Part of these have been walled up in the new arrangements of the choir. The altar table is carved, with large bossed legs, similar to others before described, and the rails inclosing it are of carved open screen work. The whole of the chancel floor is laid with Minton's tiles.

The font, which is octagonal, with quatrefoils on each face, stands on an octagonal base or shaft. In the tower are three bells.

In 1860 the interior of the church was restored to something of its ancient state, by the removal of high pews and a gallery, and the substitution of open benches in the body of the church. The old pulpit has been removed, and

---

used to be sung, before the change of religion. Very few of the ancient rood lofts remain perfect in parish churches, strict injunctions for their demolition being issued in the first year of the reign of queen Elizabeth.

4. These stalls have been removed and the best portions fixed at the east end of the south aisle. The carvings were particularly well executed, and the most prominent, a lion and a unicorn, are now fixed on two iron brackets under the tower.

replaced by a richly carved one on the south side, with a reading desk on the north. The chancel seats, with finials of elegant foliage, have been renewed, and the Commandments, Lord's Prayer, and Creed, richly illuminated on a slab, placed under the eastern window. The cost of these restorations was upwards of 1000*l.*, raised by the subscriptions of the inhabitants and friends, stimulated by the zeal of the present incumbent: They were carried out very successfully by the contractor, Mr. Corbett, from designs and under the superintendence of Mr. Neville, of Coventry.

This old collegiate church was once exceedingly rich in monumental slabs and inscriptions, and its windows equally so in coloured glass, nearly the whole of which time and the ruthless hand of man have destroyed. Dugdale particularizes and engraves the arms of Aylesbury, Somerville, Belknap, Brome, Ferrers, Marrow, and others then in the windows, as also a kneeling figure of Thomas Dabridgecourt in armour, in a window on the south side of the chancel. Separate inscriptions also existed, in various windows, calling on the faithful to "Pray for the souls" of Nicholas Brome, Edward Ferrers, Thomas Dabridgcourt, Thomas Marrow, Johanne Arnot, William Wigston, and Lawrence Eborall. He relates, also, that a fair marble lay in the chancel whereon had been a figure in brass, which tradition stated to have been of Walter Cooke, the founder of the church. Near to it was another, having brass effigies of a man, his two wives, and twelve children, and the following inscription:

> Of your charity pray for the Souls of Mr. John Dabriggcourt, Esquire, who deceased the xvi day of July, An. MDxliiii, and for the soules of Katherine and Elizabeth his wives, on whose soules Jesus have mercy. Amen.

One other monument was to the memory of Elizabeth, wife of Thomas St. Nicholas, of Ashe, Kent, *obiit* March 9, 1631.

Of these, the first, considered to be the founder's, still remains in the centre of the chancel entrance. It is a circular grey stone, four feet in diameter, and had formerly a circular border of brass, and, in the centre, a scroll and two shields. The Dabridgecourt slab lies near, but the figures and inscription have been stolen.

Mr. Vincent, writing in 1592, when he visited the churches, &c., in this neighbourhood, says, "Here is the picture of a man like a country m'chant, w'th a side cassock and a square pouch, under written Rich. Wright. And this Wright was the .... upp sc old sq'ire Christopher Wright."*

Here also, sixty years ago, were monuments to the memory of the Grevilles, Greswoldes of Malvern Hall, Spooners of Henwood Hall, and Dousets. There are now in the church others commemorating various members of the Grimshaw and Wilson families, and others.

The living of Knowle was returned to the commissioners of Queen Anne's Bounty at 15*l.* 13*s.* 4*d.* It is now of the value of 126*l.* The Rev. J. Howe is the present incumbent.

THE COLLEGE OR GUILD.5

The munificent canon of Lincoln, Walter Cooke, referred to as the builder of the church, and founder of the chantry therein, conferred still further benefit on the place, by the

5. Antiquaries differ considerably as to the nature and object of these institutions. Guilds were common in England before the Reformation, and by some are supposed to have been friendly associations; by others, trading companies; and, by some, of a purely religious nature, having for their object the administration of spiritual consolation. Whatever their design, it appears certain that the general good of their members was the principal intent of these guilds, so as to produce, by union, that which could not have been accomplished by individual exertion. For an Account of Guilds, see Appendix.

* *Harl. MSS.*, No. 2129, fol. 161.

establishment of a guild, for which he obtained, 14th Henry IV, a license to himself, and others who, from devotion, should join him in the work. The fraternity was thus established at Knowle, but as the founder's preferment increased in the church, he, with the assistance of Elizabeth, widow of John, lord Clinton, obtained another license, 4th Henry V, that they and their executors might found a college of ten chantry priests; one to be the rector, to pray for the good estate of them both, in this life and after death, and for the souls of their parents and friends, as also of all the faithful deceased. The Guild had a common seal, and was famous and popular in its earlier days, many of the nobility and eminent personages in the neighbourhood, as appears by the register, being members of the fraternity, amongst whom we have mention of Aylesbury, Somerville, Brome, Belknap, Ferrers, Marrow, Eborall, &c., whose arms were in the chapel windows when Dugdale visited it. The prosperity of the college and guild appears to have declined previous to the Dissolution of Religious Houses; for 26th Henry VIII,* when the survey took place, there were only two priests and the rector, John Townesend, on the foundation, and the return of their income as follows:

COLLEGE OR GUILD OF KNOLL.

Master John Townesend, Rector or Custodian of the Chapel of the said College.

Lands and tenements belonging to the said chapel.

The same renders an account of 20*l.* 15*s.* 2*d.*, from the total rent of all the lands and tenements whatsoever pertaining to the said chapel, within the domain of Knoll, in the county of Warwick: which domain or manor of Knoll belongs to the abbot and convent of the monastery of Westminster in the county of Middlesex, and the said custodian does not receive any other rents or profits for the sustentation and for the stipend of

* *Valor Ecclesiasticus*, ii, 75.

himself and of two other chaplains there serving God, annually, and to which he is held for ever.

Sum - - - 20*l.* 15*s.* 2*d.*

Sum total of the whole - - - 20*l.* 15*s.* 2*d.*, of which

Repayment of Rent.

	£.	s.	d.
The same accounts in rent repaid to the abbot of the monastery of Westminster, for the land there, annually	1	15	0
And there is allowed to the same for rent repaid to the prior of St. John of Jerusalem in England, annually	0	6	6
And there is allowed to the same for rent repaid to the prior and convent of the monastery in the city of Coventry, annually	0	0	6
Sum - - - - - -	2	2	0

Charitable Gifts.

	£.	s.	d.
And there is allowed to the same for charitable gifts, given on the anniversary day of Walter Coke, the founder of the chapel, as appears by the foundation and ordination of the said Walter, annually 3*s.*, and on the anniversary day of Thomas Kyxley, lately rector there, one of the benefactors of the same chapel, annually 4*s.* 8*d.*, in all	0	7	8
Sum - - - - - - -	0	7	8
Sum of the allowances - - - - - -	2	9	8
And there remains clear, beyond the aforesaid allowances, annually	18	5	6
The tenth part of this sum - -	1	16	6¾

The return of the revenues of the chantry was 29*l.* 14*s.* 7*d.* per annum, there being at that time three chantry priests, daily singing in the said chapel.

In the year 1553, John Browne and John Wright, incumbents, had each a pension of 5*l.* 6*s.* 8*d.*

An old half-timbered building, west of the church, is pointed out as the ancient college or guild house, and is generally believed, by the inhabitants, to have been such college, or the mansion of the founder or his family.

The village of Knowle is larger than many in this

locality, and, like similar places, broken up into groups of a few houses, there being no continuous line of shops, &c. It had formerly a market, and still retains a fair, which is, at the present day, of little account. There is a free school for boys and girls, endowed by the Hon. Algernon Greville, and another endowment by the Hon. Sarah Greville for clothing and educating boys for three years. There is a small dissenting chapel in the village.

The opening of the Great Western Railway, on which line there is a station for Knowle, has much improved its condition. Several new houses have been built, and others are in progress, and the healthy situation, as its name implies,[6] inviting the capitalist, its population in a few years appears likely to be considerably increased. Near to the station, distant about a mile from the village, the Dorridge estate has recently been laid out in building lots, and a new colony is already forming there.

The returns in 1861 give 1200 inhabitants as the population of the whole hamlet, in 1841 there were 1208. The number of families, *temp.* Elizabeth, were included in the return from Hampton-in-Arden.

From Knowle to Temple Balsall the traveller will pass through a succession of richly varied scenery. Quiet lanes with overhanging trees, which in the spring and summer are resonant with the song of birds, abound here; whilst the hedgerows are adorned with the variegated beauty of flowers which bloom in wild profusion all along the path the tourist will pursue.

---

6. Our old English *Cnolle* signifieth the knap of a hill, or an ascending ground.—*Dugdale.*

> "From hill and dale new scenes arise:
> The distant plough slow moving, and beside
> His labouring team, that swerved not from the track,
> The sturdy swain diminished to a boy!
> Hedgerow beauties numberless, square tower,
> Tall spire, from which the sound of cheerful bells
> Just undulates upon the listening ear,
> Groves, heaths, and smoking villages,"

all in succession meet and charm the eye, and lead us pleasantly on.

A short distance from Knowle, on the right hand side of the road, a modern-built house indicates the site of the ancient

KNOWLE HALL.

From the antiquity of the latter house this place lays claim to special notice. It was a large stone building, with a good frontage, its doorway sheltered by a portico, or porch, the side wings extending from the front a considerable distance along the lawn, so as to make the edifice occupy three sides of a square. The lawn and garden was protected from the road by a stone wall, having pillars at the angles and the gate in the centre.[7] The time of its erection is unknown, but it was pulled down about fifteen years ago. The manor of Knowle being leased, 4th Mary, by bishop Bonner to Sir John Cope for ninety-nine years, he, in the following year, assigned it to his youngest son, George Cope, who appears to have resided at this hall till his decease in 1572; and there is a very curious inventory and valuation still extant of his effects, now in the possession of the Fetherston family. In it are enumerated the goods in the hall, the gatehouse, in *Anthonie's* and his own chamber, in fifteen other offices and apartments, in the mill, and a

7. Knowle Hall, before its destruction, forms the subject of the initial letter to this chapter.

long list of horses, cattle, sheep, and pigs, besides many kinds of workmen's tools and agricultural implements. It afterwards came into the possession of the Greswolde family, and then to the Palmers, of Olton End, from the latter of whom it came to Greswolde Lewis, esq. On his death the families of Wilson and Wigley, coheirs, obtained an Act of Parliament, empowering them to divide the Greswolde estates. In this partition Knowle Hall fell to the share of the Wilsons; and at the death of the Rev. — Wilson, William, his son, sold it to R. E. Wilson, esq., who now resides at the hall.

Approaching Balsall, on the left hand stands

SPRINGFIELD HOUSE,

The seat of the Boultbee family. It is a modern brick building of no very marked features, and is distinguished by the greenhouses, pleasure grounds, and fish ponds common to country mansions.

TEMPLE BALSALL.

No mention is made of Balsall in Domesday Book. At that time it constituted one of the many members of the extensive parish of Hampton-in-Arden, passing, like the rest, to Roger de Mowbray, who gave this portion of his possessions to the Knights Templars,[8] hence *Temple Balsall.* The Knights Templars, on taking possession of

8. The Knights Templars were instituted A.D. 1118, and were so called from having their first residence in some rooms adjoining to the Temple at Jerusalem. Their business was to guard the roads for the security of pilgrims in the Holy Land, and their rule, that of canons regular of St. Austin; their habit was white, with a red cross on their left shoulder. Their coming into England was probably pretty early in the reign of king Stephen, and their first seat in Holborn.—*Preface to Tanner's Not. Mon.*

this manor, erected a house and church for their order, sending some of their brethren to reside here, and making it a Preceptory,[9] subordinate to the Temple in London. In addition to this manor, they soon had grants of lands from divers devout and pious persons, viz. the manors of Barston, Sherborne, and Flechampsted, besides smaller grants in numerous other places, for the benefit of the fraternity residing here. These they continued to enjoy till the 1st of Edward II, when, according to Stow, the whole of the order of Knights Templars in England were attached by their bodies, and kept in safe custody, though not in hard or vile prison, until the king did otherwise ordain, and their lands, tenements, and goods, as well ecclesiastical as temporal, with all their charters and writings, were seized and taken into the king's hand.*

Other privileges which they enjoyed in Balsall were free warren in all their demesne lands, by charter of 32nd Henry III, a weekly market on Thursdays, and two fairs annually. Roger de Mowbray, 13th of Edward I, confirmed all their rights as granted by Roger de Mowbray, his father, for which they made him partaker of all their prayers and spiritual benefits.

The order of Templars being suppressed, their possessions reverted to the original donors; but they were shortly after given, by the king, to another order called the Knights Hospitallers.[10]

---

9. Preceptories were manors or estates of the Knights Templars, where they placed some of their fraternity under the government of one of those most eminent Templars who had been by the Grand Master created "Præceptores Templi," to take care of the lands and rents in that place and neighbourhood, and so were only cells to the principal house in London.

10. This order took its name from an hospital, built at Jerusalem, for the use of pilgrims coming to the Holy Land, and dedicated to St. John the

* *Stow's Chronicle*, 214.

In 33rd Edward III, they were in possession of fifty messuages and fifty virgates of land in Temple Tysoe, Temple Hardwicke, Newbold Pacey, and of the manor of Sherborne.* Leland, (time of Henry VIII,) speaking of Warwick, says "There is a chappell of St. John in the Bridge End suburbe, that belonged to the Priory of St. John's in London. The landes of this came to the Commandery of Balleshalle." †

The new proprietors do not, however, appear to have always held this place as a Commandery,[11] by the residence of any of their fraternity; for, in the time of Edward IV, John Beaufitz, esq., was the farmer of the house at Temple Balsall, and resided in it. Some of the customs and services of the tenantry in early times (on which we have remarked at p. 24) were in operation here; for, among other obligations, the tenants of the Hospitallers were yearly to mow three days in harvest, one at the charge of the house, and to plough three days, one at like charge. They were also to reap one day, at which time they were allowed one ram, or eightpence, twenty-four loaves, and a cheese of the best in the house, together with a full pint of drink. They were not allowed to sell the horse colts, if

---

Baptist. They were instituted about A.D. 1092, and were very much favoured by Godfrey of Bulloigne, and his successor Baldwin, king of Jerusalem. They followed chiefly St. Austin's rule, and wore a black habit with a white cross upon it. They soon came into England, and had a house built for them in London, A.D. 1100; and from a poor and mean beginning, obtained so great wealth, honours, and exemptions, that their superior here in England was the first lay baron, and had a seat among the lords in Parliament."—*Preface to Tanner*, p. 24.

11. Commanderies were the same among the Knights Hospitallers as Preceptories were among the Templars, viz. societies of those knights placed upon some of their estates in the country, under the government of a Commander, who were allowed proper maintenance out of the revenues under their care, and accounted for the remainder to the Grand Prior in London.

* *Dugdale's Monasticon*, vii, 800. † *Leland's Itinerary*, iv, 65.

foaled on the land belonging to the Temple, without the consent of the fraternity, nor to marry their daughters without their license.

The dissolution of the monasteries swept this, together with their other manors, from the possessions of the Hospitallers. Temple Balsall, like Rowington, was assigned for the dowry of queen Katharine, last wife of Henry VIII. In the 1st of Edward VI, the reversion was granted to Edward, duke of Somerset, and his heirs, to hold by the fortieth part of a knight's fee; but he being attainted in the 6th of the same reign, it came again to the crown, and was given to John Dudley, earl of Warwick. Upon his attainder, in Mary's reign, the queen granted it to Edward, lord Dudley; but it came again to the crown; for the queen, intending to restore the order of Knights Hospitallers in London to part of its ancient splendour, and having made Sir Thomas Tresham, knight, lord prior thereof, bestowed the manor of Balsall upon the order. Dying, her successor, queen Elizabeth, by letters patent, in the 8th of her reign, granted it to Robert Dudley, earl of Leicester, and his heirs. Coming to his granddaughter lady Katherine Leveson, she, by will, gave the whole of this estate, in trust, for the building of an almshouse for the perpetual sustenance of aged and infirm females, for ever, which endowment amounts at the present day to a large income.

THE TEMPLE.

The ancient hall, or refectory of the knights, is situate near to the church. It is now a receptacle for lumber, but was formerly a magnificent apartment, framed wholly of timber, and divided by large wooden pillars into a nave and two aisles, with crossbeams supporting the roof, which still remain. It is 140 feet long; and was, without doubt, when furnished and decorated with the arms of the most eminent members of the fraternity, a goodly room. At the west end is a small room, with several coats of arms, where the Court Leets are now held. Affixed to the walls of the room are thirteen emblazoned shields taken from some former building. One is the coat of arms of William Weston, the last prior of St. John's previous to the Reformation. Dugdale engraves five coats as here in his time, and describes them as painted on the ceiling of a chamber of the house. They have lately been correctly restored, and attached to the wall.

The most perfect relic of the institution of the Knights Templars here is

THE CHURCH,

Dedicated[12] to St. Mary, and standing a short distance east of these buildings.

After the suppression of the order, it fell into decay, the dilapidations increasing till the year 1677. When the property became lady Leveson's, she directed by her will that it should be put into a complete state of repair. By means of this reparation it is thought that the roof, gable terminations, and the upper part of the tower, were rebuilt. The church was further restored in the year 1849, when the upper part of the tower, then square, and not in harmony with the other portion, was taken down to the head of the supporting buttress, rebuilt in a like octagonal form,

---

12. "There was no dedication of our Christian churches to saints, until praying to saints was in use; and after churches began to be dedicated to saints, their dedication feasts were usually kept on that day, which was the feast day appointed in the calendar, for commemoration to that saint to whom such church was particularly dedicated. This time was called with us *The Wakes*, for waking, as the Latin word *Vigilæ*, or *Vigilando*, because at such times the people prayed most of the night before such feast day in the churches."—*Antiquarian Repertory*, ii, 425.

and surmounted by a turret, having apertures on each face under it, and smaller ones on four of the faces of the turret. A continuous parapet, with a course of finely carved heads, corresponding with that on the west end gable, was run round the tower, and extended along the southern side, with the addition of pinnacles at the head of each buttress. The interior was restored at the same time. The arrange-

ment of the tower, as will be seen by the engraving, is not what is usual in ecclesiastical buildings, so that it constitutes one of the principal features of this interesting church, which forms one continuous and noble apartment, or hall, of equal width and height throughout. The roof is a semi-circular timber frame, with battens above, supported by carved stone bosses.

At first entrance the extraordinary beauty of the *tout ensemble* of the interior instantly arrests attention: its noble windows filled with varied tracery, (only two being of the same pattern,) completely captivating the eye. The fine west window of five lights, the centre one extending to the top of the arch, the whole length, with the tracery over the other four, filled with richly stained glass, has a remarkable effect upon the spectator, and one which it is impossible adequately to describe. The subjects in glass are Our Saviour and the four Evangelists.

Over this is a fine circular, or wheel window, similarly ornamented. At the east end is another window of five lights, with a small one over it. On each side are three large pointed arched windows, of three and four lights, with varied patterns of tracery. At Dugdale's visit the arms of England, Peche, Revel, Weston, prior of St. John's, and another, were in the church. There is no division of the chancel, which is defined by the three raised platforms, paved with Minton's tiles, leading to the altar, and by the two most easternly windows on the north, the sills to which are built above the level of the other. On the south of the west window is a canopied niche, which probably once contained the effigy of the patron saint of the church; and on the northern wall are three modern mural tablets. Near to the altar, under the eastern window of the south side, are the sedilia and a piscina of exquisite beauty, which have been restored. They are divided by open stone pillars, with capitals, arches, and finials, beautifully carved, the leaves and stalks of the foliage being cut clear of the supports and edges.

The whole of the interior was renewed at the last restoration of the building; and its open seats with carved heads, stone octagonal pulpit, having figures cut on the three front faces, stone altar, and graceful font, convey an impression of delicate beauty which it is highly desirable to see imitated in the renovation of other churches in the locality we have described. The only entrance previous to 1849, was by the western pointed arched doorway; but on this occasion the south doorway was reopened, and a priest's doorway added in the chancel. The south doorway had formerly a stone porch, a portion of the corbels, and part of the springers of the groined roof, still remaining on the western side.

The remarkably handsome church of Temple Balsall is now supposed to be in the same state of completeness as when it was erected by those military knights whose former location here conferred its distinctive name upon the village.

The church is the private property of the governors of the hospital, and the Rev. John Holbeche Short the chaplain.

The chaplain, or minister, is also the master of the

HOSPITAL OR ALMS HOUSES

Founded by lady Leveson. These stand on the north side of the church, and were endowed by her with "the manor of Balsall, *alias* Temple Balsall, with all the lands, tenements, and privileges whatsoever." They are built of brick, and occupy two sides of a quadrangle, the house of the master occupying the third. An ample green and pleasant walk from the road to the church, runs in front of the building; and the evidences of neatness and comfort enjoyed by the inmates, are an agreeable testimony to the munificence of their noble benefactress. The revenue has so increased in value, as to provide for a number of poor widows, or women not married. A new arrangement of the charity has recently been made by an Act of Parliament, confirming a scheme of the Charity Commissioners. The almswomen are now thirty-five, twenty from Balsall and the others from Barston and Hampton-in-Arden. Each person receives 6*s.* per week, a cloth gown, shawl, and a bonnet annually, with such quantities of bread, milk, and fuel as the governors direct. A medical practitioner and nurse are also provided when required. Formerly the poor of Long Itchington in this county, Trentham, Staffordshire, and Lilleshall, Shropshire, participated in the benefit of residence. Four persons, of suitable qualification, from each of these parishes now receive 8*s.* each per week, payable through the officiating minister and churchwardens of those places. The schools at Balsall are maintained, subject to a preference given to the children of the hamlet. The master of the hospital, who must be an ordained clergyman, receives 200*l.* per annum. He is also visitor to the school, and may act as perpetual curate of Balsall. The bailiff, for superintending the estates and property of the charity, has a salary of 100*l.* a year. The almswomen are selected according to the will of the foundress of this wealthy charity, from "the lamest and poorest persons" in their respective parishes.

The population of Temple Balsall in 1861 was 1140, being twenty less than in 1841, when the number was 1160. It was included in Hampton-in-Arden, A.D. 1563.

Northward of Knowle, on the Birmingham road, are two places of considerable interest to the antiquary. About a mile distant, the traveller will see, on the left-hand side, and two fields from the highway, *Langdon Hall;* and some distance down a lane on the right, he will find the site of the *Nunnery of Henwood.*

LANGDON HALL

Belongs to the manor of Langdon. At the Conquest it was held by one *Almar*, of Turchil de Warwick, and was then certified to contain two hides and a half, worth 20*s*., and woods one mile long and half a mile broad. In Henry I's time it was held of Siward de Arden, son of the above Turchil, by one *Chitelbern*, sometimes called *Ketelbernus de Langdona*, founder of Henwood Nunnery, a tenant and servant in the office of sewer to this Siward. His son dying without issue, it vested in his daughter's posterity, who had, however, by this time, assumed the name of de la Launde. James de la Launde, 37th Henry III, had grant of free warren here, but disposed of this estate, with the advowson of Henwood, to Gilbert de Kirkeby: This Gilbert sold his interest here to William de Arden, and his heirs, for 112 marks of silver, particularizing the capital messuage, or manor place, pertaining to the property, with all the lands thereto belonging, reserving to the before-mentioned James de la Launde, and his heirs, all such services as belonged to the same. After this, it appears to have followed the same line as Knowle, the monks of Westminster, 22nd Edward I, paying to John de la Launde, son of James, five marks of silver yearly. In the distribution of monastic property at the Dissolution, this manor was added to the revenues of the see of London. Soon after it passed into the possession of John Greswolde, esq., and from him, by one of his coheiresses, to Thomas Dabridgecourt. This family was descended from Sir Eustace Damprecourt, who came into England with Philippa, wife to king Edward III, and whose son, by a daughter of John, lord Wake, and widow of Edmund of Woodstock, earl of

Kent, was one of the founders of the order of the Garter.* This Thomas Dabridgecourt was a justice of peace, and high sheriff of the county, 29th Elizabeth. Dying[13] fourteen years after without male issue, the manor came next to John Fulwode, of Ford Hall, who had married Katharine, his eldest daughter: Through her daughter, married to William Noel, of Wellesborough, esq., it passed into their family, and came by marriage to lord Byron, descending to his daughter, the late countess of Lovelace, and is now the property of the earl of Lovelace.

There are no remains of the old manor house, but a gabled farm house, with high brick chimneys, built near to the site, now bears the title of Langdon Hall. Towards the west of it is a complete moat, filled with water; but not a vestige of the ancient edifice appears within the space which it incloses: In size and width, the moat is very similar to Codbarrow, already described: It now serves as a boundary to a garden, access to which is by a bridge.

HENWOOD NUNNERY

Was a Benedictine establishment of considerable importance. The nuns of this order, according to a legend of early date, were first settled at Polesworth, in this county, by king Egbert, in consideration of the cure of his only son, by Modwen, daughter of the then king of Connaught, whom

---

13. He was buried in Knowle church; and when Dugdale visited it, there was in a window on the south side of the chancel a male figure in armour, kneeling, and under it the following inscription:

Orate p. bono statu Thome Dabridgcourt
filii Johis Dabridgcourt et Elizabethe
uxoris eius que fuit soror Willi Wigston
militis, qui hanc fenestram fieri fecit.

See also inscriptions to members of this family in Knowle and Solihull churches.

* *Harl. MSS.*, 1100, f. 22.

he invited over to England, promising to found a monastery for her. On her arrival, with two other nuns, the king is said to have placed his daughter, Edith, with her for instruction in the rules of St. Benedict, giving her a dwelling place in the *Forest of Arderne*, and soon after, according to his promise, founding a monastery for them at Polesworth, constituting his daughter abbess. However questionable this statement may be, this is certain, that the Benedictine nuns had numerous establishments in this neighbourhood soon after the Conquest. This, at Henwood, was founded in the reign of Henry II, by Ketelberne, lord of the manor of Langdon, and was called *Estwell* on its first foundation. It was built near a spring, eastward of Langdon, and was dedicated to St. Margaret,[14] the boundaries of the gift being particularized in the charter disposing of it. The founder also granted to the nuns a free court, with all customs and liberties, as free as he had from Hugh de Arden, his superior lord. Also pasturage for all their cattle, horses, sheep, goats, and hogs, in every place where his own fed, without pannage or any custom to be paid for them: They were likewise permitted the privilege of cutting timber in Langdon wood for building their church, house, and other offices, and of erecting a mill, where they could find a suitable place on their own land, his lying opposite thereto.

The name of Estwell soon ceased, and it took the name of *Hean-wood*, from the tall oaks then and there standing, and the establishment advanced rapidly in material prosperity. Pope Gregory IX, A.D. 1228, confirmed all the tithes they had obtained in the parish of Solihull, and all their other possessions. These consisted of lands, woods,

14. St. Margaret, a native of Antioch, for refusing to marry Olybrius, president of the east, under the Romans, and renounce her religion, was cruelly tortured and beheaded, A.D. 278.

annuities, and advowsons given, at sundry times, by William de Arden, Ralph and James de la Launde, Roger de Camvill, the abbot of Westminster, the bishop of Coventry, and kings Richard II and Henry IV, the whole of which, at the dissolution of the monasteries, was valued at 21*l.* 2*s.*, with 2*l.* 6*s.* 7*d.* payments. Their property, at that period, consisted of holdings in Langdon, Hill Bickenhill, Church Bickenhill, Rodburn, Curdworth, Shustoke, Ansty, Stretton on Dunsmore, Whitnash, Barford, and Solihull, in the county of Warwick, with Appleby, in the county of Derby, and other smaller possessions.

According to Tanner, 5th Henry IV, there were twelve nuns in the convent, and in great poverty; and when, 27th Henry VIII, it was dissolved, as one of the lesser monasteries, its prioress, Johanna Hykford, or Hugford, was allowed a life annuity of 3*l.* 6*s.* 8*d.* At this time there were only the prioress and four or five nuns.[15] The prioresses were

Kath. Boydin, resigned 1310.
Margareta le Corzon.
Milisanda de Fokerham, March 30, 1339.
Johanna Fokerham, August 22, 1349.
Johanna de Pichford.
Alianora de Stoke, April 20, 1392.
Jocosa Midlemore, 1400.
Joecia Midlemore, January 8, 1438.
Alicia Waringe, 1460.
Eliz. Pultney, 1498.
Alicia Hugford, 26th Henry VIII.
Johanna Hugford, 28th Henry VIII.

The site of the convent, together with divers lands belonging to it in Knowle and Solihull, was disposed of,

15. Great doubt exists in the minds of several writers, whether many of the charges brought against the monastic establishments were not invented for the purpose of bringing those institutions into disrepute, and to prepare the common people, who profited much by their charitable offices, for their suppression. The desires of the monarch, and the cupidity of the nobility and gentry, who so largely benefited by grants of the possessions of abbeys, nunneries, &c., hastened their downfall; for, as a recent writer has observed, "a

31st Henry VIII, for 207*l.* 5*s.*, to John Hugford and his heirs, to be held *in capite* of the crown, equal to a yearly payment of 1*l.* 3*s.* 1*d.*, by the twentieth part of a knight's fee. This person pulled down the church, and appropriated the monastic buildings to the purposes of a dwelling house, in which he resided. John Hugford was descended from an ancient family settled at Emscote, near Warwick, and married Catharine, daughter of John Heneage, esq., of Hainton, county of Lincoln, by whom he had a son, John, who also resided here, as did John Hugford, son of the latter, by Margaret, daughter of Sir John Hugford, of Bindleston, in the county of Gloucester. This John Hugford, by his first wife Lettice, daughter of Edward Holte, of Duddeston,* left another John, aged twenty-one, in 1619. The estate was sold by this family to William Spooner, esq. It is now the property of Jacob Wise, esq.

In 2nd and 3rd Philip and Mary, it was found that Thomas Somerland had an annuity of 1*l.* 13*s.* 4*d.*, and Johanna Hugford a pension of 3*l.* 16*s.* 8*d.*

All that remains to identify the site of the Nunnery of Henwood is a number of grass-grown mounds, on the elevated portion of a field contiguous to the farm house called Henwood Hall: a large walnut tree marks the spot. The foundations have been dug out, and these elevations are, doubtless, formed of the rubbish left. Indications of a moat, on the east and north, remain, part of it, on the latter, being banked up to form a pond. The present Henwood Hall is small and of modern construction; and, with the exception of a carved head, inserted in the front

---

cruel king, and a greedy nobility, could not afford to wait for their prey, but turned out, helpless and homeless, on the mercies of the world, of which they had become ignorant, the aged inmates of the nunnery and of the monastery."

* *Herald's Visitation, Harl. MSS.*, 1100, f. 99.

wall bears no trace of the monastery adopted as his mansion, by John Hugford, in 1540-41. About A.D. 1600, when Belchier visited Warwickshire, there were several coats of arms emblazoned in Mr. Huggeford's house at Henwood.* In the walls, however, of the garden fronting the house are many vestiges of the former ecclesiastical buildings: These walls, indeed, appear to be composed wholly of stones taken from the priory, many of them being sculptured, such as the capitals of pillars, portions of arches, niches, &c. On one side of the gate leading into the garden is a pointed arched niche, with crockets and finial; and on the other side, a full length carved draped figure, without the head, two pieces of sculpture which the mason appears to have placed thus prominently in view, as being the most perfect relics of the old conventual abode. The farm buildings afford many traces of the plain slabs and stonework being incorporated in their walls. On the little river Blythe is still a mill, no doubt representing that erected by the nuns, in pursuance of the license they received from their patron Ketelberne, whose name is still preserved in that of a tract called *Kettleburn Heath.*

Returning to the Birmingham turnpike road, the traveller can either retrace his steps to Knowle, or proceed onward to Solihull, where we shall await him on the morrow.

* *Belchier's Notes: Bridges' Papers in Bodleian Library, Oxford.*

Eighth Day.

THE town of Solihull, with its several hamlets, rich in historical associations and architectural interest, will alone occupy our attention this day. The approach to this place, from Knowle, is of a highly sylvan character. Overhanging trees, with a beautiful and fertile country stretching beyond, will here richly recompense those who delight in

> "The rural walk through lanes
> Of grassy swarth, close cropped by nibbling sheep,
> And skirted thick with intertexture firm
> Of thorny boughs."

These, indeed, are the prevailing characteristics of

SOLIHULL,

From whatever point the tourist may reach it. It is about six miles and a half south-east from Birmingham. Formerly it possessed a considerable market, which has for some years been declining; and the place now ranks as a large and pleasant village, rather on the increase since the opening of the Oxford and Birmingham Railway, affording an agreeable place of residence for the families of

Birmingham merchants and others. Three fairs are still held at it.

The distinctive name of this town does not appear in any document prior to the reign of king John, at which period, in a record of the profit of the leets kept for several hundreds, one mark is set down to the account of Solihull. Dugdale considers it to have been reckoned in Domesday Book as *Ulverlie,* belonging, in Edward the Confessor's days, to Edwine, earl of Mercia, and, afterwards, to one Cristina, who held it by gift from the king. It comprised eight hides, twenty carucates of arable land, twelve of meadow, and a wood four miles in length and half a mile in breadth, with a church, twenty-two villeins, and four bordars. It was worth 4*l.*, and had been worth 10*l.* From this Cristina the manor came to the family of Limesie, which is supposed to have had its seat at *Ulverlie,* subsequently written *Wulverle;* and after the rise of Solihull, altered to *Olton,* or *Old Town,* distant a mile from Solihull. In the tenure of this family of Limesie it remained for four generations, and then came to Hugh de Odingsells, who had married one of the coheiresses. From him it fell to his youngest son, in whose time Solihull, out of the decadence of Wulverlie, became a town of some magnitude, as appears by his obtaining for it a charter, 26th Henry III, to establish a weekly market on the Wednesday, together with a yearly fair, for three days, commencing on the eve of St. Alphege: In 34th of the same reign, a charter of free warren in all his demesne lands here, was also granted him: In 13th Edward I he claimed a court leet, gallows, tumbrel, and assize of bread and beer, in this lordship, by charter of Henry III. He founded a chantry in the chapel of St. Alphege, and, dying 23rd of the same reign, left a son and heir, who surviving his father but a few months, the manor came, the same year, by marriage of the coheiresses, to Sir Peter de Bermingham, knight, and Richard de Perham, from whose descendants it was transferred to John Hotham, bishop of Ely, and his heirs. This bishop obtained a charter, 23rd of February, 13th Edward II, for the continuance of the market, and the holding of the fair at Lammas, instead of at the feast of St. Alphege; and again, in 1st Edward III, one of free warren.

Early in the latter reign a serious dispute arose between the inhabitants of Solihull, King's Norton, and Yardley, with the earl of March, relative to pasturage in King's Norton; for, 6th Edward III, an inquisition was held, and a fine which had been adjudged as damages to the earl, remitted, by the following writ from the king: "Since we have learnt by an inquisition, &c., that the inhabitants of Kyngesnorton, Yerdeley, and Solihull, from time immemorial, have possessed the right of common pasturage for all their cattle and sheep, at a certain time of the year, in the pasture lands of Kyngesnortonwode, which is on the borders of Worcestershire and Warwickshire, and that these men, and others also having the right of pasturage in the said pasture lands, as it was quite lawful for them to do, destroyed a certain ditch in the said pasture lands which had been lately made, to the injury and disinheriting of themselves, by Roger de Mortimer, late earl of March, and for this that, on the day of holding a certain inquisition, lately made, by our writ of *nisi prius*, in a certain plea made before us at the suit of the aforenamed earl against the aforesaid men, [inhabitants] respecting the destruction of the said ditch, they did not dare to appear, and 300*l.* have stood adjudged to the said earl for his damages on this account; with respect to which we have pardoned the said inhabitants respecting the said sum."*

* *Rot. Orig.*, r. 20.

In 45th Edward III, Robert Burgoloun recovered in the King's Court at Warwick, from Thomas Bulkemore, and Alice his wife, possession of a messuage and four acres of land, with 4*s.* 5*d.* of rent, and the appurtenances.*

From bishop Hotham the manor was transmitted through different members of his family, by descent and marriage, until the 5th Henry V, when it was resumed by the king: It continued in the crown till 16th Henry VI, when the custody of the manor was given, by that monarch, to Thomas Greswolde for seven years. This term had not expired before it was granted, 22nd same reign, to John, duke of Somerset, and his heirs male; but he dying without issue, the king granted it next to Edmund Mountford, esq., for life, on payment of fifty marks sterling per annum. He, however, held it but one year. After him, it was successively held by different tenants of the crown, up to the 5th Henry VIII. At this date, Thomas Howard, earl of Surrey, had letters patent, from the king, of this lordship, with the advowson of the church, in consideration of his eminent services against the Scots, at Flodden Field. He was followed in possession by his son, Thomas, duke of Norfolk, who passed the inheritance to Edmund Knightly, esq., and Eustace Kitteley, gent., in trust for the use of Sir George Throckmorton, knight, and his heirs. Sir George Throckmorton's grandson, 2nd James I, sold it for 1080*l.* to Edward Hawes, of Solihull, gent., and Humphry Coles, of the Middle Temple, from whom, by purchase from divers persons, it came to Sir Simon Archer, of Umberslade: In his family it remained till the estates were divided among the coheiresses, when this portion of them fell to the share of the earl of Plymouth, and from him to earl Amherst,

---

* *Rot. Orig.*, r. 29.

who sold the manorial rights to Lieut.-Col. Short, *obiit* 1859, who bequeathed them to his nephew, the Rev. John Couchman.

THE CHURCH,

Dedicated to St. Alphege,[1] is the finest ecclesiastical structure in this part of Warwickshire. It consists of an

intersection tower and spire, lofty nave, north and south aisles, north and south transepts, large chancel, and sacristy

1. St. Alphege, of a noble Saxon family, was brought up in the monastery of Deerhurst, in Gloucestershire. He became successively abbot of Bath, bishop of Winchester, and archbishop of Canterbury. He was stoned to death at Greenwich by the Danes in 1012, and not long after canonized.

with a chapel over it. The tower is embattled, having pinnacles at each corner. The spire, which is octagonal, was rebuilt after the old model, the former one having been blown down by a hurricane, on the 15th of March, in the year 1757. The south aisle has a modern plain parapet, the northern one being embattled. The nave, transepts, chancel, and chapel, are without parapets, and have all high ridged roofs. There is a porch on the north side, entered by wrought-iron gates, of good workmanship, bearing the date 1746; whilst on each side is a small window filled with stained glass, representing St. Simeon and the Royal Psalmist, with appropriate texts. The arch of the doorway is pointed. Entering the church by this porch, the spaciousness of the building, as compared with other churches, immediately impresses the visitor. The lofty pillars of the nave, the graceful arches over them, and supporting the tower, the noble transepts and chancel, with the numerous richly mullioned windows, present a *coup d'œil* that must be seen to be duly appreciated. The nave is separated from each aisle by four octagonal pillars, supporting pointed arches: it is lighted at the west end by a large pointed arched window of five lights, with elaborate tracery, under which is a pointed arched doorway. The roof of the nave is framed with curved braces, similar to the chancel, those of the aisles being straight rafters with plaster between.

The windows of the aisles are pointed, with the exception of the one nearest the east end of the south aisle, which is large and square headed, of five lights, divided by mullions and transoms, the centre upper portion being filled with stained glass, representing the Saviour as the Good Shepherd, and an inscription, "Dedicated to God and the church in memory of Mary Ann Lynn." At the east end of the south aisle is a stone reredos, having carved panelling; and on the left is a small niche, the figure gone. In the south wall is a piscina, the carving much dilapidated; and behind it are two carved brackets, the uses of which have been before described. In the northern aisle there are traces of a carved wood reredos, and a piscina. These eastern ends are the sites of the altars of some saints. The tower forms the division of the nave, transepts, and chancel, by four pointed arches resting on semi-octagonal jambs, or piers.

In the south transept, formerly the chapel of St. Mary, the ancient altar slab and the remains of the piscina still exist. It is entered by a carved screen. The organ, formerly in the gallery, is now placed in the south transept.

The north transept, once the chapel of St. Catharine,[2] is separated from the church by another screen. The four lights of the north window are filled with modern, and the tracery with stained, glass. The glass in the four lights was the gift of the late Colonel Short, in memory of his parents and other members of his family. The transepts do not open into the aisles, which is a peculiarity in the plan of this church.

The chancel is the most interesting part of the building. It is distinguished by a large pointed east window, filled with richly stained glass, the five lights containing representations of Our Lord and the four Evangelists, with their emblems at the foot. The tracery, filled with the débris of an older window, produces, with the above, a beautiful effect in the interior. It was executed by Mr. Wailes, of

2. St. Catharine, born at Alexandria, was, in the reign of the emperor Maxentius, tortured with four sharp-cutting wheels, and afterwards beheaded. From this the sign, &c., of the Catharine wheel was derived.

Newcastle-upon-Tyne, and the cost defrayed by a legacy of the late Mr. Chattock, and the liberal help of the late rector, the Rev. Archer Clive. Four smaller pointed windows occupy the south side; and on the northern are two windows similar in design, and two others now blocked up by masonry. The windows of this chancel

are adjudged to be very early specimens of the Decorated style. The arches of the side windows are connected by the hood mould, with trefoiled arches rising in the plain portion of the intervening walls: They have under each of them an elegant bracket, beautifully carved with foliage. On the south is a sedile of three stone benches, independent of the walls from which it projects. The piscina on the east of these is larger than usual, and enriched with a beautifully carved bowl, the triangular crocketed canopy being supported by shafts. In the north wall is a large opening, at present without carving or ornament, which served, in ancient times, as the Holy Sepulchre,3 a description of which has been given at p. 156. The roof of the chancel is esteemed a fine specimen of wood work, differing from most structures of the kind, by the employment of curved braces affixed to the under side of the trusses. The lower part of the walls is covered with oak, and the chancel fitted with open stalls. The communion table is similar in character to that of others that have been described, and the altar rails are of fairly carved wood work, the sacrarium being paved with Minton's tiles.

A door on the north side of the chancel leads to an ancient chapel or chantry, which is variously conjectured to have been originally intended for a charnel house, sacristy, &c. It is, however, more than probable that it once formed a chapel, dedicated to some patron saint, if we may judge from the numerous altars, founded by the neighbouring gentry, in this church: for besides the chapel of St. Alphege, the high altar, and the altars in the transepts, the church had, before the Reformation, others in honour of St. Anthony,4 St. Nicholas, St. Thomas à Becket,5 and others,

---

3. In the churchwardens' accounts are several items of receipts and of charges for celebrating these customs at Easter. In 1534—paid the sexton for watching the sepulchre light, *2d.* For twelve pounds of wax for the sepulchre light, *7s.* Two pounds of the sepulchre wax went to the rood light. Received for Easter box and sepulchre light, *20s.*

4. St. Anthony was born in Egypt about the year 251. He was amongst the earliest anchorets, and commonly called the Patriarch of Monks. He

as may be learnt from the entries of items of expense incurred by the parish on account of the celebration of the early ceremonies of the church.[6] This chapel has a groined roof, and was formerly lighted by two small lancet windows on the north, and one on the western and eastern sides, the latter one being still open. Under the window a stone altar is found.

Over this lower chapel is another, which is reached by a staircase from the chancel, and entered by a pointed arched doorway. This is considered to have been the

CHANTRY OF ST. ALPHEGE,

Founded by Sir William de Odingsells, knight, in the time of Edward I, for one priest to celebrate divine service for ever, for the health of the souls of his father and mother, as also for his own soul, with the souls of his progenitors, children, and all the faithful deceased. For the support of this priest, he gave certain houses and lands, near *St. Alphege's* well, in this lordship, and 3*l.* yearly rent, payable by several of his tenants here. The maintenance of this priest was successively augmented, first, by Ralph de Limesi and his wife, to the extent of five marks yearly;

---

withdrew from human society and took up his abode in a cave, and was the founder of the solitary mode of living. He is not named in the English, but is one of the most notable saints in the Romish calendar. The temptations of St. Anthony have, through St. Athanasius's Memoir, become one of the most familiar of European ideas.

5. Thomas à Becket was born in London in 1117; and became archbishop of Canterbury, in which cathedral he was assassinated at vespers. His relics, in a costly shrine, at the east end of the cathedral, attracted devotees from all parts of Europe. King Henry II, who had been privy to his murder, afterwards did penance at his shrine, and suffered himself to be scourged by the monks.

6. Among others we find, A.D. 1532 *et seq.*: For mending the censer, 7*d.* For cords for the saunce bell and for the lamp, 1*s.* 2*d.* For mending the cross and censer, 1*s.* For nine pound of wax for the rood light, 5*s.* 2*d.* For the light making, 6*s.* 4*d.* Received for the rood light, 21*s.* 6*d.* Of Our Lady's

next, by William Hawe and others, by a messuage and forty acres of land in Solihull, called Coldeford's tenement, for the chantry priest to celebrate divine service for the souls of Hugh le Despenser and Sibill his wife. This grant, being without a license from the king, the gift became forfeited, and was given, 14th Henry IV, by the king, to John Birkyn, one of the yeomen of the larder, for his life. Before 16th Henry VI other diminutions in the priest's income had taken place; for, in that year, on an addition of 3*l.* more annually made by one Thomas Greswolde, it appeared that the stipend was so poor that no priest was then serving. This augmentation was for the priest to sing mass every day for the good estate of the king, (Henry VI,) and of the said Thomas Greswolde, and for their souls after death, as also for the souls of the ancestors of the said Thomas, and all other benefactors. In 26th Henry VIII the revenues were valued at 5*l.* 13*s.* per annum, with 18*s.* yearly paid to several persons; and, 37th of the same reign, were found to be 6*l.* 16*s.* 6*d.* over and above all payments. At this time the chantry priest occasionally assisted the parson in administering the sacraments, the parish being extensive, having no less than seven hundred communicants. This chantry, or upper chapel, now the sacristy, is said to have been built at the time of its foundation, and the chancel is supposed to have been erected about the same period. It was called the chantry of Haliwell, or Holy Well, from, as is conjectured, the property given to it, by the founder, being near to St. Alphege's well, remains of which are still existent near

---

coffer, 13*s.* In pay of St. Nicholas' clerks, 3*s.* To find light yearly to feed St. Katharine and the table of St. Anthony, 3*s.* 6*d.* For the lamp of the cross, 8*s.* For repairs of the cross, 12*d.* For repairs of the canopy of the sacramentum, 6*d.* For the hour glass and its standard, 2*s.* 8*d.* For frankincense, 13*s.* 11*d.* Paid George Lynall for repairs to Becket's chapel.

to the rectory.[7] The chapel, which, 16th Henry VI, was called *libera capella sancti Alphegi*, is approached, from the chancel of the church, by a short staircase under a large pointed arched doorway, and is lighted by four pointed arched windows, of varied design, one of them, the eastern, having some remains of ancient stained glass. This consists of a centre of good colour, with a scroll ornament, in each light. One of the windows looking into the chancel now forms a repository for the robes of the minister, &c. In this chapel still remains the piscina; but the altar, with other accessories, have disappeared. A remarkably fine oak chest, in which are kept the parish records, stands in this chapel.

A further benefaction for the use of this church was made, 13th Edward III, by William de Stow, a priest and parson of Solihull, in the gift of twelve acres of land and six of meadow, in trust to succeeding rectors, for two wax candles to be kept burning in the church every day at mass, and two torches always at the elevation of the Host. For this, Thomas de Blaston, rector of the church of *Sulyhull*, paid a fine of 10*s*. to the king.*

The MONUMENTS, ancient and modern, in the various portions of the church, are so numerous, that they can only be briefly particularized. Those of ancient date still extant are the following:

---

7. Many wells were committed to the patronage of the saints, and treated with reverence, some on account of their purity, and others for the medicinal virtues of their waters. St. Alkmund's well at Derby is an instance of the former class, where the name has been continued long after the superstition which gave it had passed away. In early ages this veneration for holy wells was carried to an idolatrous excess, insomuch, that in the reigns of Edgar and Canute, it was found necessary to issue edicts prohibiting well worship.—*Hone's Every Day Book*, ii, 637.

* *Rot. Orig.*, r. 64.

On three oak panels, hanging on the south aisle, are several family arms and crests. One panel bears this inscription :

Thomas Dabridgecourte, esq., departed this lyfe ye xii of May, 1601.

Another is thus inscribed :

Alice Dabridgecourt, eldest sister and coheire to Richard Greswolde, esquire, departed this lyfe the laste daye of Februarie, Ano Dni, 1599.

This tablet was larger when Dugdale visited the church, and then had their portraits, and those of five children, with a verse of eight lines under each principal figure, in addition to what we have quoted.

On a brass plate on a slab, under the tower arch, are the figures of a man and his two wives, with those of fourteen children, in three groups, under them, and this inscription :

Of your Charitie, praye for the sollys of William Hyll, ge'tilman, and for Isabelle and Agnes his wyffys wich William d'ceased the vj daye of December, in the year of Our Lorde God, mcccccxlix, on whose soll Jhu have mercie, amen.

On a tablet of wood, at the east end of the north aisle, is painted the family arms, a Latin acrostic of GVLIELMVS HAVVES, and a long English verse, in memory of the same person. A brass plate affixed to the wall contains his effigy, with those of Ursula, his wife, and their eight children, and the following inscription :

WILLIAM HAWES, Æt. 80. 1610. URSULA COLES, Æt. 76.

Here William Hawes, and Ursula his wife,
Their bodyes lye, their soules with Christ in life,
Whose Holy Spirit did so direct their wayes,
That in his fear they lived to aged dayes.
In endlesse joy with Christ they now remaine,
By whose blood all salvation doe obtaine.

These are all that remain of those noted by Dugdale, as in the church in his time. Of those that have disappeared there were, first, a memorial " To Richard Greswolde, *obiit*

September 17th, 1537, and his wife Alicia, *quorum animabus propitietur Deus, amen,*" with their arms and effigies. Second, to Thomas Greswolde, *obiit* July 8th, 1577, and his three wives, with their figures. Third, a monumental brass on a marble gravestone, to John Botiler, *obiit* 1512. Fourth, an alabaster stone with portraiture of a man in a gowne; to the memory of Henry Huggeford, died 1592; "to whom the Lord grant a joyfull resurrection, Amen." And a fifth to William Plasted and his wife, 1591.

In the chapel, at the eastern end of the north aisle, now converted into a spacious pew, and called "The Malvern Pew," are several hatchments, arms, and inscriptions commemorative of the owners of Malvern Hall, who have been buried in this and other places. The north transept contains numerous monuments of the Holbeche family, heretofore of Bentley Heath, in this parish. The modern tombs, tablets, and memorials, are very numerous, and chronicle the deaths of several of the rectors, of divers branches of the families of Chattock, Welshman, Harborne, Palmer, Doley, and others, connected, by birth and alliance, with the parish.

Before leaving the church, a few other particulars respecting the interior deserve notice. The pulpit is of the usual carving of the sixteenth century, and the body of the church with a portion of the north transept is pewed, the free seats being open sittings. A large gallery ranges over the entire width of the nave, under the western window, the front of which is formed of the old rood loft in the middle, the two sides being of cast iron of the same pattern. A large chandelier hangs from the centre of the nave, bearing an inscription to the effect that it was the donation of one of the Holbeche family. The font is octagonal, supported by a central shaft, with eight small pillars, one at each angle. In the tower is a fine peal of eight bells, cast in 1686, by Bagley.

The church, or living, was valued, 19th Edward I, at thirty marks, over and above two marks paid to the priory of Hertford. In 26th Henry VIII the annual value was assessed at 23*l.* 18*s.* 4*d.*, after deduction of these two marks, 1*s.* 10*d.* yearly to the chantry at Solihull, and 10*s.* 10*d.* for synodals, &c. The tithes are now commuted for 1455*l.* The Rev. P. M. Smythe is the present rector.

When the survey was taken of the goods, plate, jewels, &c., in all the churches, chapels, guilds, brotherhoods, and fraternities in the county of Warwick, by Sir George Throckmorton, knight, John Digby and Thomas Marrow, esquires, 6th Edward VI,* the return made from Solihull was

two chalices, iij belles, a clock, and ij sacring belles.
a pix, latyn.
two cruets, pewter.
two paxes of glas and wood.
two corporys cases.
two sensers, bras.
two candlesticks, bras.
a frount for thaltar of paynted clothe.
iij altarclothes.
xviij towells.
iij sut vestm'ts, oon veluet, oon silke, oon wulsted.
vj copes, two veluet, two silke, oon wulsted, oon dornix.

The church-yard, like the edifice it surrounds, is large, and contains many monuments and memorials of humbler pretensions; but as none are of any particular interest, the traveller may on leaving it muse on the equality of all who here find a resting place.

On the south side of the church-yard stands the rectory house, a commodious brick building erected by the Rev.

* *Papers, "Warwick," in Record Office.*

Archer Clive about thirty years ago. In a field below the garden some remains of the holy well may be traced, the spring still bubbling up. This was anciently called St. Alphege's well, the patron saint of the church, to whom allusion has been made at p. 257.

In Solihull the curfew still "tolls the knell of parting day," and may have done so from the time of the Norman Conquest.[8] Two pounds a year is paid to the clerk for ringing the curfew from a general fund, formed out of several old benefactions to the church and poor.

The means of gaining a glimpse of the "old world" every-day life of small and isolated towns in this country are not too abundant: In the carefully preserved accounts of the churchwardens of this parish, however, materials exist for attaining a tolerably accurate idea of our ancestors' mode of life. It appears from an entry in these accounts, of *4d.* paid in 1534, for "a broiderer, who came to mend the vestments," and another of "*12d.* to a tynker for mending the cross and censer," that no permanent settlement of such artificers had then taken place in the smaller towns. A century later, 1657, during the Commonwealth, *4s. 2d.* is paid for eight charges at three times for s . . . . . the Papists' names at Coleshull, and *6d.* given to Mr. Palmer, by a Parliamentary order, to travel into Ireland. In 1661, *1l. 2s.* is paid for the *goale martialsie,* and maimed soldiers, and *1s. 2d.* in paying the *Polemoney,* and in the

---

8. From an order of William the Conqueror, the custom of ringing the evening and morning bells is derived. In order to suppress those nocturnal compotations to which the English were so much addicted, and which afforded them an opportunity of conspiring the better against his government, he required that they should extinguish their fires and lights at the hour of eight in the evening. A bell, called the curfew, (quasi *couvre feu,* or cover fire,) was rung, to give notice of the same; nor was it lawful to enkindle them again until the sounding of the morning bell, which was rung at four o'clock.

year following, 1*l.* 0*s.* 3*d.* for maimed soldiers and the *marrins.* In 1658, 4*d.* is paid to Henry Davies to watch in the church-yard to prevent the burying of Wid. Willson (probably dead of the plague). In the same year 1*s.* is given to Mrs. Penruddock, whose husband was taken by the Turks, to prevent collection; and in 1662, 1*s.* 6*d.* to John Searle that had been taken a slave to the Turks, as the half moon burned in three places on him made apparent. In 1664, 1*s.* to widow Bird, pitifully complaining, and in 1667, 2*s.* 8*d.* for a shirt for William Bate, and making it, as also 1*s.* 6*d.* for calf skins to mend the said William Bate's breeches.

Some discipline appears to have been exercised by the authorities of the parish over scolding wives and refractory youngsters; for, in 1658, a charge of 10*s.* 4*d.* is made as paid to Robert Haywood, for making the cucking stoole,9 and for beer at the drawing it up to the crosse; also 4*d.* for a lock to lock it to the cross. In 1714 the sum of 1*s.* 2*d.* for going before Justice St. Nicholas with the young people "which would not goe to service." In 1712 a charge is also made for going before Mr. St. Nicholas to squash Sam Larence.

The loyalty of the place is shown by the numerous charges, from 1*s.* to 10*s.*, made for ringing on occasions of St. George's Day, the king's birthday, thanksgivings, the peace, &c., in various years: On the restoration of

---

9. The *cucking stool* was an engine for the punishment of scolds and unquiet women, by ducking them in the water, after having placed them in a stool or chair fixed at the end of a long pole, by which they were immerged in some muddy or stinking pond. They were much in use formerly, and there are charges made, &c. They appear to have been in common use when Gay wrote his Pastorals; they are thus described in the Dumps:

> "I'll speed me to the pond, where the high stool
> On the long plank hangs o'er the muddy pool,
> That stool, the dread of ev'ry scolding quean."

Charles II, 4*s.* is paid to the ringers upon a thanksgiving day, 10*s.* to William Baynton for painting the king's arms in the church, and 2*l.* 10*s.* lent to Charles Causton, constable, for "drumes and collors by consent." And to the horror of modern sportsmen, be it known that 2*s.* were given to squire Dilke's man for the heads of two foxes, in 1662, a premium which extended to 1762, when 4*s.* were given for four others. Hedgehogs and sparrows also had their price. In 1659 a pennyworth of paper is bought for the parishioners; but the most curious is one which records that, in 1663, 2*s.* were "paid to William Stretch, to stop his mouth," and a further sum of 1*s.* 8*d.* to the same person "for the proclamation for the observance of the sabbath."

The town of Solihull consists of one long street, with small arms branching from it, and is cheerful and agreeable in its general aspect. Many of the houses are modern, whilst a few of them are large and surrounded by grounds of a pleasing character. A few old half-timbered houses, one dated B.C. 1571, and an ancient inn, complete the *tout ensemble.* A small building called the town hall is near to the church. Here is also a Roman Catholic chapel, erected in 1836, a smaller one having been taken down at that time, after standing nearly sixty years. The Independents have, likewise, a neat place of worship, built about 1828.

Education[10] has been amply cared for by liberal endowments. The Rev. H. J. Bennett, M.A., is the present head master of the Grammar School. There are schools

10. Two Latin entries in the parish accounts show that provision for education was made here before the year 1562, of which we give a translation. 1562. Hamlet Fetherstone requires an allowance of 6*l.* 6*s.* 8*d.* which he has paid to Edward Pole, the schoolmaster, on account of his salary as he shows by his four receipts. 1569. 9*l.* 10*s.* paid to Ranulph Hayworth, lately schoolmaster in the same place, for his salary for one whole year.

for boys, girls, and infants, all partly supported by endowments. The present number of children in attendance is about 180.

At the end of the street, and east of the church, stands

MALVERN HALL,

Long the seat of the Greswoldes. The descent of this family is from John Greswolde, of Kenilworth, married to a daughter of William Hugford, of *Huldenhall*, in the parish of Solihull:* he was followed by Ralph, the father of Richard Greswolde, who died before 13th Henry IV. The next in succession, Thomas, is recorded, 12th Henry VI, as one of the persons of quality in this county, sworn to observe the articles concluded in the parliament then held, being a justice of the peace for the same from 21st to 36th of that reign. In 16th Henry VI he had the custody of the manor of Solihull and Sheldon, seized by the king on the death of Edward, duke of York; and thirteen years after, the custody of the lands of Robert de Arden, attainted of high treason for siding with the Yorkists, and executed the year following. From this Thomas descended John Greswolde, of Langdon Hall, who was succeeded by Richard Greswolde, *obiit* 1537, and Thomas, *obiit* 1577, as recorded on their monuments in Solihull church in Dugdale's time.[11] The Greswolde estate, after passing through a long succession of direct heirs, ultimately fell by marriage to Henry Greswolde Lewis, esq., who, dying in 1829, was succeeded by Major Meysey Wigley, who assumed the

---

11. In the church register is the following entry, relative to some member of this family: "The xxth daie of September, beinge Sondaie, 1606, Richard Griswolde, yeoman, came into the churche of Solihull to divine service, and there openlie made his submission, accordinge to the statute in that case provided."

* *Herald's Visitation, Harl. MSS.*, 1100, f. 91 b.

name of Greswolde. He died unmarried in 1832, and was succeeded by his uncle, Henry Wigley, esq., who also assumed the name of Greswolde. Dying in 1848, the estate fell to his three daughters, one portion coming to the youngest, Anne, married to F. E. Williams, esq. The two eldest died unmarried, one leaving her share to Mr. Williams, and the other hers to his eldest son, Wigley Greswolde Greswolde Williams, esq., and they are now joint proprietors.

The hall is in the midst of a park, from which it is separated by a sunk fence. It is a large and well-built mansion, but of no great antiquity, the front entrance facing an avenue of trees running up to and beyond the Warwick road. On the gateway pillars are quarterings of arms, and on two pillars flanking the entrance hall door are full length sculptured figures. The gardens and pleasure grounds are extensive, and in keeping with the requirements of such a residence. Portions of the once extensive park, which bounds for a considerable distance the left hand side of the road leading from Solihull to Bentley Heath, have been converted into a farm. It was formerly stocked with deer.

The Greswoldes, as we have stated, had the custody of the manor of Solihull in the time of Henry VI; and it is more than probable that, from the circumstance of their armorial bearings being carved on the stables, some branch had once residence at *Hillfield Hall*, in the parish, a description of which, though some distance south-west of Malvern, may, from this connection, be fittingly introduced here.

HILLFIELD HALL

Is an interesting relic of a mansion of the sixteenth century, to which reference has been already made in the introductory chapter. The engraving represents the oldest part of the structure, viz. the northern front, which, before its restoration by the present owner, T. E. Williams, esq., was defaced by several unsightly lean-tos and obliterated windows. This part of the building is wholly of brick, and of the castellated order, a style of edifice which did not go out of fashion for many years after such defences were no longer required. This part presents two crenelated towers, with a gabled centre, and two wings right and left of the towers. The southern front is of later date, and is of the Italian order, with brick pillars having stone capitals.[12] Over a bay window in this part, were formerly the arms and crest of the Fieldings, who were living here in the time of the Stuarts. To the Fieldings this southern front may therefore, with reason, be attributed. When Belchier* visited the neighbourhood, he found here five

12. It is supposed to have been built by Inigo Jones.

* *Notes, Bridges' Papers in Bodleian Library, Oxford.* They are partly undecipherable.

coats of arms, (most probably in the windows,) which he thus describes:

1. John Hawes of . . . . . . 1371.
2. Thomas Hawes, married Ann. d. of John Greswold, 1465.
3. . . . . . . Hawes, married . . . . . . 1529.
4. . . . . . . empaling Hawes—arms, a dagger between stars, a crescent for difference.
5. William Hawes, Ursula d. of Wm. Cole, of com. Warwick, 1562.

This last appears to have rebuilt, or enlarged the house, as

may be inferred from the following inscription[13] over the doorway of the eastern tower:

HIC HOSPITES
IN CŒLO CIVES
W H V
1576

The interior has undergone considerable alterations. The

13. This may be rendered "Here we are guests: in heaven citizens." W. V. H—William and Ursula Hawes.

spacious old hall has been converted into rooms more suitable to the requirements of modern times. A long chamber still remains at the top of the house, under which was formerly a corridor or passage running the whole length of the building. In the western tower is an ancient oak spiral staircase, winding round a straight oak extending from the basement to the summit.

Hillfield, according to family documents, was first purchased, 5th Edward II, (1465,) by Thomas Hawes of Shirley, "skilled in the law." But the first member of the family resident at the place, as appears by the pedigree,* was William Hawes, of "Hilfield in Solihull, living in 1563." His father was Thomas Hawes of Edlicott, a descendant in the fourth generation, of the same name and of the same place, one of whom, as above stated, married a daughter of John Greswolde. William Hawes, who lies buried in Solihull church, was a benefactor to the chantry of St. Alphege there. He was succeeded by his son Edward, living in 1619, whose posterity at that time included William his son and heir, aged fourteen, three other sons, and eight daughters. This Edward Hawes purchased the manor of Solihull, 2nd James I, but afterwards sold it to Samuel Marrow, esq., of Berkswell. Since then Hillfield has come to the Greswoldes, and is at the present time the property of their descendant. The family of Hawes is now represented by the Honourable Swynfen Parker Jervis, of Little Aston, in the county of Stafford.

BERRY HALL,

Another ancient mansion, furnishing the subject of the initial letter to this chapter, lies north-east of the church.

---

* *Herald's Visitation*, *Harl. MSS.*, 1100, f. 119.

It was once of considerable size, what remains being turned into a farm house. It is said to have originally formed the chapel; but this is merely conjectural, there being no internal evidence to prove what part of the building it constituted. Berry Hall was long the seat of the Waring family, the first mention of whom in connection with this residence dates from 21st Henry VII. They were descended from a family located at Tanworth: One of this family, John Waring, 51st Edward III, was in the commission for assessing a subsidy of Pole money; in 2nd Richard II, for collecting another subsidy; and in the 7th of the same reign, for the assessing and gathering of the half of a tenth and fifteenth. He was succeeded by Thomas Waring, styled *armiger*, 12th Henry VI, in the 36th of which reign Alice Waring was prioress of the neighbouring nunnery of Henwood. The Warings contracted alliances with many of the principal families in the county, and continued to reside here for several generations; but no records or monumental inscriptions exist, by means of which to trace their fortunes up to the time when this estate fell into other hands. It is now the property of S. Warner, esq.

SILHILL HALL,

A corruption of Solihull, stands west of the town, and though still bearing the old name, is only a farm house. Traces of a moat once surrounding a much older building are still visible. The present house has nothing remarkable about it, and no data are found to connect it with any of the ancient families of this parish. It is probable that it was built on the site of a house belonging to the Middlemore family, since in the account of the repewing of the church in 1656, still preserved in the parish chest, it is stated that Richard Middlemore, esq., erected a pew near to Mr.

Dabridgecourt's tomb in the south aisle, "to be appropriated to Solihull Hall for ever." The estate is now the property of H. H. Chattock, esq.

The account of this parish can scarcely be considered complete, without some reference to two ancient members, *Forshaw* and *Widney*. They contain but little to attract the traveller. The former of these,

FORSHAW,

Was given, in Edward I's time, by William de Odingsells to his younger son, Nicholas. Here, *temp.* Henry VII, was a manor house, a park, and a warren, reputed to be a chase. Of this manor house nothing has been visible for many years, a coppice growing on its site in 1656, surrounded by a double moat of large extent. A farm house, called Forshaw, now denotes the spot, and the moat is still readily defined. The manor is owned by R. Morrall, esq.

WIDNEY

Was granted by Philip de Cumtune, *temp.* Henry III, to his kinsman, William de Parles, whose son, another William, in the reign of Edward I, granted it to Walter de Aylesbury, who obtained a charter of free warren here. His posterity, seated at Edstone, held it till the 17th Henry VI. From them it came to Thomas Somervile, esq., of Somervile Aston, Gloucestershire. In 25th Elizabeth, Widney reverted to the crown, by the attainder of John Somervile, a younger son of the family. Since this time, both Widney and Forshaw have passed through various hands. The manor of Widney is now in the possession of John Stubbs, esq., who succeeded to it by the will of J. Smallwood, esq., who purchased it from the Honourable Mrs. Musgrave, one of the coheiresses of lord Archer. Widney now consists of two or three farm houses. West of Solihull is

SHIRLEY STREET,

Another member of this parish, situate on the road from Stratford-on-Avon to Birmingham, from which it is distant six miles: It has, however, no historical features beyond being a portion of the ancient road referred to at p. 10. It consists of houses built on each side of the street, extending to a considerable distance. Several neat residences have, of late years, been erected, which gives to the place a more prosperous appearance than it formerly exhibited. It is now constituted into a district under the Ecclesiastical Commissioners' Act. The principal object of interest is

THE CHURCH,

Which, dedicated to St. James, was erected in the year 1831, considerable additions and alterations having been made in 1862. The structure consists of a tower, nave, and chancel, the nave having a high ridged roof, from which projects a row of dormer lights. The living is a perpetual curacy, value 120*l.* per annum, of which the Rev. Nash Stephenson is the incumbent.

There is a National School, accommodating about 150 scholars, and a small chapel of the Baptist denomination.

Returning to Solihull we now come to the *Old Town*, or *Wulverlie* of Domesday, which lies northward, and deserves more particular mention. Old Town End, now

OLTON END,

Vulgarly Oken End, is about a mile distant from Solihull; and, as before stated, was the original colony of the parish, and then called *Wulverlie.* After the rise of Solihull, the locality of which being more favourable, and its progress rapid, this place, as early as the 19th of Edward I, became known as the Old Town, or Olton, in which Roger de Someri is certified to have had lands. In the 23rd of the same reign, Ela de Odingsels and her husband are stated to have been jointly enfeoffed of the manor of *Oulton.* From the Odingsells it passed by one of the coheiresses to the family of Grey of Rotherfeld; and, in like manner, from them it fell, 2nd of Henry IV, to the wife of Sir John Deincourt, knight. From this family it came by descent, fine, &c., to the families of Lovel Boteler, and Arundel. In 33rd Henry VIII it had become the property of Henry Ogard, esq., and afterwards of Oliver Briggs, esq., who sold it to Mr. Middlemore, of Birmingham, and it afterwards came to the Palmers, and from them to Miss C. Meysey Wigley, who married the Rev. Archer Clive, rector of Solihull. He sold it in 1847 to W. C. Alston, esq.

In describing Olton, Dugdale states "I found a large moat, containing within it at least an acre, whereon they say a castle long since was situate, though now nothing be left thereof (a parcel of old oaks growing where the buildings stood); which tradition hath the more colour of truth, forasmuch as there is a lane near at hand bearing the name of Castle Lane. Which grounds, being at least a mile diameter, have heretofore been a park, as the country people say, and is probable enough from the large bank that lyeth on the outside of them, environed with lanes. Not far from whence are the vestigia of three very large pools, long ago converted to meadow ground."

Time has dwindled this ancient settlement to a mill and several groups of houses. The remains of a triangular moat are still traceable, within which stood the manorial residence of the early lords of the place, referred to in the account of Solihull, and above. One side of the moat now forms part of Castle Lane, rendering it highly probable that a castle was built here in the early Norman period; and, from the moat being still called Hobb's, formerly Hog's, or Odingsells' moat, it may be conjectured that, so long as the family of Odingsells continued the proprietors, they resided here. The present mansion is situated at some distance, and is called Olton Hall, and was purchased by Mr. Alston with the rest of the property.

The population of the whole parish of Solihull in 1841 was 3404, and only 3331 in the year 1861. In 1563 the number of families was 160.

Resting from our tour of this extensive parish we shall visit the other places in the neighbourhood on the morrow.

Ninth Day.

CONTINUING our journey we shall have for description the villages of Elmdon and Bickenhill. These, with the once more important town of Hampton-in-Arden, and other places of minor note, will complete our tour through the district of Arden. Leaving Solihull and passing to the right of Olton we come to some beautiful rural lanes and roads, the branches of the elm, oak, and ash forming in many places a complete canopy and lengthened avenue, affording in the hottest days of summer a grateful shade; whilst from many an eminence extensive wooded prospects open upon the view. Crossing the canal,

ELMDON HALL,

The seat of W. Alston, esq., is seen on the left. It is a handsome stone mansion, occupying a site on a gentle ascent from the road, overlooking a large extent of parklike ground, bounded with ornamental timber. It has a northern and southern front: the general features of the latter will be best understood by the engraving. It was erected by the late Isaac Spooner, esq., in 1795. After the death of Mr. and Mrs. Isaac Spooner the house became the residence of their eldest son, Abraham Spooner Lillingston, esq., who was killed in his own grounds by the fall of a tree, May 29, 1834, living only long enough to show to his relatives, and labourers who had assembled round him, that for a death thus sudden he was yet prepared. On the site of the hall stood a former mansion built by John Boteler in the time

of Henry VIII. Dugdale states that the arms of Whitacre, Waldeiff, Hore, and Boteler, successive proprietors, were cut on a beam of this hall, when he visited the place.

ELMDON

Has passed through various fortunes. Before the Conquest it was the property of *Tochi:* after that event it was granted by William I to Turchil de Warwick. In Domesday it is stated to have contained half a hide, the woods being one furlong in length and breadth, and the whole of the value of 5*s*. In the reign of Henry III it was held in fee by Simon de Whitacre, of Simon de Bercheston, and by him of Thomas de Arden, heir to the before-named Turchil. In 4th Edward I William de Arden died, possessing the manor in fee. It afterwards came by heirs female from the Whitacres, successively to the families of Waldeiff and Hore; and then, by a daughter of Alan Hore, to her husband John, son and heir of Richard Boteler of Solihull, in the time of Henry VI. John, his son, sold the manor to Thomas Marrow, gentleman, whose son, 34th Henry VIII, parted with it to Henry Mayne, of Berrington, county of Hertford, in whose family it remained several generations. It afterwards passed to the Spooners, and was sold in 1840 by Isaac William Lillingston, esq., to William Charles Alston, esq., on whose death in 1862 it passed with the principal part of his landed property into the possession of his eldest son.

THE CHURCH,

Dedicated to St. Nicholas, was entirely rebuilt in the year 1784, by Abraham Spooner, esq. The structure is situate near to the hall, and is partially concealed from view by the trees which surround, on every side, the peaceful churchyard. It is a neat stone building, consisting of a tower, nave, and chancel. The tower is embattled, with small pinnacles at each corner, an obtuse arched doorway on the west being the principal entrance. Over this is a two-light window, and one of a similar design on each face of the belfry. The nave has an embattled parapet, having on the south side three two-light windows, and two on the north. The chancel, which is semi-octagonal, has on the east angle a three-light, and on each of those adjoining a single-light window, all filled with stained glass. The interior is fitted with pews, a gallery, and a pulpit and reading desk of rather large dimensions for so small a building. These are all of oak, and of excellent workmanship. The font is small, and stands in a pew at the north-east angle of the nave.

The monuments are numerous, belonging principally to the family of the Spooners, of whom four generations are interred in the vault beneath the church. One tablet is to the memory of the late Archdeacon Spooner, who was for fifty-five years rector of the parish, and died in 1857.

The arms in the windows of the old church, when Dugdale visited it, were Clinton of Maxstoke, Clinton, earl of Huntingdon, and Hore.

In 6th Edward VI the Church Goods were stated by the commissioners to consist of

> oon chalice and two belles.
> an old cope.
> a vestm't complete, silke.
> two altarclothes.
> a crosse, latyn.
> two candlestickes, bras.
> oon old s'ples.
>
> Md. That the p'ishe owethe for oon of their stude belles, liijs. iiij*d*.

The living in 1291, 19th Edward I, was valued at 2*l.* 13*s.* 4*d.*; in the 26th Henry VIII at 3*l.* 8*s.*; and it is now returned at 230*l.* The Rev. H. C. Boutflower is the present rector.

The rectory house stands a short distance north-east of the church, and was built in 1803.

The population in 1841 was 167, and 206 in 1861.

Journeying onward, this road leads direct to the Birmingham and Coventry turnpike. Turning to the right, and keeping the high road till the toll-gate is reached, the traveller must there make another detour to the right, which, in a few minutes, will conduct him to the village of

CHURCH BICKENHILL,

So called to distinguish it from Hill and Middle Bickenhill, two of its hamlets. In the Conqueror's time the whole of the parish appears to have been computed as two villages, one containing two hides, with woods of four furlongs long and as many broad, formerly the freehold of *Alwardus;* and the other also two hides, with woods twelve furlongs in length and six in breadth, the property of one *Aluric,* in Edward the Confessor's time. These were given at the Conquest to Turchil de Warwick, who was the ancestor of all the family of Arden; for his grandson and heir, Henry de Arderne, made deed of certain lands in this place for the dowry of Letitia his wife, and grants unto her *servitium Eustachii de Arderne de Bychenhulla,* which he held of him. It appears probable that the descendants of this Eustace changed the name of Arderne to Bykenhull, their place of residence; for, 33rd Henry II, Thomas de Bykenhull is found in connection with this place; and early in Henry III's reign, Alexander de Bykenhull bound himself in the sum of fifteen marks of silver unto Sir Hugh de Arden, of Hampton, knight, not to sell or encumber any part of his lands, without his consent. This Alexander was one of the justices of assize for this county, in 19th Henry III. In 23rd Edward I Alice de Langley signed herself *Domina de Bygenhull,* though Thomas, son of the above Alexander, styled himself lord at the same time. The next owner appears to have been Walter Parles, to whom succeeded William Parles, who, 1st Edward III, sold his title to Sir John Peche, of Hampton-in-Arden, knight, whose grandson, Sir John Peche, 28th Edward III, obtained a charter of free warren. Little is known of the descent of this manor after this period. It is now the property of the earl of Aylesford.

THE CHURCH,

Dedicated to St. Peter, is, from its lofty spire, a marked object to the eye from whatever way it is approached. In Henry II's reign, at the foundation of the monastery of Henwood, this church was given to the nuns of that establishment; but it did not long remain in their possession, being shortly afterwards granted to those of Mergate, Bedfordshire.

The church consists of a tower with spire, nave, north aisle, north chapel, and chancel. The tower is rather lofty, with an embattled parapet and small pinnacles at the angles, from the interior wall of which rises a plain spire of graceful proportions. The summit of the tower is approached by a projecting staircase, over the door of which is carved 1632—2—EB. RA. The interior arch of the nave and tower is walled up, and the only entrance to the tower is by the staircase door. The west window in the tower exhibits some fine tracery, and is of four lights, in two ranges or lifts. The nave and chancel are of equal height, and, with the aisle and chapel, have all ridged roofs, without cross or ornament of any kind. The chapel and chancel eastern windows are pointed arched, and each of five lights with open tracery. The windows of the nave and aisle are flat headed, with mullions and tracery. The chancel south window is a pointed one of two lights. The entrance to the body of the church is by a pointed arched doorway, covered by a modern wooden porch. The interior arch of this doorway is a fine specimen of early architecture. Previous to the alterations, hereafter referred to, the original entrance arch was hid by plaster, and not known to exist. On the removal of the mortar it was found that a smaller doorway had been inserted, which remains the present entrance to the body of the church. The semi-Norman arch discovered has been cleaned and the dilapidated portions restored. The arch, which is sculptured in two rows of alternate billet, springs from pillars with plain oblong capitals, bearing one simple zigzag mould running across them.

In stepping into the interior, the traveller will do well to rest at the door, and take a survey of the fine semi-Norman pillars and arches which divide the nave and northern aisle. The pillars are three in number, two cylindrical and one square. They are very low and massy, and have slightly sculptured and escalloped capitals. From these spring four semi-circular arches, without ornament or sculpture, the underside, or surbase, being cut flat, the angles forming the outline of, and even with, the wall over.[1] The flat ceiling, which conceals the roof of the nave, very much mars the effect of the alterations of the interior. The pointed tower arch has been walled up, and an organ and singing pew placed against it. The tower buttresses are in two tiers, having slightly depressed trefoiled niches, to which formerly brackets for images of saints appear to have been attached. At the west end of the aisle is a doorway blocked up, having a richly carved pointed arch, with sculptured finial and headed corbels. There is no separation of the nave from the chancel by an arch; but an obtuse arch divides the chancel from the north chapel. This arch is of more elaborate character than those before-named, the outer plinth or hood mould being terminated by a griffin and an angel's head as corbels. The timber roof is open. The priest's door, like the others, is walled up, and the chancel exhibits nothing remarkable except the encaustic tiles in the sacrarium.

The chantry, or chapel, separated from the chancel as already stated, and communicating with the north aisle, is nearly the size of the chancel. The extreme end of it is now parted off by a stone wall or screen, (perhaps, the former reredos of this chapel,) which has evidently been removed to its present situation from some other part of the building, and which now forms the west side of a small sacristy or robing room for the incumbent. The doorway of this screen, or wall, is pointed, having a carved finial heading, and sculptured corbels of two king's

1. An engraving of these arches, &c., will be found in the initial letter to this chapter.

heads. The centre is an oblong panel without ornament, and on each side of it a richly sculptured niche on carved pedestals; but the effigies once filling them are gone. On the north side of this portion is a depressed surbast arch, and on the south side two smaller ones.

On the floor of the north aisle, is a large incised slab with an inscription in old text on the border; but quite defaced. A slab in the south wall, near to the organ, commemorates George Smith Cooper and his wife, benefactors of 10*l.* to the poor in bread.

The modern monuments are few, and of no particular interest. One mural tablet, in the north chapel, is to the memory of Fettiplace Nott, esq., *obiit* April 22, 1726; and three others, in the chancel, north of the communion table, record the deaths of several children of Carew Thomas Elers, vicar of the parish. The font appears, from the perfection of its sculpture, to be a modern addition. It is, however, of ancient date; and has been painted white. It is octagonal in shape, having quatrefoils on each face, with heads on the incline to the shaft, which is also octagonal. The general appearance of the church is highly creditable to the parishioners, for its neatness. It has lately been reseated with open benches and restored. There are five bells in the tower. In the windows were formerly the arms of Peche, Waver, and Erdington.

A curiously cut gravestone stands in the church-yard, "To the memory of Miss Anne Smith, who lived a maid, and died, aged 70.8, A.D. 1701." Near to the tower lies a very long oak chest, in two partitions, all cut out of the solid oak, and strongly bound with iron, but fast going to decay. It is a pity this relic of ancient native workmanship has been removed from its former position under shelter.

In 1291 (19th Edward I) the vicarage was valued at nine marks, and in 26th Henry VIII was estimated to be of the value of *7l. 17s. 2d.* It is now returned at *222l.*, and the Rev. C. T. Elers is the present incumbent. The Church Goods, *temp.* Edward VI, were

> oon chalice and iij belles in the steple.
> a frount for thaltar, wulsted.
> a cou' to the altar, silke.
> iij altar clothes, lynen.
> two towells.
> a pix, bras.
> two candlesticks.
> a cope, silke.
> a vestm't of veluet.
> a corporis and the case, veluet.
> a crosse, bras.

THE CASTLE.

About a mile north-west of the church, in a field near to a farm house, called "Castle Hills," is the site of the castle built by Nigel de Albani, or Roger de Mowbray.[2] Though nothing of the building remains, the entrenchments, part of which are traceable, furnish a tolerable notion of its extent when in existence. No historical reference to this castle is to be found after its erection, and the scanty notices of many other of these strongholds of the Norman barons tend to show that the destruction of some, and the reduction of others as castellated dwellings, was very general and complete in the time of Henry II. This at Bickenhill it is, therefore, highly probable came under the same category as Studley, (see p. 93,) and was at least dismantled under the decree of that monarch. Thus reduced, it, perhaps, became the mansion of one of the

---

2. Dugdale says it was "called Bevenchesley, in which was a castle, still called 'Castle Hills,' and lyeth in the parish of Bickenhull, though it be a member of Hampton Lordship."

Ardens, as, in an inquisition taken 4th Edward I, one of the parks belonging to William de Arden, stated to be about a mile and a quarter distant from Hampton Church, "towards Elmedon," was situated here, but no allusion to any castle is made therein.

> "Unsparing Time,
> Stern miner of the tower sublime,"

has done his work so thoroughly, that the sheep and ox now graze quietly over its obliterated foundations, which are here and there indicated by a slight elevation of the surrounding surface, by mounds of earth, and by traces of a moat.

The population of Church Bickenhill with its hamlets, was 767 in 1841, and 740 in 1861. There were 46 families in 1563. The parish is large, the village proper consisting of the vicarage, a school for poor children, and a few farm houses and cottages.

The hamlets referred to are Hill and Middle Bickenhill, Kingsford, Wavers Marston, Marston Curley, and Lindon. These at the Conquest became the property of Turchil de Warwick, and falling to the Ardens were afterwards granted to other proprietors, under various tenures, &c. A considerable portion of the first-named was bestowed upon the Henwood nuns; but, on the dissolution of religious houses, was granted to Edward Aglionby, of Balsall, and Henry Hugford, of Solihull. In Kington, or Kingsford, which is a very ancient place, though now consisting of but a few scattered houses, there appears to have been a church in the reign of Henry III; for the advowson of it was granted, 5th of that reign, to the nuns of Mergate, by one Henry de la Notte. In

16th Edward II, it was called the chapel belonging to Bickenhill.

Proceeding through Church Bickenhill, the road to Hampton leads, like so many others we have pursued, through woodland scenery of much beauty, and bringing us, in the course of two miles, to that place.

HAMPTON IN ARDEN.

This is a very extensive parish, comprehending many hamlets, some of them, as we have noticed in Nuthurst, being wholly isolated, and distant miles from the mother church. The property of this parish before the Norman Conquest was vested in one *Luevinus*. At that period it was given by the Conqueror, with many other lordships, to Geoffrey de Wirce, of Little Brittany in France, who had assisted in the Conquest. At this time it is stated in Domesday Book to have had ten hides of land, a church, a mill value 3*s.* 4*d.*, and woods three miles in length and breadth, all worth 5*l.* From this proprietor, who does not appear to have left any issue, it is probable the lands returned to the crown. By grant of king Henry I they were bestowed upon Nigel de Albani. This Nigel, the progenitor of the de Mowbrays, had issue Roger, surnamed de Mowbray, by whom the Ardens, as lords of the manor, were afterwards enfeoffed thereof. Of these Radulphus de Hamptone, 5th of Stephen, was the first writing himself *de Eardene.* It continued with this family in 35th Henry III, when Hugh de Arden possessed it. They had, in the meantime, acquired other property in the parish, since the manor house, demesnes, and advowson, which had been given by Roger de Mowbray to Ralph de Haia in exchange for other lands, were bought by Robert de Arden for fifty marks of silver. This Hugh de Arden obtained a charter of the king of free warren for all his lands here and in Knowle, as also for a weekly market at Hampton, and a fair for three days, to be held on the eve, day, and day after the feast of St. Luke. To him succeeded William de Arden, who is supposed to have been slain, 4th Edward I, by one Richard de L'Isle. By the inquisition taken after his death it appeared that he had at Hampton a manor house, two gardens, four hundred and sixty acres of land, a meadow value 7*l.* 12*s.*, two parks, one pool, two water mills, and fishing in the river Blithe, with other rents, &c., in this and various places in the county, of the value of 7*l.* 12*s.* 5*d.*, the whole, excepting the advowson of the vicarage, being valued at 52*l.* 6*s.* 4*d.* Richard, his brother, the heir, was not only a minor but being an idiot the inheritance fell to his aunts, Hawise and Olivia, sisters of the before-named Hugh. Part of the lands were afterwards purchased by the crown; but ultimately came again into the possession of a member of this family, Sir John Peche, knight, son and heir of Hawise. With them the manor of Hampton continued till the 10th Richard II.* Then, through a daughter of this house, it passed to the Montforts of Coleshill; but was estreated to the crown, 11th Henry VII, on the attainder of Sir Simon Montfort, for high treason in sending money to Perkin Warbeck.3 In the following

3. The revolt raised by one Richard Simon, a priest at Oxford, by training up Lambert Simnel, a baker's son, to counterfeit the person of the son of the duke of Clarence, smothered in a butt of malmsey, was scarcely put down by Henry VII, when the old duchess of Burgundy put forward one Osbeck, or Warbeck, the son of a converted Jew, whose name, Peter,

* *Inq. Post Mort.*

year it was granted by letters patent to Richard Pudsey, esquire to the king; but, as he had no issue, it reverted to the crown. In the 4th of Henry VIII, that monarch granted it to Sir Henry Guildford, knight, who dying childless, it reverted again to the crown. In the 15th Elizabeth, the queen granted it to her favourite, Robert Dudley, earl of Leicester; but he having no *allowed* lawful issue, it once more reverted to the crown, and remained a royal appanage for many years. During this period it was assigned as dowry to Henrietta Maria, queen of Charles I, but after his execution and her flight, it was, A.D. 1649, ordered by the Parliament to be sold.[4] It is uncertain that a sale was effected; but, whether or not, the property after the Restoration was again a royal demesne, and remained a crown possession till purchased by Isaac William Lillingston, esq., who sold it to the late Sir Robert Peel, baronet, whose son, the Right Honourable Frederick Peel, is now lord of the manor.

---

was corrupted into Peterkin, or Perkin, to personate the duke of York, murdered in the Tower, reporting previously that he was still living. The plot succeeded for a time, spreading through England, Scotland, and Ireland, many of its supporters being tried and beheaded, whilst the wretched dupe of this conspiracy was at last hung at Tyburn, with several of his adherents.

4. For this purpose, as shown by a MS. of fifty-one pages, lately in the possession of Mr. Job, bookseller, Birmingham, a survey was taken, which enumerated the name of the tenants, and the houses, lands, woods, &c., in their occupation. It is entitled "A Survey of the Manors of Hampton-att-Arden, with the Rights, Members, and Appurtenances thereof, lying and being in the County of Warwick: Last Parcell of the Possessions of Henrietta Maria, Queen of Charles Stewart, dec'd, made and taken by us, whose names are hereunto subscribed, in the month of December, 1649, by vertue of a Commission grounded upon an Act of the Commons of England assembled in Parliament, for the Sale of the Honors, Manors, and Lands heretofore belonging to the late King, Queene, and Prince, under the Hands and Seals of five or more of the Trustees in the said Act, named and appoynted." It is a curious document, extracts from which, however, would not be of much interest here.

THE CHURCH,

Dedicated to the Virgin Mary and St. Bartholomew, stands on an eminence, close to the road leading through the village. It consists of a tower, nave, north and south aisles, and chancel, with a chantry chapel on the north side of it. The tower, which is low, is embattled, whilst its roof is reached by an outer circular staircase. This tower had, formerly, a tall spire, which was a noted landmark in this

woodland district. In the year 1643, during a violent storm of thunder and lightning, it was thrown down, great damage being thereby done to the tower and to other parts of the building. The west, or tower window, is of three lights, under a pointed arch, and the belfry has a two-light pointed window on each face. The nave has a crenelated or embattled parapet, under which, on each side, are four clerestory windows of two lights. The chancel has a ridged roof, without parapet, but the northern chapel is embattled. The stringcourse of the chancel is semi-hexagonal, and of early date. We enter the church by an obtuse arched doorway, under a modern porch: The general aspect of the interior impresses the visitor with a suspicion of the parsimonious spirit that must long have prevailed amongst the parishioners of this comparatively wealthy town. Many of the ornamental windows have been allowed to decay; and the floor of the chancel paved with bricks and tiles, square and oblong, broken stones, and other odds and ends, is anything but creditable. The aisles of this church are each separated from the nave by three circular pillars, higher than, but not so massive as, those of Bickenhill. From these rise four pointed arches. The nave is, too, divided from the tower by a similar arch, bricked up, and from the chancel by another. The south aisle windows, with one exception, have been suffered to go to destruction, and are now filled with plain leaded lights, the original mullions and tracery being gone. A stone seat runs along the side of this aisle, a peculiarity we have not noticed in any other church we have visited. In the north aisle are two circular headed windows, and one pointed, of two lights each, whilst the north doorway is also pointed. Leaving the body of the church, which is pewed and galleried, we enter the chancel, which is the most ancient part of the building, presenting many features of the Anglo-Norman style. On the north side are two plain semicircular windows, without ornament, (one filled with lattice glass,) and a lofty circular headed doorway of like character, blocked up with masonry. The east window is pointed, of four lights, and with fair tracery heading, filled with stained glass of recent date, the subjects being the Dove, Cross,

&c. The windows on the south side are flat headed, the priest's door being pointed. The windows formerly contained the arms of de la Bere, Peche, Albani, Bradstone, and Say. On the east side of the priest's door is a pointed arch, with a trefoiled one under, containing the bust of an angel bearing a shield, on which are the arms of Erdington, two lions passant. Dugdale speaks of these and other arms as then being "on gravestones in the church," mentioning an inscription on one in the chancel, commemorative of "Sire Johan Peche et Johan sa feme gisant icy Dieu de lour almes eit mercy." This shield is, most likely, the sole remnant of this monument. On the floor of the nave is a large slab, on which two brass figures formerly existed; but only one now remains. This is, doubtless, the stone noticed by Dugdale as having the "portraitures in brass of a man and his wife," and the following inscription:

Hic jacet Ricardus Brokes Balinus de
Hampton in Ardena et Isola uxor eius.

Man it behoves thee oft to have in minde
That thou dealest w'h thy hand that shalt thou find
Children bin sloathfull and wives bin unkinde
Executors bin covetous and keepe all that they find.

This caution, and the portraiture of Richard Broke, are both gone. The few monuments now scattered here and there are modern, and principally to the memory of the Eboralls of Balsall, whilst the slabs, in the chancel, commemorate several of the vicars.

The chantry chapel presents little deserving of notice. Every token of its former purpose has been diligently removed, in order to adapt it to its present use as a vestry. The entrance from the chancel is by a pointed arched doorway, having a moulding with ornamental finial and sculptured corbels. It is lighted by square windows. The exterior doorway being square, and cut for this purpose, does not correspond with the architecture of the building. The font is circular, standing on a similar pillar and shaft. In the tower are six bells.

In the Conqueror's time, Geoffrey de Wirce, to whom the lordship had been given, granted to the monastery of St. Nicholas, at Angiers, of which Monks Kirby was a cell, a third part of the tithe corn, wool, cheese, and pannage; but Roger de Mowbray, when he came into possession of the lordship, recalled the gift; bestowing upon the canons of Kenilworth the church, tithe, and glebe wholly, and all chapelries belonging thereto. This grant was confirmed by several of his successors. Disputes arose, afterwards, between the monks of Kirby and the canons of Kenilworth, as, too, between the latter and the then lord of the manor, William de Arden, which were settled, through the mediation of the bishop and others, by certain payments, and the giving license to the said William de Arden and his heirs, with their family, to hear divine service in his chapel at Knowle, saving the indemnity of the mother church of Hampton. In 21st Henry VIII William Wall, abbot, with the canons of Kenilworth, let to farm to Sir Edward Ferrers, knight, and Thomas Jackson, clerk, for forty years, all the tithe corne, and greynes, with all other fruits and profits in anywise growing in Hampton, Balsall, and Knowle, belonging to the parsonage at Hampton, payable yearly 9*l.* 6*s.* 8*d.*, in two instalments.*

In the year 1291 this church was valued at eleven marks; and, 26th Henry VIII, the vicarage, with the chapel at Nuthurst, at 15*l.* 6*s.* 8*d.*, over and above 20*s.* pension paid to the canons of Kenilworth, and 11*s.* for

---

* *Thomas's Dugdale.*

procurations, &c. It is now returned at 578*l.* The Rev. J. A. Morris is the present vicar.

The Commissioners, 6th Edward VI, found here at their visitation,*

oon chalice and iij belles in the steple.
two altarclothes of bokera, and a cou'ing clothe thereto.
a front clothe.
two towells.
two altar clothes, lynen.
two candlesticks, latyn.
two cruett.
ij copes, dornix.
iij vestm'ts, the first for the p'st, deacon, and subdecon of dornix clothe, of bustyon and wulsted, w' oon albe and thimplem'ts thereof.
a pax, mastlyn.
a crosse, coper.
a ban' clothe, silke.
a syndrex of chaungeable silke.
two supleses.
It'm, an other vestm't of silke.

Near to the porch is a very old tomb, composed of huge stones, and one of similar character is found in another part of the church-yard. Here are also the remains of the church-yard cross, which was usually erected near to the south porch. This stands eastward of the chancel, and has an octagonal pedestal, with quatrefoils on each face. The shaft is broken off at about two feet from its base.

The vicarage house is a modern erection, standing on the opposite side of the road, eastward of the church.

West of the church, and adjoining the church-yard, is the site of the "Old Manor House" of the Ardens, referred to in the inquisition taken 14th Edward I. A portion of a half-timbered dwelling remains, incorporated with a farm house, which partly occupies the site. It is still called

* *Papers in Record Office.*

"The Old Hall." A considerable extent of the moat, once surrounding it, is discoverable, forming a fence to the garden. As this house presents nothing to distinguish it from other such dwellings, we will proceed to the newly-erected mansion, which has taken the place of its predecessor, and which is known as

HAMPTON HALL,

Built by, and the residence of, the Right Honourable Frederick Peel, the present lord of the manor. The edifice, standing on a commanding eminence, west of the old

manor-place, is built in the castellated style, from designs by — Giles, esq., of Derby, and the engraving will give a notion of its general appearance, which, when the trees and shrubs which fill the gardens and surrounding plantations, have attained a larger growth, will materially contribute to the interest and beauty of the locality.

The charities of Hampton are numerous, the principal one being left by George Fentham, of Birmingham, in 1690, by which relief is given to the poor, and a good education imparted to the youth of the place, under suitable masters and mistresses.

The general appearance of the village has been much improved of late years. Several houses and cottages have been erected by the lord of the manor, and a large school built by the feoffees of Fentham's Charity, all giving a more lively and cheerful appearance to the place. The erection of a station on the North Western Railway has added also to the accommodation and considerably advanced the prosperity of the town.

We have already visited Nuthurst, Baddesley, and Knowle, ancient members of this extensive parish. The other smaller ones of Kinwaldsy, Chadwick, and Diddington, are of no sufficient interest or importance for the tourist to visit. Those places were inherited by the Arden family, in the same manner as the parent parish. *Kinwaldsy* was granted to the nuns of Mergate, Bedfordshire, who, with their prioress, Christina, devised it and *Diddington, temp.* Richard I, to William de Arden, reserving for themselves the yearly rent of 20*s*. Hugh de Arden, his son and heir, afterwards purchased the inheritance of them from Isabel, the next prioress, and the convent for thirty marks. The property, with Knowle, afterwards came to the monks of Westminster. *Chadwick* also belonged to the Ardens, being granted to Peter de Arden by Roger de Mowbray to hold by the tenth part of a knight's fee. From this Peter it came to Roger, his brother, whom he made his heir. Coming next to William de Arden he granted it in dower to his wife, Amicia de Tracey, as *tota villa de Chadelswiz.*

In 36th Henry III it was certified to be held by the eighth part of a knight's fee by Peter de Montfort, but in 29th Edward I it had descended by marriage to Sir John Peche, in the same way as was described in speaking of Hampton-in-Arden.

As, from their having been at one period proprietors of a great portion of the northern part of this locality, it has been necessary to introduce this family of Arden, taking their name from the district, and to give many details of their history, it will not be irrelevant to make some further remarks relative thereto, before terminating our labours in leading the tourist through the country at one time known as the Forest of Arden. Descended from Turchil de Warwick, branches of the Ardens settled in various parts of the county, viz., at Curdworth, Hampton, Kingsbury, Rodburn, Ratley, and other places, all dying out, or leaving female issue, in a few generations, with the exception of the branch at Curdworth, which continued till the year 1643, when Robert, great grandson of Edward Arden, executed, 27th Elizabeth, for high treason in connection with his son-in-law Somervile (see p. 58), died in his youth, leaving the inheritance to his sisters.

The population of Hampton-in-Arden in 1841 was 2306,* and 689 in the year 1861. In the year 1563 there were 140 families.*

It will be no unfitting conclusion of these wanderings in Arden, if we request the tourist especially to mark the yet strictly rural character of the district we have attempted to describe—more particularly of the southern and northern

* This included the whole of the hamlets. In 1861 they were returned separately.

portions of it. Although so close upon large seats of manufacturing industry, its peculiarly rustic features have been preserved almost intact: The dense and shady woods about Wootton, Morton, Bushwood, Umberslade, Baddesley, and Hampton, and the great abundance and richness of the hedgerow timber in field, lane, and road, everywhere, except in the mid portion of this district, justly claim for this part of Warwickshire, if not a pre-eminence of sylvan beauty, at least an equality with any other part of any other county. The spreading prospects, the gentle hills, the beauty of the valleys that intersect in every direction the Forest of Arden, must afford, to every true lover of the country and its tranquil scenes, an unfailing fund of enjoyment and delight. Here too, in many a mossy lane, shadowed road, and secluded byway, may the naturalist find ample scope for the exercise of his taste; whilst in purling brooks and winding streams, the disciple of "Old Isaak" may forget the town, as he plies his art to circumvent the finny tribe. For the healthiness of the neighbourhood, the ruddy countenances of the villagers are a sufficient voucher: And, whether seeking health or pleasure, whether worn by the toils, or wearied with the cares, of business, or of state, here may "all sorts and conditions of men" find, for awhile, the solace suited to their varied circumstances, needs, and infirmities. Here may the visitor realize the poet's words:

> "The statesman, lawyer, merchant, man of trade,
> Pants for the refuge of some rural shade,
> Where, all his long anxieties forgot,
> Amid the charms of some sequestered spot,
> He may improve the remnant of his span,
> And, having lived a trifler, die a man."

Statesman or lawyer, merchant or man of trade, who seeks these "cool sequestered shades," we heartily wish him the fulfilment of the desire so well expressed by the poet: And when official, professional, or business exigencies summon him to say farewell to these scenes,

> "Where smiling spring its earliest visit pays,
> And parting summer's lingering bloom delays,"

we bid him "God speed" on his journey, be it north, east, west, or south, as, forsaking Hampton-in-Arden, he pursues his homeward course, under the London and North Western Railway, and turning round to the stations on that line and the junction line to Whitacre on the Midland Railway, takes his seat in the train which will bear him to his destination.

Appendix.

I.

CHARTER OF KING HENRY VI, A.D. 1449, TO SIR RALPH BOTELER, KNIGHT. SEE PAGE 33.

HENRY, by the Grace of God, King of England and France, and Lord of Ireland, to his Archbishops, Bishops, Abbots, Priors, Dukes, Earls, Barons, Justices, Sheriffs, Reeves, Ministers, and all his Bailiffs and faithful Subjects to whom these present Letters shall come, GREETING. Know ye, that whereas our trusty and beloved Ralph Boteler, lord de Seudeley, knight, is tenant and owner of the town and manor of Henley-in-Arden, in the County of Warwick, and he and all his ancestors tenants and owners of the town and manor aforesaid, and all others whose estate he hath in the same manor, have had, and from the time whereof the memory of man is not to the contrary were wont to have, amongst other things, the liberties and franchises underwritten, that is to say, view of frankpledge of all the tenants and resiants within the same town and manor, to be holden twice in the year at Henley aforesaid, and waifs and strays and all things which appertain to view of frankpledge within the precincts of the town and manor aforesaid, and a certain market there to be holden every week, namely, on Monday: and we of our special grace, by our Charter, for us and our heirs as far as in us lies do accept, approve, ratify, and to the same Ralph and his heirs by the tenor of these presents grant and confirm, all and singular those liberties and franchises; willing furthermore and granting for us and our heirs aforesaid to the same Ralph, that, albeit he and his ancestors, lords of the manor aforesaid, or others whose estate the same Ralph hath in the same town and manor, before these times had not, nor ought to have had, the liberties and franchises aforesaid, or any of them, or did not fully use them, nevertheless the same Ralph and his heirs shall hereafter fully use and enjoy those liberties and franchises and every of them, without let or hinderance of us, our heirs or successors, or the justices, escheators, sheriffs, coroners, or other ministers of us or our heirs whomsoever. And furthermore forasmuch as the tenants of the same Ralph, and the resiants in the town and manor aforesaid, and within the precincts of the same, before these times have been often grievously and unjustly vexed, arrested, and disturbed by our sheriffs, escheators, and other ministers, and the ministers and servants of the same sheriffs, escheators, and other our ministers aforesaid, by their entry into the town and manor aforesaid, and the precincts of the same, to execute their offices therein, to the manifest disturbance of our people there, and to the no small loss and grievance of the same Ralph, as it is said: and we, being willing on that account out of our royal magnificence to impart our favour to the same Ralph, so that his tenants aforesaid and the resiants within the town and manor aforesaid, may the more quietly dwell and reside there, of our especial grace have granted, and by the tenor of these presents for us and our heirs do grant, to the aforesaid Ralph and his heirs aforesaid that they may have for ever by themselves, or by their bailiffs or ministers, within the town and manor aforesaid, and the precincts of the same, the return of all writs and precepts of us our heirs and successors, and of summonses of the Exchequer of us our heirs and successors, and of estreats and precepts of the Justices of us our heirs and successors of either Bench, of the Justices in Eyre of us and our heirs as well of Pleas of the Crown as of the Common Pleas, and of other Justices of us and our heirs whomsoever, and also attachment as well of Pleas of the Crown as of bills and precepts of the steward and marshall and clerk of the market of the household of us our heirs and successors, and also the execution of the same writs, estreats, summonses, attachments, and precepts within the town and manor aforesaid, and the precincts of the same, so that no sheriff, under-sheriff, coroner, bailiff, or any other minister of us or our heirs, shall enter into the said town and manor, or the precincts of the same, to do or execute anything there in anywise, nor intermeddle in aught within the same, unless in default of the same Ralph or his heirs aforesaid. We have granted also for us our heirs and successors as far as in us lies, that the aforesaid Ralph and his heirs may have infangthief and outfangthief, and all chattels of felons, fugitives, or persons in anywise condemned or put in exigence for treason or felony, and the chattels of outlaws, whether it be at the suit of us or our heirs or at the suit of a party, the chattels of felons, of themselves, chattels confiscated or in anywise forfeited of all their tenants, resiants and non-resiants, and of others resiant within the town and manor aforesaid, albeit the same tenants, resiant or non-resiant, and others resiant elsewhere, have held of us or our heirs or of any other person whomsoever; so that if any one of them ought to lose his life or limb for his offence, or shall flee and not be willing to stand his trial, or commit any offence or contempt for which he ought to forfeit or lose his chattels, wheresoever justice ought to be done therein, whether it be in the court of us or our heirs or successors, before us or our heirs or before the Justices of us or our heirs of one Bench or the other, the Justices assigned to hold the assizes and gaol delivery, or before any other Justices, Officers, or Commissioners of us or our heirs, the same chattels shall belong to the same Ralph and his heirs; And that it shall be well lawful for the same Ralph and his heirs, by themselves or their ministers, to seize those chattels, and that they may have, convert, commit, and apply them to their own proper use, without let or hinderance of us or our heirs, or the justices, sheriffs, escheators, or other ministers or officers of us or our heirs whomsoever; And that no buyer or purveyor for the household of us or our heirs do take any goods from the aforesaid Ralph or his heirs, or from any tenants of the same, resiant or non-resiant, or from others resiant of and in the town and manor aforesaid, and the precincts of the same, without the will of the same Ralph and his heirs and the tenants aforesaid, that is to say, of those whose goods so to be taken they shall be; And that all and singular the tenants of the same Ralph and his heirs, of the town and manor aforesaid, as well resiant as non-resiant, and all others there resiant, and all others who hereafter may be resiant there, shall for ever be quit of toll or tollage, stallage, pontage, paviage, weighage, murage, keyage, and cheminage, in all places, as well by land as by water, throughout our whole realm of England and elsewhere within our dominions and power. We have granted also to the same Ralph and his heirs, that they shall have within the town aforesaid every year two fairs, namely, one fair to be held on Tuesday in the week of Pentecost and the two following days, and the other fair to be held on the day and feast of St. Luke the Evangelist and the two following days, with all and singular the things to such fairs appertaining, so that the same be not to the nuisance of neighbouring fairs. Albeit express mention is not made in these presents of the true value of the premises or of any of them, nor of any other gifts and grants to the same Ralph by us or our progenitors before these times made, or any statute, act, ordinance, restriction, or mandate to the contrary made in anywise notwithstanding.——These being Witnesses: The Venerable Fathers John, Archbishop of Canterbury, Primate of all England, our Chancellor; Marmaduke, Bishop of Carlisle, our Treasurer of England; and Adam, Bishop of Chichester, Keeper of our Privy Seal; our most dear Cousins Humphry, Duke of Buckingham and Duke of Suffolk, our Chamberlain of England; Richard, Earl of Salisbury; and Thomas, Earl of Devon; our trusty and beloved Sir Ralph Cromwell and Sir James Tenys, Lord de Saye, Chamberlain of our Household, Knights; and others.

GIVEN under our hand at Westminster the 16th day of May, in the twenty-seventh year of our Reign.

[With a seal.] ROUS.

II.

TRANSLATION OF ANCIENT DEEDS IN THE AUGMENTATION OFFICE, RELATING TO LAPWORTH. SEE PAGES 134 AND 135.

BE it known to people now and hereafter, that I, William Catesby, Knight, son and heir of John Catesby, Esquire, and of Margaret his wife, have given, granted, and by this my present charter have confirmed, to Robert Catesby, senior, Esquire, and to John Wattson, Clerk, the half of the manor of Lappworth, with its appurtenances, which formerly belonged to Rose Mowntforde, and all the lands and tenements, rents and services, together with the reversions, which I have in the villages and grounds of Lappworth aforesaid, Henley, Wotton, Beldesert, and Wellesburne, which lately have legally and hereditarily descended to me, after the decease of the aforesaid Margaret, my mother, with their appurtenances in the county of Warwick. And I have also given and granted to the aforesaid Robert and John all the tenements, lands, and rents, with their appurtenances, which I have in Brawnstone and Falkeles in the county of Northampton. To have and to hold the aforesaid half of the manor of Lappworth, with its appurtenances, and all the aforesaid lands and tenements, rents and services, together with the aforesaid reversions, in Lappworth, Henley, Wotton, Beldesert, Wellesburn, Brawnstone and Falkeles, with all their appurtenances, as is aforesaid, to the abovenamed Robert Catesby and John Wattson, their heirs and assigns, for ever, from the chief lords of those fiefs by the services thence owing and legally customary. And I, the aforesaid William Catesby, and my heirs will warrant, and for ever defend against all persons, the aforesaid half of the manor of Lappworth, with its appurtenances, and all the lands and tenements, rents and services, together with the aforesaid reversions, in Lappworth, Henley, Wotton, Beldesert, Wellesburn, Brawnstone, and Falkeles, with all their appurtenances, as is aforesaid, to the abovenamed Robert Catesby and John Wattson, their heirs and assigns. In testimony of which I have affixed my seal to this present charter. Dated at Lappworth aforesaid in the feast of Saints Simon and Jude, in the thirty-sixth year of the reign of King Henry the Sixth after the Conquest of England. The witnesses being: Bawdewin Mowntforde and Edward Dodyngsils, Knights; William Leucy and Thomas Huggeforde, Esquires; Thomas Assheby of Lappworth; John Blythe of the same; John Stalye of Henley; and many others.*

LET people now and hereafter know, that I, Ivo Pippard, parson of Lapworth, have given and granted, and by this my present charter have confirmed, to Master Henry de Brauncestone, and to his heirs or assigns, all my part and all the pasturage which I have from the feoffment of William de Harecurt, in the Great Park of Lapworth.

* Marked Warr. No. 1 (25).

Also all my part which I have from the feoffment of the same William in the meadow which is called Havenesham, in the same village of Lapworth, with the hedges and ditches adjoining the aforesaid park and meadow, and with all other appurtenances of the same. Also three shillings of an annual rent from land which Walter de la Wode and William Gardelop formerly held from me in the same village, which land is called Snelleslond, with the homages, wards, relevies, and all other appurtenances and escheats, which can hence, in any manner, occur, as well in the land itself, as in the coppices, meadows, hedges, and ditches, and all other appurtenances of the same land, for ever, without any hinderance of myself or of my heirs. Rendering thence annually the same Master Henry and his heirs, to me and to my heirs or assigns, one head of cloves at Easter, for all service, exaction, custom, or secular demand. And I, the aforesaid Ivo, and my heirs the aforesaid part of the park and meadow, with the pasturage, and the aforesaid rent of three shillings, with all the other things abovementioned, will warrant, acquit, and defend against all men, to the aforesaid Master Henry, and to his heirs or assigns, for ever; excepting only the dowry of Matilda la Potere, the wife of the aforesaid William, if she shall survive her husband and ought to have her dowry from the aforesaid. In testimony of which I have affixed my seal to the present charter. These being the witnesses: Richard de Wroxhulle; Walter de Wynterton; John the Archer; Richard de Fulwode; Geoffrey le Mareschal; Robert Pippard; Walter Stikeman; Walter le Fraunceis; and many others.*

Be it known to people present and to come, that I, William de Harecurt, formerly Lord of Lappewored, have granted, and by this my present charter confirmed, to William de Bissoppesdone, my relative, son and heir of the late Sir Thomas de Bissoppesdone, for his service, all that land at Lappewrd which Henry Pippard formerly granted and confirmed by his charter to Simon Bagot of Prestone: And all that land in the same village which Luke Sorel formerly gave and confirmed by charter to Sir William de Bissoppesdone: And all that land which Henry le Bonevile formerly gave and confirmed by charter to Sir Thomas de Bissoppesdone in the same village: And

* Marked Warr. No. 1 (26).

all the land which Henry Sorel formerly gave and confirmed by charter to the said William de Bissoppesdone, my relative, in the same village: And the advowson of the church of the said village of Lappewrd, together with two marcs of yearly rent at Thorneton. To have and to hold from me and my heirs or my assigns, to him and to his heirs or his assigns whomsoever, all the aforesaid land, and the advowson of the said church, and the said rent, with all the liberties and their other appurtenances, freely, quietly, honourably, in peace, and in fee, for ever. Rendering thence annually to me, my heirs or my assigns, himself or his heirs or his assigns, one barbed arrow on the day of Pentecost, for all services, exactions, suits of courts, claims, and for all secular demands. And I, William de Harecurt, and my heirs or my assigns will warrant, acquit, and defend, for ever, the whole of the aforesaid land, and the advowson of the said church, and the aforesaid rent, with the appurtenances, to the said William and to his heirs or his assigns, by the aforesaid service, against all mortals. But for this concession and confirmation the aforesaid William has given to me in hand one mark of silver. And because I desire that this my concession, confirmation, warrant, acquittance, and defence may for ever retain its binding effect, I have confirmed the present charter with the impression of my seal. These being witnesses: Sir Bardulph de Cestreton, Sir Thomas de Caunvile, Knights; Peter de Wolwardinton; John de Cairly; Richard de Wroxhul; John de Bruly; Robert Pippard; and others.*

[With a seal.]

HENRY de Brauntestone to all his faithful, free, and customary tenants of Lapworthe, greeting. Since I have lately given to Sir John de Bisshopisdon, Knight, all my manor of Lapworth, with the whole of the domain belonging to the said manor, I strictly charge and direct you, all and singular, that you henceforth regard and consider the same Sir John as your Lord. And that you may be able to do this well and securely, I send to you these my letters patent, sealed with my seal. Dated at Bishwode on Sunday in the feast of Saint Andrew the Apostle, in the fourteenth year of the reign of King Edward the son of King Edward.†

[With a Seal.]

---

* Marked Warr. No. 1 (31). † Marked Warr. No. 1 (23).

III.

GUILDS. SEE PAGES 41, 68, AND 233.

GUILDS were founded at a very early period, and were originally associations of the inhabitants of particular districts, for the purpose of furthering the general welfare of the brotherhood, and assisting each other in cases of sickness. They were of two kinds, religious and secular, the former being the character of those guilds referred to in the above pages. These guilds were established for the performance of works of charity, and for the regular observance of certain religious services, and in the middle ages they had also the management of the public amusements of the people. These amusements were considered by the ruling powers of those days to be so intimately connected with the peace and welfare of society, that they were placed under the protection of religious guilds, for the purpose of perpetuating their existence; for it was thought that if suffered to fall into disuse, the people, being bereft of their customary sources of relaxation, would employ their vacant time in schemes of mischief. They managed also the religious processions and shows. The heathens had their mysteries, so had the christians, and divine worship, in like manner, was accompanied with flowers and perfumes, and clouds of incense, and the religious edifices were adorned with images, pictures, and symbolical designs. In processions and public shows the clergy bore a conspicuous part, hence guilds were established for their particular direction. Miracle plays were performed, and contributed a splendour to the rites of religion peculiar to the times in which they flourished. The celebration was usually kept at one of the annual fairs, or feast of dedication of the church, which, by increasing the number of visitors, brought additional profit to the trades associated in the secular guilds. On these occasions pleasure was in the ascendant with the masses, and no feeling indulged but anxiety to witness and give increased splendour to the ceremonies.

To establish a guild, or other religious institution, it was necessary to obtain the sanction of the sovereign, the parties being subject to heavy fines if founded without this authority (see pp. 41, 117). The constitution of the guild was formed of an alderman, brethren, and sisters, and the vicar or rector, as well as the principal persons in the town and neighbourhood, were enrolled among the members. They frequently met, but at the annual assembly they went to the church, offered up their prayers for all the members of the society, dead or living, and concluded with a dinner at the guild house. Many of the guilds accumulated considerable property, by grants from individual members, or parties friendly to the institution. The priests generally resided on the foundations, receiving an annual stipend, and on the dissolution of the monasteries, when guilds were suppressed, it will be seen that those described in these pages were in possession of considerable property, taking into account the value of money in the reign of Henry VIII.

IV.

NAMES OF THOSE IN THE DISTRICT WHO CONTRIBUTED TO THE DEFENCE OF THE COUNTRY AT THE TIME OF THE SPANISH INVASION, A.D. 1588.

William Skynner, gent., of Rowington -	- £25.
William Fetherston, gent., of Packwood	- 25.
Gabriel Poultney, gent., of Knowle -	- 25.
William Somervile, gent., of Edstone -	- 25.
Andrew Archer, gent., of Tanworth -	- 25.

V.

FOREST LAWS. SEE PAGE 19.

No written English Forest Laws existed previous to the time of Canute the Dane. This monarch framed a code about the year 1016, by which the king had the power to take possession of any tract of land, and to use it for his own purposes. While the timber and trees were little cared for, the greatest strictness was enforced by these laws in respect of the wild animals with which the forests abounded. Death was the punishment awarded to those who killed a deer, and if any one merely chased a deer until it panted, a fine was inflicted, the lowest being ten shillings, which, comparing the value of money in different periods, was a severe penalty at that time. The verderers were also protected by stringent regulations, and if force were used against them, the offender, if a freeman, lost his freedom, and if a villein, then, for the first offence, his right hand was chopped off, and for a second offence he lost his life. These laws continued in force for upwards of two hundred years, totally restraining all rural pleasures and manly recreations.

William the Conqueror confirmed the code of Canute, and soon after his arrival in this country formed the New Forest, by dispossessing the proprietors of the land, and driving the population to other localities. William Rufus followed his father's example with regard to these laws. Stephen, on his accession, promised to redress these grievances of the people, but failed to do so after he had secured the crown. Richard I also administered the Forest Laws with severity. In king John's time, and that of his son Henry III, they were so strictly enforced that they occasioned many insurrections of the barons, or principal feudatories, which had the effect of obtaining the two great charters of English liberties, viz. *Magna Carta* and *Carta de Foresta*, 41st Henry III; and though the Forest Laws were stringent for many reigns after, the latter charter swept away the cruel statutes of Canute and William.

VI.

ARMS IN CHURCHES AND MANSIONS. SEE PAGE 273.

AMONGST the Bridges' Papers in the Bodleian Library at Oxford are two volumes of Heraldic Notes by W. Belchier of Guilsborough, *obiit* 1609. They refer to the arms, &c., in various churches and private dwellings in the counties of Warwick and Northampton. In this district were the following. The arms are very badly executed in trick, and some of them scarcely to be made out.

Arms in the windows—Knowle Chapel and College, Lapworth Church, Henley-in-Arden Chapel, and in the Churches at Bickenhill, Hampton-in-Arden, Temple Balsall, Tanworth, Studley, and Claverdon.

Arms in Mr. Hugford's, Mr. Hanlope's, Mr. Hawes', and Mr. Danby's houses at Solihull, at Langdon Hall, Baddesley Hall, Mr. Fulwood's house at Tanworth, and Mr. Spenser's house at Claverdon.

Index.

NOTE.

By a mistranslation of a Latin document in the Record Office, an error has arisen at pages 34, 110, and 168. The date of the rentals should be read 23rd and 24th Henry VII.

CPSIA information can be obtained
at www.ICGtesting.com
Printed in the USA
LVHW100437110522
718424LV00003B/148

9 783375 003715